Relative Justice

Eleri Thomas

Copyright © Eleri Thomas

The right of Eleri Thomas to be identified as the Author of the Work has been asserted by her in accordance with the Copyright, Designs and Patents Act 1988.

First published in 2024
by Eleri Thomas

Apart from any use permitted under UK copyright law, this publication may only be reproduced, stored or transmitted, in any form, or by any means, with prior permission in writing of the publisher, or in the case of reprographic reproduction, in accordance with the terms of licences issued by the Copyright Licensing Agency.

To my mother, Menna Thomas

and her two sisters

Nesta Jane Jones

and

Enid Eluned Thomas – a writer of Welsh books and dramas

Also by Eleri Thomas

Treasured Valley

Chapter 1

'Your case has been put back until this afternoon, Mr. Morgan,' the Clerk of the Court informs me as I make my way into the courtroom. 'Apparently, the prison van has been held up on the M56 but should be here in time for Alys Roberts' hearing to go ahead at three o'clock.'

My first encounter with Alys was as duty solicitor. I was called in to represent her during an interview at the police station, after she had been arrested for a Public Order offence. She was obviously distressed at the time, but I was impressed with her self-possession and how she managed to keep it together, despite finding herself in a situation which would have terrified most girls at her age of eighteen.

After the police had interviewed all those involved, Alys, along with others, had been remanded into custody, albeit at different establishments. They were charged with Affray, which involved a vulnerable victim. She vehemently insists she was not involved in the crime but cannot provide an alibi for where she was when it was committed. Her next court appearance will be her second community bail application.

Alys is estranged from her extended family. Tragically orphaned as a baby, she had been brought up by her *Nain*, whose sudden death has devastated Alys, the two having been very close. Her *Nain* had always told her not to worry about the future, as apart from some investments, she was planning to leave everything to her in her Will. But instead, Alys was shocked to learn that the Will left everything to the twin sister of her late mother, who was also executor of the estate.

With unseemly haste, Alys' aunt had sold the house and all its contents, leaving Alys homeless and destitute. Prior to the alleged offence, she had been living temporarily with her aunt and her cousin, Lena, while she saved for a deposit for her own place.

The offence occurred in the early spring of 1985. In the period leading up to it, Alys had already come to the conclusion that the friends she was hanging about with were becoming increasingly reckless, especially one of them. They drank rough cider down on the beach in the evenings, sometimes lighting a fire to sit around. Alys did not want to be a part of this scene and was trying to distance herself from them. But as she had no real close family or any other friends, she knew she would feel completely isolated if she didn't meet up with them occasionally, so she kept a tenuous link with those she did like.

'In that case, I'll stroll into town and get myself a sandwich,' I say to the court Clerk. 'See you later.'

I don my black long-coat, put my briefcase in a locker and make my way out of the court building. It's quiet around town today, which is not unusual, given it's a Wednesday. Maybe the forecast of heavy rain has kept people indoors. I walk quickly towards the sandwich shop, taking a shortcut down backstreets, as the broody black clouds make it feel it could rain at any moment.

As I near the Auction Rooms, a sudden blustery squall starts, so I nip inside to wait while it passes – but I am easily tempted to look around. Such places always fascinate and intrigue me; I think about the tales these pieces of furniture could tell if only they could talk to me. I tend to be drawn to these types of historical relics of a bygone age – in fact I sometimes think that I may have been born into the wrong century.

Who has sat on these chairs and eaten at this trestle table? Whose clothes have hung in this mahogany wardrobe? Who has sat at this dressing table looking in the mirror, maybe dreading the day ahead? But nobody wants this dark brown furniture now. It's considered dated even though it's generally far better made than most of the modern stuff you can buy these days. There is, of course, a lot of tat here but interspersed are some very nice antique pieces: a smallish oak knee-hole desk with a beautifully embossed green leather top; an ancient studded-leather office swivel chair, shiny with use; a beautiful pitch-pine Caernarfonshire dresser, including a full blue and white transfer Abbey-pattern dinner set, possibly by Thomas Jones of Stoke. I would love to have a traditional house suitable for furniture such as this one day.

As I go down the next aisle, I notice people starting to gravitate towards the centre of the auction room floor. I watch as the auctioneer steps up onto his podium, where he can be seen by all, so presume the auction is about to start. People begin to clamour around him, ensuring they can be seen by him should they bid.

'Good afternoon, Ladies and Gentlemen,' he announces, picking up his gavel. 'Welcome to this afternoon session of the auction. We'll continue with Lot 51.'

But I turn away and continue to browse; I'm not here to buy. He will have to compete with the heavy rain as it continues to lash in waves onto the corrugated iron roof of the auction room. But I'm sure he will manage; he has one of those penetrating voices. His assistant, wearing a white coat, lifts the various pieces aloft for people to see as the auction proceeds.

I spot a set of beautiful, leatherbound, first-edition, classic poetry books but I guess these will go at a premium – certainly out of my reach.

Then as I wander down the next aisle, I see a large black embossed book, which I deduce is a Bible. As I get nearer, I see it has brass clasps to keep it closed and gilded-edge pages. Idly opening the clasps and lifting the front cover, I see a family tree, handwritten in black ink, showing numerous names and dates. At least this can talk to me in a fashion – through the information on this page. I think it looks pitiful in this setting, diminished and disrespectfully discarded. This was once somebody's pride and joy, a treasured family Bible. It looks well used and lovingly cared for, despite the dust now engrained into the patterned front cover. Given its size, I wonder if it had originally been a chapel or church Bible, it being well over a foot long.

Generations of gentle hands have respectfully turned these pages, seeking out an appropriate verse or passage for comfort, as well as guidance on how to live a moral life. I am not very into religion, describing myself as more spiritual – but I believe Christianity has been a force for good through the ages. It has guided people and inspired them to live good lives; but I also know that it has harboured dark forces, which have taken advantage of trusting, vulnerable people in order to feed and stimulate their own twisted perversions. I have come across many of the victims of these perpetrators during my time training and practising as a defence solicitor.

On the next page is the title. 'The Holy Bible' is printed in a large gothic-type script, surrounded by beautiful religious artwork, depicting angels, cherubs and an overarching golden spectrum of light. I deferentially close the cover and start to move down the next aisle but there is something compelling about it; an intrinsic quality which I can't quite put my finger on, as if it wants to communicate with me. It draws me back again. I note that the earliest entry is a date of birth in 1819 for an Efan Jones of Llan Farm in Eglwysbach. The next line names his children and their spouses, followed by four more generations of his descendants, with the last birth being in 1950. Are these last-born people still alive somewhere?

How sad to think that a family's history, once carefully and beautifully recorded here on this page, has ended up unwanted in an auction room. Maybe the family has died out. But surely somebody, somewhere, even a second cousin twice removed, would want to know about their noble forebears and may love to be in possession of this very tome, if only they knew of its existence.

I scan the furniture around me and wonder if some of these pieces also came from the same property as the Bible. Such a shame for someone's treasured belongings to end up in this damp, dusty auction room, for vultures such as me to pick at, then discard like a wasted carcass. As I ponder this, one of the auction room assistants moves past me, picks up the Bible and holds it aloft.

'How much am I bid for this lot, a Bible and a box of old photos and documents, all in excellent condition? No one interested? Who will give me a fiver?'

I look around and see the disinterested faces, mentally willing him to hurry up, so he can get to the lot they are interested in.

'I can't let it go for less than two pounds,' he says to silence, as he scans the room.

With uncharacteristic impulsiveness, I put up my hand.

'I have a starting bid of two pounds. Thank you, sir. Can someone offer me two pounds fifty?'

Another sweep of the room tells him an emphatic 'no.'

'Very well. Sold to the gentleman on my right.'

The gavel sweeps down with a sharp whack onto its circular sounding-block. I hadn't previously realised there were photos included in the lot. Maybe they will be of the people in the family tree.

Time has moved on since all the drama and I have yet to buy my sandwich. I pull out two pound notes from my wallet and rush over to the cashier's office.

'What's your name, sir?'

'Morgan, Gareth Morgan.'

Are you paying cash or cheque?'

'Cash.' I hand over the two one-pound notes.

She hands me my receipt, then kindly gives me a large carrier bag which was lying around, to carry my purchases in. Thankfully, the rain has stopped but large puddles sit in the deep potholes on this back road and water lies along the kerb where the drains are solidly blocked by years of dirt and debris. I quickly make my way out towards the sandwich kiosk.

Back in court in the afternoon, Alys' bail hearing is unsuccessful, leaving us disappointed. The address offered was not considered suitable due to the proximity to the victim's family, along with the violent nature of the offence. I rue the loss of this second chance to get her out and know that she will only have one more opportunity to apply. Our final bail application must therefore be absolutely watertight.

After the hearing, I go down to the holding cell to speak to Alys and find her looking forlorn, hugging her knees in the corner of the green padded bench. She is in a very low mood, leaving me concerned that her despondency and hopelessness about her situation may lead her to a dark place.

'This is so unfair. I don't want to go back to that place. I didn't do it, why won't anybody just believe me? I was nowhere near them when they injured that lad. Yes, I admit I had been with them late that afternoon, but then I left to have an early night,' she reiterates to me.

'The problem is, we can't actually prove that, Alys.'

It is considered a serious offence, plus the aggravating factor that the victim is deemed vulnerable. Although there were quite a few girls involved, no one is admitting they actually did it. It seems they were playing a game where they were spinning the victim around until he lost his balance, then he fell over, badly injuring his head on a nearby rock. He's very poorly in hospital and we just have to hope he recovers, or it could well become a charge of manslaughter. No one is admitting to the offence. They all blame each other, as well as Alys for what happened.

'Anyway, Alys, the police tell me they are still actively cross-checking information from their various interviews and following up on any further leads. Even if you didn't actually do anything, they claim you are still involved, as you did nothing to prevent it happening. You were known to hang around with these girls. If what you say is correct and you were not there at the time the crime was committed, we must find someone who can absolutely prove that. Did you talk to anyone on the phone that evening? Did you speak to anyone on your way back?'

'I can't remember, but I was home all evening. I had a long soak in the bath 'cause I was feeling rotten, then I went to bed to study. I knew my cousin was downstairs. I could hear she was watching some TV programme I didn't like, so I didn't bother going down.'

'I wonder why she won't just say I was at home,' she adds pensively. 'It's almost as if she wants me to be in trouble and out of their way.'

'She says she didn't actually see you, so could not vouch that you were in all evening.'

'I'd love to know why she is lying then. She knew I was in. She would have heard the front door opening and closing when I came in and me moving about upstairs on the squeaky floorboards. She would have heard the bathwater draining. You have to help me get out of this nightmare! If I had been involved, I would admit it. They were drinking cider and I could see that things could start to turn nasty, so I left.'

Her voice sounds both wretched and desperate at the same time, which leaves me with an uneasy feeling. I tend to trust my instinct on these things; it is telling me that she is being utterly truthful. Mind you, an objective flicker of doubt still lingers, as I know there are many accomplished liars who are very convincing – especially in my line of work. But I sense she is different somehow, almost incapable of lying successfully. She would probably give herself away with a guilty look if she was lying. Maybe she is too honest and naïve for her own good, without guile or deceitfulness. Maybe this is what comes of being brought up by her *Nain*, from the older generation, which may have had stricter morals.

For these same reasons, she does not 'fit in' the prison environment. She is not particularly streetwise. She has, so far, managed to stay out of the usual prison dramas by keeping her head down, herself to herself. But for how long can she keep that up before she is dragged into another inmate's argument?

I found it unsettling when Alys had said it was as if her cousin 'wants me to be in trouble and out of their way.' This statement is to resonate around in my head, off and on, for the next few weeks.

As I make my way out of the court to my car, I suddenly remember the Bible and photos, which I'd left with the court usher earlier. Cursing under my breath, I return to the building to retrieve them, just as he is locking up.

'Quite a tome you've got there, sir,' he utters, as he hands me the carrier bag.

I nod wryly, wondering now what on earth had possessed me to bid for it; little did I know that I would become obsessed with it – and that in time, it would prove to be critically important.

I put the Bible and the box of photos in the boot of my Golf GTi, along with my briefcase, then jump into the driver's seat and head for home. I will look at it properly when I next have some free time. Meanwhile, I must review where I am with my other cases, then start to work on Alys' final bail application.

As I drive out of the car park, I see Ruth, the court probation officer.

'Ruth, can you suggest a more suitable bail address before Alys' next appearance?' I ask, winding down the window as I pull up alongside her. 'Although the offence is considered violent, I don't believe she poses any risk of harm – and she has no previous.'

'Leave it with me, we've got time until the next bail app. Let's speak next week sometime. Meanwhile, I'll give it some thought….... I'm on my way to meet up with some colleagues in that new wine bar on the prom. You can join us if you like.'

'Thanks – but no, I'm planning to get a takeaway, then do some catch-up work, so need a clear head.'

I like Ruth; she is usually helpful and always does her best for her clients, plus I have a sneaky feeling that she might just fancy me a little. But being ambitious and newly qualified, I have put my social life on hold just for now, while I get myself established in my career. Plenty of time later to play the field – not that I am in any way a player.

As a treat on Sunday afternoon, I take a break from my legal work and settle down at the kitchen table with the old Bible. Lifting open the large front cover, I feel as if I am stepping back into a long-forgotten world; it seems almost disrespectful to be snooping on the lives of these people. Then I justify it to myself by thinking they are long since gone from this world, so cannot mind too much.

I look in more detail at the names. Entered on the first main line, in the normal script of that time, are the names of Efan and Myfanwy Jones, whilst the entry of their first-born son William is written below in a beautiful copperplate script. Usefully, Efan's date of birth and the date of their marriage are there, so I decide I should go to their local church soon to try and look them up.

Then, on rifling through the box of photos, I find their actual marriage certificate. Myfanwy's parents' names are recorded on it but 'Unknown' is written across the section for Efan's parents on the certificate. Having started a reference file for my research into the family, I carefully place this document into it.

I could take this certificate with me when I drive up to Eglwysbach to try to get a look at the Church Records there. Maybe while I am in the village, I may even be able to find the whereabouts of this Llan Farm.

Family Tree

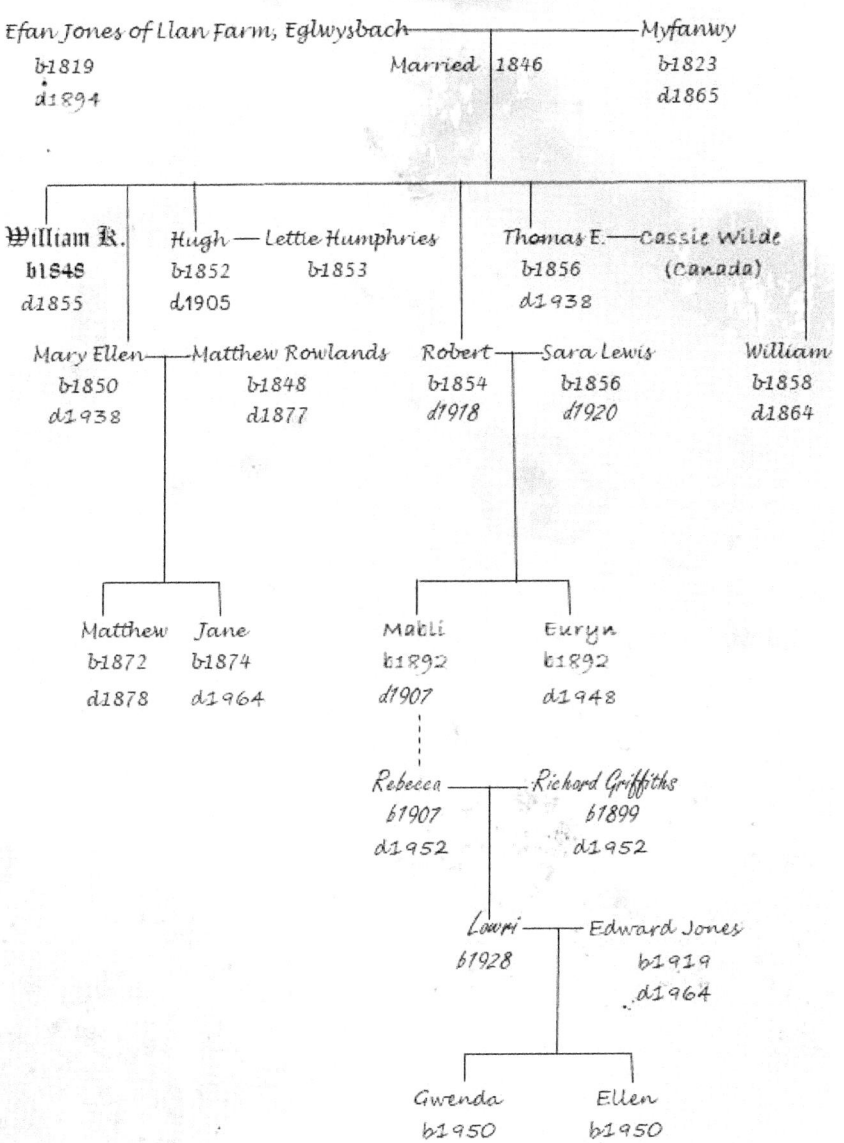

9

Welsh / English Glossary

Nain	Grandmother
plentyn siawns	illegitimate (literally 'child of chance')
Afon	River
Hen Efail	Old Forge
Helo eto	Hello again
Sut wyt ti?	How are you?
bach	little
ffenester	window
Fe ddaeth yr Athraw, ac y mae yn galw am danat	The Lord has come, and he is calling for you
gwas ffarm	farm hand
penderfynol	stubborn
gwialen fedw	birch rod
Ti eisiau reid i Gyffin, blodyn?	You want a ride to Gyffin, flower?
Oes, diolch	Yes, thank you
Wyt ti'n cadw'n dda	Are you keeping well?
Iawn, diolch	Fine, thanks
hen lanc	old unmarried man
Hedd Perfaith Hedd	Peace Perfect Peace
Bws Bach Hên Bentre	Old Village Small Bus
fy'n ghariad bach i	my little love
panad	cuppa

Efan's Story

'I thank the Lord that we were offered the tenancy of this farm, with its existing stock. It's in a fine position. Mixed arable and livestock – a large dairy herd of Welsh Blacks and a flock of hardy Welsh mountain sheep, plus it has a stream running through the fields. It supplies the meat, milk, cheese and butter to the big house, the villagers and local shops, as well as the nearby weekly farmers' market. If we can break even this first season, we will be well set up but it's going to take a great deal of sacrifice and back-breaking hard work.'

Fanwy smiled fondly at Efan's enthusiasm and nodded her tacit agreement. It was a life she knew well.

They walked around some of the near boundaries of the farm, familiarising themselves with its forty-seven acreage – hardly able to believe their good fortune. Timing was everything, and they had been in the right place at the right time, for reasons that frankly baffled Efan. He was sure there must have been plenty of others, more experienced, who had wanted it.

'Seems Old Tom has been working here for over sixty years, but as he said, he can't manage it on his own now because of his arthritis. But there is one condition to the tenancy – he asks to live out the rest of his days on the farm. He says he'd like to convert one of the outhouses into his accommodation and will carry on working to earn his keep. I have no objection to that – his being here will be a real bonus – he knows every acre of the place and every individual animal.'

The frontage of Llan farmhouse was unassuming, blending in as part of the High Street. The front door was on the road at the side, which went up a hill past his fields. The farm barn and outbuildings were behind the main house, where the land sloped gently upwards towards a small deciduous copse. Originally, the farmhouse had been freestanding, abutting what would have once been the farm track. But gradually, houses, shops, chapels, inns and taverns were built alongside. The track became the main road, creating the High Street. A small hamlet developed, housing workers for the surrounding hill farms and mills in this mainly rural area.

The next building along from the farm was Llan Grocery shop. Then a few hundred yards further along the road again, set back in its own grounds, stood a large manor house called Ty Mawr Llan. The farm itself had belonged originally to the house and had provisioned it, but now they were separate entities. Sadly, Ty Mawr Llan had long been boarded up, abandoned and left empty for many years. It was in a sorry state, overgrown with bramble, weeds and self-seeded saplings growing up between holes in the roofs of the various outhouses.

Efan's wife, Fanwy, came from solid farming stock, so the life was as natural as breathing to her. Her family owned a large sheep farm further up the Conwy Valley, selling the meat and the wool of the hardy Welsh sheep. The couple had met one day, quite by chance. She was out foraging for mushrooms – whilst Efan was on his way to see his eccentric friend.

'Those look good,' he said. 'Can I buy some to take to my friend, who lives in that house over there?'

'Take two with my blessing,' she replied. 'He always greets me politely when I pass by.'

That day, they had sealed their destinies.

Fanwy was pivotal to his plan. Some people admired her handsome face, her hourglass figure, her voluminous dark-blond hair. But these were not the main qualities Efan valued in her, although he knew she was undeniably striking. He loved her to her very core. He valued her abundance of fortitude, sound judgement, common sense, and her ability to make anything out of almost nothing. Her innate farming knowledge was inherited from generation upon generation of pastoral ancestors, whereas Efan's skills had been acquired from the various farms he had worked on as a boy and young man. But he knew he couldn't have taken the farm on without her. He felt very lucky the day she had decided to settle on him, given that locally he was considered more than a little odd.

Efan had never known who his real parents were and guessed he was a *'plentyn siawns.'* He had never bonded or ever been close to the estate's forester couple who raised him; he knew instinctively he wasn't of their flesh and blood, or intellect. His personality was too different; neither did he bear any physical resemblance to either of them. He thought that maybe he was the result of an indiscreet dalliance; the dirty secret of a respectable, well-to-do family, which needed hiding away in the dark remote place where they lived. Whenever he broached the subject of his parentage, they clammed up, so he assumed they had been warned or paid not to disclose who his parents were, if indeed they even knew. He guessed they were given money to raise him, not that he saw much benefit of that and had to work very hard for his keep.

Their cottage was dark and dank with very little natural light, due to the dense umbrella of trees shrouding it. After finishing his wood-chopping chores, on which he vented his many frustrations, he got out into the light and sunshine as often as he could. He spent days digging up peat clods on the surrounding moors, then bringing them back on the cart to the woods to store in a pile, which as commoners, they were permitted to do. Once dried, the peat, along with the chopped firewood and logs, was sold to locals; these were all a major source of fuel for most families. He also made roof tiles out of the wood, when he had some particularly good oak.

During his wanderings as a young lad, he had befriended 'The Professor', an elderly, eccentric man who lived alone in a beautiful gentleman's residence on the edge of the large forest. Initially, they conversed and passed the time of day over his garden wall, then later he invited Efan in for some tea.

'You look as if you need something to eat, my boy,' he would say. 'Come in, I have some ham which needs frying and my hens have just laid some fresh eggs.'

With his strange, tasselled hat, fingerless gloves, half-moon wired spectacles and clearly superior intelligence, he was a curious mix of healer and astronomer. He was often in the middle of some scientific experiment and liked to tell Efan all about it. They seemed unlikely friends, but quickly bonded and were kindred spirits. He liked Efan's insatiable curiosity about absolutely everything. He found his thirst for knowledge refreshing and he was always pleased whenever Efan called by to see him.

Over the years of their friendship, The Professor taught Efan how to read and write, know his numbers and how to identify the various constellations in the sky. Considering Efan never attended school, his general knowledge was excellent. Sadly, and possibly because of this, he was considered locally to be a curiosity, as well as a 'know all' by his contemporaries.

'Walking through the wood on my way here today, I managed to bag myself a vixen in pup with my sling,' Efan told his mentor one afternoon. 'I should get five shillings from a trader for her,' he announced proudly.

'You must be an excellent shot. What will you spend the money on?'

'I might buy myself a gun, so I can catch some more. It could turn out to be quite lucrative.'

'How will you learn how to use a gun?'

'I'll go and speak to one of the gamekeepers on the estate. I'd be doing them a favour in helping to keep the vermin down for them.'

Once Efan was old enough, he left the cottage and worked as a farm hand on various farms in the Eglwysbach area. Each year in May at the Hirelings Fair, he would offer his services to local farmers for the year. He found that some of the farmers he worked for were fair – but others exploited him. This Fair, as well as the others held in February, August and November, was very popular, due to the various stalls which sold seeds and an assortment of implements, as well as the usual livestock.

Efan was resigned to the belief that this would be the pattern of the rest of his life – but at the age of twenty-eight, he was shocked to suddenly be offered the tenancy of Llan Farm. Without his knowledge, his natural father had covertly watched his son growing up. He was pleased to see that the apple had not fallen far from the tree and knew that Efan had inherited his better characteristics. He was impressed by Efan's self-reliance and his drive to improve himself. He realised that all Efan needed was the opportunity to prove himself to the world.

Llan Farm had become slightly run-down – but Efan was confident he would soon get it in good order. The farmhouse itself, fronting the main street, was a substantial building. Upstairs there was a bedroom over the front parlour and another over the dairy. There was a third at the back over a milking parlour, which was next to the main kitchen. Behind this were the stables with their frontage of cobbled stones, a goodly barn, a hay shed and some open-fronted farm sheds.

'Hopefully we will get a good crop of lambs in the spring, God willing, and a decent mix of calves – heifers to add to the dairy herd and some bullocks for beef,' said Fanwy. 'The half dozen pigs will provide us with the hams.'

'There is just enough hay-feed left for the animals for the rest of the winter,' Efan replied. 'In the meantime, we'll have to be very careful. But luckily Old Tom has a whole side of beef hanging in one of the outhouses and there are still a few sides of bacon hanging from the rafters, curing over the fire in the kitchen. We also have a field full of turnips ready to be lifted – all of these will ensure none of us, or the animals, will starve this winter!'

Efan took over the farm in January 1848. Life was hard then. Most people lived off or worked on the land, on small, mainly self-sufficient farms. What they couldn't make or grow, they bartered for, or bought at the local farmers' markets.

Life was even harder on the outlying hill-farms of the parish in the mid eighteen-hundreds – with very little change or improvement in conditions from how it had been in the previous century. A typical farmer's wife would walk about five miles each week to Llanrwst Market, often carrying a baby on her back, where she sold her butter and eggs. Eggs were sixpence a dozen and a pound of potatoes cost one penny.

Harvesting was done by hand with a scythe and sickle, while wooden rakes were used to form upstanding stacks for the sun and wind to dry off. Later they were loaded onto flat carts with pitchforks, for storing in the barns for the winter. Thankfully, there was a small hand-powered threshing machine on Llan Farm to separate the corn from the stalks, rather than the hand-flailing they previously had to do on the barn floor.

The introduction of these machines, following years of low wages for farm labourers, meant fewer labourers were needed to tend the crops. This had triggered farm labourers in southern England to revolt in 1830, because of widespread unemployment and starvation. Some so-called Swing Rioters were hanged, while more than five hundred were transported to hard labour in Australia. Although the Swing Riots spread northwards, they did not reach Wales. However, a few years later in 1838, farmers and labourers in Wales took part in the Rebecca Riots. Men, dressed as women, rioted in response to the levels of taxation and the imposition of turnpike tolls, which provided a focus for discontent.

Efan was inordinately pleased that he was finally about to become established in his own right in life – but was also aware of the creeping industrialisation underway, luring farm hands away from farming for higher wages in the belching factories of the North. He could never be tempted to go and work in such a place for any amount of money. After his claustrophobic childhood in that dark, suffocating forest, he needed to be able to be outside in wide spaces and open fields.

'Running this farm will be a big responsibility to take on but with the help of Old Tom, we'll make it work,' said Fanwy, not letting show her slight disquiet regarding the risk they were taking on. It was quite a gamble. She knew how unpredictable farming life and landowners could be. 'But if the owner is willing to wait for the rent until after harvest time as he's agreed, we have a good chance.'

Fanwy was truly at one with her environment and seemed to experience it differently from other people. She blended in and was permanently tuned in to her surroundings, picking up signals via an innate, inbuilt antenna. She interpreted these messages through a continuum of sights, sounds, smells and atmospheres, and sub-consciously analysed them. She read body language and heard what people were not saying. She possessed an inherent ability to tune in to the joys and sorrows of others and knew instinctively how they were feeling. To her, Efan was an open but endlessly interesting book, which she never tired of reading.

Fanwy would occasionally walk down the dell, through the Bodnant estate, where she watched the white-fronted dippers feeding amongst the pools in the stream, which eventually spilled out into the banks of *Afon* Conwy. On the banks, if she was lucky, she would see brilliantly-plumaged kingfishers darting low over the water. Sometimes, she would throw a hook and line into the water while she foraged and occasionally caught a nice fat river trout to take home for supper.

The area was carpeted by an abundance of wildflowers. Myfanwy knew all these by name, as well as their uses for healing and in cooking. She knew to avoid the poisonous ones such as Wild Arum and Dog's Mercury, which grew alongside the bluebells in the dell, while the roadside abundance of cow parsley was, for her, a harbinger of spring and hopefully warmer weather.

She sat down on a carpet of celandines and watched the bees gathering the pollen from their golden centres. She knew that common pennywort, once boiled, was helpful for urinary illnesses. She picked and dried the wonderfully beneficial wild garlic in early summer and occasionally feasted on a patch of sweet wild strawberries. In the autumn, she would harvest the riverside hazel bushes, fallen acorns, small wild damsons, sloes and over-ripe rosehips. She knew them all – but one of her favourites was the delicate smell in early spring of the wild honeysuckle.

She heard the men shouting to each other as their flat-boats laboriously hauled goods across onto the opposite riverbank near Tal-y-Cafn. Sometimes, she saw the drovers swimming the cattle across at low tide to the livestock market, close to the coaching inn.

But she wasn't as safe there as she had once thought. On the last occasion she had gone to the riverbank, a man who had once begged her to marry him, stole up behind her. Putting his hand over her mouth while threatening her to be quiet, he threw her roughly onto the ground.

'Thought you were too good for me, didn't you? Whore! You took that idiot, Efan, a nobody, a bastard. But you're not too good for me now, are you?' he said menacingly.

She had hit her head hard on the pebbly ground when she fell and was momentarily stunned. He fell on top of her and pinned her arms down above her head.

'Let's see who's good enough now, shall we?' he said, as she struggled to get out of his grip.

As he forced his knee between her legs, her dog, Taff, seemed none too keen on what was happening and clamped his jaws into the man's forearm, then tugged. The man shouted out in agony then let go of one of Fanwy's arms as he tried to swat the dog away. The dog then bit into his calf and tugged, making him scream out again in pain. In utter fury, he turned on the dog and rolling sideways, picked up a rock to throw at it – but missed. Now apoplectic with rage, he rose to pick up a large stick to beat it with.

Seeing her chance, Fanwy scrambled to her feet. Picking up her bundle as well as her skirts, she ran for her life, quickly followed by her hero, Taff. She turned around once, to see the man sitting on the bank, holding his injured leg, while swearing obscenities.

As she walked, exhausted, into the farmyard, Efan looked up.

'You're back early.'

'Yes, not much there today.'

Taff went up to Efan for his usual fuss. Efan noticed blood on his beard.

'I think he got hold of some creature or something while I was foraging,' she said.

No more was said. She did not tell Efan about the encounter as there was no real harm done – not to her anyway. She did not think the man would be talking to anyone about it either, given that she and a dog had got the better of him. Had she told Efan, it would probably have ended in a severe beating or worse for the man – and Efan would be no use to her in the county gaol.

During the dark early evenings of winter, Efan regularly brought in now-dried peat clods he had dug up from a nearby marshy area soon after they had moved into the farm. This source of fuel took the edge off the harsher weather of winter. Fanwy had managed to turn the once unwelcoming, bare farmhouse into a cosy, comfortable haven. Meanwhile, Old Tom had finished converting one of the outhouses into his own living quarters and was quite content there.

Despite some deprivation, they survived until spring. Once the frosts had passed, the fields became bathed in sunshine and drenched in soft soaking rains. Wild crocus, snowdrops and daffodils – the harbingers of spring – started to appear in or near the hedgerows. New grass sprouted and a few early lambs were born, giving a feeling of hope and continuity.

The time came to till the soil ready for spring planting.

'First, you need to turn over the top field next to the trees,' Old Tom advised Efan. 'It's been left fallow for a few years, so is now ready for use.'

'I'll harness the cob in the morning and get to it,' Efan replied, 'but first I'll check the plough is in good order.'

In one of the open farm sheds, he sanded the rust off the plough discs, then sharpened them, using a fine whetstone. He replaced one of the woodworm-ridden plough handles and beeswaxed the leather harness ready for fitting onto Betsan, the Welsh Cob.

'Weather looks set fair,' said Fanwy, as they rose well before the sun next morning.

Conditions were good and ploughing easy. Efan sowed seed potatoes for an early crop to cleanse the soil after it had been left fallow. Then he turned over two more fields, which he left to dry out.

The domestic hens as well as the wild birds were grateful for the newly exposed worms, which fortified them as they built their nests for the eggs they were soon to lay. They were also glad when the trees began to sprout their buds, as the soft new leaves, once fully grown, would eventually provide camouflage for them from the scavenging jackdaws and crows, which raided their nests for eggs and chicks. Smaller birds such as chaffinch, goldfinch, robins and sparrows were canny enough to nest within the safety of the farm hedgerows, into which the larger birds couldn't enter, and would make an enormous racket if they ever tried.

Sticky horse-chestnut buds, usually the first to leaf, were closely followed by sycamores. In late April, their leaves created welcome shelter for the sheep, until a couple of months later, when shearing relieved them of their heavy woollen winter coats.

The more vigorous lambs were delivered as normal. The weaker ones and those rejected by their mothers, were nursed and hand-fed in the kitchen by Fanwy. Life was vigorously rubbed into the sickly ones with an old hessian sack; every single one was worth the effort of saving. Dead wood, the bounty from winter storms, along with the dried-out peat clods, kept the black range burning through the day and overnight.

One evening, after a late supper of bread and cheese, Efan watched as Fanwy bottle-fed a lamb, using a glass bottle with a rubber teat on. Suddenly it dawned on him that her waist had thickened somewhat.

'Fanwy, is what I am suspecting true?'

Her beautiful blush confirmed his suspicion and he was

overjoyed. Their first son! He knew it would be a boy – and sure enough William was born later that year; a new life bringing new joy and hope into theirs. They had no inkling then of the raw heartbreak they would suffer a few short years later.

Chapter 2

I decide to visit Alys in prison to discuss her final bail application and to see if I can glean any more information regarding her movements on that fateful evening. I want to get a proper feel for the feasibility of her version of events.

As she enters the Visitors area of the prison, she clearly stands out among all the others. She is stunningly beautiful in an elfin sort of way, in this grim dystopian setting, with its grey painted walls and orange plastic tables and chairs screwed into the floor by thick steel brackets. I worry that in this environment, her looks and her nature could unfortunately attract attention from some other inmates.

Her whole face lights up when she recognises me. I am strangely and inexplicably touched by this and to be honest, slightly disconcerted. What does this mean? Has she formed an attachment to me? Uncharacteristically, I feel an unfamiliar sense of response, a weird stirring inside me, as if something undeniable is recognising a kindred spirit – a compatible soul. Did hers just communicate with mine on some deep, subconscious, other-worldly level – in a way that is completely out of the control of both of us? I feel momentarily flustered by this experience as I walk over to her. In that brief moment, I conclude that maybe I don't have a choice about playing the field; perhaps the choice is being made for me by unseen forces.

Putting aside this strange experience, and composing myself I quietly ask, 'How are you doing?'

'Oh, you know, I'm getting by somehow. Making the best of it, I guess. But I felt so depressed just sitting in my cell, looking at those four grey walls around me; the bunk's hard, the ranting of my cell mate and having to use the toilet in the same room – ugh! – is so disgusting. So, I find ways to get off the wing as often as I can. First, I started as the hub food server at lunch and supper time, which meant bringing up the hot trolley from the kitchen, then dishing out the food. Night-time is the worst, when they start shouting to each other from their cells. There's no chance of any sleep then. It's like they are afraid of the silence and have to hear their own voices and those of others.'

'But since then, I've been made a Listener,' Alys continues, 'because I'm now considered a trusted inmate. I can get called out anytime of the day or night to talk to a prisoner who is having a hard time adjusting. Most are missing their families, their children. One is only here because she hadn't paid her TV licence. Can you believe that? What danger is she to anyone? Depriving the BBC of their funds? She probably had to prioritise the family food bill over the family babysitter!'

'It's good that you are keeping your head down and your spirits up,' I say.

'I'm also going to the gym in the mornings. In the afternoons, I work in the library, so I get the pick of the best books, which is great. I'm keeping myself as busy as I can, to fill my time. That way I don't spend too much time thinking depressing thoughts.'

'This is all excellent, Alys,' I reply encouragingly. 'It will go in your progress report for your next court appearance. Keep up the good work, it's very important to make a positive impression on the Judge – the sooner we can get you out of here, the better. We're working on it.'

She smiles, then inordinately pleased by my praise, she blushes ever so slightly, which is sweet. I try to bring up the subject of the offence but as she says, she can't tell me anything else, she wasn't there. I am becoming more convinced now that she is being totally honest.

'There's also information in the library about how you can study for qualifications,' she tells me, changing the subject, 'so I'm looking into that. The Librarian is being very helpful. She told me you can now study for a degree in prison but it's mainly the long-termers who get into that.'

'Well, let's hope you won't be in long enough to take advantage of that! Ruth, the probation officer, is looking for an acceptable bail address for you. If you do get bail, you'll have to stick to some very strict conditions.'

'I don't care how strict they are, as long as I can get out of here,' she replies wistfully.

* * *

As a distraction from work, I look at the Bible again at the weekend. I notice once more that the entry for William, the first-born of Efan and Myfanwy, is beautifully written in a scholarly script. William was born in 1848 and there is also a note at the foot of the page in the same script that the Vicar of Eglwysbach baptised him in 1849. The date of his death in 1855 reveals their probably longed-for first-born died very young. I wonder if the Vicar who baptised him then buried him those few short years later.

Looking through the bundle of photos and papers, I see a black and white photograph of what looks like a Welsh, slate-roofed, longhouse. A handsome couple is standing proudly outside the porch. Going by their attire, it looks as if it could have been taken in the late eighteen-hundreds. I wonder who these people are and where this house is.

Flicking through the rest of the photographs, I see that most are of people from about the late nineteenth to mid-twentieth century, mixed up with some faded colour polaroid ones of what look like hippies from the nineteen-sixties and seventies.

I decide that if the weather is good next weekend, I will drive up to Eglwysbach Church. Perhaps I will find some clues there about the Llan family in the church records. I'm now beginning to feel that my mission is to reunite this Bible with descendants of this family.

The drive up the Conwy Valley to Eglwysbach is always very beautiful, no matter what time of year. After a prolonged winter, there are finally signs of spring. Little green shoots are appearing, the hawthorn is flowering, and daffodils, crocus and cuckoo flowers are already out on the verges. Cheerful clumps of primroses, with their delicate pale-yellow petals quivering in the chilly wind, have made an appearance and even last year's blanket of dead bracken up on the hillside slopes, wet from a recent shower, adds a dramatic deep rust colour to the scenic backdrop.

Mid-morning, the village is very quiet. I park close by the church and enter through the rather impressive gateway. There are graves surrounding three sides of the church; some look very ancient, whilst others are made cheerful by freshly cut flowers. Many generations of Valley people are buried here. The gravestones, mainly slate and granite, are a variety of shapes and sizes. The elaborate statues clearly belong to the more illustrious and important people, whilst tombs hold the bodies of the titled and wealthier families.

I turn the round black metal handle on the church door and enter, to be met by a wave of ancient musty coldness. It is Saturday. The Sexton is inside laying out the hymn books on rows of pews for tomorrow's services. After I tell him my mission, he kindly leads me back to a dusty part of the vestry.

'We have some parish records in here as you can see,' pointing to some very old ledgers, 'but as you have not made an official arrangement, I cannot really show them to you – you need to speak to the Vicar first about getting to view them. Any viewing has to be supervised by him, as they are very old and fragile.'

'But there should also be copies of all these records in the local archives,' he adds helpfully. 'You can ask them to help dig them out for you by district. There is also a local historian living in the village, who knows a lot about the history of the place. Maybe speak to him?'

I scribble down his details and thank the Sexton for his help.

As I need to be in Conwy shortly, I decide to drive back down the other side of the river, so head for the Tal-y-Cafn bridge. Before driving over the railway level-crossing, I notice the animal pens of a livestock market and wonder how long it has been here and whether Efan had brought his livestock here to sell, more than a hundred years ago.

I relish imagining the sort of lives the people I am researching had lived. I think about what Efan and Myfanwy's first-born son's life must have been like and want to find out about the lives of the rest of their children. This is a perfect antidote for me to the sometimes 'drudge' of reading tedious legal argument. As a junior, I know I need to do the groundwork to get myself properly established in the small practice which thankfully took me on. But sometimes now, it's beginning to feel as if my legal work gets in the way of what I really want to be doing, especially when I am in the middle of focusing on a particular member of the family. For example, I would love to know about the short life of little William and what caused him to die at such a young age.

* * *

William's Story

'What is the child to be named?' the Vicar of St. Martin's, John Efans asked, looking gravely at Efan over his round and ancient-even-then, wire-framed spectacles.

'His name will be William Kyffin Jones,' replied Efan, standing proudly beside Fanwy at the font.

'In this year of our Lord, 1849, I baptise this child in the name of the Father, Son and Holy Ghost.'

He then poured the holy water, cupped in his hand from the church font, onto the top of little William's head. At this, the baby let out an almighty cry, shocked by the iciness of the water but quietened down after being returned to and soothed by the comfort of his mother's arms.

After the service was over, Efan went back to the vestry to thank the Vicar for his ministrations. He stood there awkwardly twisting his cap in his hand as he joked, 'I shall have to buy a Bible now so that I can start recording the births of all my children.' Then he quickly added, 'God willing, He will grant me more,' so as not to appear overly presumptuous.

As he spoke, the Vicar began rooting in a cupboard and Efan, believing he was being dismissed, turned to walk towards the vestry door.

The Vicar then turned around.

'It just so happens that there is a Bible here,' he said. 'It is no longer being used since the new version came out, which I prefer to read from. I will gift it to your family willingly, so long as you agree to read a passage from it each day and attend church regularly.'

'Vicar, I don't know what to say,' Efan mumbled, stunned at this offer. 'You truly are a good and Godly man. Such kindness overwhelms me. I promise faithfully that we, as a family, will read a passage each evening after supper, if you see your way to bestow this gift on us.'

'Then take it with my blessing,' holding it out with both hands, adding, before Efan could take it, 'Would you like me to write in your first entry for you?'

Efan did not like to dissuade the Vicar of his assumption that he could not write it himself, so nodded and quietly watched as William's birth was duly recorded on the front page of the Bible. Later that evening, using quill and ink, Efan wrote above it, recording his own marriage to his beloved Fanwy.

Because of the kind gesture of the gift of the Bible, Efan remained faithful to the Church in Wales for the rest of his life, despite the fact that many of his contemporaries had left the church in droves to join the fledgling non-conformist sects, for which he had no time.

In 1850, their daughter, Mary Ellen was born, followed by Hugh in 1852, then Robert in 1854. In 1856, they were blessed with Thomas. He was a lively one and turned out to be brave and fearless – a very independent and self-reliant little soul.

By aged seven, their first-born, William, had become a bit of an explorer and wanderer. He was wont to go about on his adventures around the farm – once his chores were done. He was fascinated by insects. He loved to play by the stream where he watched bees burrowing into their nests on the banks and the wasps and insects coming to the water. His favourites were the beautiful tiger-striped, double-winged dragonflies, with their big bulbous eyes. He also liked watching the dazzling electric blue and red damselflies darting about. He wondered where they laid their eggs as he watched them suddenly land on stones in the stream, to enjoy the warmth of the sun on their gossamer wings. Then just as suddenly, they would dip their heads for a drink and quickly dart off.

One afternoon, after he had been out for a couple of hours, he began following one particularly large tiger dragonfly, which flitted from stone to stone in the stream, before it flew up onto the boundary wall, as if it was leading him somewhere. Climbing up onto the wall to see where it had gone, William suddenly lost his balance and fell down onto the other side. He lay still for a moment, winded, checking he was not injured.

His father had warned him never to go on the estate land – but he really hadn't meant to. It was an accident. He knew he shouldn't be there so he wandered along the inside of the boundary wall, trying to find a place he could get a foothold to climb back up onto the top of the wall. Then he would be able to quickly fall back down onto his father's land without anyone knowing. As he searched, looking upwards, he was oblivious to what was hidden below in the long grass.

Later, his parents began to fret about where he was, as he was always back by suppertime. Calling out his name, Old Tom and Efan set off to find him. First, they checked the barn – but with no joy. Then, taking the dogs with them, they expanded their search outwards to the other farm buildings, spanning further out again into the fields, until they finally reached the boundary wall.

'The dog's sniffing something over the other side,' Efan suddenly heard Tom shout to him. Then, 'Over here, quick, he's injured!'

Efan rushed towards him.

William lay there on the other side of the stone wall boundary of the farm with the Bodnant Estate. Efan had never in his life experienced the sheer and utter horror he felt at that moment, as he looked down at his young son. His leg had been caught in a metal-toothed mantrap. It was bloodied and mangled. The steel teeth of the trap had cut right through the muscle, exposing the bone, which had been snapped in half. Sweating with the effort, Tom forced open the two halves of the trap while Efan gently pulled out William's mangled little leg, now hanging onto his thigh by a bloodied bit of skin and muscle. Efan lifted and cradled his little son's limp body in his arms – but looking at the grey pallor of William's face, he guessed that he was probably already dead. He had bled to death from his horrific injury.

As Efan walked back to the farmhouse carrying William's dead body, he held him close to him, as if trying to transfer his own life force into him, to bring him back to life. He could barely see where he was walking, for the stinging salt tears blurring his vision. His heart was drained of joy. It began to fill instead with a deep, dark, numbing sorrow at the disbelief that his young son had died such a violent death. How much pain had he suffered while he lay trapped there all alone?

Efan was racked with guilt and sorrow, knowing that as his father, he was meant to protect his child. The contrition he felt was immeasurable. He imagined him lying there, calling out in vain for his parents to save him, until his life force had eventually drained out of him. He imagined his pleading voice, with all expectation of being saved, gradually weakening. Then silenced forever. Efan hoped fervently that God had been merciful enough to let him lose consciousness quickly from the shock of the injury, so that he had not suffered any more pain than necessary.

Disgustedly, and with downright loathing for those who had set it, Old Tom bent down and picked up the evil instrument with sheer revulsion and carried it home, so that no other human being or animal would ever need to suffer such a grotesque death again.

The estate's gamekeeper had laid the trap to deter poachers. Instead, his actions had resulted in the brutal taking of the life of a small defenceless child. The use of these traps had been made illegal in 1827 – except on large estates between sunset and sunrise, ostensibly to prevent house burglaries, so some were still in use – but this was in broad daylight.

Rumour had it that the gamekeeper who had set the trap, left his employment as soon as word reached him about what had happened. He threw a few possessions into a game bag and quietly stole away that night. Although he thought he was acting within the law, he was no doubt afraid of a local reprisal, believing that trouble could be brewing for him. Maybe a lynch mob would be formed to track him down.

News of William's tragic death shocked everyone in the district, despite their being well used to many tragedies in their lives. But this was the most shocking type, it was the death of a child. News eventually reached the ears of the Prime Minister. A law was subsequently passed to completely prohibit the use of these traps, thereby outlawing the practice – and promised a heavy penalty for anyone who still chose to use them.

The violent death of her son left Fanwy broken. She had watched as they walked back across the fields, carrying his mangled body to the house. After gently taking him off Efan, she cradled and rocked him in her arms for hours. It was difficult to get her to relinquish his body, to wash the blood off him, in readiness for him to go to his maker. She was never quite the same afterwards.

Their daughter, Mary Ellen, was also badly affected. She saw just how quickly somebody so full of life could be snuffed out, making her feel insecure and afraid. After that, the children tended to stay closer to the farmhouse, except that is for Thomas when he grew older. His adventurous spirit became difficult to keep dampened down.

Although Efan had stipulated a private 'family only' burial, locals and people from the surrounding area, every one of them dressed in black, had lined the High Street to show their respect and sympathy for the family. Efan walked up the whole length of the High Street from the farmhouse to the church, carrying his son's small coffin on his outstretched arms. His subdued family walked behind him in utter silence, their eyes fixed to the ground. Mr. Beverley, the schoolmaster, stood outside the Hall with his pupils as the family passed by. All had black bands tied around their upper arms and their heads were lowered in respect. Men removed their hats then bowed their heads as the little coffin passed by.

Suddenly, halfway down the street, a beautiful tenor voice started to sing a mournful hymn; then others joined in, in unison. Efan nodded his acknowledgment for their empathetic thoughtfulness – but inside he was numb and utterly broken, while he fought hard not to show his tears.

The enormous pride he had felt the day his first son was born had made him finally feel that he belonged somewhere – in the heart of the little family he had created. Having been a foundling, farmed out to be raised by strangers and belonging nowhere, he had at last felt whole. Had God been angry at his pride? Was this His way of punishing that sinful pride, by taking away his little son?

The Vicar, who had Christened baby William a few short years ago, was now burying their little son in the hallowed grounds of St. Martin's Church. After a short service at the graveside, a wooden cross was placed at the head of the tiny mound of earth. Later, a simple granite stone was erected with the inscription:

In memory of
William Kyffin Jones of Llan Farm
died tragically in 1855 aged seven years

Their last-born son, also named William, was born in 1858. He was a sickly child, whose birth Fanwy never seemed to get over. William became even more poorly as the years went by and eventually succumbed to a chest infection, already weakened by tuberculosis. The death of her first born and now her last, seemed to have sucked the life out of Fanwy. She eventually died of a broken heart in 1865, leaving her other children motherless and Efan grief-stricken. Mary Ellen had no choice but to step into her mother's shoes to raise her younger brothers and care for the family.

Following the death of his last-born son, then his beloved wife, Efan again endured the crushing wave of grief he had felt from losing his first-born, rising up once more to overwhelm him. He became despondent and downhearted. He wondered just how much more sorrow he could absorb but knew he must put his feelings aside to work and support his living children.

Not long afterwards, Old Tom was found dead in his bed one cold morning. He hadn't turned up to milk the cows, which had come in from the fields on their own and taken themselves into the milking parlour. Efan heard them lowing in pain from their swollen udders and had rushed out to milk them. Afterwards, he went to look for Tom in his accommodation, only to find that he had passed away peacefully during the night. The family felt his loss more keenly than they could ever have imagined; he had always felt like family. Little did they know.

* * *

Efan had expected the tenancy of the farm to continue indefinitely, so it came as a complete shock when he received a letter from a solicitor requesting him to call at his office in Llanrwst in one week's time.

'Are you going to tell me that the tenancy is to be ended?' he asked the solicitor as soon as he arrived.

'On the contrary,' he replied, 'the owner of Llan Farm has bequeathed it to you in his Will.'

'But... but... I don't understand,' Efan stammered, utterly stunned. 'How? Why even? Who is he? This can't be right. Have you mistaken me for another Efan Jones?'

'I am afraid that I am not at liberty to divulge his identity, as I have been sworn to secrecy. What I can tell you is that he has been observing you for years and acknowledged to me just how hard you have worked to improve the farm and that he was very pleased and proud of you.'

It looked like Efan's luck was finally swinging the other way, from all the sorrow and despair of the last few years. But despite Efan again begging the solicitor to tell him the identity of his benefactor, he was never to disclose it.

Efan guessed the bequest must be linked somehow to his own surreptitious birth but he had no idea how. Because he had been left the farm, he thought it likely that his birth father had died, and with him, any chance of ever finding out who he really was. Despite this, it was comforting to know that he had been secretly minding him throughout his life and knew of his good character and achievements. He wondered if he had ever come face to face with him but reasoned that he would, by some deep instinct, surely have 'known' him if he had. He also reasoned that he must have been an influential man to have been able to keep his birth a secret, as every effort to find out about him had been met with a stone wall of silence. Either that, or he was protecting the identity of someone else, possibly Efan's mother.

Although Efan felt no emotional attachment to the adoptive parents who had raised him, he sometimes visited them out of a sense of Christian duty, taking food from the farm to supplement their meagre income. But each time the subject came anywhere near his birth parents, the proverbial shutters came crashing down. Even when he told them his father had died, they still refused to tell him his identity.

During the next few years, the farm remained well established, despite the constant underlying sorrow of the family's numerous losses. Efan kept abreast of the modern farming methods of husbandry and the farm ran like clockwork. It became very profitable, despite having to pay the tithes demanded by the Church.

Mary Ellen had taken responsibility for running the house and caring for her brothers but a dairy maid was now employed to produce the butter and cheese. As the brothers Hugh, Robert and Thomas became older, they helped their father to rear the cattle, milk the cows, feed the pigs, and gather, shear and brand the sheep. They also broadcast the seed, then later on, harvested the hay and crops.

They attended the local school for part of the day, where Mr. Beverley reported that they were all very capable students – when they were actually there. It was a National School, built by the Church of England in Gothic style in 1832, five years before Victoria ascended the throne. Mr. Beverley would become very cross when the children were kept home from school to help during the busy times on the farm but grudgingly accepted that 'needs must' in such a community. And to be fair to Efan, he acknowledged just how important it was for the children to be educated, so did not keep them away unless it was strictly necessary.

Despite their cruel losses over the years, the family's faith remained strong. In truth, it was what kept them going through the difficult times. Efan kept his promise to the Vicar; every evening after supper, one child would choose a verse to read from the Bible, which would then be interpreted and discussed by the whole family.

Chapter 3

I have again come to the end of a busy, sometimes chaotic week. My probation officer friend, Ruth, has finally managed to find a suitable bail address for Alys to be released into, together with a comprehensive but stringent bail package. It will necessitate her residing at the stated address and adhering to strict curfew times. She would also be prohibited from contacting any of the other accused or the victim's family – not that she would anyway. Alys would be released into Ruth's supervision and be required to report for regular weekly appointments with her for the first few weeks. This would then be regularly reviewed, to monitor her progress and adherence to the conditions.

The final hearing is next week. I hope I have done enough work to warrant her release into the community. I am now convinced she is innocent, so am determined to get her out of custody. This is my final chance to help her. I cannot fail her.

The big day comes – her final bail hearing. Alys, having been transported here by prison van, is brought up into the court from the holding cell below. She looks anxious and nervous but still lovely to me and I wish I could just put my arms around her to shield her from the awfulness of what is happening to her. But with luck, the custodial nightmare might hopefully end today.

The judge considers the prosecution and defence submissions and reads the progress reports from the prison.

'The court has carefully considered the bail package which has been proposed for you,' the judge says. 'I am impressed with the excellent progress report from the prison, monitoring your behaviour, and the good use you have made of your time there. The court probation officer, Miss Fowcs, has arranged a suitable supported bail address for you and has also contacted a prison charity which has agreed to escort you from the prison gates to the nearest railway station. Once there, a ticket will be purchased to your destination. You must report directly to the Probation Office on your arrival, which should be no later than three o'clock in the afternoon. You must observe the set curfew hours and must not contact any of the other offenders or any member of the victim's family. Do you understand, Miss Roberts?'

'Yes Sir, I do.'

'Therefore, the court agrees to your application for community bail. If you breach any of these conditions, you will be returned immediately into custody – and it will go against you at sentencing.'

I see Alys smiling and can imagine her saying to herself that she has absolutely no intention of letting that happen; having finally gained her freedom, she would not be jeopardising it again. As her solicitor, I am very relieved the court has agreed to the arrangements.

Unless I need more information from her, I do not really need to see Alys again until her next court appearance. This makes me feel a bit sad, as I enjoy talking to her and listening to her plans. Then a couple of days after her court appearance, I am unable to resist any longer and decide to give her a quick phone call.

'Hello Alys, it's Gareth. How are you settling down in your new digs?'

'I'm massively relieved to be out of that place,' Alys replies. 'I've reported to Ruth on release and am sticking to all my bail conditions. The people I'm living with are really helpful and supportive.'

Alys understands it is in her best interest in the long run to comply with the conditions but I remind her that sticking to them will also help mitigate the length of any sentence she may receive later, if she is found guilty.

'That's just not going to happen,' she says resolutely. 'I have to trust that our legal system will get to the truth in the end.'

Meanwhile, I am assured that the police continue to follow various lines of enquiry, and further interviews have taken place in other establishments where the other girls are presently being held.

I'm told that during one of these interviews, one girl let slip that before the offence occurred, she had heard Alys saying she was leaving to go home to study. But the police had argued that wasn't actual proof she had really left the scene prior to the offence being committed, so it did not really help her. However, it did show that this girl had been somewhat duplicitous by holding back this information at her initial interview. As they had not tried to stop the main protagonists committing the offence, the others were also considered culpable. Alcohol tests had been taken initially at the police station, which proved that the offenders had a high blood alcohol level, except Alys, whose negative test also went in her favour.

Come the weekend and given our successful bail application, I think I deserve a bit of a distraction from work. To me, this means dipping into the old Bible's family tree and box of photos again. I enjoy the opportunity to lose myself for a couple of hours in the lives that I imagine they may have lived. I find I am becoming strangely intrigued and a little obsessed with this family. I'm fascinated to know what has happened to the descendants. Ultimately, I want to find a modern-day family member, so I can gift the Bible and reunite them with their past.

While rummaging around in the box of photographs, I find my favourite, which is the black and white one of the couple standing proudly outside premises that I now think must be a Victorian tea garden. I pick up my large magnifying glass to look more closely at it. The house behind them looks vaguely familiar – but maybe I am just imagining that, as many Welsh long-houses look just like this one.

The couple look very happy and at ease with each other. This is despite the semi-formality of the pose, which is enhanced by the white frilly mop cap and large, seemingly stiffly-starched white apron the woman is wearing over a buttoned-to-the-neck, light-coloured dress. The man looks very proud to be standing next to her – maybe they are the owners, man and wife. He is tall and handsome in a tweed suit and sports a large handlebar moustache, while his hair, parted on the right, is greased down flat to his skull. He is smoking what looks like an ivory curved-stemmed, elaborately-carved tobacco pipe.

To the side of them, I can see a number of garden tables, covered with spotless, probably starched, white tablecloths, with wicker chairs tucked in beneath them. Further back and to the side, there is a covered but open-sided sitting area containing more tables and chairs. This has fancy black wrought-iron lattice detail at the corners, almost like spiders' webs – and two ornately cast column-like upright metal posts at front, holding up the roof. The setting looks relaxing and idyllic – with its backdrop of indigenous trees. Full sunshine falls beautifully onto the front of the house and alongside it, causing the complementary flowers in the border in front to open wide, which adds to the tranquillity of the place.

They stand before a centrally-placed, apex-roofed front porch, with small window-panes in the top half and a white, wooden tongue-and-groove bottom half. A heavily-blossomed, pale-coloured climbing rose grows up one side wall, then across one half of the house. There are two sets of small-paned sash windows each side of the front door and five similar windows across the upstairs level, the middle window presumably throwing light onto a landing inside. The narrow border of what I imagine are various coloured cottage-garden flowers, separates the garden from a lower, perfectly-mown lawn area; beyond that is a drop down to a smooth-bouldered river.

Putting this down, I pick up another photo of a large, impressive country house. Posing outside the front entrance are what I believe to be the resident domestic and grounds staff, given the uniforms they are wearing. This building is unique and should easily be identifiable if it's local to the area, which I am guessing is likely given these items came from the local auction rooms.

Next day, I take this photo into work with me, thinking that maybe a staff member will recognise it and sure enough, one of our amateur historians tells me that he believes the building is Pendyffryn Hall in Dwygyfylchi, once the residence of a well-to-do family, but now a holiday caravan site. He agrees the photo could be of the then household staff of the Hall, he thinks probably in the late eighteen-hundreds. On closer inspection, I notice a resemblance between one of the maids and the woman standing outside the tea-rooms alongside the handsome man and wonder if there is any connection, or if they are related in some way.

* * *

Mary Ellen's Story

One of Mary Ellen's earliest childhood memories was of her brother, William, dying at the tender age of seven. Together with the whole family, she was shattered by his tragic death. Later, she came to realise that her parents had been extremely affected and never really got over it. Simple joy had been extinguished from their daily existence. She likened this to the wind having stopped blowing their sail forward – and instead, a heavy anchor was dragging them back, causing them to go around in endless circles in the doldrums of their lives. They were stuck, riddled with the guilt of those who believe they had failed in their main duty in life – to protect their children. They put on brave faces when the other children and people were around – but she saw their sorrow finely etched into their expressions, almost hidden but undeniably deep, unextinguishable, inescapable and eternal.

Further pain, stabbing even deeper into their souls, was added to the already unbearable sorrow, when a few years later, her youngest brother, also named William, was to die suddenly, aged six. He had always been a sickly child with a congenital lung problem, so it wasn't a complete shock. They were therefore slightly better prepared for the next onslaught of emotions which followed his death – but nothing could really shield them from the exposure to raw pain once more. They buried him in the churchyard, alongside his older brother, William.

Happier memories for Mary Ellen were of when her mother was still alive; they went foraging around the pine copse behind the farm. She taught her the names of the many herbs found there, as well as their healing qualities and their culinary uses. They often made a tea out of pine needles, which they sometimes gave to William, as they believed it helped fight off infections and illnesses such as his chesty cough. The needles had to be the white pine variety, with two needles joined on each sprig, distinguishing them from other pines.

Her favourite foraging was for the large field mushrooms, often found in the stubs of recently harvested or riddled fields. She remembered vividly the meaty smell they gave off when being fried in butter. She soon learned which mushrooms were safe to eat and which were best avoided. In the autumn, they harvested ripened, deep-red rosehips to make cough mixtures, and the clusters of black elderberries to make a tonic wine, which was full of iron to see them through the winter.

In her eighteenth year, she was devastated when her father told her, 'It's time you went out into the world to live your own life, Mary

Ellen. The farm runs very well now. I've been told that there is a live-in position for you at Pendyffryn Hall, in the Parish of Dwygyfylchi, which you must take up.'

'But I want to stay here with you and my brothers. This is my home. I don't want to go.'

'The others can now run the farm, together with our daily domestic help,' her father insisted, 'and you need to be earning some money and making a life for yourself.'

Sadly, she had no choice in the matter. Her father's word was law.

A week later, she was taken over in the cart to the Hall by her father to start work. She was to have two half-days off a month, but as her home was too far to get there and back in half a day, it was inevitable she would stay locally.

'Just give it a go; if you don't like it, you can come home.'

But this never happened.

The squire of Pendyffryn Hall was a quarry owner and magistrate. He had built the Hall in 1840. It was a striking, two-storied, stuccoed building with hipped roofs. It had the look of a handsome Italian villa, with tall, large-paned arched windows and many bedrooms for guests. It was situated in a raised position on the lower slopes of Alltwen Mountain, facing westward out to the Irish Sea and Anglesey.

The squire was a very sociable man. Originally from South Yorkshire, he had a large family and a wide variety of guests who stayed at the Hall. This meant a lot of work for Mary and the rest of the staff. His two older sons farmed the land of the estate around the Hall.

Mary Ellen had been told that in 1855, William Gladstone was a guest at the impressive home. Over the years, this Prime Minister often holidayed in Penmaenmawr, as he enjoyed hill walking, swimming in the sea and indulging in his love of reading.

'Hurry up and get that buffet table set in the Main Hall, Mary, the shooting party will be back soon. I want it laid, so all we need to do when they arrive is to bring in the chafing dishes.'

The housekeeper was a hard task-mistress but Mary was glad in one way that she had been sent to work there, as she had learned so much from working under her – mainly how the other half lived.

To enter the main reception hall, guests climbed up the few wide steps to an imposing panelled double front door. A large brass bell-pull hung on the right-hand side. This was rarely used, as the Hall butler sat on guard for arrivals in his high-backed rattan butler's chair, which did little to keep out any cold draughts.

Once inside the main hall, eyes were drawn to the impressively high ceiling, with its beautifully-painted ornate plasterwork. The walls were clad half-way up with opulently-carved oak panelling, and wonderfully large Palladian-type windows allowed the light to flood in. At one end, there was a beautifully carved wooden fireplace, with a welcoming roaring fire burning in the hearth, useful for the shooting party to warm their buttocks and backs by. A very large oak refectory table with intricately carved legs stood in the centre of the room, which Mary was in the process of laying with all the fine crockery, silver cutlery and crystal glassware the guests would need. Once the food was brought out from the kitchen, the colourful and varied fare would look spectacular and impressive – as was intended.

'The beaters and gamekeepers will eat in the staff kitchen – but make sure first that everything is perfectly set up in here. I want the cut-glass brandy glasses placed on silver trays with the warmed brandy already poured to offer the guests when they arrive – it's very nippy and damp out there this morning. Then the chafing dishes can be brought in. Waiting staff will assist the guests to fill their plates if necessary.'

The three-day pheasant-shooting party had been planned to coincide with the owner's birthday. All his important friends, who had arrived the previous evening, were now out shooting on the estate and surrounding hills, following a hearty breakfast of kedgeree.

As Mary Ellen went back to the still room to fetch more condiments, Nancy, the undercook said to her, giggling, 'His eyes light up and follow you around the room every time he sees you!'

'Stop your moidering will you? He pays me no more heed than anyone else.'

Although Mary scolded Nancy for teasing her, she was secretly pleased that the handsome gamekeeper who had accompanied his master to the Hall, appeared to have taken a shine to her.

Everybody joined in the general banter in Servants' Hall at mealtimes; conversations were not generally on a one-to-one basis – but on the very last day, as Mary passed him in the corridor on the way to the Servants' Hall, Matthew asked her if he could have a quiet word.

'Would it be alright if I was to write to you, once I'm back in Norfolk?'

Under his close, intense scrutiny, Mary began blushing furiously, despite keeping her eyes fixed to the ground. Delighted with this confirmation that he did like her, she hoped he would not notice the flushed colour she was feeling in her cheeks. She knew ears would be waggling close by, trying to catch what was being said, so she nodded her agreement.

'Yes, alright,' she then ventured, more confidently.

'I know we haven't had a chance to speak to each other,' Matthew went on. 'I don't even know much about you – except that you are very pretty and hard-working, given the way you dash around this place. I would be very pleased if we could stay in touch!'

'Yes, I'd like that too.'

Mary had felt herself being imperceptibly drawn to him since the party had arrived but thought nothing would come of it. She wasn't sure if her feelings were being reciprocated but she now had her answer.

'I will write to you if you like,' she volunteered, 'but we don't get much idle time here.'

A big smile broke out across his handsome face – and it was at that moment she fell hook, line and sinker for his cheeky grin and unfathomable gold-flecked eyes; but at the same time, her sensible side warned her not to get her hopes up, as these 'flash in the pan' big house, inter-staff attractions rarely came to anything.

Three weeks later, after she had disappointedly decided the handsome gamekeeper would not be writing to her after all, the Housekeeper had said casually, 'There's a letter for you on the side dresser in the servants' hall,' as she walked past her.

Mary curtsied a 'thank you' then rushed to the servants' hall to get it.

'Read it in your own time,' said Cook crossly, as Mary picked it up to look at her name on the envelope, 'there's a lot to do this morning.'

So she slipped it into the pocket of her work dress and had to put off the thrill of reading it until later. Seeing the penny red stamp and the unfamiliar handwriting on the envelope, she felt a nervous frisson of excitement for what she would read later:

Oxbury Hall
Kings Lynn
Norfolk

My Dear Mary Ellen,

The winds blow a cruel cold over the flat fens of Norfolk, where there is little shelter for neither man nor beast. I find myself fondly remembering the gently rolling hills and majestic grandeur of the North Wales mountains that I walked over in late autumn. I can picture the dying bracken, the heather clumps and the ancient lichen-covered stone walls of the hill farms and ffriths, with their sturdy weather-defying stiles.

From the tops of these, I could see for miles across the open uplands as well as out to sea. The sheep-cropped grass, the small, babbling dark-watered streams and the occasional isolated farmhouse are still imprinted clearly on my memory; but it is the memory of your dear sweet face which draws my thoughts back to that place, even more than its grand beauty. I like to imagine us walking those gentle hills hand-in-hand in summer, with the heady, honeyed smell of the heathers filling the air.

Work on the estate is long and hard with plenty to do – but the old Colonel is a fair employer. His health is not good at present – but I hope he will pick up come the spring. My daily routine consists of minding and feeding the pheasants, checking the estate boundaries and fetching wood for the house fires. I spend hours cleaning and polishing the guns and boots. But minding the horses is no chore. Their soothing, undemanding company calms my soul.

Well, enough of me. Let me know how you are and what is happening in God's own country.

Hoping to hear from you soon.

Your servant,
Matthew Rowlands

After reading this, Mary felt a bubbling of excitement of what might come of their correspondence, but she did not share it with any of the others. She did not want to appear too keen so let a couple of weeks go by before she answered:

Pendyffryn Hall
Penmaenmawr

Dear Matthew,

I was surprised but pleased to receive your letter. I didn't even know your surname until I saw it written down! It sounds Welsh; was your family originally from here? Maybe this is why you are drawn to – and love it here.

It is always busy in the Hall with plenty of house parties going on, seemingly endlessly. I have been promoted to the grand title of Assistant Housekeeper, although with no more money to go with the position!

The weather has also turned cold here, with a light sprinkling of snow covering the higher hills. It will soon be Christmas – meaning even more to do! But in truth, I'd rather be busy than idle.

I wish you all the best seasons greetings,

Your good friend,
Mary Ellen

* * *

Dear Mary Ellen,

I don't know why you were surprised to receive a letter from me, given I said I would write. I would also like you to be more than my 'good friend.'

It is dark here early now, so not much can be done outside after 4pm. So I spend my evening time whittling and polishing.

Christmastide came and went. Celebrations were very muted, as I am afraid that the Colonel's health has taken a turn for the worse. We continue to pray for his eventual recovery.

The foxes have been a problem this winter, breaking into the pheasants' shelter and seemingly killing them for the sake of it – they are vermin – not like other animals which kill because they are hungry. They have devastated the stock and we must start from scratch again in the spring.

However, cook was very pleased that I brought her a brace of rabbits this afternoon!

Yours,
Matthew

They continued to correspond regularly, but Mary then received a letter from him which disturbed her:

My Dear Mary Ellen,
I have sad news to impart. My kindly employer died unexpectedly a few days ago. It would appear that his only nephew is going to inherit the Hall. I am not one for passing on gossip but am informed that his nephew has large gambling debts – owed to some very unsavoury characters.
I am worried that he may intend to sell the Hall to pay off these debts, leaving me and the others without gainful employment. I have a small amount of savings which could tide me over until I find another position – but I have no family as such, to which I could return.
I feel as if the proverbial rug is being pulled out from under my feet – and that my life is about to be thrown into turmoil. This fills me with apprehension.
I will write again when I know more clearly what the future holds.
Yours, as ever,
Matthew

After reading this letter, Mary regrettably concluded that it would probably be the last she would hear from or of him. Her dream for the future had died little by little as she read the letter. After that, she went about her chores with a heavy heart.

* * *

In the evening following the Colonel's funeral – which his nephew did not attend – the staff were summoned into the Staff Hall by his trusted, long-time butler. Everyone sat down, agitatedly apprehensive, wanting to know what it was all about. Were they all about to be dismissed?

Once they were all seated, the butler handed out a high-quality cream envelope to each one of them. These were sealed with the red wax monogram of their newly-deceased employer and contained letters written previously by him.

'Do not open them now,' he instructed the staff as he handed out the letters. 'I advise you to go somewhere quiet to read by yourselves. Do not discuss your situations with each other, just follow the instructions in the letter. If any of you has a problem reading or understanding it, come to me only. I will be in my office and will explain everything to you. It is your business only – nobody else's.'

Matthew went outside and found a quiet place in the stables where he settled down to read his letter. In the envelope, together with the letter, was a bank draft for £500 made out to his name! Matthew's hands visibly shook as he opened up the letter, causing the bank draft to flutter down onto his knee.

Dear Rowlands,

I would like to take this opportunity to thank you for your loyal, diligent service whilst in my employ, in particular the way you cared for my beloved horses.

My nephew will be my main beneficiary and will inherit the Hall. I expect he will sell it immediately, as he has incurred vast debts to some very disagreeable people.

I apologise in advance to you as you will probably lose your employment as a result of this.

I hope the enclosed bank draft will ease the difficulty you will find yourself in. I would prefer it to go to you rather than some hellhole of a gambling den, as I know you will do something worthwhile with it. I have noticed that there is great potential in you and that you will do well with a bit of money behind you.

In addition to the bank draft, I advise you to take a horse of your choice plus the tools of your trade and leave quickly, before my nephew is able to challenge the bequests. If anyone else does, you can show them this letter of authorisation.

Very gratefully yours,
The Colonel

Matthew rose well before dawn the next morning. He had slept badly – his mind racing with problems but also with possibilities and opportunities. On dressing, he tucked the envelope containing the letter and bank draft safely in the hidden inside pocket of his waistcoat.

He had decided that Bessie, the Welsh cob, would be the most practical horse for him to take; what good were sleek hunters where he was going? Besides, he may be suspected of horse theft if he was seen riding an expensive pedigree racehorse. He then loaded the tools of his trade plus his shotgun, cartridges and a large sack of oats, onto a serviceable cart. The clothes he stood up in were the only ones he possessed but he took a large black oilskin cloak and a sou'wester hat, which were hanging on the inside of the stable door. Then he covered the contents of the cart with a large tarpaulin and walked over to the kitchen, where a sleepy-eyed cook was just stirring herself.

'What in the world is to become of us all,' she lamented, shaking her head sorrowfully, 'now the good Master has gone to his Grace.'

Below her mop cap, from which stray wisps of grey hair were escaping, her normally cheerful face looked forlorn, almost tearful. She expected her life would never be the same again.

'Don't worry too much. It may look bad now, but things always have a way of working out somehow. Excellent cooks such as yourself are rare to come by and you will soon be in demand elsewhere.'

She smiled wanly at him.

'Is there any chance of some early breakfast?' Matthew asked, knowing she had a soft spot for him. 'I'm planning to leave soon – and if you're of a mind, could I also have some food for the journey?'

'What, you're going already?' she asked, horrified. 'I've hardly had a chance to take it all in yet.'

'Yes, I'm going before the young master arrives and stops me taking what the Colonel has lawfully bequeathed me. He's aways had an edge to him, that one. I wouldn't trust him an inch and he is cruel to the horses; too handy with the whip.'

'I'm not one to gossip about my betters, as you know,' said Cook, lowering her voice confidentially – 'but I have heard say that he's got big gambling debts and that the debtors are after him.'

'Well, the Colonel's death has come just in time to save him from the debtors' gaol then. But unfortunately, it will just encourage him to carry on with his bad habit, if he gets bailed out this time.'

Cook was the absolute law in the kitchen and rumour had it that she could whiplash you with her tongue if you crossed her – but Matthew had only ever seen her softer side.

'Seems to be just us two around the place this morning,' observed Matthew.

'Perhaps the rest of the staff are taking advantage of there being no master about and have stayed abed later than usual,' Cook suggested.

'Or maybe they are thinking about how things are about to change and are making plans,' he responded.

But Matthew, acting on instinct and his late master's advice, was convinced that the sooner he was gone from there, the better.

Having downed a satisfying breakfast of fried ham, fresh eggs, large field mushrooms and yesterday's bread, plus a large steaming mug of sweet tea, he was handed a straw hamper of food for the journey.

'Here, take this billycan and a small skillet as well. There's a screw of tea leaves and half a bag of flour, so you can brew yourself some tea and make some damper bread on your journey.'

In thanks, he pecked Cook's cheek, which promptly turned bright pink with embarrassment, as she wiped her hands down her ample body's apron.

'Take care of yourself, young man,' she said, changing the subject, although inordinately pleased. 'Which way are you headed?'

'Don't know for sure, I'll just follow my nose,' he said, not wanting to give any information which could result in the new master sending someone after him. Even though he was not doing anything wrong or illegal, he just felt anxious, so the less he said and the sooner he left and put a fair distance between him and the Hall, the easier he would feel.

But in truth, he knew exactly where he was heading. In the small hours of the night, he had decided. He was going to Wales, to court Mary Ellen – if she would have him. He didn't have time to write to warn her and was sure she would be shocked – but would she be happy to see him? Circumstances could have changed for all he knew. If that was the case, he would just have to face it when he got there.

As the cart slowly pulled away down the drive from the stately house, Red Sion, known for his fiery colouring and quick temper, came running down after it, shouting, 'Wait for me, Matthew!'

'Which way you headed then?' asked Sion as he neared, reaching out to grab the cart.

'Due north-west,' Matthew replied, as he slowed the cart. 'Jump up now if you want a lift. I'll not wait.'

With that, Red Sion clambered up onto the footstep, then slid onto the front bench of the cart, next to Matthew. He placed his knapsack, which held his few possessions, by his feet. A red rag was tied around his neck. His wide-striped collarless shirt with rolled-up sleeves had not seen a wash tub for many months. Neither had his brown moleskin trousers, which were held up by twine.

'I'm headed back to Shrewsbury to see me old Ma. Nothing for me here now.'

Both men nodded their solemn agreement as the cart trundled down the track where it joined the main highway. They did not discuss what was in their employer's letters.

'D'ya know your way then?'

'Vaguely,' replied Matthew.

'Well, I knows the way to Shrewsbury; you can ask folk from there onwards.'

The journey would take four days in total. Each time they came to a crossroads, Red Sion indicated with his arm which way to go, otherwise the hours, then days were spent in relative silence. Neither was known for their conversation – and each was deep in their own thoughts about what was to come. As well as the provisions Cook had given Matthew, they were able to buy food such as bacon and eggs and sometimes bread from the small farms they passed on their way.

Their first stop from Norfolk was near Peterborough, where they rested for the night. Then early next morning, they headed for Leicester.

In some parts, the roads were badly rutted and puddled after the recent winter rains. They deliberately kept to the lesser-known roads, where they felt safer, as there were fewer thieving footpads abroad. Matthew had decided to keep his shotgun next to him just in case, and whenever they neared groups of people on the road, he would speed up Bessie, so they could not be boarded and robbed.

On the second night, they pulled up on common land next to a village green. A colourful Romani caravan was already there, with a tethered piebald pony grazing nearby. Once they had settled and fed Bessie, a man ambled over to speak to them.

'Where are you boys from then?'

They explained that they were on the road because they had lost their jobs in the Hall.

'Where are you heading?'

'The north-west.'

'Why don't you join us for a bit of supper then?' he asked, seemingly satisfied with their answers and having decided they were genuine. 'We've a brace of rabbits we caught earlier, roasting on the spit. But bring your own plates and a mug – I have a cask of home brewed.'

Their Romani hosts were very congenial. The food was excellent but after their long journey that day and not being used to beer, they began to feel very relaxed and told him something of their backgrounds. Their host then told them about the Romani's cultural history and language.

'People call us 'gypsies because they think we are Egyptian,' he said laughingly, 'but our real origins were in the north-west of India.'

Their teenage daughter was exotically dark and alluring, with very long corkscrew curls in her raven-black hair. Her arms were adorned with many gold bangles. Hanging from her ears were large-hooped gold earrings. Given the influence of the homebrew, Matthew could easily have let himself fall into those deep, unfathomable, almost black eyes; but then Mary Ellen's face floated into his fore vision and the fleeting spark quickly fizzled away to nothing.

Aware of the glances their daughter was giving Matthew, the father soon hinted that the Romani lived by strong social codes and could not marry out to a Gadjo. Matthew felt he was being more than subtly warned off her – but their daughter seemed to have other ideas and continued to flirt with him.

As they sat around the embers of the campfire, the mother told Matthew to hold out his right palm, so she could read his 'fortune.' Matthew did not hold with such nonsense but did not want to appear churlish and offend those who had so kindly shared their fare with him.

'I can see you are lucky. Someone has been kind to you. You will do well for yourself. You will own property and be married within the year – you have already cast your eye on her – and lost your heart to her. But your lifeline……' She suddenly dropped his hand as if it was burning her own and declined to continue.

Turning to Red Sion, she said, 'What about you, young sir? Shall we see what the future has in store for you?'

But he could not be coaxed to have his palm read.

'No. I don't hold with knowing what the future will be, I'd rather leave it to fate, if it's all the same to you. Thank you for the offer – but no thanks.'

The daughter huffed, then rose and entered the caravan. Matthew wondered if her mother had said about him having 'lost his heart to someone' to warn their daughter off him. But whatever the reason, he did not take much heed of the information which had been imparted to him by her mother, believing that what will be will be in the lap of the Almighty.

The father rose to put more wood on the dying fire, causing more flames and a shower of sparks to rise. The flames threw out long, eerie shadows around them and Bessie nickered gently. Then he went into the caravan and came out with his fiddle. He began playing a mournful tune, evoking thoughts of sadness, loss and longing – echoing the persecuted lot of his people.

'Why don't you play something more cheerful, Alfonso?' his wife suggested after a while.

So, to lighten the mood, he struck up a lively tune. Their daughter then reappeared and began to dance, as if the music was drawing her forward, then hypnotising her into a trance-like state.

Her supple dancing form was silhouetted by the light of the campfire, while her gold bangles sparkled and set off hypnotic flashes of light. Matthew and Sion seemed transfixed, as if a mesmeric spell was being cast on them, which was only broken when the music finally stopped.

* * *

When they woke next morning, the caravan and piebald were gone. The blackened cinders were scattered and cold.

After a breakfast of bread and cheese, they headed for the smoky Potteries, skirting Tamworth, then on to Market Drayton, where they camped the next night. On their final morning as travelling companions, they ate a hearty breakfast, then parted company.

'I thank you for your company and directions for the journey and I wish you and your family well,' Matthew said in farewell, shaking Sion's hand warmly.

Matthew then headed for the market town of Whitchurch, while Red Sion headed for Shrewsbury and home. Matthew wondered what Sion would find when he got there. Would his family still be there?

Although they had not spoken much, Matthew soon began to miss Sion's physical presence sitting alongside him, as it had been reassuring.

'It's just you and me now, Bessie,' Matthew thought, as he fed her the breakfast bag of oats. Then he checked her shoes were intact. She still seemed to be full of energy, despite the length of the journey she had travelled thus far.

By the end of that day, Matthew had finally crossed the border into Wales, hopefully on the last lap of his journey. He would now head due north-west for the coast. He also wondered what he would find when he got there. Would Mary Ellen still be there? Would she still want anything to do with him?

As darkness fell that night, he lit a fire and using Cook's pan, fried himself a piece of ham and threw in a finely diced potato for good measure. Satiated, he climbed up onto the cart to prepare for sleep. Just as he was drifting off, he heard a rustling noise in the undergrowth. In the dim light, he could see that the cob was still tied up where he had left her quietly grazing, so had not broken loose. Suddenly fully awake, with his nerves now on tenterhooks, he very slowly reached down for his shotgun, then cocked it. The noise stopped instantly but it had put him on edge, so he sat upright in the cart, alert now for anything untoward.

'Don't shoot me, mister,' came a piping young voice from the bushes. 'I means you no harm. I smelt your ham frying and thought you could spare us a crust of bread. I's very hungry.'

Be careful, Matthew thought. The child may be a decoy; part of a gang.

'Are you on your own child?' he asked. 'Where is your family?'

'Just me sir,' claimed the as-yet, bodyless voice.

Then a small shadowy form came forward from the

undergrowth. He could just make out a ragged, scruffy-haired waif of a child, who could be either a boy or a girl – it was hard to tell through the unkempt layers of clothing and dirt.

Matthew decided the child was genuine enough, so he reached into his coarse linen sack and literally pulled out a crust – the last of his bread. He reached out to give it to the child, who snatched it greedily and began eating. Then he cut and handed over a chunk of cheese from the round that Cook had given him.

'What's your name, child?' thinking he would get a clue as to the gender.

'It's Sammy, sir,' which did not help at all.

'What happened to your family then?'

'We was travelling the roads lookin' for work when me sister got the pox, then the others got it one by one, all except me. So, I's got nobody now.'

'When was this?' aware that the child could still be contagious.

'Must be 'bout a fortnight ago that me Dad died. He was the last of 'em. I had to leave him there, I was too small to bury 'im.' Tears tracked down the cheeks, through the dirt.

'Well, you can't stay on the roads by yourself, there are all sorts of bad people about.'

He thought of the gypsies he'd met and how they would probably have taken in someone like this. He wondered idly if that would be a good or a bad thing.

'I know, sir, but me Ma always said I was a good girl though.'

Aha! thought Matthew. A girl.

'Well, get some sleep now, girl, we'll talk about what to do with you in the morning.'

With that, Sammy melted back into the darkness she had come from, her hunger temporarily quelled.

When Matthew woke in the morning at first light, she was busy making the acquaintance of Bessie, who was lapping up the attention.

'Her name's Bessie,' he said. 'She's waiting for her oats. Here, you can hold the bag while she feeds if you like.'

'Do you have any other family anywhere?' Matthew asked, as she held onto the feed bag with both hands while Bessie munched contentedly.

'Nobody, sir, and if the Child Catcher finds me, he'll put me in the workhouse for sure. Me family was running away from being taken into the workhouse. I can't bear to be banged up. I likes me freedom see.'

'Well, we can't let that happen, can we?' Matthew said, while frying some mushrooms with the last of the ham.

'You can ride with me until we think of a plan,' Matthew volunteered when he had finished cooking. 'I'm travelling up to the north coast of Wales. It's up to you if you want to come along.'

With her mouth full of breakfast, Sammy nodded her head vigorously in assent. Then, after a big noisy swallow, 'Oh, thank you sir, I will feel safe with you. Can I ride on Bessie's back?'

'Yes, but if you want to ride with me, first I want you to take yourself off to that brook over there and have a good wash. Here's a bar of carbolic soap and a rag to dry yourself. Get that ingrained dirt out of your skin and wash your hair.'

* * *

Mary Ellen was busy polishing the silver for a dinner party to be held later. This mindless task allowed her to daydream about what her life might have been. She did not expect to see Matthew again and wondered if what she had now – her job and her small attic room – would be enough for the rest of her life. She longed for more from life. She could practically do her job with her eyes closed now.

On her Sunday afternoons off from working in the big house, Mary Ellen was unable to go home to see her family in Eglwysbach. It was too far for her to get there and back in half a day, so sometimes she helped out a friend who ran a small village café for tourists in the nearby little hamlet of Capelulo. She found that she enjoyed talking to the many interesting people she met there. On one particular Sunday, closing time finally arrived after a very busy day, so Mary Ellen went out to bring in the pavement menu board.

She wondered wistfully once more if what she had now was all her life would ever amount to. She sighed heavily, before her attention was caught by the sound of horse's hooves coming down the Pass towards her. She saw a man driving a horse and cart. At first glance he looked strangely familiar. Looking up again, she almost dropped the sign as he came closer – and realisation dawned. It was Matthew.

On seeing her, he hurriedly pulled the wagon to a stop and jumped down, his face a picture of pure happiness, despite the fatigue of the long journey.

'What are you doing here?' he asked.

'I could ask you the same question?' she replied.

'When I lost my job, I decided to come up to see you, so here I am,'

'But. . . why? . . . where will you stay? . . . how long are you here for?' She blurted out the questions all at once.

'That depends entirely on you,' he said, smilingly taking her hand. 'I will stay forever if you'll have me. I've thought of nothing but you since I left here. Losing my job was the nudge I needed to do something about you.'

At these words, Mary Ellen started to cry.

'Have I upset you?' said Matthew, instantly mortified. 'Have I done the wrong thing?' as he put his arms around her.

'I'm so very happy to see you, Matthew. I'm so very glad you're here,' she said as her head bobbed, between gulps of swallowing air. 'I thought I was never going to see you again. My life has been so empty.'

Untying her pinny, she threw it to one side in the hall, while running inside for her cloak. After a few moments of explanation to her friend, she reappeared, just as a sleepy young girl's face peeked out from under the cart's tarpaulin.

'Oh, this is Sammy,' said Matthew. 'I'll explain in a minute. Come on, climb up. I'm blocking the road here,' as the local carter pulled up behind him.

Mary climbed up onto the cart and happily sat down beside him. It felt good. It felt right – she felt she belonged there.

Just along where the road widened, in front of Glyn Abercyn, Matthew pulled up the cart so they could talk properly. Catrin Jones, the owner, was sitting outside the farmhouse, shelling peas in the late afternoon sunshine.

'Lovely day, isn't it, Miss Jones, we're just stopping here for a moment,' Mary Ellen called over to her.

'What happened to her was very tragic,' Mary Ellen said quietly, turning to Matthew. 'She's on her own now. John, the man she hoped to marry, was killed when a horse kicked him in the head.'

'Anyway,' Mary Ellen said, changing the subject, 'tell me what's been happening to you.'

First, Matthew explained to Mary Ellen about how he had been left money by his deceased employer, then about his urgent but necessary leaving of the Hall. He told her about his journey across the country, the people he'd met on the way, and how very glad he was to finally be there at last.

'What were you doing in that café?' he asked.

'I help out on a Sunday when she's very busy. The charabancs bring in hundreds of sightseeing tourists who like to walk up the Fairy Glen. To be honest, there are far more people wanting cream teas than we can ever cope with. Some won't queue and leave disappointed.'

'Do you like doing that work?'

'I love it; you get to meet all sorts of interesting people.'

'What about opening your own tea-rooms then?'

'What do you mean by that?' she said, looking at him sideways, thoroughly confused.

'I passed a house on the left coming down the Pass with a 'For Sale' sign,' he said, pointing back the way he had come. 'Shall I buy it and turn it into a tea-rooms for you to run?'

'You … buy a big house like that … for me?' Mary Ellen was wide-eyed and astounded.

'Why not? I have the money now. I'll do it as long as you'll live in it with me.'

'But that would mean…….'

'Exactly, I want to marry you; didn't you even realise that?'

She looked at him, open-mouthed.

'I just need time to take all this in,' she replied, with both hands fluttering by her face to cool it down.

'Take all the time you need,' he said grinning. 'Now I'll take you back to the Hall,' flicking the reins for the cob to start walking, as he waved goodbye to Catrin Jones.

'By the way, Sammy is an orphan who attached herself to me on the road. I just didn't know what to do with her.'

Mary Ellen glanced back at the child, who she thought seemed like she needed some proper looking after. Sammy looked up sulkily, not sure what was to happen now that this new person, who seemed very important to him, had appeared in Matthew's life.

'But for now, you'd better start looking for some lodgings. Sammy can stay with me tonight while I clean her up. I think Mrs. Pritchard at Tan-y-Graig takes in lodgers. We can call there on the way. Ask her if she would take in Sammy as well, when she's more presentable.'

'Lodging will be a drain on my resources,' he said, while nodding in agreement, 'so the sooner I buy the house, the better. I will go and enquire about it tomorrow.'

Mary Ellen's head was in a whirl. Matthew arranged to stay with Mrs. Pritchard, who reluctantly agreed to take Sammy in on a temporary basis.

Matthew went next day to enquire about the property. The owner told him it had previously been a Post Office and showed him around. He told him he was now a widower, so was moving to live with his daughter in the North. He said he did not need the house now or any of the furniture.

'Even better. How much do you want for the lot?'

During the viewing, Matthew saw that there were some lovely pieces, mostly of mahogany and pitch pine. The owner quoted him a price including everything, with Matthew not quite believing the bargain it was. As the house was already furnished, all he needed to do was build a little tea-room at the side and sort out the kitchen.

He reflected that if this idea worked out as planned, he would have really fallen on his feet in all aspects of his life. Most importantly, Mary Ellen had agreed to marry him.

Mentally, he recapped: he would have a fully furnished home; be his own boss, beholden to and at the whim of no one; and have a potential business in the offing. And best of all, he was going to marry the girl of his dreams. How was that for luck? All this had been made possible by his former employer, to whom he silently sent a thankful prayer.

'You've got a deal,' said Matthew, shaking the man's hand

warmly. 'I'll take the lot for the price you want, including all the furniture and fittings.'

He then drove Bessie and the cart down to the main village. On enquiring with a local, he was directed to the office of a solicitor, who he instructed to draw up the legal paperwork, stressing that both parties wanted to complete the sale quickly.

On his return, he asked Catrin Jones if he could keep Bessie and the cart in her field for a small consideration, which was agreed.

Next Sunday afternoon, instead of helping her friend, Mary Ellen found herself raising the brass knocker on the front door of what would soon be her new home. The setting was delightful, with full sun to the front of the house and gardens. It was a detached, double-fronted, whitewashed long-house with a purple slate roof. It had pretty stained-glass panes in the half-glazed porch, which reflected beautiful prisms of light in the sunshine. An as-yet-to-bloom climbing rose grew around the porch.

Downstairs there were two reception rooms and a galley kitchen at the back. Upstairs were three main bedrooms and a small one above the kitchen. In the cosy sitting room, a fire burned in an open hearth, which was surrounded by beautiful, floral Victorian tiles. A Welsh oak dresser with a full dinner set stood to one side of it. The parlour was a little more formal. At the cooler side of the house, there was a large walk-in pantry, lined with shelves and cupboards, mostly empty.

We'll soon fill those, thought Mary Ellen, who enjoyed pickling and jam making.

Mary Ellen fell in love with the place instantly. She was impressed that Matthew had such a clear vision of what it could be made into.

Later, in the small hours of the night, she kept pinching herself to check she wasn't actually dreaming about all of this. Her own place, with the man for whom she had fallen head over heels. Who was it who had suddenly waved their magic wand? She knew her brothers would never believe her when she told them what had happened.

Whilst the sale progressed, Matthew told her he was busy drawing up plans to build a small extension to the side of the house, next to the road. This would serve as an indoor café area for rainy days – but he envisaged that when the weather was good, most of the customers would be sitting outside on the lawns. He thought he could also build some open-fronted outdoor shelters on the boundary of the garden.

'If the Bedol Bach café in the village is as busy as you say it is, there will be more than enough custom from tourists for two cafés, so don't you be fretting about taking customers away from your friend. The other little place, Nant-y-Glyn, only sells home-made sweets such as fudge, treacle toffee and boiled sweets, as well as nettle beer and ginger beer, so we won't affect their trade either. Besides, it will take me a few months to alter it to how we want it, so we couldn't possibly open until the spring.'

The owner had told them that in the spring, all sorts of plants in the garden would start blooming – a typical cottage garden mixture of tall flowers such as lupins, poppies, phlox, hollyhocks, delphiniums and dog daisies. These flowerbeds edged the lawns in front of the house. To one side of the property was a small copse of ancient woodland. At the back of the house was a large sloping meadow belonging to the Red Lion Hostelry, which was a hundred yards or so further up the road. A river, which they were told was called Y Gyrach, contained large, smooth boulders and ran along the boundary of the garden in front.

The long galley kitchen running the full length of the back of the house could serve both the indoor café and the outdoor seating. A large black range was sunk in an inglenook fireplace in the back wall. This emanated a warm comforting glow and on top, a large black iron kettle was gently simmering. A bread oven was offset on one side of it and the main oven doors below seemed sturdy and robust. Up above the range was a pulley-system clothes rack on which gingham tea towels and some long-johns were drying and airing. Against the opposite wall from the range was a long deal table, with four wooden chairs tucked beneath.

'Well, Mary Ellen, do you think you like it?' Matthew said, once they were back out in the garden. 'Could you run the house and a café? Although I am buying it outright, we still have to turn it into a paying business for us to live on. The owner has already accepted my offer – but it is you who will run it. I can't do it without you. I can only make it happen for you. I can make the alterations needed for it to be a more practical café kitchen – but you are the one with the practical skills to make it all work.'

'By the way, do you know how to make scones?' he joked, lightening the tone.

She gently smacked his arm, knowing how he liked to tease her.

'We can get married as soon as you like,' he continued, 'then work to get it ready for the spring, if you are agreeable.'

'What am I going to tell them at the Hall? They are not going to be happy when I tell them I'm leaving.'

'They'll manage. They wouldn't begrudge you the happiness of marrying me, would they?'

'You're impossible – but I suppose they might even be happy for me once they get over the initial shock. And after all, they've got time to find somebody to replace me. What are we going to do about Sammy?'

'Well, she can help us out with the alterations and cleaning the house and then work in the tea-rooms once it's ready. Or we can try and find her work in one of the big houses. Maybe the Hall?'

'Let's ask her which she prefers.'

Unsurprisingly, she chose to stay with Matthew, who she now considered her substitute father.

The following Sunday afternoon, they took Bessie and the cart to Llan Farm, where Mary Ellen introduced Matthew to her father and brothers. They took to him straightaway.

'We're glad you're taking her off our hands to be honest,' teased Hugh. 'But do you know what you're letting yourself in for?'

'Give over, will you,' she said, knowing the teasing was a sign of their affection for her.

A replacement for Mary Ellen at the Hall was found sooner than expected. They were married in St. Gwynan's Church and the Hall provided a wonderful wedding reception buffet. Some of the Hall's family joined them later to raise a toast to the happy couple.

Mary Ellen, blushing furiously and self-conscious from all the attention, was glad when it was all over and farewells had been said. The two of them finally set off under a shower of dried rice and shouted-out good wishes. Bessie pulled the gaily-decorated cart up to their dream home in Capelulo. Sammy, who had been their bridesmaid, moved in with them, bagging for herself the small warm bedroom at the back of the house over the kitchen range. She then worked tirelessly with them to help build up the business. They were her family now.

Matthew started work straightaway on building the indoor tea-rooms. The small bay window he fitted gave the room a feeling of space and let in plenty of light.

As soon as Mary Ellen had cleaned the house from top to bottom to her satisfaction, she started thinking about what sort of food she was going to serve in the tea-rooms. She couldn't be too ambitious as they would have to make all their own bread and cakes. They would churn their milk, which they could buy from Catrin at nearby Glyn Abercyn farm, to make butter, and cream for the cream horns. She consulted the local butcher to see if he could provide potted beef for the sandwiches. She planned to make Madeira cakes, scones, rock buns, bara brith and delicate Battenburg cakes which she would serve with wafer-thin bread and butter.

She purchased elegant, silver-plated, three-tiered cake stands with etched glass plates, and the finest bone china tea-sets she could find. She made tablecloths and napkins from a bolt of cotton and bought some robust baking trays.

'I think I'll go down and see cook at the Hall. My mother taught me basic farmhouse baking but I also need to make some fancier cakes,' Mary Ellen said to Matthew one afternoon. 'It's time I paid them a visit anyway. She might give me a few tips and recipes.'

'How will I know how much to make each day?' she asked him after some thought. 'I don't want to be throwing away food people don't buy.'

'Well, it would certainly be better if we knew how many to cater for.' He paused, deep in thought. 'Maybe we should speak to the coach trip companies who bring the people here in charabancs. They will know how many they are bringing, so we could offer to serve refreshments for the parties on the afternoon outings. That way we would know roughly how many. When they bring them to the village, they could allocate about an hour for them to go sightseeing up the Fairy Glen, then they could come here for their afternoon teas. They will mainly be the people who are staying in the fancy hotels in the Llandudno resort. They will see the pavement boards advertising the day excursions outside the booking office of Red Coaches on the pavement on Mostyn Street. I will go and speak to the organisers.'

'They could include afternoon tea as part of the excursion price,' Mary Ellen suggested. 'We could offer this to the company at a set price per head. That way we'll know how many to cater for and the company can pay us directly. We can still have some casual customers but at least we'll know in the main how many there will be.'

* * *

Mary Ellen remembered that Matthew had said in his letter he had enjoyed the scenery when he was here with the shooting party and that he wanted to walk the hills with her. So the next Saturday, she packed a small picnic hamper and surprised him at breakfast.

'We are going for a walk today. Get your boots on!'

Leaving Sammy in charge, they walked up between the Cross Keys and Y Bedol. They passed the bridge which went over the River Gyrach to the Felin Newydd, then walked up the narrow track between the small miners' cottages of Y Nant. They reached the junction which went left to Nant Ddaear-y-Llwynog and the so-called Fairy Glen – but they bore right, up the steep track through the pine trees, finally reaching the tiny cottage of Pen Talwrn. The owner was busy planting early potatoes in the walled garden and exchanged pleasantries with them as he leaned heavily on his gardening fork.

'If you keep following the track upwards, it eventually levels out a bit. Then it's quite a pull to the top of Tal-y-Fan – but not for you youngsters! Well worth the views from the top, right across the Conwy Valley and westwards across the Caerneddau.'

They thanked him for the directions and set off once more.

Just up from Pen Talwrn, they turned around to look back. The panorama which opened up in front of them made them stare in wonder.

'What a beautiful place we live in!' declared Matthew, as they looked seaward over the rolling farmland below. In the distance they could see Ynys Seiriol, named after the monk who had founded a monastery there.

Then onwards and upwards they went along the winding zig-zag track, despite the sun beating down on them. Sheep belonging to the local farmers grazed contentedly on the common land around them. On their left, they passed stone-walled ffriths which dropped down steeply to the riverbank of the higher reaches of Afon Gyrach. The river, already swollen after recent rains, would soon fall in dramatic waterfalls through the glen below, carrying on downwards to skirt the foot of Alltwen. It would continue running through the more level farmland of the coastal valley floor, before eventually spilling out to sea on the beach.

Just before reaching the upland farm of Ty'n Ffrith, they bore left and came to a stile over a stone wall. Climbing over, they walked down to the river, where they stopped for a rest and to cool their feet in the icy water. They crossed the river there and continued their climb upwards past the smallholding of Halfway House. On the way, they saw some local reservoir water works and above that, a quarry.

On finally reaching the base of Tal-y-Fan, they began the hard climb upwards. Just when it seemed they were on the final climb, they found that there was another rise, then another. They longed to rest and have their picnic but were determined to climb to the top first. Eventually, they mounted the final hill, reaching the summit at about midday.

'Look, you can literally see for miles and miles in all directions,' said Mary Ellen. 'That must be the Isle of Man northwards and Sir Fon to the west – and over there on the right, we can see right up the Conwy Valley.'

Matthew stood there in utter awe, stunned and seemingly mute. He was reminded of just how beautiful it had been when he was previously up in the mountains with the shooting party. They stood there for about five minutes, just soaking up the panoramic view. Then hunger from the walk began to gnaw at their stomachs, so finally, throwing down a plaid blanket, they settled down to eat their picnic of egg and cress sandwiches, Dundee and walnut cake, washed down with cold ginger beer. Bliss.

'Mary Ellen, it was the best day of my life when I first clapped eyes on you,' said Matthew, replete and using a grassy tussock as a back cushion for his head. 'You make me so happy; I feel so complete with you. Just to think, my old master made this miracle possible.'

Coming from a reserved family, which considered it vain to compliment each other about anything, particularly their appearance or achievements, Mary Ellen was unused to hearing anyone declare their feelings like this and she still blushed with embarrassment whenever he told her how he felt.

Again, Matthew sent a silent prayer of thanks up to his benefactor in heaven as he quite often did. He wondered what had happened to the old estate and the other staff members since he left; sold to pay gambling debts no doubt. He felt glad he was able to get away from there when he did.

'Let's make the most of today; we have a busy summer coming up,' said Matthew. 'We can tell our customers about the lovely walks along these hills. I could even offer them guided local walks. Also, what about making a couple of the bedrooms suitable for paying guests who may want to have a walking holiday? It's a perfect spot for that.'

Mary Ellen, nodded. She loved to listen to him talking and telling her of his plans and ideas. She just loved him full stop.

Then Matthew's thoughts began to wander elsewhere.

'You know there's not a single person around here for miles except us,' reaching across and pulling her gently down beside him. Kissing her softly in the afternoon stillness, with only the sounds of a far-away bleating sheep, chirping chitchats and soaring skylarks high up in the endlessly blue sky, they made the sweetest love, then both fell into a drowsy sleep.

Later, they walked along the high ridge of Tal-y-Fan towards the west, then dropped down once they'd avoided the marshy area below. They passed Red Farm, then turned west again and eventually came to the Meini Hirion, a circle of large ancient granite standing stones.

'These may have been erected thousands of years ago,' speculated Matthew.

'There's another smaller, even older circle over here,' said Mary, exploring close by.

After the last swig of ginger beer, they set off once more, dropping down the Green Gorge, near the ancient axe factory at

Graiglwyd, then down to Mountain Lane, before reaching the main road home to Capelulo, happy but exhausted.

'What a wonderful day. I will remember it forever. I shall certainly sleep tonight,' said Matthew – unless you have other ideas of course.'

Mary Ellen picked up a tea towel and threw it at him.

'Behave yourself, you insatiable scoundrel,' she said laughing.

* * *

Matthew had finished the small extension onto the side of the house where they could serve customers on cold or rainy days. It was only large enough for a few tables – but an attractive three-paned overhanging picture window gave the room a feeling of space.

Mary Ellen was enchanted with the kitchen in the house, where the black cast-iron range stove dominated the long back wall. She lead-polished it to a high colour and its large brass hinges shone like sunshine. The warmth it emitted was comforting on colder days – but it would also make the kitchen almost unbearable to work in on hot summer days. The stove was never allowed to go out; this was Matthew's responsibility. Above the stove on the ceiling pulley-maid, numerous linen tea towels were hung to dry.

The floors were covered in highly-scrubbed and waxed red quarry tiles and the walls were limewashed. The larder had a multitude of shelves, now holding the delicate florally-decorated bone china teacups, saucers, side plates and large serving platters. Open-topped wooden trays held teaspoons and side knives in their different compartments. Another shelf held small, medium and large teapots, as well as milk jugs – all the accoutrements that a tea-room could require. A higher shelf held recently-made jars of jams and pickles.

Soon the customers began flocking into the tea-rooms and trade was brisk. Their reputation grew and the coach excursions brought even more people into the village.

On a quiet Monday about six weeks later, they decided to have a break from the tea-rooms and walk in the direction of Conwy over the mountain. After an early breakfast, carrying a packed lunch and a newly-acquired Ordnance Survey map, they set off at a brisk pace up Bwlch Sychnant. As they neared the first bend, they noticed large iron rings plugged into the rock and wondered what these were used for.

'It might be something to do with the coaches going down the Pass. Maybe they use ropes to act as brakes to stop the coaches going down too fast. Or were they used in the construction of the road?' suggested Matthew.

'I'm told this rock on the right is called Echo Rock,' he said, when they were further up the road. 'Apparently, if you shout loudly, your voice will bounce off the rocks opposite.'

'What shall we shout?' giggled Mary Ellen.

'I love Mary Ellen,' he shouted at the top of his voice, as she scolded him with embarrassment. Sure enough, his voice bounced right back at him a few times from further away.

'There you are, even the rocks agree with me, they love you too.'

'Daft a'porth,' she said, as they set off once more.

Matthew was admiring Mary Ellen in her walking outfit. The oversized bloomers, cuffed at the calf were ideal hiking gear. It was easier than wearing a long skirt, which shortened her stride, and petticoats which could get snagged on gorse bushes. She wore long socks and sensible brogues. Her double-breasted jacket, nipped in at the waist, showed off her hour-glass figure and the jaunty cap on top of her pinned-up hair finished off the outfit. She had no idea just how lovely she looked and could still not take a compliment without blushing furiously.

Matthew sported a pair of practical plus-fours, thick knee-high stockings and stout shoes, with a light-coloured linen summer jacket over a paisley waistcoat, which had a fob watch chain hanging across it. Clothes were their one extravagance – now they could afford them.

On nearing the top, as Mary Ellen noticed smoke coming from a chimney high up on the right, they saw a lady in a black dress and a crocheted grey shawl, walking down towards them.

'Good day to you both,' she said cheerfully as they neared. 'Lovely weather for walking.'

They returned her greeting.

'I'm going to Pensychnant Farm to buy some milk and cheese for my charges,' as she headed for the small pedestrian gate that was built into the estate wall.

They both looked blank.

'I run Murddyn Potas – it's just up there. I take in waifs, strays and destitute families.'

'How charitable of you,' responded Mary Ellen. 'We own the tea gardens in the village. Sometimes we might have food left over we could send up to you.'

Matthew thought it was a shame he had not known of this place for Sammy. But anyway, she seemed happy now where she was. They had left her in charge at home – although the café wasn't open as it was a Monday. She had been a godsend during the whole time they were converting the place into tea-rooms and happily worked as a waitress, cleaner, washer-up, laundry maid – whatever was asked of her.

At the top of Bwlch Sychnant, they headed left onto Alltwen. They followed the track as it bore right along a dry-stone wall belonging to the Pensychnant Estate, skirting a field of grass, which rippled beautifully from a light breeze. They saw Pen Pyra farm nestling snuggly up against the side of the mountain, sheltered from the prevailing north-westerlies.

'Look at those ponies,' said Mary Ellen. 'Aren't they beautiful.'

A small herd of three adults and two foals grazed peacefully, not far from the footpath.

'I wonder who they belong to,' said Matthew. 'This is probably common grazing land.'

Little did they know that these ponies and their ancestors were wild and had been living on the Caerneddau Mountains and the uplands of the North Wales coast since at least the Bronze Age. The breed had developed a hardiness and robust waterproofing to shield them from the harsh winter weather experienced on the higher hills. They had big manes and tails and grazed on rushes, gorse and sweet mountain grasses.

The path looked directly down onto a quarry and beyond this was a stunningly beautiful bay which sparkled with turquoise spangled light. White-sailed yachts were busy tacking as they headed back towards Deganwy beach. Further out they saw the headland of the Great Orme, which completed the curve of the bay. They saw the rooftops of the shining white hotels which flanked the North Shore of Llandudno, which was fast turning into a tourist haven for people from the north and north-west.

'Most of our customers are coming from those grand hotels on the North Shore this summer,' Matthew pointed out, 'but the small fishermen's and quarrymen's cottages dotted randomly along the West Shore look more picturesque to me.'

A few longboats were pulled up onto the stony shore, their deployment depending on the tide and weather conditions. In the distance, they could see people picking what were probably whelks, oysters and clams from the nearby sandbanks which were exposed at low tide.

They found a sheltered, semi-sunken spot out of the breeze under a large boulder to eat their picnic on the blanket. Apart from the intermittent drone of a pollen-laden bee flitting between the heather clumps, and gulls occasionally crying far overhead, they were surrounded by utter silence.

Feeling the warmth of the sun on her face and the breeze cooling her, Mary Ellen was very relaxed and felt herself starting to doze. Life was good.

'Here,' said Matthew, rousing her from her reverie, 'have a windberry,' as he popped one in her mouth.

'They're called *llus* in Welsh, or bilberries' she said.

'Not where I come from.'

He picked and ate quite a few more of the tiny dark blue berries, which were both sweet and sharp at the same time.

'We should have brought a jar with us to collect some to make jam – but I suppose we'll just have to eat them instead!'

The berries had made her lips blue, so he leaned over to kiss them.

'Temptress,' he said.

'Get away with you, you're incorrigible. People might be watching.'

'Not a person for miles around; we'd be safe if we wanted to …….'

* * *

Matthew and the new estate manager of the Fairy Glen had become firm friends due to Matthew's experience of working on a large estate. The manager allowed him to shoot and fish on the land and in turn, Matthew advised him on how to breed the pheasants for the shoot and trout to feed the ponds.

'Did you know that the Romans originally imported pheasants from Asia, through France, nearly two thousand years ago and bred them for the table? My old Master at the Hall told me that. He offered the public what were called 'daily bags,' and in their best year, they were able to offer about eight hundred pheasants for large shooting parties. It seemed a bit of a waste to me as they were never able to eat that many.'

'Well, we don't want to go into it on that scale,' the manager responded. 'We just need enough for the estate owner's family and friends to enjoy shooting up on the moors above the glen and also to do a bit of trout fishing.'

'I'll show you how to capture a female trout by tickling its belly. Between November and January, you put the females into a smaller pond with some males to fertilise the eggs. They usually lay between four hundred to a few thousand eggs each. Then it takes between twenty-eight to eighty days for fertilisation to occur. You will soon stock the river with enough trout for the family to enjoy fishing.'

'As for the pheasants,' Matthew continued, 'once the eggs hatch, they are graded. Then the chicks are carefully reared and finally, when ready, are released onto the moors. It will be a year-long commitment but I will be here if you want me to steer you through the various stages.'

Although Matthew was officially allowed to fish, he didn't doubt that some of the locals also tickled the brown trout when they could get away with it and occasionally bagged a pheasant.

* * *

The tea-room was having yet another successful season and September had just arrived. On a lovely sunny autumnal morning, Mary Ellen stood back and admired the outdoor setting. It was so picturesque, so inviting, so lovely and she had been reassured many times that the food was excellent. Trade was flourishing and she had been blessed with two children, Matthew junior and Jane.

Every Monday morning, when the tea-room was closed, Sammy

put the tablecloths, napkins and tea towels into the old boiler to soak. She used a three-legged wooden agitator to wash them and a 'dolly blue' to keep their pristine colour. Then she rinsed and starched them, before hanging them all out to dry in the wind and sunshine, or under one of the covered seating areas if it was raining. Once dry, she put them on the airer above the range, where the black smoothing irons were heating. She sprinkled cold water onto them if they were too dry for the iron to get the creases out.

Next day, the tables were laid with the clean starched tablecloths and small bunches of flowers placed in the middle. After that, Sammy was in the kitchen, baking trays of blackberry scones, sultana biscuits and a yeast-based Bara Brith. Then she took out the Madeira fruit cake which had been baking slowly overnight in the range oven.

Trays were made up in the pantry with the pretty floral tea-cups, saucers, plates, milk jugs, small bone-handled butter knives and apostle teaspoons, ready to lay when the customers arrived. China teapots were placed on the cast iron shelf above the range to warm. Everything was arranged just so – and the business ran like a well-oiled machine.

They were expecting two charabancs from the Hydro Hotel in Llandudno mid-afternoon, so it was going to be a busy day. All went smoothly as planned and the last of the satiated stragglers finally left to walk back to their waiting charabanc.

Then without warning, Mary Ellen's idyllic world was to be suddenly shattered and she would find herself going out of her mind with grief.

The next morning, her beloved Matthew, who sometimes lent a hand to the Fairy Glen estate manager, went to help saw up a massive scotch pine which had come down in a recent storm. It was blocking the narrow footpath alongside the full-flowing river, so had to be moved urgently. He and the manager had just started cutting it with a two-man saw.

'The teeth on this saw need a bit more sharpening,' Matthew shouted over to him. 'It's not cutting very well because the wood is still damp.'

The manager watched as Matthew turned around to pick up his honing stone but instead, Matthew suddenly grabbed at his chest with both hands, lost his balance, then fell over backwards towards the river below. He landed on his back a few feet down, splayed out on a massive black river boulder, as if ready for sacrifice. As the deafeningly turbulent river went thundering by him, he must have thought that he had descended into Hades, unless of course, he was already dead before he landed.

Desperately, the manager scrambled down the bank as near as he could to get to Matthew, who was lying there prone and lifeless. But he was unable to cross the treacherous stream to reach him, because of the massive volume of amber-coloured storm water raging through the boulders between them. The glen acted as a conduit for all the storm rainwater which ran off the mountains higher up, sending copious amounts of the peaty-coloured water charging down at breakneck speed. Also, the green moss made glossy by the constant splashing of water droplets falling onto it, was treacherously slippery and impeded his progress.

'Don't just stand there gawping, you fools,' he screamed at his labourers in his frustration. 'Go and get help from the locals. Tell whoever you find that we need a short ladder ……. and ropes and a winch. Go, for God's sake, go!'

He decided he would have to build some sort of a bridge over to Matthew and then somehow winch him back over to the bank on the ladder. He came to the conclusion that Matthew must have broken his back in the fall. 'Poor bugger', he thought.

By the time they had finally strapped him onto the ladder, they realised that Matthew was already dead. Even if he had initially been alive, the hypothermia would probably have finished him off. But the manager insisted to anyone who would listen, that before falling, Matthew had clutched at his chest in pain. He said he thought it wasn't just an accident but probably a heart attack that had caused him to lose his balance.

As soon as Mary Ellen heard there had been an accident in the Glen, she had thrown off her apron, grabbed her shawl and run up to watch helplessly from the nearby riverbank. Silent tears streamed down her lovely face when she saw it was Matthew lying there. She watched the rescue mission with increasing desperation, realising early on that he wasn't moving or breathing as he lay there, prone; her beautiful, beloved Matthew.

She watched as the body of the love of her life was gently lifted off the boulder, placed then tied onto a ladder and winched across to the riverbank. Her dream was dead; her nightmare had begun.

In utter silence, he was reverently carried by the labourers through the village back to their house, as the villagers stood by and watched in shock. The men gently placed Matthew onto a bed, then left. Mary Ellen lay down next to him. She gently traced the profile of his handsome face with her forefinger, as if to imprint it onto her memory forever. She could not bear to see him cold and lifeless – he had always been so energetic, so warm and alive.

A doctor arrived, already far too late. There was no way that he could know if his heart had caused him to fall but agreed it was possible.

Gone. Just like that. Like an instantly invisible puff of wind; with a click of fate's fingers, along with the idyllic life she had known. What was she to do now? She couldn't imagine her life without him in it. It would be a half-life. She knew instinctively that the joy she had felt with him would never be felt by her again with any other man. Her two little children, Matthew junior and Jane, were now fatherless.

The funeral was a heart-breaking affair throughout, with Mary Ellen just about coherent and functioning. Her soul had gone into a dark, sad place and only Sammy, who arranged nearly everything, managed to encourage her to keep going, a day at a time. At night she welcomed the oblivion of sleep.

As they stood surrounding the mound of fresh earth under which Matthew's cold body now lay in a wooden box, she wished she could lie in there beside him, warming him. Only the thought of her children being orphaned stopped her from digging up the mound of fresh soil with her bare hands, to lie next to him once more. To hold him. To be with him. To be safe. His arms around her. Shockingly, she felt completely abandoned by him. He had made himself her rock and now the rock was gone.

Thankfully, her little family was neither destitute or homeless – as some widows were when they lost their husbands – just as long as she continued to work hard. They had their home and a source of income. She resolved to dedicate her life to the well-being of her children, making sure they would never feel the overwhelmingly numbing sorrow she was now feeling. He had made every day special for them all and she vowed to keep his memory alive in her children.

* * *

    Mary Ellen, now a young widow, carried on with her life, despite all joy having been sucked out of it. She warned her little son, Matthew junior, numerous times against playing in the river – but he was drawn to the water, just as his father had been. He would secretly climb over their boundary fence, then slide down to the riverbank to catch tiddlers and stick insects in the stream. He would plop them in his jam jar, which had a handle made of twine tied around the lip at the top.

    Then one day, as they were marking a year after Matthew's death, history repeated itself. In a similar tragedy to that which had befallen his father, little Matthew slipped on a river boulder which was covered in slimy green lichen, banging his temple hard on a rock as he fell. As he lay in the stream on his side, a small, slow trickle of blood ran down from his temple, then entered his open mouth. The friend who was with him saw this and screamed, which brought adults running out of their homes on the opposite bank.

    'He slipped on that green rock, he's not moving! There's blood!' his friend shouted hysterically, pointing at Matthew.

    On hearing the scream from the house, Mary Ellen ran down the road over the bridge and down to the river, only to see a man carrying the limp body of her son in his arms. The nightmare had been repeated. She rushed over and took little Matthew off him. Noticing the blood on his face, she held him close, as she carried him carefully back home.

    'Go fetch the doctor,' she shouted at Sammy, as she went in through the front gate. 'Quickly!'

    Once she'd laid him down gently on his bed, Mary Ellen realised his breathing was very shallow. She began to gently dab at the wound on his temple with a piece of clean linen moistened with tepid water. She could clearly see the injury on his temple – but who knew what damage had been done inside his little head? His face was a deathly white, his pulse a slow, barely perceptible beat. She held his small hand while rocking herself to and fro for comfort – and to stop herself from going mad with rage and anger at the unfairness of it all. Then she dropped and prayed fervently on her knees beside him, until the doctor burst into the room.

After carefully checking him, he slowly shook his curly-grey-haired head and looked gravely over his half-moon spectacles at Mary Ellen.

'Could be concussion,' he proclaimed, 'or it could be much more serious. Time alone will tell.'

As the doctor was packing his medical bag and preparing to leave the room, little Matthew's eyes started to flicker, as if fighting to reach back up into consciousness.

'Daddy, here I am. Pick me up, Daddy. Hold me. I'm hurting,' he uttered.

Mary Ellen imagined Matthew stepping forward, lifting him up into his strong arms, to take their baby with him to heaven. She knew he would be in safe hands – but at the same time, was desperate not to lose him. Maybe she had to let him go, to let him be safe with his Daddy.

Then little Matthew finally let out a long, shuddering final breath and quietly slipped away from her. The doctor certified the cause of death as 'head injury' and quietly left the room, leaving Mary Ellen to her shattering grief.

Tragedy had repeated itself.

If Matthew's funeral had been difficult to get through, this one was ten times worse. Mary Ellen was overwhelmed by the number of people from the village, especially the local chapel members, who offered condolences, comfort, sympathy and practical help. But none of this would bring him back. They railed against his death. The death of a child was not the natural order of things. They were appalled it had happened. But Mary Ellen somehow again managed to get through the funeral and at the end of the long draining day, she finally got to the sanctuary of her bedroom. She collapsed onto the bed, seemingly paralysed, her spirit crushed – unable to rise.

She had suffered yet another devastating loss. How was she supposed to deal with all this shored-up sorrow and grief? Where could it all go? It felt like a dam which needed to burst. She needed desperately to feel Matthew's arms around her, needed him there next to her, to comfort her. How could she cope with all this without the man she had adored and idolised, and her precious little son who she had worshipped? Why was God punishing her? What had she done wrong? Had she been too happy? Had she wanted too much? Was it her time to suffer now? Had she used up her life's quota of joy too early?

Sammy let her grieve while she looked after little Jane. It was as if their grief was secondary to hers, so they comforted each other. They waited quietly and patiently for Mary Ellen's raw emotions, which saw her biting her knuckles until they bled, to ease.

'There are bookings this weekend for the tea-rooms which we need to honour,' Sammy, ever the realist, eventually said to Mary Ellen. 'I will do what I can for the casual trade – but you are needed to start the preparations for the charabanc parties.'

Thus, gently rebuked, in a 'pull-yourself-together' sort of way, Mary Ellen remembered how Sammy had suffered the tragic loss of her entire family all within a matter of weeks and left alone in the world, so she dragged herself from her bed. She could indulge her grief no more. She needed the income. But more importantly, in her mind, she could hear Matthew's voice gently persuading her:

'Come on Mary Ellen, you can do this, my love.'

So she ordered the provisions and set to work baking once more, albeit totally mechanically, devoid of any of the previous joy. She put on a brave face in front of her customers but when alone, any little trigger or memory would cause her to give way to the waves of grief which frequently engulfed and overwhelmed her. Was this now to be the new pattern of her life? Would she ever heal?

Chapter 4

Pleased that Alys is finally out on bail and doing well, I now need to prepare for her next court appearance. The more I get to know her, the more impressed I am with her strength of character, and the more convinced I am she is being utterly truthful. Since her release from custody, she is less anxious and more relaxed – which shows in her lovely face.

What I need to get to the bottom of is why her cousin could be lying about Alys not being in the house on the evening of the offence. I have the beginning of a vague stirring of a suspicion, which I need to explore further.

Alys is sticking faithfully to her bail conditions and is working for a few hours in a local café in between Probation appointments. She tells me she would like to study for qualifications to work with young people who get in trouble with the law, so I ask Ruth to speak to her, to explain how she can go about it. I don't want to discourage her by telling her that should she be convicted of the offence, she will never be allowed to work with young or vulnerable people.

On a bitterly cold, sleety grey Sunday afternoon, with heavy snow forecast, I toast some comforting muffins on my open fire, smear butter on thickly and pour myself a cup of tea. This, for me, is pure gluttonous indulgence.

After wiping my hands on my napkin, I pick through the box of old photos again and come across a landscape one in black and white, mounted onto stiff card. It is of a row of twelve men facing the camera, wearing ponchos over their black jackets and waistcoats, while sitting on the backs of small ponies. It looks somewhat comical. All the men are wearing black trilby hats and sport large droopy moustaches. On the back of the photo is stamped the details of a photographic studio in Buenos Aires, so I assume it was probably taken somewhere in Argentina by a travelling photographer. I've read about Welsh settlers who had established a community in Patagonia around that time.

Then I notice that the number 88, preceded by an apostrophe, is written in the corner on the back. Judging from the style of clothing, perhaps this means the photo was taken in 1888. Also written on the back is 'Thomas E. Jones'.

Looking at the family tree again, I realise that one of the men in the photo might be Thomas, the fourth son of Efan and Myfanwy, and wonder what his life had been like.

* * *

Thomas' Story – Part 1

Thomas and his family have just celebrated the birth of the Lord Jesus and tonight, it is the Eve of the New Year 1880. He has gathered and locked the pigs into their pens for the night on his father's farm in Eglwysbach, then made his way towards the farmhouse for supper.

'You coming to this meeting later or not?' called out his older brother, Robert, who was washing his torso under the pump in the yard.

'Not sure it's worth it. It holds no real interest for me. Besides, it's too cold to be standing about.'

'The meeting is at Bedd Garrog. Sara will be there with her sister, Megan.'

Thomas felt a sudden flush rush up his neck to his face on hearing Megan's name, so he carried on walking, hoping that Robert would not notice – he teased him enough as it was without giving him more cause. Just because he was the youngest, his brothers thought they could mock and make fun of him; they thought it was all good natured – but he hated it.

They no longer had a mother to scold them and take his part. He would have had two more brothers – had they not also died while very young. There had been no lack of sorrow, grief and loss in their home earlier in his life, so he had resolved to live life to the full while he could.

Once gathered at the supper table, they all respectfully bowed their heads to give thanks for the food. They would not be discussing the forthcoming outdoor meeting, as the subject was taboo. Their father did not hold with itinerant preachers encouraging gullible potential emigrants to go to 'foreign parts,' promoting the benefits of establishing a new Wales in a desolate backwater of South America.

Yet as the youngest of three brothers, what future did Thomas have here? The eldest, Hugh would inherit the farm. At forty-seven acres, it would not be viable to split it between three. If Robert wooed Sara, he would move to her farm. She was the older sister, with elderly parents who would in time need a man to carry on the work. Life was hard and Thomas knew there was no place for him here. Neither did he want to live in his father's house all his life. This was the dilemma he faced.

Thomas finally succumbed to pressure from Robert, so the brothers later walked together across the field, to avoid meeting neighbours on the street.

'I'm only coming to this stupid meeting with you because you don't want to go on your own,' Thomas made clear to Robert. 'You're obviously only going on the off-chance of speaking to Sara. I know you're soft on her.'

Neither brother was particularly interested in the subject of the meeting – but any social occasion was welcome in this quiet little backwater, where their only real alternative was church.

Finally, the brothers climbed over the last stile, which brought them to the field where the meeting was being held. Legend had it that Bedd Carrog was the grave of a mythical flying dragon-like creature with long sharp talons, a sharp beak and fiery red eyes. Locals in medieval times were very afraid of it, as it would swoop down to take, then eat, lambs, sheep, goats, calves and even toddlers.

Legend also had it that a reward was offered to anyone who killed it. So Local Chieftain Bach ap Carwed devised a plan. He identified its preferred landing place, then made a quiver full of poison arrows and lay in wait to attack it. Bach succeeded in fatally shooting down the beast but was unable to enjoy his reward. In his moment of glory, he proudly kicked at the corpse with his foot. Unfortunately, it struck one of the arrows, which led to him also being poisoned, followed by a slow, agonising death.

Other versions claimed that the creature was an extremely large dangerous wild boar. But whatever it was, it was no longer there to trouble those at the meeting that night.

The brothers saw that a small crowd had already gathered.

Thomas spotted Megan straight away; she always stood out in any crowd for him. He knew there was not a chance she would look his way or speak to him – in truth, he would have been mortified and astounded if she had. Standing near the back, he could already see a few young men casting furtive sideways glances her way. Why then would she look at him, the runt of the family litter, when she could have any prize-winning pup she wanted?

Robert was already gawping at Sara. Thomas dragged him by the arm to the very back of the crowd to stop him making a fool of himself, and so they would be ready to leave before too many people saw they were there and told their father.

Megan was Sara's younger sister. As an adult, she would have very little prospect of anything except to marry a local farmer and this thought frankly appalled her. She did not want the endless drudgery of farm life. She wanted much more than that. She wanted excitement and travel. Her sister, Sara, could well marry Robert from Llan Farm, who would then eventually take over their family farm, when her parents got too old to manage. But Megan was a free spirit and she wanted to fly.

She loved to ride her horse across the lower slopes of the Conwy Valley and it was on one such ride that she had met up with the son of the nearby estate owner. She had stopped for a drink and a rest by a large stream. As she watched the kingfishers dip in and out of the water, he rode up to her, dismounted, then joined her on the riverbank. They met up quite often after this first encounter and Megan felt herself falling for the dapper young man. He was exciting and very different from the local men she knew.

One day, he asked if she would like to see a cave he had discovered behind a waterfall. She agreed and followed his horse to the spot below the cave. They tethered the horses and walked up a narrow track to the cave. She was enchanted by the waterfall, over which a permanent rainbow was formed. But exhausted from the climb up in her riding attire, she sat down to rest at the entrance to the largish cave. Sitting down beside her, he started to tell her that she had bewitched him, that she was beautiful and that he would like to kiss her. Thrilled by what she thought was a declaration of love, she succumbed to his advances.

They met more regularly after that. After a few weeks, she hinted at the possibility of their getting married – but did not get the response she had expected. He pulled back in horror, proclaiming that he thought they were just having a bit of fun. He told her that he could not possibly marry her, as his parents would not approve nor ever allow it. Indeed, they would in all probability disown him if he did. Angry but too proud to show it, she got up on to her horse and rode back home.

Later that day, Sara asked Megan to accompany her to the meeting at Bedd Carrog, so she could see Robert. Even though she was still upset from the earlier incident, Megan agreed, so as to take her mind off the brutal rejection.

Soon after they arrived, a hush fell over the crowd as a short, black-suited, unprepossessing man stepped up onto a makeshift platform. He introduced himself and stated his reason for being there. His deep baritone voice resonated with a musical quality.

'Greetings, my fellow countrymen and countrywomen. I am here this eve to talk to you about our Welsh colony, Y Wladdfa, in Patagonia. As you know, in 1865, the Mimosa took the first brave pioneers to settle in the untamed, heathen land of the Argentine and landed in what they named Porth Madryn. It was named after the Madryn estate of Sir Love Jones-Parry, who together with Lewis Jones, travelled to Patagonia in 1862 to scout for suitable land for emigrants to settle.'

The speaker's strong, oratory style was instantly spellbinding. His dramatic pauses and stirring words were able to raise passion in the most indifferent of men. He was one of an army of volunteers who delivered orations on behalf of the Welsh Emigration Society, encouraged by Michael D. Jones, the man who motivated the first cohort of settlers to 'found' the Welsh settlement.

'They bravely sailed the treacherous seas, then endured untold deprivation and hardship, motivated as they were by the need to establish their new colony. They wanted to protect their way of life, their culture and most of all, their language, which had been affected by the relentless Anglicisation, brought about by the Industrial Revolution. We are traditionally a nation of farmers – but the factories of the North lured away our young men to their dark satanic mills in a search for higher wages.'

He dropped his voice and shook his finger, to emphasise that to be working there would be doing the work of the very devil himself.

'Our pioneers also went to escape the oppression of the Church of England, which commandeered tithes from them to upkeep their churches. Churches, which as non-conformists, they did not attend!'

At that, a vibration of anger rippled through the crowd – many calling out indignantly and enthusiastically to agree with the sentiment.

Whipping them up even further, he continued, 'The British Empire seeks to kill off our language by forbidding our children to speak their mother tongue in school, then vilify and humiliate them for inadvertently but quite naturally doing so. Our motherland, founded by the ancient Celts and ruled over by the Welsh Princes, our beloved land of poetry and music, is no longer the land of my childhood and this saddens me greatly.'

He paused, before dramatically declaring, 'But we are replicating our former way of life in Y Wladdfa.'

He briefly paused again, sweeping his eyes over his listeners for theatrical affect, making each of them feel as if he was addressing them individually.

'Now, on the eve of the year of our Lord 1880, I beseech you to join our cause. Sail forth to help your brethren to build on what they have started. Build up the Utopia for the Glory of God. Strong men are needed to help create even more channels to irrigate their crops. They have already built dams and two-hundred miles of canals to bring water to the farmsteads but more are needed.'

'Farmers are needed. Trades people are needed. There is free land there in the Chubut Valley for those who are motivated to work it. The valley floor is already divided into three hundred and fifty farm plots and is close to a large river.'

'Those who unfortunately chose to migrate from these parts to North America have witnessed the demise of their language, as they become more assimilated into the American culture. Some of those expatriates are now seriously considering moving from there to Patagonia, because Y Wladdfa is the only place to keep our language pure.'

While Robert was distracted, feasting his eyes on Sara, Thomas felt the speaker's voice pulling him in, mesmerising him and reaching into his very core. His words felt urgent and magnetic. The speaker had the innate ability to inspire nationalistic fervour, making the pioneers' cause seem noble. His plea for more skilled people to emigrate there to help them continue their quest for the Welsh colony was finding fertile ground in Thomas' mind. He had not intended nor expected for this to happen – but it suddenly seemed to be a solution to a problem he didn't really realise he had until now. He was suddenly open to the idea of emigrating.

Finally, the speaker thanked the people for coming and stepped down from his podium to loud cheering and heart-felt applause. Others were walking through the crowd handing out pamphlets. Thomas took one when Robert looked away and quickly put it in the inside pocket of his jacket to read later.

Although Thomas helped out on the family farm, he had recently finished his stonemason's apprenticeship and had been taught basic joinery by his father. He was given paid work locally now and then – but was not yet established or earning enough to be independent of the family's farm.

One of his first jobs had been helping a local builder to erect a new outhouse for the thatched-roofed Bee Inn, previously known as the Pennant Arms. As they were finishing off the job, Thomas had watched the builder carve his initials and the year of 1876 into one of the new lintels they had put in. While he did, he told Thomas the story about the Inn being haunted but Thomas did not pay much heed to stories of the supernatural and had laughed it off.

Thomas had already begun to think that this small Parish of Eglwysbach, seven miles long and four miles wide, was getting too small for him. He felt that he needed more space to flex his muscles – to see a bit more of the country, if not the world. He had some savings but knew he would never be able to save enough to buy his own farm in Wales. He could possibly get a farm tenancy but he would still have to save a lot more than he already had for a down payment. So, he surprised himself by thinking that maybe emigration really was the answer to his predicament. He could be the owner of a farm in Patagonia and the thought was very tempting.

'You're quiet – cat got your tongue?'

'Just thinking.'

'About Megan?'

'No, as it happens.'

After climbing over the stile towards home, Robert challenged him.

'Come on, race you home……'

Once Robert was asleep, Thomas covertly read the pamphlet by a lit candle stub. His mind was much too agitated for slumber after the preacher's talk. The pamphlet informed him that if he was interested, he should write to the Welsh Emigration Society in Liverpool.

The idea of leaving for a new country began to steadily take hold and grow in him. He felt as if he was emerging from a chrysalis like a butterfly, getting ready to stretch and expand, to escape his cocoon, then fly away. With each passing day, he was becoming increasingly tempted to leave. He mentally argued with himself for hours. It was appealing to the adventurous spirit in him while his sensible side was advising caution. The very idea made him feel daring and brave – like a pioneer; he had always wanted to travel to see more of the world but never thought it could actually happen.

He reflected on his current situation; the thought of being stuck here for the rest of his life suddenly appalled him. He had itchy feet and now craved adventure. He had no dependents or relatives who would miss him or tie him down. He thought how challenging it would be to establish and run his own farm, to make it just as he wanted, as his father had done. He had useful skills with which he could subsidise his income if needed.

He knew really that his mind was already made up even as he considered the idea.

After about a week of thinking about it, he decided he would write to them; then it would be in the lap of the gods. If it was meant to be, it would happen. Although he was a bit out of practice, he had a fair hand at letters and knew his numbers – his sister Mary Ellen and Mr. Beverley had made sure of that – so one night he quietly crept down to the kitchen to write the letter which would change his life forever.

* * *

'What's this I hear about you thinking of leaving?' a voice behind him asked a few weeks later, as he was coming out of church.

Everybody knew everybody else's business in this small village, he thought.

Turning, he saw Megan, a vision of pure loveliness. He stood there mesmerised, momentarily lost for words.

'Are you really going half-way across the world? I am so envious. I wish I could go on such a journey. That speaker made it all sound very brave and exciting, didn't he?'

Dumbfounded, Thomas said nothing.

She continued, 'To be honest, I can't bear the thought that I will have to spend the rest of my life in this small corner of the world, lovely as it is, living the relentlessly hard life of a farmer's wife. I've seen what it has done to my poor mother.'

Thomas didn't know what suddenly possessed him:

'You can come with me if you want,' he blurted out.

* * *

'But Megan, I know I said it – but on reflection, I think it's a really foolish idea. I was wrong, the idea is totally impractical. They say they will only allow married couples, so you can't go as a friend.'

Megan looked directly at Thomas. She found his lack of guile so endearing – he had absolutely no idea just how handsome he really was.

'Then we'll have to get married on board ship,' she said. 'Can't a sea Captain do that?'

Again, she had managed to utterly shock him with this suggestion. Trying not to look nonplussed, he swallowed hard, then deciding to be practical, he continued, by telling her the arrangements.

'We would need to be ready to leave here and make our way to Liverpool docks in just two weeks' time. How will we do that? If you keep on insisting on not telling your family you are leaving, it is going to be very difficult. We cannot go by horseback. It's too far to walk and coaches are expensive.'

'I have a plan,' Megan interjected. 'Here's what we'll do. The night before the sailing, we'll each take a horse from our farm stables, then meet at the crossroads on the Llanrwst road at about two o'clock in the morning. We'll then ride down the valley to the railway station and take the first train to Liverpool. There's a milk train at five o'clock. We can leave the horses at the Station Livery and give one of the grooms a coin to lead them back home. I will leave a letter with the groom to give to my father explaining everything but by then, it will be too late for him to stop us. We will have already sailed.'

Thomas was thoroughly bewitched by Megan. She had a way of making things happen. She made the irrational seem normal. While he was sometimes thrown by problems, she saw them as challenges, situations to be overcome, beneficial even. Consequently, he gave in to her and wrote to the authorities to book their passages out.

The berths were confirmed by return. He was also informed that he would be allocated a square plot of land of about 250 acres near the river in the Chubbut Valley, west of a place called Gaiman. That will be good for irrigation, he thought. Little did he know how much irrigation he would actually get.

He should have realised then that there was a slight air of desperation about Megan's insistence on going with him along with her determination to leave secretly, which seemed irrational. Granted, if her father had known, he would no doubt have tried to stop her. What father wouldn't? But Thomas was much too bewitched to thwart her.

* * *

'I thought you were never coming,' Megan giggled nervously, as Thomas finally rode up to her at the crossroads.

She had a carpetbag and a bedroll strapped to her horse. She wore a thick full-length double-breasted coat of Welsh wool, split at the back to the waist, and long leather riding boots. As they set off for the station in the light of a half-moon, she looked majestic, with her black wavy hair blowing back gently in the breeze as they rode. Anyone would be proud to be seen with her – but at that moment, they were in the business of being invisible.

'I don't think anybody heard me leave. Father did come out with his lantern to the porch to look around the yard when he heard the horse whinnying. I had to give the dog a meat bone to distract him from barking and I laid straw down on the cobbles to muffle the horse's hooves. These were all part of my plan as I had already thought about the things which could go wrong. I have written the letter to explain everything to the family. They will be furious when they find out but there is nothing they will be able to do about it by then.'

To be conversational, Thomas said, 'I took this horse down to the *Hen Efail* yesterday, to make sure its shoes were sound. I had to wait quite a while because Thomas Pierce already had four other horses waiting to be shoed. He really should get some help there to speed things up a bit. Did you know that he makes all his own nails as well as the shoes?'

The conversation died and they travelled on in the broody silence of the semi-moonlit night, to the sounds of far-away owl calls and the hypnotic clip-clop rhythm of horses' hooves. Thomas sensed that underneath Megan's bravado, there was a hidden air of anxiety mixed in with excitement.

Parts of the road were so rutted that it took them more than an hour to ride the seven miles to the station. There, they handed over the horses at the Livery, while instructing the stable boy who was on duty. There was a train already at the platform, so they dashed across the tracks to buy train tickets. They just about managed to board this earlier mail train by running alongside it and grabbing the back carriage handrail, just as it was starting to slowly pull out of the station. Then they threw on their bedrolls and bags and scrambled into the rear guard's carriage.

'Phew, that was close,' Megan said, as they entered a third-class carriage. This 'by the skin of our teeth' moment seemed to have given her another little thrill. But within a few minutes she was quietly napping, lulled by the rhythmic motion of the train wheels on the track, with the side of her head resting on Thomas' shoulder. He revelled in the closeness of her and the feel of her soft breath on his face.

But given the time to think, the doubts crept in once more. Had he lost the good sense he had always been known for, in all of this? They could still turn back now to the safe bosom of their humdrum lives and families; but somehow, he did not think Megan would let him – she may even go on alone, given she was so headstrong. He wondered what this strange power was that she seemed to have over him – she knew he was obsessed with her and could bend him to her will.

Then he thought of the soon-to-be exploding anger of his father and hers, when they discovered she had gone with him; he hoped they didn't think too badly of him. His loyalties felt conflicted but then, at the same time, he sensed that the further he travelled away from his home, the more he was slowly becoming detached from it. It was a new, heady sort of freedom.

'Wake up, Megan! We're here! Quick! We need to find a hansom cab to take us to the docks.'

As she rubbed her eyes, he lifted their bags down from the stringed overhead storage rack. Then he opened the window of the carriage door and turned the T-shaped brass door handle on the outside, as the train came slowly to a halt. He looked up and saw a huge station clock telling him it was exactly seven o'clock. Once at the docks, they walked along the last few hundred yards towards the beginning of their new life, shrouded by an early damp fogginess coming in off the River Mersey.

'Look out for a ship named Hipparchus,' he said as they walked along the busy docklands service road. They did not need to look too hard as they heard mingling animated Welsh voices, well before they spotted the ship.

Thomas, however, could hardly understand a word the dockers were saying, as their heavy accent was unfamiliar to his ear. There was a palpable excitement amongst the crowds gathered at the quay and he wondered how things got done in this seemingly chaotic disorder of people, carriages, horses, trunks and porters.

Nearing the ship, they heard even more amongst them speaking Welsh – the voices of those who were leaving their beloved land, as well as the tearful, unhappy cries of those they would soon leave behind. Thomas was glad that they did not have to deal with upset, weeping relatives. His family had been fairly resigned to the idea of him leaving, although he hadn't told them the actual date of the sailing. When he told his father he would be sailing on the ship

Hipparchus, he surprised him by telling him Hipparchus was the name of an ancient Greek astronomer. His father often came up with nuggets of knowledge like that, which he attributed to a friendship with an old man when he was himself a young boy.

Thomas now felt that they would have been surprised if he had not left at some time or other. He recalled his father telling him he should not have listened to the romantic claptrap of fanatics. But by then, it was too late. Thomas had become hooked on the righteousness and morality of the idea of saving his culture, ever since he had attended that fateful meeting.

Shockingly, reality suddenly struck home. It dawned on him that it would be a very long time before he saw his homeland and family again, if ever. This made him feel a bittersweet sadness. But this was no time to become maudlin. The queue was moving towards the gangplank.

Eventually, they were let through the roped area at the bottom of the gangplank and walked up to the deck.

'Come on, follow me up; we'll find ourselves a space in steerage,' said Thomas.

As they made their way up, the crew directed them to the women's section on the 'tween deck. They were crestfallen by the sudden realisation that the men and women would be occupying different spaces on the ship. They eventually found a bunk for Megan with two other Welsh-speaking women and agreed to meet up later on the upper deck, once the ship was ready to sail and the ropes were released from their capstans. He was annoyed that he was unable to stay near her and was later to come to deeply regret this arrangement.

Thomas then left Megan there to go to find himself a space with other young men from North Wales.

The bunks were made from rough boards and covered with straw-filled mattresses. He had been warned by an old sea captain that the bunks which were situated athwartships caused seasickness and discomfort in rough seas, so he had chosen a bunk along the fore-and-aft line of the ship.

Both light and ventilation in steerage were poor, so conditions soon deteriorated. He noticed buckets for use as toilets, which would have to double up as sick buckets in stormy seas. The thought repulsed him. He had heard that diseases spread easily on-board ship – but he was hopeful that being young and healthy, they would both endure.

As the ship set sail out of the port with the tide, they stood side by side on deck, watching their old life slip away from them and took their last lingering view of the British coast.

'How are your bunk mates then?' asked Thomas.

'They are really friendly but I'm not sure my stomach agrees with all this rolling around.'

'We're not even out in the open sea yet! I expect it will get a lot rougher than this.'

Thankfully, his stomach seemed to be made of sterner stuff – but he decided he would spend as much of his time up on the top deck as he could. It was too stuffy and claustrophobic down there and the air was quickly becoming fetid.

That night he settled down to sleep but before long, he was furiously scratching at his skin and was soon covered in red bites. He realised that the mattress was infested with lice and fleas. His sister, Mary Ellen, would have been horrified by the thought of that! He decided that weather permitting, he would sleep up on deck on his bedroll as often as possible.

'Bring your own plate if you want food,' shouted a crew member next morning, walking through steerage, banging a gong. Thomas made his way to the galley and queued up with his tin plate. He looked around, becoming concerned as he could not see Megan.

'There, that's your lot,' said the galley hand as he dumped a smallish ladleful of porridge onto the plate. 'You'll get some more food later on in the day.'

Dismayed, Thomas looked at the small portion on his plate, then dipped his enamel mug into a barrel to scoop up drinking water.

By mid-afternoon, he had still not been able to see Megan and was beginning to feel sick with worry. Suddenly, he recognised one of her below-deck companions from yesterday.

'How is Megan?'

'Her sea-sickness has got worse. She wretches almost constantly and can't even keep fluids down.'

'Please keep an eye on her and let me know how she is.'

By two weeks into the voyage, Megan was too weak to rise out of her bunk to be up on deck where it was healthier. Thomas worried that she was not getting enough water, as she continued to wretch. He asked the girl to insist she drank but she said the water is not always fresh there.

Then the weather conditions suddenly improved as they were picked up by the trade winds. The ship creaked into sleek action, seemingly alive as she glided majestically up and down, through the water. Now that the rolling choppiness had gone, he thought that hopefully, Megan would perhaps begin to improve at last.

But still he didn't see her on deck and became increasingly worried, not knowing what was happening with her. He was not allowed in the women's quarters or he would have gone there himself to carry her out. He was frustrated that he could not go there to see for himself how she was. Out on deck, he began a conversation with another girl of about Megan's age.

'Will you please go to the women's quarters and ask about a Megan Lewis?' he asked her. 'I need to know how she is.'

'Of course, I'll go there directly.'

She could see he was quite desperate to know, so she headed straight down the ladders to the women's section.

'Megan's in a bad way,' she said on her return. 'The surgeon is with her now. He doesn't think he can save the baby, as it's nowhere near full-term.'

Reeling at this information, Thomas caught hold of the bow rail as his legs began to buckle under him from the shock,

'Baby?' he repeated incredulously as he sat. 'Are you sure you've found the right Megan? I know of no baby!'

'I'm quite sure. They told me she keeps on calling out for a Bleddyn, over and over in her delirium.'

'Who on God's earth is this Bleddyn? – and why was she calling his name?'

He tried to remember who he knew from home with that name; the only one he could recall was the son of the local gentry in nearby Maenan. Could it be him? Had she been secretly seeing him? He had come to realise just how secretive she could be by the way she had schemed to get away from Eglwysbach. Or had he forced himself on her and she hadn't told anyone? Maybe when she confronted him with her news of a baby, he told her he would not marry her. Was this why she was so keen to get away from home, before the baby became evident?

He suddenly felt sick at the thought that he may have been exploited by her. He had trusted her – but it looked like she had been deceiving him. What should he do now? He felt his heart begin to harden towards her; she had her bunkmates to look after her – he would no longer worry about her. He knew he would find it very hard to forgive her now, if ever, for this. He could no longer see a future with her. But sadly, he soon discovered he would not have to forgive her after all and that there would be no future with her.

About an hour later, the girl came back with a shocked look on her face.

'I am the bearer of very sad news,' she said, wringing her hands, as tears trickled down her face. 'The surgeon tried to save her but she was very weak from lack of food and the sea-sickness. I was standing close by when I heard him proclaim that both Megan and the baby boy were dead. Typhus, I think he said. I heard him order the women there to wrap her body in a sheet and get it tied securely with rope.......'

Her voice petered out as she could see that Thomas was in shock and no longer taking in what she was saying.

Thomas was shattered by this information. Then the wind suddenly dropped, as if appalled by his devastating news, quietening, so that Thomas could hear his own thoughts properly. Thoughts which were bouncing about wildly in his head. But they were thoughts he did not want to be thinking. Her sickness had obviously been far more serious than he had originally imagined when he had been considering whether to forgive her or not. What a fool he had been to be taken in by her. His dreams of their future life together were now irretrievably shattered into a thousand pieces. Scattered to the wind.

News of the tragedy quickly spread throughout the ship. People had come out on deck and were now openly discussing it. A funeral was expedited, as required on board ship.

The captain, who was supposed to have married them, was now

preparing a burial service for her instead, along with their previously planned futures. Her sheet-wrapped body had been sewn into a canvas shroud and weighted with lead to ensure it sank. It was then carried out on deck by crew members on a plank to the stern of the ship, where an elderly gentleman stepped forward and draped a Welsh flag around her body for the service. At first, a small crowd gathered around, as the captain began to read, then more joined them.

'Forasmuch as it hath pleased Almighty God in his great mercy to take unto himself the soul of our dear sister, Megan, here departed, we therefore commit her body to the deep, in sure and certain hope of the Resurrection to eternal life, through our Lord Jesus Christ...'

The crowd crossed themselves and collectively, sombrely said 'Amen.'

Instinctively and without prompting, a lone tenor voice began to sing:

'*Arglwydd arwain trwy'r anialwch...*' Lord lead us through the wilderness.

Other voices soon joined him in four-part harmony. The music's spontaneous and utter beauty in the midst of such tragedy touched Thomas' heart and he knew he had never heard such heartfelt singing, even in his old Church. This pathos came from deep within the souls of those who were glad they still clung on to the preciousness of life.

This young death was a stark reminder to them of how precarious the act of living was. They all knew they were vulnerable to the vagaries of life and for their need for God to protect them. Fate had been cruel. She was far too young to be going to meet her maker and in the natural order of things, should have had the whole of her new life ahead of her.

The gathered mourners continued to sing from that deep place inside of themselves, their eyes shut tight, their hands pressed together in prayer, as her body slid slowly seaward down the smooth plank, into the wake of the waves of the cold sea – to slowly, silently sink finally into the depths of a deep, indifferent ocean.

The general atmosphere on board ship remained quietly subdued for a while afterwards. Even the usual banter between the crew was subdued. Then suddenly, as if to put an end to one phase and to begin another, the sails began to unfurl and fill out, as a fresh storm blew up, ready to move the lives of those still living on to the next stage of their perilous journey.

Passengers and crew became distracted from the recent tragic event, as the captain called for 'all hands on deck' to fight to keep the boat headed south-west.

Thomas was astonished at how quickly people could get back to supposed normality and the business of living – whilst he still remained stuck in the shock of his unexpected and appalling loss, which had suddenly splintered his very soul to the core.

He a was broken man. He grieved for the life that might have been. But then again, that life would have been a lie. He smarted from the knowledge of her easy deception of him. The destructive seed of their future together had literally been planted by another, months ago. His situation and the life he had envisioned had changed on a whim. He was now on his own. He was unable to share what he knew with anyone. The only ones who knew, apart from the surgeon, were a handful of bystanders and the girl who told him of Megan's passing, with those immortal words that still echoed over and over in his head:

'Baby? I know of no baby.'

Thomas knew that he could not tell his family or Megan's, what had happened. The scandal and shame would mortify them and destroy their peace of mind.

He stayed on his bunk for days, having no reason or incentive to rise. He went over and over in his head the conversations they had had, searching for any clues, hints or nuances he had failed to pick up on earlier. Shock had now turned mostly to slow anger, along with acute feelings of having been used, and he felt deeply that he had been stupidly trusting and gullible.

Soon, he felt his heart harden. He knew he would find it very hard to trust anybody in the future and decided that he would now only ever depend on himself, as he had since his mother died when he was young.

'Why do those I love abandon me?' he asked himself plaintively.

He knew that it was his responsibility to write to Megan's family to inform them of her death. But he decided it could wait a while longer, until he was in a better frame of mind – with less anger in his heart to cloud his words. He wondered again if he should tell them of the dead baby – but decided not to. There was no other way they could find out, unless this Bleddyn, whoever he was, blabbed, which seemed unlikely. He decided it would be best to keep it from them, to spare their feelings, so that they could remember her with love and pride, not everlasting shame. He did not think there was any other way that the news could reach her parents. The people who knew her on board did not know where her home was, because she had decided not to tell anyone.

A week had passed since Megan's death. Thomas, finally driven by hunger clawing at his stomach, slowly began to return to the land of the living. He sat out on deck for hours. He slept mostly but when he awoke, the feeling of deep regret was still heavy with him. Then one bright, breezy day, he became aware of a child's soft touch on his upper arm. He turned his head sideways to see a scruffy young lad sitting beside him. His clothes were patched and threadbare, his trousers too short for his spindly legs, his feet sockless, his boots laceless and holed. The child did not speak but Thomas instinctively felt his concerned empathy reaching deep to touch his shattered heart, only as someone who had suffered the same immeasurable heartbreak and loss can.

'What's your name, boy?' Thomas asked idly, not really wanting to know.

'Josh, sir.'

'And where's your mam?'

'Don't have one no more.'

'You are on your own? How on earth did you get on board? Are you crew?'

'No, I was living rough in the docks. I ran away from the farm the orphanage sent me to work on. They were mighty cruel to me. Had the lash on me back every day, so one day I just started walking and didn't stop. I wanted to run away to sea for an adventure. Once I got to Liverpool, I heard the Welshies talking about going to Argentina to start a new life, so I thought maybe I could go as well. I sneaked up the gangplank with one of their families, so crew wouldn't notice I was on me own and have kept out of their way ever since.'

As Thomas looked sideways at him, he brought to mind his younger brother William, who had died years earlier. He felt sorry for Josh; he was completely alone in the world. At least I have a family, Thomas thought, albeit back in Wales.

From then on, the lad seemed to latch onto him, seeking him out when on deck. He did not bother Thomas with idle chatter but rather sat in a companionable, empathetic silence next to him. He wondered indifferently where the boy slept and how he managed to feed himself.

They were nearing their destination now. The ship docked briefly in Buenos Aires to drop off some passengers and cargo, then continued on its way to Patagonia. Porth Madryn was now ten days or so away at most, if a fair wind prevailed.

'What are your plans when we dock, Maldwyn?' Thomas asked, when speaking with a group of other young men one evening.

'I'll be looking for work in Porth Madryn or Rawson – maybe as far as Gaiman in the Chubbut valley or even beyond. I'm a builder, so there should be plenty of work there for me. I have the tools of my trade with me in my carpenter's chest.'

'Gaiman is a very new town,' said another, well-built young man called Rhys. 'I've heard there are plans to build a railway spur-line to take the produce from the farms in the valley down to the docks for export. Trelew will be the terminal which will link to Porth Madryn. I'm hoping to get work building the line there.'

'What are your plans, Thomas?' one of the group asked.

'I've been promised a parcel of land by the government and organisers, so I can start farming. I am a stonemason by trade but grew up on a farm in the Conwy Valley. Maybe I'll combine both.'

Carpenters, engineers, stonemasons, preachers, teachers, traders and others all spoke of their plans. Some were going there for good, others transiently to make their fortune.

Presently, one of the main organisers, Gwyndaf, who would be leading the farmers to their plots, joined the group.

'When we dock and disembark, you will be processed by the official immigration authorities. The potential farmers amongst you will also go through the Land Registration section, to be allotted your land. Surveyors have already divided up the lower Chubbut valley into plots – there should be enough for all. We will then make our way south towards Gaiman, which is a smallish town at the beginning of the narrow Chubbut valley.'

'Where will we get our supplies and provisions?' one of the men enquired.

'There is a general store which sells just about everything you can ever think of – but you will pay a bit more there than you would expect to, because everything has to be transported in, nothing is manufactured. Some of the smaller forges will make implements and nails for you but even the metal they use has to either come from Buenos Aires or it comes in by sea.'

'I will stay with you until every one of you has safely reached your plot,' Gwyndaf continued, 'so first you will get your immigration paperwork ready, then get your land deeds sorted. After that you can go and buy your ponies, horses and carts. You can also buy your supplies and tools in Porth Madryn or wait until you get to Gaiman. We will meet up by the general store and ride south the day after we land. This should give you time to get what you need for the journey and everything you will need to get you started for developing your plots. Any questions?'

Finally, the long voyage was coming to an end. They approached Porth Madryn on a beautiful sunny but cold day. The atmosphere on board was highly charged, the excitement palpable. As they had sailed down the coast, they had looked at the lowish hills as well as those surrounding the port as they sailed in. They all agreed that this land was nowhere near as majestically beautiful as Wales. Just miles and miles of low, scrubby, treeless hills, stretching as far as the eye could see. Once the boat was secured to the quay and the gangplank fixed, the passengers began to slowly file off, most of them heavily laden with all their worldly possessions.

'Well, this is it,' Thomas thought, as he stood, swung his bag over his shoulder and lifted his chest under his arm. He stopped to survey the landscape immediately in front of him and wondered what the future would have in store for him now. Taking a deep breath, he made his way down the gangplank and onto Argentinian soil.

Passengers were guided into the Immigration Office where they showed their original embarkation papers. They gave the information required for their registration: name, occupation, date and country of birth and where they had travelled from.

Thomas was then directed down a corridor to the Land Registration section, where details were checked against a list of those who were to be allocated a land grant.

'Where is your wife?' the official asked Thomas when it came to his turn.

'She died on the passage out,' he replied flatly.

'That changes the situation. You are now no longer eligible for a full plot, only a half plot. As you have no wife, your entitlement is now for land as a designated 'single person' rather than as part of a family.'

Thomas' eyes widened and his jaw dropped as the shock registered on his face.

The clerk scribbled something down. After a moment, Thomas was handed an important-looking document, which stated that he was now the half-owner of Plot 352.

'You will share the plot with a Juan Hughes.'

This was a bitter disappointment but given the circumstances, what could he do? Those were the rules. Nevertheless, Thomas asked him if he could reconsider and give him a full plot.

'Take it or leave it, it's your choice,' replied the official, shrugging his shoulders. 'Your half is on the west side. Next please.'

Defeated, disappointed and dejected, Thomas walked round-shouldered out of the Immigration Office.

Others, coming there for work only, had already been allowed through and were on their way. Thomas cursed that the best horses and supplies would probably have already been taken.

Out on the wide, dusty, mainly wooden-built main street, he soon found the horse dealer's corral. Thomas thought that the horses for sale looked as if they had only recently been taken from the prairie and were barely broken in. Some still had a wild look in their eyes.

'These ponies can ride twenty leagues in a day. Good value,' he was told.

But Thomas was not going to make his decision based solely on the seller's sales talk. He considered himself a good judge of horses and spent a great deal of time looking for ones which he thought would give him the least trouble. Deep in thought, with one leg up on the lower plank of the ranch fencing, he suddenly heard a voice at his elbow.

'*Helo eto*. Remember me?'

'Josh! How did you get off that boat without being seen?'

'Same way I got on,' he grinned cheekily.

'What are you going to do now you're here? I'd get back on the boat and go home if I were you. This is no place for a boy on his own.'

'I have nothing to go back to – and I won't be on my own. I'm coming with you!'

'Oh no you're not,' Thomas said emphatically. 'I can't be responsible for you. You have to register with the authorities. See if they can find you a work-place with somebody.'

'That would be no different from what I left behind. I don't want to register; I don't exist as far as they know, so it doesn't matter. I can be useful to you. I can hunt for food and help you build your house.'

Looking at the puny lad, Tom doubted he was up to much. Impatiently, the dealer interrupted their conversation to ask Thomas if he had chosen yet.

'I'll take a pack mule and the piebald, she seems a little less wild than the others. I'll take that light saddle as well.'

Thomas paid him, then led his new acquisitions away by the ropes tied to their halters.

'For now, they'll both be pack-horses,' he said to Josh. 'I'll try to break in the pony for riding later.'

Next, he walked over to the general store.

'Josh! Here, make yourself useful; hold the reins while I go in to buy some supplies.'

Josh hoped that by making himself useful, he would be able to accompany Thomas to his new plot.

'I need pans, tools, feed, seeds and a tent,' Thomas said to the storekeeper. 'A good strong axe, chisels, a saw, planes, an assortment of nails, a wheel, calico, a decent rifle and warm blankets. Most of all, I want the best knife you have with a belt.'

Showing him one, the dealer told him, 'It's called a gaucho belt which has a knife sheath built in. You will also need to purchase a poncho to keep yourself warm riding the plains.'

'Throw in two ponchos,' Thomas replied, looking at the lad.

Handing one to Josh, he told him, 'Don't think that this means you're coming with me, though.'

Next morning, Thomas rendezvoused with the leader and the others to begin the walk to their plots. When he got there, they were getting ready to leave. The leader opened up a surveyor's map of the valley floor and showed the land divided into numbered plots.

'The river basically runs from the west to east along the base of this escarpment,' he said, pointing to the map with the stick, 'so we'll follow that westward when we get to Trelew. The lower numbered plots will be reached first, so those owners will peel off from our main group as we reach them. Obviously, the owners of the higher numbers will have further to travel.'

They set off, heading inland towards the featureless landscape.

'Who's your little friend, Thomas?' said one of the group.

He turned around and there was Josh, his shadow, tagging along.

'Go! You can't come with me where I'm going. It'll be enough for me to look after myself, without another mouth to feed.'

Thomas continued to walk westward with the main group, while the lad looked crestfallen.

'He could be useful,' said one of the men.

'Why not let him tag along?' said another.

Encouraged by this, Josh started to walk again behind the group.

'You take him then,' said Thomas, scowling his disapproval.

'He doesn't want to be with me,' he laughed. 'Looks like you're stuck with him.'

Thomas shrugged his shoulders resignedly.

Once away from Porth Madryn, they got their first real look at the country where they intended to create their utopia. It appeared to be mainly low scrub desert with poor quality grass, surrounded by low undulating hills. Not at all what they had been led to believe. The landscape was vast, endless and dry, with an immense blue, cloudless sky. Trees were few and far between. As they moved southward, Thomas wondered how he was going to build a cabin without trees, wondering if he may have to rethink the build entirely.

'There are several nomadic Tehuelche Indians in the area,' their leader, Gwyndaf, informed them, conversationally. 'They helped the first settlers to survive by bringing them food but some can be unfriendly. However, they are happy to trade if you have something they need.'

No sooner had he said this than they looked up to see a group of six Indians high up on the nearby ridge, astride their steppe ponies. They were watching the Welshmen intently. A cold shiver travelled through Thomas' spine as he imagined one of those spears thrust into his back. He told himself always to be wary of them – even the friendly ones.

'Don't worry, you'll soon get yourselves established,' Gwyndaf went on. 'Water is the main thing. You'll either need to try to run water in off the main irrigation system, or depending on where you are, build channels to bring your own supply in off the river. As soon as you've done that and cleared the land, you can start sowing your seeds.'

After many more hours travelling south across the Argentinian pampas, daylight finally began to fade, so Gwyndaf ordered them to strike camp for the night. Darkness falling was shockingly sudden – no gentle fading into the night here. The stars soon came out, spattering the vast blackness of the sky with stars of such clarity and magnificence that they took Thomas' breath away. The temperature also dropped rapidly.

A campfire was lit, then after eating, they sat around the dying embers talking excitedly about the possibility of reaching their plots in the next few days. A feeling of real camaraderie prevailed in the camp, while the coyotes barked and howled around them in the distance.

Exhausted by the trek and the strangeness of everything, Thomas pulled out his bedroll. After a drink of infused yerba leaves, which Gwyndaf brewed for them, Thomas slept soundly. The night was uneventful but with the dawn, there was more talk amongst the men. They had become unsettled by the sight of the Indians the day before. There were fears that they would try to steal from them, or worse. They agreed that vigilance must always be utmost in their minds.

Initially, Josh had kept out of Thomas' way until he believed it was too late to send him back. Then, as the days went by, he made himself useful by loading and unloading supplies on and off the mule and pony. He also helped to pitch the tent made from the calico and some poles. Thomas noticed he had a good way with the horses and soothed them whenever they were spooked by wild animals lurking nearby. Occasionally, from his wandering, Josh would bring something back to add to the communal pot.

At their pace of travel, Thomas believed they would reach his plot later that day. That morning, he made some damper bread from the flour in his supplies by cooking it on a hot stone, then shared it with Josh. With this breaking of bread, it seemed their fates were finally sealed.

They continued trekking westwards and by midday, the merciless sun was pounding down on them once more. Thomas was glad he had bought a wide-brimmed hat at the store. As they neared Thomas' shared plot, he wondered if Juan Hughes would already be there, working his section. Would they be working together or would they subdivide their plot? Thomas would prefer to work his own section but there could be some advantages to working with others. He wondered why Juan had a Spanish Christian name and Welsh surname. Thomas also wondered why he had not travelled out to his plot with him and the others. Maybe he would follow later on.

In the late morning, they finally reached the boundary of his plot and Thomas bade a fond farewell to his remaining fellow-travellers; all vowed to meet up in the not-too-distant future.

More trees grew here nearer to the river and there was a small copse on the northern side of the plot. They first walked along the four dirt roads which edged the square plot, then Thomas chose a spot near a small spring to set up camp on his section. There was no visible evidence of any prior development on any of the land. Having worked out where the midpoint of the plot was by pacing it out, he divided the plot straight down the centre of the square.

Irrigation would be his first major task. As Thomas' deeds showed his was the western side of the plot, he saw it was possible to irrigate it from the river. As there was no one else around to consult, he decided to dig out an irrigation trench along the side of the dirt road on the west, eventually continuing across the north and south sides of his half-plot. Juan would have to dig his own channel to irrigate his side of the land.

To test the soil, Thomas took the pickaxe and dug a small channel near the river. It appeared to be a mixture of alkaline and clay, which he knew would hold the water well, preventing it from seeping away into the ground. The clay deposits would also be useful later for the manufacture of bricks and roof tiles. To fire them, they would also need to dig out a largish claypit.

'Here, if you want to be useful, take this machete and start clearing the scrub up there and set up camp,' he said to Josh.

Josh gladly set to the task and worked hard for a few hours, until the sweat was running in rivers down his back, soaking his shirt. He left some of the more mature trees standing to create shade from the relentless sun.

'When you get the fire going, I'll show you how to make some damper bread, so we can eat. Then if you know how to, you can set some traps hereabouts, for the pot later. Tomorrow, we'll start digging the main irrigation channel.'

Josh was proving to be a great asset and an antidote to the silence which surrounded them much of the time. Thomas was now very glad that he was there, realising how lonely he would soon have felt alone.

It took a few weeks before they finally got the water flowing in from the river. Once the land was cleared and the water channelled, they dug the claypit to fire the bricks and roof tiles they needed to build the house. They lifted large chunks of clay from the riverbank and used fine wire to cut these into bricks, before they were fired.

They collected as many large boulders as they could find, to build the footings of the dwelling and a chimney stack, using a wheelbarrow that Thomas had fashioned utilising a wheel and axle bought at the general store. Then, using axes, they cut down and trimmed some tall cypress trees which grew along the riverbank and planed them into roof beams, before leaving them to season.

That was their routine for the next few months. They built, they ate, then fell exhausted into their bedrolls at nightfall. The finished one-roomed building with the chimney on one side, proved substantial. Next, they built a long-drop a few yards from the main dwelling to replace the hole in ground they had been using.

Their next task was to build a barn, which also had stone footings but was finished in wood. Thomas was proud of his little abode and the progress he and Josh had made over the months. The completion of these buildings gave them a feeling of being more established and secure, should any Indians come calling.

Over time, they tilled the soil, planted orchards and established vegetable plots. They built pig pens and kept a few cows and a small flock of sheep which were mainly for their own consumption – they did not have enough grazing land to breed animals in large numbers.

In the spring, there were masses of blue, purple, pink and mauve lupins growing along the banks of the Chubbut River, which was a beautiful sight for sore eyes after the drabness of the pampas. It lifted their spirits to see them.

After about six months, when the co-owner of the plot had still not appeared, Thomas was highly tempted to cultivate the other half, but decided against it as he could appear at any time and claim the crop. So it was left fallow, although they did burn off the weeds close to the boundary to stop them seeding onto Thomas' half.

They had hens and had managed to trap and breed some native turkeys. Eventually, they were self-sufficient enough to only need to go into town to buy flour, implements, nails, seeds and oats for the ponies, as well as to sell their produce.

Thomas had broken in the pony, so that she would now let them ride her but the care of both animals had somehow become Josh's responsibility. He had a gentle way of handling them as if they were his friends – and they seemed drawn to him.

* * *

Once established, things went well for a few years. Thomas was busy, happy and prosperous. Fruit crops were plentiful.

Then disaster struck.

A sudden snowmelt high up in the Andes had gathered momentum, causing the valley floor to flood. The dwelling was spared but their hard-earned harvest was washed away from inside the barn.

They had to rebuild from the ruins but eventually, all was well once more.

Then a few years later, a similar disaster struck again and heartbreakingly, they had to rebuild the barn once more from scratch. This seemed to be becoming a never-ending pattern of life in the valley for many of the settlers.

* * *

After a few more settled, productive, well-established years, Thomas once again found himself perched on his roof in the dead of night. But this flood proved to be far worse than any previously experienced. The night was pitch black – the blackest of black. He could see no shapes, and apart from feeling a slight breeze on his face, he could only hear, smell and sense. The Chubut River had started rising again that morning for the third time and by early evening, it was again breaking its banks. The valley floor was completely flooded and everything in its path was being destroyed. His worst recurring nightmare had become reality once more.

Earlier, as the water level began to rise rapidly, he had let the animals loose. They would have to fend for themselves and be lost to him – but some of the turkeys had managed to perch high up in some poplar trees. But there was no high ground nearby for the other animals. They would eventually be carried down by the overpowering flood, then out to sea, along with all the other flotsam of the storm from higher up in the valley. Sadly, he thought about when he'd bought them at the local market and was told that some were probably descendants of those which had come over with the first settlers on the Mimosa in 1865 and had landed at Porth Madryn.

He expected that yet another harvest, laboriously tended and carefully stored in the barn, would be ruined; as would he, for the third time. A toxic mix of torrential downpours from a cyclonic storm along the coast at the end of winter had coincided with the snowmelt on the Andes, doubling the usual volume of water in the river and causing it to flood the pampas once more. This occasionally recurring pattern, together with the violent dust storms common in the summer, made this land virtually impossible to farm consistently.

By sun-down, the water had risen so high that Thomas had

finally climbed up onto the ridge of the house roof for safety, taking food and water with him. His important papers and what money he had were in his leather satchel which was strapped to him. He felt the comforting presence of his knife in its sheath around his waist. As the temperature dropped, he despondently threw his llama-wool poncho around his hunched shoulders, to keep out the cold damp. His situation was utterly hopeless once more. He even began to wonder if this time, the water would actually get high enough to wash him and the house away as well.

He had learned the drill from previous flooding events; all he could do was to sit it out until the water finally receded, then assess the carnage.

Thomas' half-plot was only big enough to sustain a small herd of cattle and a small flock of sheep. Thousands of acres were needed to support the grazing of sheep and cattle on a large scale. Existing sheep barons from earlier immigrations now owned huge tracts of the land but even their sheep would not have been spared this devastation, unless they were already safe up in the higher pastures, on the lower slopes of the Andes.

The flood flowed silently, furtively by as he dozed fitfully, sitting upright, leaning against the chimney. But sudden, sporadic sounds in the silence startled him awake: creaking timbers, metal scraping on stone – he tried to imagine what was happening around him. He listened for animal sounds. But there was no lowing or bleating from them now. Their plaintive earlier cries as some were swept away, powerless to resist the strong current, still haunted him.

Suddenly, he heard the thunderous cracking of the main uprights of the barn, as they slowly succumbed to the overwhelming power of the rushing water. All would now be swept away, along with the barn roof which had covered his precious harvest, his winter feed gone.

Thomas reflected that when he had first arrived in this God-forsaken country, he had just suffered the worst trauma of his young life. The heavy stench of deceit and a general disappointment in people had been metaphorically pressing down on his broad shoulders. Had he known then what would be in store for him, he may have left immediately, but he had decided to make the best of it. He couldn't face going back then and in the main, despite life being desperately hard at times, he had fared reasonably well for quite a few years.

'Help! Help!' A weak, female voice passing close by, broke into his thoughts, then faded into the distance. Someone was mercilessly being swept along in that all-powerful churning body of icy water, its source hundreds of miles away up in the Andes. Thomas knew he could not help her, but he squeezed his eyes tightly shut and prayed fervently to God that she managed to latch onto an overhanging branch or some flotsam. The likelihood was that she would soon succumb to the intense iciness of the water and eventually lose consciousness. That would be merciful.

The house had been solidly built on the highest point of the plot, using backbreakingly-cleared stones off the land and others carried up from the riverbank. It had stoically resisted past floods, so it should survive once more. Thomas had also built a bulwark in the water's path to redirect it away from the main buildings. But these thoughts gave him neither comfort nor hope; his mood was one of utter despair. Dark thoughts arose – a part of him even wanted to be swept away, along with the ruins of his life. But it was not his choice whether he lived or died, he knew it was the Lord's.

What he had with him on the roof was once again all he owned in the world. The farm would once more be worthless until re-established. What arrogance to believe man could tame this wild desert. The Argentinian government authorities who had allotted the land, must have known that this whole area was a floodplain and he felt real anger towards them for misleading his countrymen in this way. They had been sold an impossible, unachievable dream.

Thomas decided there and then. That was it. He was done with the place. He could not face building it all up, only to be destroyed once more. If there was anything left, he would leave the farm to Josh and his Tehuelche woman – if they survived this onslaught. He wondered then if this was why the Indians were nomadic.

Thomas could not condone their relationship, as they were not married in the sight of God but both were good people who had worked hard for him. Josh was away at the time collecting supplies and Thomas wondered what he would find on his return. His woman must have known through ancient tribal instinct what was about to happen, as she had decamped earlier to higher ground with her people.

It had been a lonely life out there in the pampas. Apart from Josh and the farm animals, the only other large living creatures were ostrich, guanacos and llamas. The homesteads were some distance apart, which meant that he did not have much opportunity to socialise. Since his arrival in Patagonia, his lot had been one of relentless hard work, to keep his head literally above water. He reflected on the cruel irony of that thought.

Although he had recently been helping to build their little Welsh chapel in the nearest town, which had been named Bethesda by the Welsh settlers, it would take time for the congregation to grow. He wondered, disinterestedly now, if it would even endure this flood. What was the point of building anything for it just to be washed away every few years? He liked to make things that lasted. He remembered that the previously, almost completed school in Gaiman had been washed away by the flood of 1899. He wondered if the new Intermediate Welsh Language School now being built as a replacement, would survive this Biblical deluge.

Those who had cultivated their estancias had done well. The wheat, fruit and vegetables grew in abundance with irrigation – but those with a surplus of produce had no means yet of transporting it to the coast to sell. So until the new railway line was completed, they grew only what they could sell locally or could preserve and store.

In desperation and anger, Thomas cried out plaintively to the Lord: 'What was it all for? Why do you allow us to build it up only to destroy us time after time? What sort of God are you?'

He immediately felt guilty for this doubting thought.

He sat for hours in this black darkness, thinking even blacker thoughts. His limbs became stiff and sore from being in the same position for hours in cold, damp conditions. The chill had slowly crept through to his bones. What was the point of all his endeavours? He reflected on the wasted years with nothing to show for them. Nature was too powerful in the valley where he had sought to make his home for more than twenty years. But this time he knew he would not rebuild. He no longer had the energy that he had as a young man in his prime. His spirit, heart and soul were now broken beyond repair.

Despairingly, he wondered why he had ever wanted to come to this forsaken land. Why did he listen to the seductive rhetoric of those who peddled their dream of a new Wales, where culture, language and religion would be safeguarded? They weren't told that the climate was frequently inhospitable; the land was practically treeless, generally rainless and sterile. Floods, swarms of locusts and dust storms could destroy crops – but the Argentinian government was deaf and unsympathetic to their needs when it came to rebuilding after these catastrophic events.

There had also been some talk locally that the Welsh immigrants would soon have to bear arms for the Argentinian army and be required to do drill practice on Sundays. This outraged them, as Sunday was set aside for the worship of the Lord. Besides, they were simple farmers, not fighting men. The government was also talking about establishing Spanish-speaking schools to replace some of the Welsh ones. Furthermore, some settlers had recently been having problems securing the deeds for their properties from the Argentinian government.

Despite the Welsh and other nationalities having given blood, sweat and tears to irrigate the valley to make it productive, they now felt they were discriminated against. It had become clear that the powers that be no longer wanted his people to continue as a Federal Welsh Government, which had originally been formed in 1878. Instead, they were downgraded to an Administrative Region of Patagonia in 1894.

Tello, the Governor, quietly resented the power of the Calvinistic Welsh Methodists, particularly given that he was a Catholic. He had recently decreed that all Argentinian males must attend military exercises on Sundays; those who refused were to be imprisoned. Some Welsh families had already sent their sons back to Wales to avoid the call-up, as they had settled this land to farm, not to fight. Thomas knew that despite his age, they would in time come for him. Maybe Josh would avoid it, given that he had never registered as a citizen on entering the country.

Thomas believed he was still young enough to start a new life elsewhere in a gentler country and had read reports of farmers needed in Canada. He'd heard that Joseph Chamberlain had sent a delegation to Buenos Aires to recruit farmers for Canada. There was the promise of thirty-six square miles of land to form a Welsh colony. Temporary housing would be provided while the immigrants built their own and they would be allowed to cut down Crown trees for this purpose. The funds to enable this migration were already being raised by public subscription.

Sitting on top of his house in the pitch black of night, Thomas decided that this is what he would do. He would leave Argentina. He would go to farm in Canada.

But first, he wanted to go back to visit his family home in Wales.

Heartbroken and defeated, Thomas had decided he could no longer take any more of this distress, of building things up only to have everything destroyed time and time again. Nor would he remain under this new autocratic government regime. It was too much to bear. He would leave this God-forsaken country. This country had had enough of him – and he of it.

He did not know where Josh was but he would return when he could. Luckily Josh had taken the pony and mule with him to fetch supplies. He hoped he had reached higher ground. Josh could build the farm up again if he wanted to. Thomas no longer had the stomach for it. There was nothing left to stay for but more despair and heartbreak in the future. He felt wretched. He hated failure but he felt this life had been a failure beyond his control.

Once the water level had dropped enough, Thomas threw the few of his tools he could find into his trunk. Then carrying his few possessions, he began the long walk along the river into Gaiman. He could not bear even to survey the damage the flood had done to his farm. He just started walking eastwards and never looked back once.

On the badly rutted, flood-damaged road, he was lucky enough to be given a ride by a Tehuelche, who was leading a spare pony to a dealer in Porth Madryn. On the way, they saw the bloated bodies of dead animals and people, washed down by the flood. Vultures and flies were now feeding on them. Other items had also been washed downstream and carelessly dumped by the water on the banks of the river as it receded. The flotsam of once-precious possessions had been unceremoniously scattered along the flood's path and left abandoned, high and dry. There were several pieces of furniture, some of which may very well have been brought out by the original Welsh settlers on the Mimosa.

Once Thomas reached Porth Madryn, the first thing he did was to book his passage out of Patagonia on the Orissa, bound for Liverpool on the fourteenth of May, 1902 – on which he would be joined by more than two hundred other disillusioned and disheartened people. In the week before he sailed, he settled his legal affairs regarding the farm.

During the homeward voyage, many of the traumatised people exchanged their horrific experiences of the flood. Many were bound for home, while others would be going on to pastures new in other parts of the world.

Once Thomas arrived at Liverpool, he enquired about a possible passage out to Canada. He also made enquiries with the Colonial Office to express his interest in acquiring some land there.

But first, he would visit his family in North Wales, before leaving home once more for his new adventure in Canada where he had once more been promised land.

Chapter 5

Alys has been out on bail for some time and there is still no indication from the police as to whether the case against her will proceed. As she complies so well, we return to court to ask for some of the more restrictive conditions to be lifted and our application is granted.

She will be allowed to sit her A-Levels, and achieving her predicted grades will enable her to apply for the course she is interested in. Her plan is to study part-time for a probation or social work qualification, as her latest idea is to be a probation officer. She is impressed with the structured way that Ruth has helped her get back on her feet after being released on bail. The only dark cloud is that the case is still ongoing – and any criminal conviction would obviously put paid to all her plans.

I continue to think about Alys more than is healthy in our relationship between solicitor and client. I still can't forget that look on her face the day I visited her in custody. What did it actually mean? My reading was of someone who has become far too attached to her lawyer – but this thought in itself does not really concern me and I am strangely flattered.

What does bother me is what if this attachment is only about my ability to help her legally? She has no parents or family to support her through this, only me. And what if she is convicted? What then? There could be no possibility of a relationship then. In my line of work, I could not be involved with someone who has a criminal record. I could of course take up a different career but all those years of reading heavy legal tomes could then be wasted.

With all this stuff swirling around unresolved in my head, I hold myself back from admitting even to myself what my real feelings are, never mind sharing them. Strangely, this saddens me but then I decide I will just let things work themselves out. I decide it is out of my control; what will be will be.

I wonder then if my own upbringing is influencing my thinking and behaviour. I was an only child and my parents were in their early forties when I was born. They were intensely devoted to each other, leaving me to often feel isolated within the family, but I was devastated when they died within months of each other when I was twenty. At least I had started my legal training by then and was fortunate enough to inherit their house. I never knew my grandparents, so to all intents and purposes, am alone in the world, as is Alys. Maybe we are lost, isolated souls which have recognised each other.

Continuing my research, I take a look through the local archives for the early nineteen-hundreds. Quite by chance, I stumble across a local newspaper article, which tells the story of a Thomas Jones from Eglwysbach, setting off from Liverpool on an outward voyage to Canada in 1902, on board the 'Nubian.' His brothers and family were there to see him off. The story also mentioned that a month or so earlier, he had travelled back from Patagonia, to where he had previously emigrated in 1880.

Looking at the family tree, I see that 'Canada' is written in brackets after the name of Thomas' wife, Cassie, so Thomas clearly had a connection to Canada – and I already know about his connection to Patagonia. It seems very likely that this newspaper article is indeed about him.

* * *

Thomas' Story – Part 2

As Thomas rode into the sleepy village of Eglwysbach in 1902 on his hired horse, he saw it had changed very little since he'd been away. Everything seemed just as it was. A few more houses here and there but nothing fundamental. Thomas, now forty-six, was still in his prime. He seemed to be one of those men whose looks improved, the older he became; he still cut a handsome figure, despite the hardships he had endured. His dark hair was now sprinkled with grey at the edges but he had kept his lean physique, earned through hard physical work.

His brother, Hugh, with his wife, Lettie, were at Llan Farm to welcome him. Lettie was new to him and she seemed an unlikely choice of wife for Hugh.

It felt strange that his father, Efan, was no longer there at the farm and he regretted that he was away when he had died. There was now a new regime on the farm. On the following Sunday, they all attended the morning service, then took fresh flowers to their parents' grave, next to that of their two little sons.

'In his later years, father told me about the circumstances surrounding his birth,' Hugh told Thomas later that evening, after Lettie had gone to bed. 'He was brought up by a woodland couple who made shingles for roofs and sold logs for firewood. He knew he wasn't theirs and had never felt he belonged there. He believed he was a *plentyn siawns* and believed they were paid to rear him on someone else's behalf. But they would clam up whenever he asked them about his parentage.'

'Later in his life,' Hugh continued, 'he believed he was probably the result of a scandal which involved local gentry and thinks this was the reason he eventually inherited Llan Farm. He told me he also had an inheritance from an eccentric old man he called The Professor, who he had known when he was young, which allowed him to expand and invest in new stock.'

'That's quite a story. But thinking about it now, we never knew of any of our paternal grandparents, did we, only those on mam's side?'

Sara and their brother Robert planned to come over to see Thomas in a few days, when they were less busy on the farm. He already knew Sara, Megan's sister, and felt a twinge of guilt about not having told her the full story about what had happened on their sea voyage all those years ago. But of course, it was much too late to tell her now. It would only disturb her peace of mind to know.

They'd all got older of course but there was no awkwardness in their coming together. He liked Lettie well enough but began to think she was a little odd and that she held a part of herself back from them all.

Thomas realised that it was only he who had changed from the adventurous lad he once was; now less optimistic and enthusiastic – and a deal more cynical about life and people in general.

Over a delicious roast lamb dinner, using the best dinner set, Thomas told them about his life in Patagonia and how the farm kept getting flooded until he reached the point when he'd had enough.

'My plan now is to sail to Canada, where I have been promised land by the government to farm in the Northwest Territories. But first I wanted to come home to see you all, as it may be the last chance I ever have.'

'I was half hoping you'd stay and help me run the farm,' Hugh responded despondently. 'We could expand if you were with me; buy some more land.'

Thomas looked at him apologetically.

'I have some gifts for you,' Thomas announced after dinner. 'That is, what little I managed to salvage out of the whole disaster, when my farm was flooded for the third time.'

He pulled out the brown and black wide-check llama wool poncho, which he had originally purchased when he first arrived in Patagonia. It had kept him warm when riding in the bone-numbing coldness on the back of a steppe pony, as well as on the roof during the fateful night of the last great flood.

Next, he held up a hollowed-out and heat-scored wooden seed pod, the size of a large apple with a small round hole cut in the top.

'This was used for drinking the national drink called maté. It's a fiery liquid which warms up your insides in the fiercely cold mornings on the pampas.'

'Father would have been very disapproving,' said Robert, correctly assuming that this maté was alcoholic, which went right against their teetotaller principles. Thomas nodded in apologetic agreement.

Finally, Thomas showed them a longish photo, mounted onto a stiff white card.

'This is a row of Welshmen sitting on their steppe ponies. See, the men all have large droopy moustaches, waistcoats adorned with watch chains and are wearing trilby hats! I'd joined them for a three-day muster of the sheep which roam far and wide out there on the plains. They must look a little odd to you but that's how they dress there. And that's me – the fifth one along from the left. I only shaved off the moustache on the voyage back here.'

It felt good to be surrounded by his family again; for too long, Josh had been his de facto family. He wondered how Josh was getting on out there and if he was making a go of it on the farm again.

Soon he had caught up with their news, as well as the local gossip and was introduced to his twin niece and nephew, now ten years old. He realised that he had been lonely for years, isolated as he was, apart from Josh of course. He told them the story of how Josh had sneaked onto the boat and ended up working with him.

He became sorely tempted to stay in the bosom of his family, especially when Hugh suggested he wanted him to farm with him. But then there was a small part of him which felt that he did not quite belong there either. Maybe this is what going away from your home did to a person – alienated you from your roots. Unsettled you.

After he had been back about a week, Thomas and Hugh were sitting in the cosy kitchen one evening after Lettie had gone to bed.

'I want to tell you everything about what happened on the boat journey out to Patagonia,' Thomas said to Hugh confidentially. 'You know I wrote to tell you that Megan had died – but I didn't tell you the full story. Forgive me, I found it too difficult at the time.' In truth, he was also finding it difficult now, talking about it for the first time.

'I had no idea at the time of sailing that Megan was already with child before we even left Eglwysbach,' he continued '– and it was definitely not mine,' emphasising this by looking directly at Hugh as he spoke. He heard Hugh's sharp intake of breath before continuing.

'She suffered from terrible sea sickness before we even got out to the open sea, so was in her bunk most of the time, due to the inclement weather. She was sleeping with the other women on a separate deck from me, so I was unable to go there to check on her. She couldn't eat, so she gradually became weaker and more dehydrated, until the ship's surgeon was called to see her. The next thing I was told was that she had died – and that the surgeon had been unable to save the baby. I can't explain to you what an awful shock that was, given I had no idea she was with child.'

There was a long pause while Hugh digested this information.

'Do you think we should tell Sara and her parents about it?' Thomas asked quietly.

Hugh paused again.

'I wouldn't tell them,' Hugh eventually replied. 'Sara would be very angry with you for not telling us sooner and it's probably best not to sully her parents' memory of Megan.'

'Just one more thing, Hugh. Do you know of anyone called Bleddyn around these parts?'

'Only him up at the Hall I think, why?'

'Apparently, she called out this name over and over again when she was delirious.'

'Could it really be him?' asked Hugh, shocked.

'I intend to find out,' said Thomas determinedly.

They continued to discuss it, eventually agreeing it was best to keep the information to themselves. If the topic came up, Thomas would tell them that she died from Typhus, which technically wasn't a lie. Thomas and Hugh then both vowed to each other to take the information to their graves – except for one other person.

'There is just one other individual who needs to know about it,' said Thomas, '– this Bleddyn. If it is him, he will be told in no uncertain terms.'

Thomas paused before completely changing the subject.

'Who will take over the farm if you have no children?'

'Why don't you stay and help us run the farm; we'd work well together?' Hugh repeated plaintively, while shrugging his shoulders.

'I don't think that would work. You and Lettie now run it. If I stayed, it would be like it was before I left, when I worked for our father, only I would be working for you instead as a farm hand.'

No amount of Hugh's persuasive arguments could make him change his mind. By this time, Thomas had come to the conclusion that there was not enough, if anything there to keep him from leaving. Once you have had you own farm, he thought, you do not want to be beholding to another, telling you how to do things. Maybe he was more like his father in that way than he had realised.

'I don't think I could ever settle down back here, Hugh,' Thomas reflected. 'There's still too much 'them and us' here for my liking and too many people wanting to know your business. I've got itchy feet and am heading for the wide-open spaces of Canada to finally make my fortune. But first I have a score to settle.'

In his second week home, Thomas made his way towards Bodnant Hall, where he hoped to see Bleddyn, regarding the unfinished business.

As Thomas strode up the drive of the Hall, he luckily came upon

Bleddyn, who was walking across the grounds with one of his hounds. He was now a middle-aged, florid-faced, stocky man, without any redeeming features.

Although the views from the grounds to the surrounding countryside were stunning and the grounds beautifully kept, Thomas was not there to enjoy the view but to do justice to Megan's memory. He felt compelled to tell this creature, who he believed had caused her death, exactly what he thought of him.

'Can I help you?'

'You don't remember me, do you? I'm Thomas from Llan Farm.'

'Oh yes, I remember now,' said Bleddyn, with dawning recognition. 'I'd heard you were back from Patagonia.'

'You were an old friend of Megan's, weren't you?'

Bleddyn's demeanour changed and he instantly became more guarded.

'I believe she went with you……' His voiced petered out and he began to fidget when he realised who the topic of conversation was to be about. He ran his forefinger along the inside of his starched white collar and his Adam's apple bobbed up and down, as he swallowed nervously.

'Did you know she was expecting your baby when she left? Were you stringing her along? Did you refuse to do the honourable thing by her, once you knew?'

Bleddyn's previous healthy pallor drained, turning an alabaster grey colour and he refused to meet Thomas' fierce, accusatory glare.

'Had your fun, did you?' asked Thomas, who was a good foot taller, pushing him in the shoulder.

Thomas felt the years of 'slow to build anger' – the most dangerous type – rising to the surface.

'Did you know she died on the outward journey, birthing your child, which also died? So in truth, you are responsible for the deaths of two human souls.'

At this shocking information and with an acute awareness of the explosive, emotional sparks flying off Thomas, Bleddyn felt his legs becoming jelly-like under him. He staggered onto a nearby garden bench and dropped his head between his legs. Utterly traumatised by what Thomas had just told him, he turned an even ghastlier grey colour, then suddenly began to retch.

Seeing Bleddyn's response, which he interpreted as guilt, Thomas became even more worked up, feeling once again all those overwhelming angry emotions he had felt at the time of Megan's death on board the ship; the feeling of having been deceived by her, the poignant responses of the passengers and crew at her burial service, the pathos of the moment she was jettisoned to her watery grave. This all came flooding back to him.

Suddenly, he wanted nothing more than to grab Bleddyn by the collar and punch him hard on the nose. But he stepped back and reasoned with himself. This was not his way – and furthermore, it would not solve anything. He doubted it would even make him feel better.

As a young man, Bleddyn had been attracted to Megan, but their liaison was just a fling – no more than that. However, he was appalled that his careless actions had caused her death, as well as that of his child. This thought caused him to start retching violently once more.

There was not a scintilla of pity in the look Thomas gave him, only utter revulsion at his lack of moral integrity.

'Please don't tell my parents or my wife,' Bleddyn begged. 'You see, we have no children of our own. They would never forgive me – and the scandal would ruin us all.'

Thomas glared at him with sheer loathing. Bleddyn had now reached a new low in his estimation.

Sullenly, shamed into being straight with Thomas, he confessed.

'We used to meet in secret – and I liked her well enough – but I had told her right from the start that I could never marry her. But she was very headstrong; maybe she thought she could change my mind. My parents would never have agreed to such a marriage and would have disowned me if I'd even suggested it. Things became quite fraught between us because of this – and it was no longer fun. I was quite relieved to hear she had run off with you – it was quite the scandal around here for a while, you know. But I'm very sorry that her life had such a sad ending, please believe me.'

'Yes, a scandal of your making. You caused it all. I can see that her leaving with me sorted out an inconvenient little problem for you. But ironically, through your callousness, you probably killed the only son you might ever have.'

'A boy, you say……' Tears welled up in Bleddyn's eyes. It felt as if karma had decided to teach him a lesson, given his own marriage was childless. Even more so, it appalled him to think that he had caused the death of his only likely son and heir.

Thomas' look was filled to the brim with the contempt that he felt for this excuse of a man. He spat at the ground beside him, then walked away from him in disgust. All he cared about was the scandal it would cause if his family and neighbours found out.

'Will you tell anyone?' Bleddyn called out at Thomas' receding back, as he strode away purposefully down the drive, his mission satisfactorily accomplished.

Thomas ignored him, deciding to let him stew instead. It would do his soul good to be humbled and for him to fret about whether he would be exposed for what he really was.

When Thomas got back to the village, he was much too wound up to go into the farmhouse. He needed to calm down first, so he walked up to the small copse at the top of the field, which he thought of as his calming place. He sat there looking down at the little hamlet of Eglwysbach, as he had done many times in his younger days when his brothers had annoyed him. Feeling the breeze pick up and blow gently across his face, it gently latched onto his angry thoughts and sad memories. As if by magic, it took them all away, so that his mind felt calm once more.

He loved this place in which he had grown up and would always keep a part of it in his heart – but he knew that it had nowhere in it for him to be what he needed to be. He recognised that there was a drive in him, not unlike that of his father, Efan, which made him want to spread out, to have the space to be himself, to do things his way.

There was just one more person Thomas needed to visit before he left Wales for the second and last time – the sister who had practically raised him after his mother had died. Making his way on foot over the mountains by following the paths that had been used for centuries, he finally came down into the tiny hamlet of Capelulo. It was a good walk which took a few hours but it allowed him to see more of the area again.

He hoped she would be at home, or he would have had a wasted journey. He need not have worried as he got a huge welcome from his big sister, Mary Ellen, who happily embraced him, then proceeded to ply him with the best cakes she could provide.

'*Sut wyt ti, Thomas bach?*'

She stepped back and studied him closely.

'Time has not been kind to either of us, I fear, but I am very glad to see you again,' she said.

She was now fifty-two and despite various potential suitors, she had never remarried, remaining resolutely a widow. She was content with her little household and business, which she ran together with Jane and Sammy.

'It's not just time though, is it?' Thomas said. 'Life itself has not been kind to either of us. To lose your spouse and a small son as suddenly and tragically as you did, would have broken me, but you were always made of tougher stuff. I'm glad to see that you are happy here – you have a beautiful home and a thriving business.'

'You wouldn't have said I was tough at the time. I went to pieces until Sammy told me to pull myself together. Don't know what I would have done without her all these years.'

Jane came into the room. She was now twenty-eight years old and did not remember meeting Thomas before, as she was only six when he left for Patagonia. She struck Thomas as a timid, less compelling personality than her feisty mother. Neither did she have much to contribute to their conversation apart from polite replies. Quiet as a dormouse, she slipped out of the room as soon as it became politely possible, claiming to have some scones to pull out of the oven.

He wondered what had made Jane so introverted, almost afraid to live her life. Maybe the trauma of the loss of her father and brother at such a tender age had affected her more than people had realised at the time. Or perhaps Mary Ellen had been over-protective of her after Matthew died, making Jane too afraid to make her own way in the world.

When it was time for him to leave and walk back to Eglwysbach, Thomas bid a fond farewell to Mary Ellen, realising that it would probably be the last time they would ever be together, but happy in the knowledge that having finally come to terms with her losses, she was content and secure.

* * *

During the last few days, Thomas began to get very restless. He knew for sure that he couldn't ever settle back there. He began to finalise his plans to sail to Canada. He had done what he had set out to do, which was see his family and to tell Bleddyn about Megan. He hoped that the knowledge would eat away at the stuck-up, selfish prig for the rest of his life and that he would feel the need to start praying to the good Lord to forgive him when his judgement day finally came along. Why should he have peace of mind when he had caused so much harm to others?

Thomas' second home leaving was far less surreptitious and far more poignant, knowing that they may never, ever see each other again. His brothers and their families made a day out of it by accompanying him to the Port of Liverpool to see him off on the Nubian. He could not be doing with long goodbyes, so he strode purposefully up the gangplank with his trunk – away from them and towards his second new life.

'Make sure you write to let us know where you are, so we don't have to worry about you this time,' they called after him.

He turned around.

'No need to worry about me but I promise to write……'

Later, Thomas did write to them to say he had married a teacher called Cassie Wilde – but there was never any news of any offspring.

Hugh duly added her name to the family tree in the Bible.

Chapter 6

Police are still following various leads in their investigation. Apart from the other accused girls having said that Alys was there, there is not much tangible evidence, except her cousin saying she was not at home that evening. I am beginning to get a good feeling that the case against her may eventually be dismissed, due to lack of evidence. I am convinced now that she is being completely truthful. If the case was to proceed against her and she was actually convicted, I believe that it would be a grave miscarriage of justice.

On re-interviewing the other offenders involved, the police find that they are now contradicting their earlier statements, which throws considerable doubt on their original versions of events. The police also inform me that one of the group of girls confirmed that she had heard Alys say she was leaving the group to go home to study prior to the offence being committed. Although there is still no proof she actually left, it could be a reason that charges against her may eventually be dropped.

To get to the bottom of it all, I need to focus on why Alys' cousin appears to be lying. What is the motivation? How does she benefit from Alys being framed for this offence?

Next time I speak to Alys, I ask if she can think of any reason for this.

'It just feels like they want me out of the way. My mother died giving birth to me in 1967, so my Nain brought me up. We were very close – maybe my aunt resented me for that and told my cousin Lena to lie to get me into trouble.'

If that's the case, Lena has lied to the police. I'm obviously thinking clinically as a lawyer here – but on a personal level, I think they are both despicable if they have pulled a stunt like that on their orphaned, vulnerable relative.

'I don't know though,' I ponder, 'it has to be more than that. You said your Nain told you she intended to leave the house to you. Maybe that was the motive. Did your Nain ever say that to your aunt? Did your Nain ever show you a Will written by her, leaving it to you?'

'No, she was a very private person with things like that. She wouldn't have discussed it with anybody except her solicitor – but she wouldn't just say it and not do it.'

'What about your father?'

I see a sudden cloud cross her lovely face and watch as she swallows hard to hold back the emotions. I have obviously touched a raw nerve. This is a side of Alys I have not seen previously and am instantly appalled by my lack of sensitivity.

'I'm sorry Alys, I didn't mean to upset you,' I say as I put my arm around her shoulder.

'I'm not ready to talk about that just yet.'

I interpret this to mean, 'I don't quite trust you enough yet with my most personal feelings.'

Who could blame her, given how I just threw that curved ball at her.

* * *

Next time I am in the Glan-y-Coed area, I decide to drive through the Park to try to find the house that had belonged to Alys' Nain. I find the gated entry to Ty Glan-y-Coed and look up the drive at it from the road. It is a sizeable house. It looks to have about five bedrooms and is traditional with a largish garden. The place seems dark and deserted. It is early evening, so I would have expected there to be some lights on if the new owners had moved in. The agent's 'For Sale' board is still there with a large 'Sold' banner across it.

I imagine enough time has probably now passed for all the legal sale formalities to have been completed.

I make my way to town to visit the estate agent's office, which I realise will shortly be closing for the day. I want to try to find out how much the new owner paid for it but am aware that agents are generally reluctant to disclose such information.

The estate agent's assistant is sitting at the reception desk.

'I'm looking for a property to buy in Glan-y-Coed Park. Do you have any on your books?'

'Sorry. Nothing at the moment – but we have just sold one there recently.'

'Do you know roughly how much they go for there?'

'I think that one actually went for about £95,000 – very reasonable for the area.'

Damn cheap, I thought.

I am becoming convinced that the Will is the key to the whole matter. If Alys' aunt was an executor of the Will, did she know about the bequests? Maybe she had not had sight of it either. Alys was still a minor at the time and had been reassured she could stay in the house. Did her aunt suspect the Will left only lesser bequests to her – and the house and contents to Alys? Perhaps she felt she should inherit the whole lot. If she did suspect Alys was to have the house, she may have been jealous.

When writing her Will, Alys' Nain may have reasoned that her daughter was already financially secure with her own house and settled marriage, so didn't need her house as well, whereas Alys had nothing. And it seemed her Nain wanted Alys to keep it and all its contents in the family and knew that she would do this.

When I return to my research, I look again at the newspaper article about Thomas Jones travelling to Canada on the 'Nubian' and I discover that the passenger list is printed in the same newspaper. Looking at the list, I see that a Cassie Wilde was also on this voyage.

This intrigues me and I wonder if this might be the same Cassie Wilde shown on the family tree as Thomas' wife.

* * *

Cassie's Story

When she heard the echoing sound of hob-nailed boots staggering down the Liverpool street towards their house, she felt the familiar stomach-churning sense of dread, then tension building up in her body.

'What temper will he be in tonight? Who will he take it out on this time?' Cassie whispered to her sister, Erin.

Thankfully, they were already in bed – hoping 'out of sight' meant 'out of mind.' Then they heard him fall in through the front door, which he cursed as it swung back and slammed him in the shoulder.

'Get me some food, woman,' he shouted at her justifiably

anxious mother, who meekly opened the oven door. Carefully, using a grimy tea towel, she lifted out his dinner, which had been drying out there for hours, then placed it onto the bare deal table.

'What d'you call this muck?' he slurred as he sat down. 'This isn't fit for the pigs in Dawson's yard. Can't a man have a decent meal when he comes in from a hard day's work?'

Her mother knew better than to reply that she hadn't known he would be hours late, because he had gone via the pub on the street corner on his way home. With his outstretched arm, he swiped the plate of food across the table, making it smash onto the red-tiled kitchen floor.

'Get me something decent, woman,' he shouted, as she got down on her hands and knees to pick up the shattered pieces of plate.

'Ach, don't bother, I'm off to the chippy.' He rose and kicked her hard in the ribs with his steel-toe-capped boot. 'Useless bloody woman,' he muttered as he went out of the front door, slamming it behind him.

The girls, watching what had been happening from the top of the stairs, rushed down to help their mother as soon as the door slammed – but she cried out in pain when they tried to help her up, holding onto her ribcage.

'Just let me be still for a minute, I can't breathe too deeply. I'll be fine soon,' she said bravely.

Cassie bent down to clear up the mess of food and broken crockery while pretending not to see her mother's silent tears running down her face – thereby allowing her a bit of dignity.

Their father was a docker, more out of work than in. Because he earned the money, he believed that his needs came well before any of his family and that he was entitled to drink most of it. He gave their mother so little money to buy food and pay the rent that she had scrimped and saved for most of their married life. He could be very charming when he chose to be and was not unpopular with his workmates – but he was a very different person at home and was becoming increasingly violent.

'So help me God!' Cassie spat the words out, as she picked up the remaining slithers of crockery, 'if he does that one more time to you or us, I will kill him with my own bare hands. I hate him so much.'

They helped their mother get up the stairs, her breath catching in pain from her ribcage, indicating he had cracked a rib or two, as he had in the past.

They laid her down gently on the bed that the sisters shared.

'Enough now,' said Cassie. 'We must leave here before he finally kills one of us.'

'But where will we go?' wailed her mother. 'I only have my sister left and her house is too small for all of us. Besides, she never approved of me marrying him, so will tell me it's all my own fault.'

'She may well say that but all the same, I think you should still go and stay with her. Despite her sharp tongue, she lives far enough away for you to be safe from him; he won't bother looking for you there. Besides, Ma, Erin and I have been talking recently. We are now fifteen and fourteen, old enough to make our own way in the world. Not much of a life for us washing laundry forever. We have been watching the emigrants on the quays, leaving for exciting new lives in the New World. I think we should both sail to America; there is plenty of work to be had there.'

Her mother burst into tears at the thought of her girls leaving her and being left alone in the world.

'But we have no money for fares,' she cried out.

'I've spoken to Father O'Connell,' disclosed Cassie. 'He says that sometimes, wealthy parishioners need nursery maids to look after their children on the voyages out – and also for when they get there, so I asked him to make enquiries for us. He said he might have some news for us this week.'

'He'd do anything for you – even marry you himself if he wasn't a priest,' Erin giggled.

'That's as maybe but I have my own dreams and ambitions and I'm not going to waste my life married to a violent drinking docker, which is what will happen if I stay here. Do you have any money at all, Mammy, to get yourself to Aunty Fanny's in Neston?'

'I only ever have the rent money. I pay it on Fridays, so if we were to go earlier in the week, I could use that.'

'Right, this is what we'll do then. Firstly, we have to secure positions with an emigrating family. On the day of departure, as soon as he's left to find work in the morning, we'll leave for the quays and you for Aunty Fanny's place. That way, it will be a while before he realises we've gone. Oh! – to see his face when he comes home to a cold, deserted house with nothing on the table for him to eat or throw about!'

'What if he sees us at the docks – or someone who knows us does and tells him?' asked Erin.

'We need to get cloaks with big hoods on tick from the rag and bone man to hide our faces. We'll probably need those on the ship anyway!'

* * *

Cassie had often walked along the docks on her way to work at the Laundry. She had watched the ships, imagining they were bound for exotic destinations. They had engendered in her a sense of adventure in faraway places and the wish that she could be sailing out on one – to be free, and oh – anywhere but here.

A week later, a smiling Father O'Connell greeted her as she left church.

'I have good news for you, Cassie.'

Although their mam was from strong chapel farming stock, she had married a Catholic. This had dictated the faith they were raised in – although Cassie didn't hold much truck with all the pomp, idolatry and incense stuff they wafted about. Her mother's choice of husband was another reason her family had rejected her, which had led to little contact with them during Cassie's childhood.

'Your father's alright with all this, is he?'

'He's fine; says it's time we made our own way in the world,' she lied.

Father O'Connell felt strangely drawn to this woman-child, who was more grown up than most her age. Her abundance of fiery red hair grew in wayward, wispy corkscrews to halfway down her back, a legacy of her Irish forebears. Beautifully innocent-looking, chocolatey-brown eyes disguised a wise and canny character. There were no flies on her – and he wondered what had made her grow up so fast.

'I made enquiries with members of my congregation to ask if

they knew of any families planning to emigrate. I learned that an important businessman has booked a passage with his family to Quebec City in Canada on the Nubian. He is enquiring about the services of a good Catholic nursemaid to oversee the care of his four children on the voyage. There is also the possibility that if the nursemaid turns out to be satisfactory, he may engage her on a permanent basis when they reach their destination. You would have to get yourself on deck on the twelfth. He will write you a letter that you can show the authorities to let you on board. He is willing to accept my recommendation and sees no need to meet you first. You may have just landed on your feet, if I recommend you.'

Excited by the possibility of employment but with an uneasy feeling that securing it might be conditional, she was wary, as Father O'Connell's arm rested itself familiarly across her shoulder.

'That's very good news; please tell him I want the post. I have to dash now to fetch my sister from her catechism class.'

Phew, she thought, she had managed to side-step that one. Despite his so-called commitment to celibacy, she had the distinct feeling that he could conveniently cast that pledge aside momentarily, if need be.

Cassie quickly filled Erin in on what he had said.

'The job will probably only be for one nursemaid, so we will have to persuade him that he can have two for the price of one. There are four children, so I guess he might be glad.'

'It sounds like a very good plan, Cassie, but maybe you should tell them I will be with you as well?'

"We'll have to find a way around that. To be sure, I will speak to Father O'Connell to ask him to persuade the man to agree. He will only be paying one wage but getting two helpers – and we can share a bed, so I don't see the harm in you being there as well.'

* * *

It was difficult for them to act normally when the fateful day finally arrived. Cassie's stomach churned with anxiety as she placed her father's breakfast down on the table in front of him. Grunting, he picked up his cutlery and started eating.

'Where's my blerry tuck box?' he demanded of his wife, half-way through.

She placed it gently on the table in front of him, then turned back to the sink, while rolling her eyes. Cassie sensed she was feeling scared.

'Why're you all so quiet this morning?' He had an uncanny knack of picking up on tension or fear. Usually he liked to create it – but luckily, he let the thought go.

'Just tired, Pa,' Cassie said, rubbing her eyes. 'I couldn't sleep with all that brawling in the street last night.'

The last thing they needed was for him to get suspicious. Presently, he rose, scraping his chair on the quarry tiles as he did, then he picked up his box and went out the front door without a word of thanks or goodbye.

All three breathed a collective sigh of relief, then moved quickly to put their plan into action. They donned their moth-eaten cloaks and picked up their bundles, leaving the house abandoned like the Marie Celeste. Opening the front door, Erin looked gingerly down the street to make sure he'd gone. Then they quickly walked in the opposite direction to make their way to the coach stop. After leaving Ma with tearful hugs and promises to write to her sister's address, Cassie and Erin went to the church to pick up the letter from Father O'Connell – and freedom.

* * *

'That was a close shave!'

Just before walking up the gangplank, they had looked back and seen their father leaving one of the dock cottages in a row nearby.

'Seems he doesn't mind sharing his tuck box with the redhead he was talking to in the doorway. Well, maybe she can tend to him from now on. But she won't want him for long, when he starts getting handy with his fists and puts the boot in.'

Any small shred of guilt they had felt about deserting him was now well and truly extinguished. Strange how they felt absolutely no form of emotional attachment to him. He'd literally knocked out any benevolent feelings they might once have held for him.

With their bundles clutched to their chests and the cloaks causing them to overheat, they stood near the top of the gangplank, waiting apprehensively for their new 'family' to arrive. The letter provided by Father O'Connell had ensured their stress-free passage onto the vessel.

They watched as the other passengers embarked. Mostly families but also some young men heading out for a new life. She did not notice Thomas though, as he passed by them carrying his trunk on his shoulder.

'Ah, good afternoon, you must be our new nursery maid, er . . . maids?'

Clearly, Father O'Connell had not explained that Erin would be accompanying Cassie.

'And who is this young lady?'

'My sister Erin.'

Erin curtsied.

'My sister Erin, Sir,' he stressed. 'You are to address me as Sir and my wife' – who gave a barely perceptible nod in their direction – 'as Madam.'

'Yes, Sir,' Cassie replied. She wondered at the cause of the woman's frostiness towards them but was to find out much later.

'This is Alexander,' he said, pointing to the tallest child. 'Next is St. John, then Jemima and baby Clarice. I did not expect there to be two of you.'

Erin shrank back behind Cassie, trying to make herself invisible.

'Well, you'll have to share your bed, food and cabin – and I will only be paying one wage, on the final day of the voyage. If your work is satisfactory, I may consider continuing to hire your services when we land. There will be no fraternising with the crew or other passengers. Do I make myself clear?'

'Perfectly, Sir.'

'Right. Follow us to the children's cabin. Your berth is next door. Hey, you boy, take us to our cabins. This is our baggage, there is more coming aboard presently. Make sure it is put into stowage,' as he showed a crew member his booking form.

'Aye aye, Sir. Follow me if you please, Sir.'

Once they were ensconced, the boy brought in the ordered trays of sandwiches and milk for the children. Cassie was told to supervise them, then get them cleaned up to take them to their parents' cabin later. What they didn't eat, Cassie wrapped in a clean handkerchief. There did not seem to have been any provision of food made for them, so she assumed they were to eat any leftovers the children did not want.

'Yikes! This is a tiny berth and there's no porthole,' said Erin when they finally got into their cabin at the end of a frantic day. 'One small hard bed, a washstand of sorts and oh!' she giggled – 'a water closet.'

'This is obviously meant for one person,' replied Cassie, 'probably a lady's maid or the likes of us – nursery maids. One of us will have to stay with the children, but at least we can take turns sleeping in here. I must admit I am a bit wary of their father, Major Ponsonby. There's something about him I don't trust.'

'What do you mean like?'

'Not sure. But my instinct tells me that neither of us should ever find ourselves alone with him, just in case. I hope he doesn't renege on paying us. I need to make sure I get our money off him before we get off this ship.'

In the event, the parents tended to spend their time socialising in the ship's Saloon, so they didn't see much of them on the voyage. They usually came to say goodnight to the children when they had been made ready for bed. Cassie wondered why they even bothered to have them, as they seemed to want to have so little to do with raising them.

* * *

After a week or so, they had a good routine going with the children, who were fairly obedient. Alex spent most of his time with his head buried in books, as a way of shutting himself off from what he saw as his annoying siblings. Jemima was in a dreamy world of her own playing with her dolls, whilst Erin looked after baby Clarice. It was only St. John with whom Cassie spent any time. He was missing his tutor, who had been teaching him to speak French, so he decided to practise by teaching Cassie some. She was happy to go along with this and was able to pick it up quickly. She had a good ear, having heard many languages spoken down at the docks while growing up and already knew a few foreign phrases.

'You will find it useful when we land,' St John told her. 'They speak French in Quebec, you know.'

'Well, I'm glad I'll get some benefit from my hard work then,' Cassie teased.

The days passed pleasantly enough. Cassie was thankful that Erin was with her to share the burden and could not imagine having managed on her own. However, there was one dark cloud on the horizon. One afternoon, whilst she was carrying a pile of clean linen to the children's cabin, Major Ponsonby blocked her way along the corridor outside the cabins.

'Excuse me, Sir, I need to get into the children's cabin.'

'Surely a pretty girl like you can stop for a chat with her employer?'

Casting her eyes downwards, she did not reply, having judged it was best to keep her mouth shut in situations like this.

'Very surly this morning, aren't we? A bit of civility wouldn't go amiss.'

'Yes Sir, but the children are waiting to be seen to.'

'Oh, very well, make sure you settle them early this evening. We have been invited to sit at the Captain's Table, so we need to say goodnight to them earlier.'

She gave a quick curtsey and he finally let her pass but not without deliberately making her brush past his body. She smelt alcohol on his breath, which may explain why he acted as he did with her. Her original instincts about him had been correct and she comforted herself with the knowledge that given a fair wind, the journey would soon be ended.

Later that evening, the children settled down quickly. They had been sure to run them ragged around the decks during the day and the fresh air seemed to have done the rest. It was Erin's turn to stay with them, so as soon as their parents had been and gone, Cassie decided to go up on deck, just to have some time to herself to think.

It was a warm evening, with a strong breeze filling the ship's sails until they were taut, pushing her relentlessly onwards. Cassie found a semi-hidden, tarpaulin-covered space near the main mast. The earlier incident with the Major had shaken her somewhat and she now knew that she definitely had to make alternative plans for their employment once they landed. She listened to the creaking of the old deck timbers as the ship rolled along and to the ropes mercilessly whipping against the masts, while she tried to think of an escape plan.

They were sailing up the St. Lawrence River, bound as they were for Quebec City. St. John had told Cassie that Quebec meant 'where the river narrows.' Deep in thought, she suddenly heard movement close by.

'Hello, anybody in there?' came a pleasant male voice with a Welsh lilt. As a hand drew back the tarpaulin, she rose to rush out but found herself face to face with a man in his forties.

'Don't worry, I mean you no harm,' he said, holding up both hands, palms outwards.

'You don't have to go; stay a while, I could do with someone to talk to. My name's Thomas, by the way. I think I remember seeing you standing at the top of the gangplank with another young girl when I was embarking and since then, looking after some children on deck.'

Intuitively, she thought he seemed trustworthy, so she settled back down in the hideaway while he sat down opposite her.

'Yes, that was my sister, Erin.'

'What are you doing on board?'

'My sister and I are looking after some toff's children on the voyage. I just came up for some air. We take it in turns; she's with the children now. I'm a bit worried about her though as she seems to have started a bad cough recently.'

'What are you going to do when you get to Quebec City?'

'The parents expect us to carry on working for them once we get there – but I don't think I want to do that…..'

He sensed that there was a lot more to this decision not to stay with the family – but he didn't press her.

'Well, you certainly don't have to. I'm told there are plenty of jobs to be had not only in the cities and towns but also out in the prairies. They say there's also work in the oil and agricultural industries.'

'But how do I get away from them when we arrive?'

'Well,' Thomas explained, 'for a start, when we disembark, we common folk have to go through Immigration, where you'll be asked for the address of the accommodation where you are going to stay. Then you'll be checked by a medical doctor to see if you are fit and healthy for work. If you fail the medical examination, they ship you back home straightaway. So you won't be disembarking at the same time as them anyway. As they're 'First Class' passengers, they will probably be escorted off the ship first. They won't want to wait for you, so they will probably give you the address where they are staying and the cab fare to follow them on later. There's your chance, just don't follow them.'

'That sounds like a good plan but I don't think I should give them the family's address as my accommodation. I don't want there to be any connection to them.'

'Well, you could give them the address where I'm staying when we land. It's a boarding house at 73 Rue Principale. It's a bit of a walk from the port but manageable. I will only be there a couple of days while I make arrangements to travel on westwards through Canada.'

He was easy to talk to. He told her he was on his way to farm in the Northwest Territories, where he had been promised a tract of land.

'I used to farm in Argentina,' he reminisced, 'but more than two hundred of us sailed out of Patagonia on the Orissa bound for Liverpool. Many of us then embarked on this journey to Canada, where the government are assisting us to establish Welsh settlements. In Saskatchewan, there are plans to give these places Welsh names such as Llewelyn or name them after places from home such as Bangor. But I'm going to Wood River, which is a few miles east of Ponoka in Alberta.'

'Patagonia sounds a long way away.'

'Well, that's a whole other story which I won't be able to tell you as it's time I turned into my bunk.'

'Good luck if I don't see you again,' he added as he rose. 'I'll have a post box in Ponoka if you ever want to get in touch. Send it for the attention of Thomas Efan Jones, as there may be many Tom Joneses!' he laughed.

When she returned to their berth, Erin was sound asleep. She looked so peaceful and beautiful that at that moment, Cassie felt an extraordinarily sudden rush of love for her. Indeed, she had always felt very protective of her younger sister, who unlike her, had not done well at school and was still unable to read and write.

It had been nice talking to Thomas but she didn't expect to see him again. Nevertheless, she quickly scribbled down the details he had given her, just in case.

* * *

After about five weeks, as the penultimate day of the voyage drew near, Cassie was busy thinking about how to get her salary from the Major. She thought it would be best to go to their cabin when his wife was there, so she could avoid any funny business. But in the event, she was summoned to their cabin the evening before landing, to be instructed on what to do next morning.

'We will be docking early in the morning, so I want the children fed and dressed in their best and their trunks packed, ready to go by seven o'clock. This is the address you must follow us to,' he said, wrongly assuming she wanted to carry on working for him.

'Please Sir, could I have my wages tonight?' Cassie asked, with her heart in her mouth. 'You may be very busy tomorrow and might not get a chance to sort it out?'

'We can deal with that later, when we've landed,' he said haughtily, as if the thought of discussing money matters with her was quite distasteful.

Standing her ground, she plucked up more courage.

'Please Sir, I said I would wire some money to my mother as soon as we landed, as she is in desperate need.'

'Oh, very well; this is all very inconvenient and tiresome,' he said irritably, as he pulled a heavy pouch of coins out of the inside pocket of his jacket.

'Here, I'm feeling generous. I'll give you two sovereigns. You and your sister have done a good job keeping the children in order; see to it that it continues.'

His wife deigned to look over as if the sight of money disgusted her – it probably did – while he mistakenly thought that his generosity would ensure their loyalty.

Cassie had no idea if two sovereigns was generous or not but thought it would see them over the next few days or weeks until they found work. She was grateful that at least they had been able to work their passage over. She thanked him and curtsied. As she left the cabin, she tucked the sovereigns deep into her bodice.

Next morning, the children were ready as instructed by seven o'clock. Soon after, the Major and his wife arrived. Erin passed the baby to his wife a little wistfully, as she had grown very fond of her.

'Come along children, follow me,' the Major directed.

'You have your instructions,' he said as he turned to Cassie and Erin. 'See to it.'

With his brisk air of self-importance, he walked out of the cabin, with everyone else in tow.

'Bring down my trunks!' he ordered a crew member.

After the first-class passengers had all disembarked, Cassie and Erin reached the bottom of the gangplank and were directed towards a large wooden building. Its sign read 'Immigration, Medical – Clearing.' They joined the queue, eventually filing into the Women's and Girls' section, which was partitioned off from the Men's. Once there, they joined another long queue. The sun beat down on them as they sweltered in their heavy cloaks but they had no choice but to wait patiently for their turn to be processed.

'You're a very healthy specimen, you can go now,' said the medical doctor to Cassie. She put her cloak back on after she had been examined and was waved on through.

Waiting on the other side of the barrier for Erin to come through, she suddenly, she heard an almighty wail. She turned around to see an official leading Erin away by her upper arm, in the opposite direction.

'They say I have TB,' she shouted back to Cassie. 'They say I can't go with you. I have to go back home.' With her voice reaching an hysterical pitch, she screamed, 'They're sending me back!'

There was absolutely nothing Cassie could do. They barred her from going back through to talk to Erin. She could only shout desperately to her.

'Go to Aunty Fanny's in Neston – where Mam is. The Milliner's near the Cross.'

She hoped Erin had caught what she'd told her. Cassie was glad that she had given her one of the sovereigns, which she could use when she landed back in Liverpool. She worried that Erin was far too young and clearly too unwell to be travelling alone with no one to look after her. She would have to travel in steerage this time. Would she even survive the voyage back, she wondered?

'Move along there, missy.'

Suddenly, she was ushered forward again, further away from her beloved Erin to the next desk, where she had to give all her personal details. This distracted her briefly from Erin's plight.

'Where will you be staying?'

'A boarding house on Rue Principale, number 73,' she replied, straight-faced.

'What is the nature of your employment?'

'I'm to be a nursery maid but can turn my hand to anything…..'

He ran his fingers through his hair and sighed, only vaguely curious as to why she was on her own, but already bored – he'd heard it all before. With the flick of his hand, he gestured her to move along and suddenly she found she had actually exited the large clearing shed and dock area and was now outside in the street in brilliant sunshine.

Only as she stood there did she finally begin to process the enormity of what had just happened. She was now actually on Canadian soil – completely alone in a foreign country. They had been separated. How could she look after her little sister now? How would she manage on her own? Erin was so young and vulnerable. And how was she, Cassie, now supposed to cope on her own? This was not part of the plan at all.

At that moment, all Cassie wanted to do was to lie down on that dusty road and bawl her eyes out. Tough as she was, she had never felt so utterly isolated and abandoned in her entire life. But she decided she could not show any vulnerability by giving in to her dire situation as she might be taken advantage of. No, she would brazen it out. She stood still in the middle of that dusty road and decided there and then that she would not show any weakness and would have to make the best of her situation. It was all down to her now as to what she made of her life.

'Well,' she said to herself, 'you wanted to travel, to see the world, to escape your cruel father – now get on with it.'

Seeing a sign pointing the way to the centre, she left the dock area and began walking in that direction, her head held high. There were people everywhere around her, jostling and shoving. Horses and carriages were transporting people and their trunks, trying to get through the general melee.

As she got further away from the docks, the crowds started to thin out. She came to the beginning of a row of shops on both sides of the main thoroughfare. These were selling anything and everything a person could ever need or want – but she couldn't buy anything, she needed what money she had for food and a safe bed somewhere. Men called out lewd comments to her and women tittered behind their hands at her appearance as she passed them by.

Some of the shops had signs but she could not read them properly, as they were written in French. However, she saw one sign in the window of a boulangerie, which read 'Le Poste Vacant.' She found this easy enough to understand and realised that they were looking for staff. Well, what had she to lose by trying?

Her mouth watered at the display of wonderful cakes, delicate pastries, and assortment of breads and pies in the window. She then realised that she had not eaten yet that day and felt momentarily faint. Peeking inside, she saw that it was a very clean-looking establishment. Maybe they needed a French speaker? Trying to recall the smattering of French that St. John had taught her, she searched for the French words she would need to say. She tidied herself up as best she could, then waited for the last customer to leave the shop.

As the brass bell attached to the door rang out, the man behind the counter looked her up and down as if she had a nerve to even enter his shop.

'Excusez-moi, je pose un question sur le travail dans la fenêtre.' She knew it was fenêtre, as it was like the Welsh word *ffenester*, which she had picked up from her mother.

'You're obviously no French speaker,' he replied disdainfully in English, 'and didn't, or more likely couldn't, read the rest of the sign. It said I was looking for a local.'

This caused her to flush bright red with embarrassment and she was left feeling as if she had been caught out cheating.

'Oh, I'm so sorry to bother you, Sir,' she said, quickly turning to leave. I'll be on my way. Good day to you.'

As she reached the door, he suddenly seemed to have a change of attitude.

'But hang on…. you might just be the answer to our little problem. We also need someone to look after our daughter. We work all the hours God sends here and need to get her from under our feet. You would have to learn to speak French properly, as she and her mother do, but I'm the son of two English immigrants. Maybe she can teach you French and you can teach her English!' he chuckled.

Appearing inordinately pleased with his own suggestion, he continued, 'What work have you done before?'

'I've worked as a nanny but can turn my hand to anything.'

'Do you have any references?'

She decided honesty was the best policy and explained how she had ended up in this situation but did not mention that her predatory employer was waiting for her to turn up at his accommodation to look after his children. She gave him the impression that her services had no longer been needed.

He scratched his chin, deep in thought.

'I will give you a trial,' he decided. 'If you work hard and get along with Dora and her mother, I will keep you on. You might have to help out serving in the shop and we may need you to make some bread and pastries, which I will teach you.'

That would be a useful skill to learn, she thought, although he looked as if he'd eaten too many of them himself!

'That's wonderful, thank you. When shall I start? What is the wage? I will need to go to find a room somewhere first.'

'Calm down dear, no need, there is a small attic room at the back you can use if you want. It will be more convenient anyway if you are living-in. I will pay you what you are worth. Come along through to the back room; I will introduce you to my wife and Dora.'

'Maman, Dora, descendez s'il vous plait.'

As Cassie walked through, she sent up a silent prayer of thanks, though not entirely sure to which God. She now had a roof over her head and food in her belly, at least for a while.

* * *

On Sunday, Cassie had the afternoon off. The first thing she did was to write to her mother at Aunty Fanny's address:

La Boulangerie
7 Rue Principale
Quebec City

Dear Mam

This is the first chance I have had to sit and write to let you know all that has happened. I am in Canada, am well and have work in a bakery and do some childminding and cleaning. For this I get a small wage and a small room. But it is enough for now.

I have bad news about Erin. At immigration clearing, she was found to be suffering from TB, so the last that I knew, they were planning to return her to Liverpool. I know nothing more but have been so worried about her. I told her to seek you out in Neston on her return to Liverpool and she had a sovereign, which she had earned on the voyage. Did she arrive there?

I decided I did not want to keep working for the family, as the Major made me feel uncomfortable. So on leaving the ship, instead of following them to their house as directed, I sought employment. I am on a trial basis here and I have no idea whether I am paid a fair wage.

I am becoming quite good at speaking French. One of the children on the boat was teaching me and I have to learn very quickly here, so I can communicate with the wife and child, as well as to serve the customers.

This is all my news for now. Please write and tell me if you have heard from Erin. My dread is that our father sees her and takes her home to look after him – but she really needs someone to look after her.

Your obedient daughter,
Cassie

* * *

Things went well for a year or so and her French improved enormously. A couple of times late at night, she thought she heard the stairs creaking and wondered who was lurking outside her room. After the first time, she began sliding the small brass door lock across when she went to bed. Then one night, while still awake, she sensed there was someone standing right outside. She watched in horror as the brass doorknob turned, glad then that it was bolted. Occasionally, she caught the baker looking at her in a way which made her feel uneasy. It felt as though he was mentally undressing her. Maybe it was now time to leave this place, she thought.

The only man she had felt truly safe with was Thomas on the boat. Anyway, she reasoned, Dora would soon be seven and starting school. Cassie wondered if she would still be needed here then.

She never did receive a reply from her mother regarding Erin, so had decided to write to Father O'Connell to see if he could find out anything. She continued to fret, not knowing whether Erin had ever reached home safely and if her health had improved.

La Boulangerie
7 Rue Principale
Quebec City

Dear Father O'Connell

I am wondering if you have had any contact with Erin recently. She failed to pass the health test to get into Canada and was sent back to Liverpool on the returning ship.

I have been worrying a great deal not knowing what has happened to her. I told her to go to our Aunt Fanny's place, the Milliner's in Neston.

Please let me know if you find out anything.

Yours
Cassie

* * *

During one of her Sunday afternoon strolls down a leafy avenue, Cassie came across a small school. She stopped and was engrossed, reading the drawing-pinned posters on the outside notice board.

'Are you a teacher?' said a female voice behind her.

'No, but it seems a really friendly-looking school,' Cassie replied as she turned.

'You speak French well – but I can tell it's not your first language.'

She nodded in agreement. 'English is my first.'

'Have you ever considered teaching?' continued the slightly intimidating, grey-haired, middle-aged woman.

'I have no training – but I dearly love working with children.'

'Then why don't you apply for the position of English teacher here? You can train on the job and learn what you need to teach as you go along. You'd have to work hard though.'

'Is that even possible? I would love to learn to teach properly. Do you think I would be suitable?'

'I need an English teacher. I am the headmistress here and think you would make a very good candidate. You will need to tidy your appearance a little and try to tame that hair of yours. Write me an application with all your details, in English if you prefer and I will give it some consideration. Address it to the 'The Headmistress' and drop it through the letterbox. By the way, I have a small room at the back of the school you can rent if you need to.' With that she walked briskly away.

Somewhat stunned, Cassie just stood there reflecting what a strange thing to happen – and just as she had been thinking she may no longer be needed at the bakery. How strange are the twists and turns of life, she pondered. Are these happenings pre-ordained? Are we given what we need to make us better people or is it all, as some believe, just a series of random coincidences?

After posting her application, Cassie received a letter by return from the headmistress, telling her she had been successful. Maybe she had thought their conversation had served as interview enough.

When she told the family she was leaving to work in a school, they were aghast – and Dora began wailing loudly and uncontrollably.

'But we have come to depend on you; how will we manage?' the baker complained.

'Don't worry, you are now school age,' Cassie said, turning to Dora. 'Maybe you can attend at the school so we can still see each other.'

At this, Dora stomped off up the stairs in a sulk and did not speak to her again. She didn't like the idea of sharing her with lots of other girls.

'Here is my new address,' Cassie said on the morning she left, 'should any letters arrive for me here. If you can get a message to me, I will collect, or if it's not too much trouble, could you redirect?'

Later that day, a letter did arrive for Cassie from Father O'Connell but the family was still so angry with her for leaving, that they threw it on the fire in disgust.

* * *

With the wages she had saved at the bakery, Cassie managed to buy herself a decent grey dress and a shawl suitable for a schoolteacher but thought her old cloak still had some life left in it. Looking in the pitted mirror in her small room, to where she had been shown the evening before, she drew back her unruly hair into a reasonably presentable chignon.

Having partaken of her croissant and coffee breakfast from the tray left outside her door, she descended the stairs. At the bottom, a maid directed her to a door along the corridor. Seeing the sign 'La Directrice' on it, she tapped lightly, entered, then gave a slight curtsy.

'Good morning, Mlle. du Pont.'

'Ah, there you are Mlle. Wilde. Please, come in and sit down. We will first talk about what you will be doing today. Before I introduce you to the children, I want to explain to you our raison d'etre.'

Cassie obediently sat down as indicated on the green studded leather chair next to the knee-hole desk. She looked around the beautiful room, then longingly at the stacked bookshelves on three sides of the room. She felt a soft warmth emanate from the cosy, highly polished, black-stone fireplace, flanked by two inviting button-backed wing chairs.

'As you will soon learn, this is not a normal type of school. It began about two years ago when my wealthy aunt left me an inheritance, which included this house. It was too big for me to rattle around in, so I wondered what use I could possibly put it to; I didn't want to sell it for sentimental reasons. Then the idea occurred to me that I could use it to house and educate orphaned girls, to try to give them a chance in life. So that's what I did. I let the authorities know that I was setting up an orphanage and told them that I would provide an education and board for them. I don't want to educate them to just become a man's wife, but to become useful, rounded members of society.'

'So the children live here as well? I didn't hear any indication of that last night.'

'They were fast asleep before you arrived, so you wouldn't have.

Come, let me take you on a tour of the house,' she said, getting up from her chair.

As she rose, her pince-nez fell off her nose but were saved by the black velvet ribbon pinned to her silk blouse. This sported large, fashionable, leg-of-mutton or gigot sleeves, with a row of tiny pearl buttons on the elongated cuff and a high-necked lace collar. Her full-length, black, shot-silk skirt did nothing to slim down her thick-set body.

'This is the girls' dormitory.'

Six steel-framed beds lined each side of the second-floor room, with wooden lockers fitted in between each one. Sunlight poured in from a large oriel window at one end down the centre of the room onto the bare board floor. There was a plain chair beside each of the beds, which were all immaculately made. On leaving this room, they made their way downstairs into the main classroom.

'Good morning, children! This is your new teacher. Her name is Mlle. Wilde.'

The children rose, scraping their chair legs on the wooden floor.

'Good morning, Mlle. Wilde. Good morning, Mlle. du Pont.'

Their dresses, clean and neatly patched, were covered with white pinafores. To Cassie, the girls appeared slightly undernourished. However, as the weeks went by, she found they had a great hunger for knowledge, aware that education was their only respectable route out of homelessness and poverty.

Cassie had to learn fast; faster than they did, to keep one step ahead of them. She worked hard on her lesson plans the night before, so was always well prepared. The girls seemed to work at different speeds; some picked things up immediately, others took longer but were more thorough in their work. Her job was to bring out their best abilities and to build up the confidence of each individual.

They did not use cruel punishments and rule through a culture of fear like the teachers at Cassie's old school had done. Many of these girls had already been damaged by life experiences long before they arrived at the school. Cassie was well aware that resentments could build up from excessive discipline, making it less likely that the pupils would be open to learning or give of their best. If a pupil misbehaved, she kept them back after class and tried to get to the reason for the behaviour. One such pupil was twelve-year-old Francesca, the oldest in the class.

'What's the matter, Francesca?' she asked but was met with a sullen silence.

The same thing happened three days in a row.

'I'm going to keep asking you until you tell me.'

'I miss my music,' she finally blurted out.

'Explain to me what you mean.'

'My father was teaching me to play the violin before he died; then the violin was sold to pay for the funeral. And then I was sent here. And I don't know where my mother and little sister are.'

While thinking 'I know just how you feel,' Cassie said, 'My, that's a very sad story but what a wonderful gift to have music in your soul. Let's see what can be done about it, shall we? As for your sister, what is her name?'

'Naomi, Miss.'

'When did you last see her? Could she be with a relative?'

That evening on her daily recap in the headmistress's office, Cassie told her about the conversation she'd had with Francesca.

'Well, we must do something about that; leave it with me.'

'Excuse me being bold,' Cassie ventured, 'I have been thinking. I believe we should teach the girls other skills which could lead them to getting work when they are old enough to leave here. I learned how to cook and bake in my last job. I think one of the days could be spent in teaching them to plan, prepare and serve the midday meal for us all. Maybe cook could have her day off on that day. But before that, we should have a sewing class, where they could learn to make their own aprons to wear while cooking. We would only need a few yards of white cotton, gingham or even linen. They could also learn to embroider their names on them and be responsible for washing, starching and ironing them.'

As she continued, Cassie became even more passionate as she expressed her ideas.

'From there, they could go on to learn how to make simple dresses, even their underwear and how to knit shawls. These are all good practical skills to have, as well as the arithmetic, history, reading and writing they do already. I would also add geography, so they could learn all about the world. I had no idea where I was coming to when I got on that boat in Liverpool to come here. Learning from an atlas or globe would give them a sort of world map in their heads.'

'You've really thought all this through, haven't you?' Mlle. Du Pont observed smilingly. 'For what it's worth, I think we should implement your plans immediately.'

'So, to summarise: I must find a violin, a music teacher, probably a piano, find out where Francesca's sister is and also buy some linen, wool and a globe. That's a tall order!'

'Well, I could make the enquiries about her sister, if you can tell me roughly the area they were from.'

* * *

During the next year, they implemented the new practical skills plan, alongside the academic subjects. Francesca was happy now that her sister had joined them but sad to also learn that her mother had died. Cassie saw the potential in her and began to give her more and more responsibility as class monitor. Then gradually, she started to train her as a student teacher, who would be able to deputise for her. The need for this came about sooner than planned, when she received a letter from Thomas, with whom she had been corresponding on an ad hoc basis.

PO Box 137
Wood River
Ponoka
Northwest Territories

Dear Cassie

I hope this letter finds you in good health and excellent spirits. I have plenty to write to you about.

My log cabin is finally finished – and it is very handsome. It sits well in a small glade overlooking the lake. There is an abundance of good pine trees here to fell for timber.

It has been a long hard winter, but once the roof was on and the windows and doors in, I was able to spend the long dark days fitting out the inside with cupboards and a kitchen. I was glad of the woodwork skills I had gained in Patagonia. I have made tables, chairs and a bed – so it all looks very cosy. I also built a chimney at one end out of smooth stone from a nearby river, so I now have a fire which heats the cabin and which I also cook on – as long as I keep the woodpile well stacked!

I have even built an outside privy!

Our community continues to thrive and multiply. We farmers and townspeople have recently formed a local council and plan to build a small wooden village school for the children of the district, with some teacher accommodation.

This brings me to the main reason for writing. We will need a schoolteacher. I believe you would be ideal for the post, having read your letter in which you describe how you have transformed the school you are in.

Please give my proposal some thought and let me know what you decide. Come for a visit and see for yourself how beautiful it is here.

Your friend
Thomas Jones

Cassie was astonished but flattered by this suggestion. She thought the system she had developed was perfect for girls but would be less so for boys. But maybe the boys could be taught woodworking and stonemasonry, alongside reading, writing and arithmetic. She surprised herself that she was even considering the idea, given how comfortable she was in her current situation, which she had worked so hard to achieve.

And what would a move there mean? How would it change her relationship with Thomas? Would there be any other expectations on his part? She remembered how easy she felt with him and knew it wasn't his style to pressurise her in any way. Dashing off to give a lesson on breadmaking, she pushed the letter in her pocket, promising herself that she would think it through properly later.

Cassie decided her first course of action should be to visit the place; find out more about what type of school was required and see the local environment. Last winter in Quebec had been particularly severe. She knew from an earlier letter from Thomas that the winter, although long, had been less harsh where he was.

She asked for leave to visit her friend, assuring the headmistress that Francesca was very capable of filling in for her for a couple of weeks.

'Who is this Thomas person then?' the headmistress asked.

'Just a Welsh immigrant I spoke to one evening on my way over here on the ship. He was given a tract of land by the government to start his own farm. It seems the little town now needs a schoolteacher.'

Mlle. du Pont frowned when Cassie said this, suspecting that she would not be returning.

* * *

Before she knew it, Cassie was sitting in a third-class rail carriage, cross country to the Northwest Territories. Her carpetbag and her cloak were in the stringed overhead storage above her bench seat. Settling down for the long journey, she dipped in and out of the two books Mlle. du Pont had given her for the journey. She also spent hours looking at the beautiful scenery outside, some of which was quite dramatic. She saw mile upon mile of flat prairie land, interspersed with large farms, which had huge granaries. She also saw small, clustered settlements, forestry and logging operations, large sawmills, canneries and fishing industries.

The country was vast. She had read that when British Columbia became a province of Canada in July 1871, part of the agreement for doing so was the building of the Canadian Pacific Railway on which she was now travelling.

She wondered what the small town of Ponoka would be like. The pupils would probably be the children of the local tradesmen, shopkeepers and farmers. These might have to be given some allowance regarding attendance, as their parents would need them at busy times. She assumed these children would already be well versed in domestic skills, so the focus would be more on academic and arts subjects.

Reflecting on her thoughts, it dawned on her that she was more or less planning to take up the post if she liked it when she got there. She thought it would be a new adventure. If she could improve the lives of those children by opening up their minds to show them that there was a whole other world out there, then all the better.

Thomas was at the station in Ponoka to greet her with his horse and trap. She'd forgotten how handsome he really was. Farming life certainly suited him. His skin was tanned from the sun and wind from outdoor work and contrasted with his crisp white collarless shirt. He greeted her warmly and kissed her lightly on the cheek – but she still sensed that guarded aura of self-protective diffidence about him, which she had first sensed on the boat coming over. However, he seemed genuinely pleased to see her and his face lit up with pleasure at the sight of her.

'Welcome to Ponoka. Thank you for coming to visit us Cassie, it's gratifying to see you again. Here, let me take that bag.'

He put it in the cart, then helped Cassie up onto the rig and drove her to the school.

Cassie did not return to Quebec. The next stage of her life adventure had begun.

* * *

Cassie wrote occasionally to her aunt's address in Neston, hungry for any news of her mother and sister. Then, out of the blue, she received a letter from a solicitor, which had been redirected from her old school in Quebec City. It informed her that her aunt and her mother had both passed away but that her sister was still alive. She was sad to read about her mother and aunt but the news about Erin thrilled her. This was until she read the next paragraph, which stated she was chronically ill and was being cared for in a sanatorium on the Wirral. He asked Cassie to send money for her care, as the proceeds of her aunt's estate which had been paying for her care, were now depleted.

She wondered why he was contacting her now after all this time. Why hadn't she been told of her mother's and aunt's deaths before now? Why had her sister not written to her herself? Surely she could have found someone at the Sanitorium to write it for her. If she sent money, would there be any guarantee that it would go to pay for her sister's care? Indeed, this needed very careful thinking about.

The school had been quickly built by volunteers next to the Methodist chapel and Thomas had contributed by building the stone footings. Cassie helped to establish the lesson plans, school timetable and general routine. Desks and chairs were fashioned, blackboards and books bought, a piano and some music donated. She had been taught to play a little by Francesca, enough to accompany the morning assembly singing and with practice, was becoming quite proficient.

*　*　*

A year went by.

'Cass, I've been thinking,' Thomas said one day, swallowing hard. 'Do you think we ought to get married? We have been 'walking out' for a while now. I could do with your help on the farm. You like the house and the farm well enough, don't you? Could you live the life of a farmer's wife?'

Cassie had been expecting him to ask her for quite some time. She still felt that guardedness which shrouded him and thought he must have briefly suspended his need for self-preservation to ask her. She realised it would have taken him a lot of courage to even broach the subject and maybe he asked because she was expecting him to. It wasn't anywhere near what she would consider a love match – but they liked and respected each other well enough. Thomas had worked tirelessly, getting the farm into good shape and making it productive. He told her he could now really do with some help to start building it up.

While considering what marrying him would mean, she thought about the difference in their ages. He was almost thirty years older than her and she knew that in time, if he became infirm, she would be expected to do more of the farm work. This was something she would just have to accept. But how would all this change her life now? She would have to give up her job as a teacher, which she loved, to live and work with him on the farm.

In truth, in secret preparation for such an event, she had begun to train the studious young son of the local pastor, who showed good aptitude to become a teacher – and so she accepted Thomas' proposal of marriage.

Having previously been surrounded by people and children at the school, Cassie now often felt lonely for the company of other people, with Thomas out in the fields all day. She baked bread, learned how to make butter and cheeses, jams and pickles, and to preserve joints of meat. She also tended the domesticated animals. Once a week, she took the pony and trap into the town to sell their produce at the village market, except when they were sometimes snowed in during the winter months. A couple of years then slipped by unnoticed – but there was no sign of any offspring.

Although her life was now good, she still suffered from the guilt of her sister having been sent back home and not her; survivor's guilt maybe. She had no way of knowing whether Erin was even still alive. She had replied to the solicitor, asking him for receipts or proof that the money she had sent was paying for her care. She had received a reply saying that unfortunately, as Erin was illiterate, she had dictated what she wanted to say to the solicitor and her letter was enclosed. So in reality, she was no nearer the truth and had no real proof.

Cassie battled daily with her conscience but justified it to herself that she would be to blame if she didn't send money, resulting in Erin being ejected from the sanitorium. The letters had seemed to be from a reputable firm of solicitors, written on quality paper but there was just no way for her to know for sure. She would like to have had confirmation from Erin herself about her poor health, so she could be certain but that was clearly not possible, as all Erin could write was an X by her name.

She just had to trust the solicitor; she felt she had no choice. She had even written to Father O'Connell again but had never received a reply, so assumed that he had probably moved on to another parish or had passed away. She had no one else she could ask who could investigate the situation for her.

At first, she had sent money from her teacher's salary, then later, used money she made from selling some of the goods at market. But that source dried up over winter when she was unable to get to town sell her produce. As the solicitor continued to demand money, she started to send some of the housekeeping money that Thomas gave her. Later, feeling she was not managing, and still racked with guilt about Erin's health, she decided to take out a loan on the farm itself, without telling Thomas about it.

One day, a reminder from the loan company arrived, advising that a payment was due. Thomas was working out by the gate to the farm track that day. Cassie had managed to circumvent previous letters to prevent Thomas seeing the solicitor's and loan company's correspondence. Unfortunately for her, he inadvertently opened the official-looking letter, assuming it was for him. He was shocked beyond words to discover that Cassie had taken out a loan on the farm and that a payment was being demanded.

He was absolutely furious. He felt that for the second time in his life, he had been deceived by a woman. Incensed, he returned to the cabin to confront her. He did not even allow her to explain. He was so beside himself with rage that he threw her few possessions into her carpet bag and flung it out of the front door, followed by her cloak, then her.

'Get out!' he raged, his voice cold with suppressed anger. 'I never want to set eyes on you again. You know that I have never owed money to anyone in my entire life, ever. Now you have burdened me with this debt.'

Thomas seethed. He had never felt so infuriated and was experiencing that old feeling of having been made a fool of, creeping up on him once more.

'Go!' he said, with his voice cold as ice. 'We are finished. Go! Never, ever darken my door again. You are now dead to me. I have no wife.'

Cassie knew she had been wrong to deceive him and that this was no more than she deserved. She tried in vain to explain why she had done it – but he was far from being able to listen to reason.

She stood forlornly outside the little log cabin and knew that the life she had built with Thomas was irrecoverably finished. She had no choice but to leave. So she donned her now dusty cloak, picked up her bag and started the long walk towards town, convincing herself that she would survive somehow – she had always done so before.

Thomas felt betrayed once more. The emotions he had felt after Megan's betrayal resurfaced as he wallowed in uncharacteristic self-pity.

'I have nothing now to show for all my years of hard work here – no child and a mountain of debt – thanks to her.'

He felt himself slowly sinking into a flat depression. It felt that no matter how hard he worked, others – or the climate – thwarted his efforts. But he had no choice other than to carry on. He knew he alone would now have to work even harder in order to try to meet the monthly loan repayments, or have the farm taken off him.

Cassie meanwhile had arrived in Ponoka. It had taken her hours of walking and she was utterly exhausted when she finally reached there in the mid-afternoon. She had very little money but decided to buy a local news sheet to look at the job vacancies column – but there was nothing.

She needed to find a bed for the night. She thought she might go to the school where she had taught – but then realised that everybody there would then know her business. She decided it was best to get completely away from the area, so went to the train station to get the next train out. As she waited, she bought some food from the station buffet to keep her going and reflected on how she had managed to utterly mess things up.

* * *

Cassie eventually made her way to the nearest city, Edmonton, where she found work as a governess for the children of a wealthy family. Their mother, who had a delicate constitution and was not expected to live for long, wanted to travel to England to see her parents in Cheshire.

The family made plans for the journey and offered Cassie the opportunity to accompany them to look after the children. She thought this would be a good way for her to get back to England and readily agreed. Thankfully, she could travel back in better style than the way she had travelled out to Canada.

The health of the children's mother suddenly deteriorated and sadly she died on the passage back. Then shockingly, within a day or two, her husband unexpectedly asked Cassie to marry him. She didn't tell him she was still legally married to Thomas.

'You know just how to deal with the children,' he said, trying to convince her. 'They like you and she had not been a wife to me for years.'

'Yes, I see that – but they will think I am taking their mother's place and will resent me.'

'Anyway, think about it. We get on well enough, don't we?'

Cassie knew such a marriage would be bigamous but was desperate to finally find out if Erin was still alive and if her money had been going for her keep. She thought that she might even need money to hire a private detective to find Erin and to investigate the solicitor. She reasoned to herself that marriage to Charles would enable her to have the means to do these things.

Nobody knew her, or that she had married Thomas in Canada, so there was no way anyone could find out. So before they landed in England, she agreed to marry him, thinking she could change her mind later when they landed.

But Charles was so smitten with her, he had secretly asked the Captain of the passenger ship to marry them onboard. He arranged it all, before springing the surprise on Cassie.

Although feeling trapped, she knew she had no choice but to go ahead with it. Either that or tell him everything there and then. But if she did that, she knew the wedding and their relationship would be off and she would not have the means to find Erin. So she went ahead with the wedding, feeling she had to carry on the pretence.

When they landed back in Liverpool, the intention was for the family to travel straight to their family home. The familiar sounds and smells of the dockland rose up to meet her as she walked down the gangplank with the other first-class passengers. It felt strange to be back on home soil, to hear familiar voices once more and the shouted Liverpudlian humour of the dock workers. She was also aware that she needed to get out of that area as soon as possible in case she bumped into her father. Pulling up her hood she walked along with Charles and his children towards the railway platform for the journey to Cheshire.

'Do you mind if I just go to visit my family briefly in Liverpool before joining you?' Cassie asked. 'I haven't seen them for years.'

'I'd rather you come with me darling; I don't want to be without you for even a short while.'

'I really want to go and see my mother and father and little sister,' she replied, not having told him the truth about her dysfunctional family. 'It would only be for a few days.'

Reluctantly, he gave into her, giving her some money to tide her over and to enable her to join him later.

Once she had seen Charles and his children safely onto the train, she needed to work out what to do next, so she sat down at a table in the station Waiting Room and ordered herself a cup of tea and an iced bun. Critically, she needed to know if Erin was still alive. She decided that the first thing she would do would be to ditch her old cloak and buy a more respectable one, using some of the money Charles had given her. Then she would take a train to the Wirral.

'Could you please tell me the nearest station to the TB Hospital on the Wirral?' she asked the attendant in the ticket office, wearing her modern new cloak.

'Certainly Miss. You need to take the next train on platform three and get off at Heswall. The Sanitorium is about a mile's walk from the station. Would that be a single or return?'

The journey did not take very long and she soon alighted. Having made enquiries about the directions, she made her way there. In the grounds, she could see convalescing patients sitting outside in the shade of the trees on wicker-work bath chairs.

'Can I help you, Miss?' asked a rather prim and starchy looking nurse, as she entered the foyer of the impressively large building, with its tall white columns and beautiful terrazzo floor.

'I'm looking for my sister, Erin Wilde. I've been led to believe that she is being cared for here.'

'That name is not familiar to me but I shall check the register if you can just wait a moment.'

As Alys waited in the hall, she could see into one of the wards which ran off it and was surprised to see that it had no windows.

'Miss, I'm sorry to have to tell you that we do not have, nor have we ever had anyone of that name staying here.'

Bitterly disappointed, Cassie made her way back to the station for her return journey. Her worst suspicions had finally been confirmed; she had been duped by the so-called solicitor for years.

Once back in Liverpool, she went to the office of a firm of solicitors in the city. She was dismayed to be told that they had never heard of the solicitor who had been writing to her in Canada. Nevertheless, they offered to contact the Law Society to enquire whether there was a solicitor of that name registered to practise. She was devastated when they informed her that there was no such solicitor.

Next, Cassie made her way to the Registry Office in Liverpool.

'I wonder if you could help me,' she asked a member of staff.

'I'm trying to find out if the death has been registered for an Erin Wilde. It's possible that she may have died on the Nubian, returning from Quebec City in Canada to Liverpool in the summer of 1902. It's also possible that she may have died later, following her return.'

'Well, since 1874, registration has been required for all deaths aboard ships registered in Britain or its colonies. Please take a seat and I will check the Death Registers.'

Presently, the staff member returned with the news that Cassie had dreaded.

'I am very sorry to have to tell you that an Erin Wilde did die on board the Nubian on the first of August, 1902. The cause of death was recorded as TB and pneumonia.'

Cassie swooned and almost fainted from the shock. She was beside herself with grief and anger. Her little sister had actually been dead all these years. She had paid all that money she could ill-afford to a scoundrel who she would never be able to trace.

Cassie was heartbroken. She sat down to absorb what she had just been told. At least she now finally knew the truth – but she felt such a fool. She had lost her husband and her life in Canada because of this conman and there was nothing to be done but to get on with her life and start yet again.

Before leaving the Registry Office, she asked them to check if her mother's death had also been registered and was devastated to be informed that it had been.

After she got outside the building, she just stood there. Once again, she experienced the same overwhelming feeling she had felt when she had arrived on that hot day in Quebec City, totally alone in the world. Her mother and her little sister were dead. As far as her father was concerned, whether or not he was still alive, he was already dead to her anyway.

Would she have to make a new life? What would that life look like? Would she return to her bigamous marriage? Is that what she really wanted? Deep down, she already knew that she would not join Charles in Cheshire. She knew she wanted more from life than being a mother to his children.

She then thought, wasn't there something about a marriage having to be consummated to make it legal? Consummation had been impossible aboard the ship as the children shared his cabin and Cassie was already travelling in a communal cabin. She also reasoned that an annulment would have the additional benefit that she would no longer be illegally married.

Cassie made her way to the nearest newsagent and bought a copy of The Lady. Looking at the classified advertisements, she saw positions available for governesses, schoolteachers and nannies. She fully intended to apply for something better paid now as she had far more skills to offer.

She decided that she would start yet another life for herself with a clean slate and would go wherever her life took her. She was ready for her next big adventure, maybe in Europe. After all, she now had the French language.

Cruelly, she wrote to Charles to let him know she would not be joining him. She told him that she had applied for their marriage to be annulled and he would be hearing from her solicitor.

She left no forwarding address.

* * *

A few years earlier, on the rare occasion that Cassie's father went to mass, he had bumped into Father O'Connell.

'Ah, Mr. Wilde. How are you?' he asked. 'How is your lovely daughter getting on in Canada?'

He looked blankly at the Father.

'How is Cassie getting on with her teaching?' Father O'Connell continued. 'She wrote to me about the school where she was working. It was very sad that her little sister had to return on the ship.'

This was all news to their father, who had not seen hide nor hair of them since that day he came home to find them all gone.

'Cassie wrote to you?'

'Yes, I still have the letter if you'd like her address to write to her yourself. I'll bring it with me to Friday Mass if you like.'

'Yes, yes, Father, thank you, you do that, Father. I'll be here Friday to get it from you.'

'Those scheming little bitches,' he thought. 'So that's where they went. Just upped and left, abandoning their old father. As for their mother……'

'So Cassie's in Canada and Erin had to come back here,' he seethed. He wasn't sure what to do about it so resolved to wait to get the letter before deciding.

Next Friday evening, after getting the letter from Father O'Connell, he met up with a conman he knew in the pub.

'I think she owes me big time, disappearing like that,' as the conman read the letter. 'Bitch! How can I screw her for some money?'

'Leave it with me. I'll put some thought into it and maybe draft a letter to her. I want half of any monies we get, mind.'

'It's a deal,' Cassie's father replied, spitting into his hand and shaking the proffered hand of the conman.

* * *

Whilst collecting the mail from his post box, Thomas was surprised to see a letter addressed to Cassie. She had been gone quite a few weeks now. He had no idea where she was and he had no forwarding address, nor did he want one. The less he had to do with her, the better.

But what was he to do with the letter? He would never open someone else's mail in normal circumstances. But as she was not there, he decided to read it:

Fotheringay Solicitors
32 Church Lane
Neston
Wirral

Dear Mrs. Jones

I am concerned that you have not forwarded me any funds for several months, I will be unable to prevent your sister being evicted from the Wirral Sanitorium if these funds are not forthcoming urgently. They have been very patient to date – but have informed me that if they do not receive anything from you by the end of the month, they intend to discharge her.

As you will be aware, she will then be homeless, destitute and without medical care.

I urge you to send the funds by return.

Yours sincerely
Edward Fotheringay

Thomas sat down on the milk churn stand. His legs felt weak, given the shock he had just received reading this letter. As he read it again, it brought back all those feelings of having been deceived by her.

Although still very angry with her, he was now able to better understand her motive but this still did not make what she did right. However, he slowly began to appreciate things from her point of view and felt perhaps that he should have given her the opportunity to explain what was going on.

But then again, he thought, he was her husband. She should have been totally honest with him from the start and should have explained the situation to him. Perhaps they could have worked something out between them…….

* * *

Many months went by. Then just as Thomas was at his wits' end and had almost reached the point when his farm was about to be repossessed by the bank, he received an official-looking letter from Patagonia, which had been redirected from North Wales by his family. It read:

My Dear Friend
I write to your family home in the hope that they will know where you are and will forward this letter to you. You will remember me, first as the orphan boy – and later the man you kindly (although initially reluctantly) took under your wing, as you set off on your journey to lay claim to your plot of land in Gaiman, Patagonia.
Much has happened since you left after the last bad flood. We had a few stable seasons, so I was able to buy the other half of the plot from Juan Hughes. He had settled elsewhere and offered to sell it to me cheaply.
My woman and I had developed the plot by planting a variety of fruit trees. In time these became 'fruitful' and we had a ready market for our produce in Buenos Aires, once the railway to Trelew was completed. Business was good and we prospered. Then sadly, my woman just disappeared one day and no one has

seen or heard of her since.

In time, I started to socialise more with the other Welsh farmers hereabouts who then began to accept me as their equal, no longer shunning me because of my squaw. A wealthy sheep farmer, who owns a nearby farm, has three daughters. Strangely, one of them took a fancy to me during an assado at her farm, which she inherited from her mother. There were many lambs on the spit that day and the maté and home-made wine was flowing freely. Well, she asked me if I would be her husband! You could have knocked me down with a feather. I knew there was a shortage of men here – but still, I was strangely flattered to be propositioned thus.

To cut a long story short, we were married and I moved in with her and we are very happy. Then a Spanish couple approached me to ask if I wanted to sell our farm. Well I thought, you will not be coming back and I have no need for it now, so I agreed.

Hence why I am writing to you. I feel that rightly, the farm is still yours. So, I am sending you the proceeds of the same for your half at current value. I am sure you would say keep it all but I would not have been where I am today but for you taking in this ragged orphan back then.

So there you have my story. I know you were destitute when you left Patagonia and hope you have prospered since but if not, this money may ease things for you. You were a friend to me when I was in need.

Yours very gratefully
Josh

Thomas picked up the bank draft and saw that it would more than cover the debt left by Cassie.

'God moves in mysterious ways,' he thought, falling to his knees and fervently giving thanks to the Lord above for saving his farm from the creditors. He saddled the horse and went straight into town to arrange to receive the funds from the bank draft. He then used it to pay off his creditors, leaving him a balance as a buffer for future difficulties.

Thomas lived on for many years after this. With his debts cleared, he was able to live comfortably and was grateful for what he had – but it was a life of drudgery and depression, with no real motivation. He was lonely but did not seek company as he had been let down too often. He had worked so hard all his life and what did he really have to show for it? He felt no real joy, only anger, regret and embitterment but he took much comfort from reading his Bible.

The Great Depression came in 1929 but Thomas continued to farm for almost another ten years, until his health began to deteriorate. He eventually became frail and unable to care for himself. On finding him in a bad state, his neighbours kindly took him into their home.

Thomas died in 1938. He was not to know of the utter devastation which would be wrought across Europe by the second world war.

His death was reported in the local Ponoka newspaper:

Thomas Jones, who had been a resident of the Wood River district since 1902 and who was well and favourably known, died on Thursday May 12th at the age of 81years, 11 months and 20 days.

The late Mr. Jones was born in Eglwysbach, North Wales on May 23rd,1856. As a young man he went to Patagonia in the Argentine Republic, South America. There he farmed until 1902. He returned to his home in Wales where he visited his family. Being imbued with the spirt of pioneering and desirous of exploring more of the British Empire, he turned his attention to Alberta. He was granted land to farm in the Welsh settlement of Wood River district where he remained until 1938. Feeling the weight of his advanced years, he accepted the kind invitation of neighbours to go and live with them to be cared for. Thomas Jones often remarked to others about the comfort and kindness he received at the hands of his benefactors and that he could not wish for a better home. Mr. and Mrs. Williams modestly affirmed that their old friend merited any kindness they could extend him.

Mr. Jones was a very interesting man and friends would often, in conversation with him, ask about South America, a subject he thoroughly enjoyed and about which he often became quite eloquent. He was generally of a retiring nature and while many differed in opinion with him, all agreed that he was a man of courage and sincerity and a devout Christian, who practised his belief in everyday life. The deceased was the last member of his family, having been pre-deceased by his only sister and two brothers.

The funeral was held on Sunday May 15th in the United Church, Ponoka with Rev. T. Jeffreys and Rev George D. Young officiating and was attended by many friends who came to pay their last respects to one who will be long remembered.

Interment took place in the Forest Home Cemetery, Ponoka, Alberta. Cline and Nelson Funeral Directors.

His neighbours initially wrote to inform his family in Wales of his death and later how settling of the estate was progressing. Jane read:

Route 1 Tees
Alberta
Canada

Dear Miss Rowlands,
We hope this letter finds you in the best of health, as we are at present. Thank you for your letter asking when you will get the money from your uncle's estate. Well, we handed your letter to the other trustee, he should have given you a statement – you folks should have had the money months ago. We went to see the lawyer after Christmas after we got your first letter. He said that he had sent a little money to you. The trustees also got a little money. They were the ones that sold the 160 acre farm - they had to look for someone with cash and the eventual buyer was the highest bidder. The sale money was put into the late Mr. Jones' account. He said he had thousands of pounds a few years ago but that his wife had spent it somehow or other and after she went, he found out there was very little money left in the account. You would not have got anything if he had not made a will.

I had been going to write to you sooner – but we have been harvesting and threshing and then we had a cold spell, frost and snow, but it has since warmed up again. How are you getting along with this terrible war? We get news several times a day from England. I think you are very brave over there. I do hope it will come to an end soon. We see aeroplanes in the sky training and everybody's busy now with the young people going away. I hope you will be safe from these air raids. Old Hitler will never land in Great Britain. You will get more help from Uncle Sam.

My husband had gone over one day, about a year ago. Mr. Jones was sick, his heart was bad, he had only a crust of dry bread in the house. The hired man left him, he didn't like it because Mr Jones didn't make his will for him. He came to live with us for a while then told us to sell the farm. He wished he had come sooner. With us he had his breakfast every morning, then got up when he liked. He seemed happy just to read his religious books. He was a good Christian man. I am going to send you a picture of your uncle soon. The doctor registered the cause of death as 'Heart Failure.'

    Mr. Jones had made his will before he got sick, everything was done as he said. We had gone there to talk to him about it, he was willing to make one and seemed happy. He wanted to leave everything between his siblings, or if they were deceased, to their descendants.

    He was too old to write it, so we helped him. He did try but he broke down crying, as he was too weak, his heart was very bad even then and he was very sick for a few weeks before he died. I will try to get a picture of the grave when I get a chance. We had this verse put on his headstone –

    'Fe ddaeth yr Athraw, ac y mae yn galw am danat.'

    He had a very nice funeral. We could have got a cheaper coffin but we wanted it to be nice for him. The Welsh came and sang Welsh hymns.

    I hope the matter of the estate is finally dealt with quickly.

I am truly yours
Mrs. Williams

Chapter 7

After a few more few weeks, I am notified by the police that the case against Alys has finally been dropped, due to lack of any real evidence and I feel a huge sense of relief. They have evidence that placed three of the other accused at the actual scene of the crime but nothing for Alys. They finally conceded that it was possible for Alys to have been at home but not seen by Lena.

'Alys, we have good news. They have dropped the case against you. You're in the clear.'

'Finally – at long last,' she says, grinning from ear to ear as she does a little jig. She is ecstatic. I realise it is a great relief for her but am hugely surprised when she throws her arms around me and hugs me. I know she has grown fond of me but am cautious, as I may be reading it completely wrongly; perhaps it is only a show of gratitude, as I imagined earlier. Or maybe she feels I am the only one who is on her side. She really has absolutely no one else.

I must be giving out a weird 'don't touch me' vibe, as she drops her arms instantly. She looks downcast, then embarrassed and doesn't look me in the eye. She probably thinks she's overreached and may have breached some sort of invisible boundary. But that is her personality; she is spontaneous, without guile. I wish I could be a bit more like her – but it is not in my nature. If it ever was, it has been trained out of me.

Who am I kidding? Certainly not myself. But am I mistaken? If she is in love with me, is it a love born out of gratitude and dependency, as I fear? Is it only because I have been representing her. In other words, is it <u>what</u> I have done or can do for her, rather than <u>who</u> and how I am as a person?

'Listen Alys,' I say, taking a more formal line. 'I sense you may have feelings for me but as your legal representative, I am not really allowed to become emotionally involved with any of my clients.'

She brightens up, instantly sensing a solution.

'That's alright then,' she says in that honest, direct way she has, that I love. 'If they've dropped the case, you are no longer my representative. I am not your client. Case closed, as they say. We are now officially friends.'

What can I say to that? I don't know how to react. I shake my head slowly, smile, then walk away still shaking my head as I have no idea how to deal with this straightforward, spontaneous affection.

One of the things drummed into us during our legal training was not to become emotionally attached to your client. The conflicting thoughts that I have, continue to be affected by this mantra. But then I recall the reaction in her face that day I visited her in prison. The light that shone out of those eyes will stay with me forever. And then, today, the spontaneous hug – well, it had felt good to be that close to her – but now I regret my insensitive reaction. And, as she says – she is no longer my client.

Later that evening, I continue to mull over what happened earlier and feel like an idiot now for responding the way I did to Alys' open, instinctive, loving emotion. To distract myself from all the conflicting feelings of guilt I am thinking, I bring out the photos and the old Bible again. My comfort blanket.

* * *

I have been able to gather quite a bit of information recently and am fortunate enough to have arranged a meeting with the Vicar to view the Eglwysbach church records at the weekend. To me, he looks like a typical country vicar, slightly stooped, with wiry grey hair. He is obviously well-educated, endlessly interesting and soon becomes fully engaged in my quest to trace the family tree. There are some fascinating documents there from the seventeen-hundreds. I could spend hours just sitting there reading them but make myself stay focused on the information I need to obtain.

In the church entries for 1882, we find a marriage entry for Hugh Jones of Llan Farm to a Lettie Humphreys. This must be Efan's eldest son, Hugh, so I decide to continue my research by investigating him.

By the time I have finished in the church, it has started to rain heavily so I am unable to look around at the graves as planned and have to head for home instead. However, I feel as if my research is progressing well. Thanking the Vicar profusely, I take my leave of him and dash to my car.

Later, I visit the county archives and search the local newspapers at around the date of his death, which is shown as 1905 on the family tree. Fortuitously, I come across a faded article about the death of local farmer, Hugh Jones of Llan Farm. The date of the article matches the date of Hugh's death.

* * *

Hugh's Story

'Well, I'm glad that's over with,' said Lettie to her husband, Hugh, on their return home from Efan's funeral. She peeled off her black leather gloves, pulled out her pearl-tipped hatpin and removed her hat. She then unbuttoned her long, double-breasted, black coat with its velvet collar, to reveal a very slender, verging on skeletal figure – unlike many of her farmer's wife contemporaries.

'That Vicar is so dry,' she complained, 'but I suppose the singing made up for him.'

That seemed to be all she had to say, as she was silent for the rest of the evening.

As she set about laying the table for a late supper of bread, cheese and pickle for herself and Hugh, she frequently sighed her usual deep, dissatisfied sigh.

Hugh and Lettie had been married for many years now, still without the babies she desperately longed for. Hugh knew that seeing Robert and Sara's twins today would have made Lettie feel insanely jealous – and this evening, the unspoken words of accusation hung heavily in the air between them. It was just the two of them living at Llan Farm now, apart from Mari, the dairy maid and Bob, the *gwas ffarm,* who occupied one of the outhouses.

Hugh had met Lettie in church and they had married in 1882, after which she moved to the farm. Today, it was still run pretty much as it had been in Hugh's father's day, but now they also provisioned the local butchers, as well as the Kyffin Grocery store, with meat and dairy produce.

Hugh, the eldest of the brothers, was the one who looked most like his father, Efan. He had his physical strength – but not his strength of character. He was tall and solidly-built, with broad shoulders and slim hips. His mop of unruly blond curly hair, which he inherited from his mother, was hidden mostly under a flat cap. Working outside in all weathers resulted in his face being tanned and the hairs on his forearms a golden blond, enhancing his good looks.

This evening, Hugh was also experiencing feelings of sadness and inadequacy, albeit for different from the usual reasons. He also mourned the fact that they had no children – but these sad thoughts came about through comparing himself to his father. This was especially so today, at his funeral, where local people and dignitaries had been eulogising him.

Efan took a lot of living up to; he was generally considered brilliant in his own particular way and had an outstanding personality. Had he received a formal education, who knew how much more he could have achieved? He may have reached a high position in the church, or even the law. But he seemed content to be a farmer, as long as he could do things his way – and do them to the very best of his ability. He was never quite the same though after the death of his wife, Fanwy; it was as if a piece of him had died with her. But he had held himself together at that time to finish raising his three sons alone, initially with the help of his daughter, Mary Ellen, before she went into service.

But with his father no longer there, even though he was now forty-two, Hugh felt desolate and abandoned. Orphaned. But shaking himself out of his maudlin thinking, he decided pragmatically that life, such as it was, must go on and he must make the best of it.

Hugh reflected that Robert seemed very settled with Sara – but those twins really were hard work and into everything. It had been good to see him today and catch up on his news. The brothers only saw each other occasionally, if they happened to be at the livestock market or at church on Sundays – or of course at a funeral, such as today. Farming was hard, demanding work. There was little or no time for general socialising.

It was not long after Thomas had left home for South America that Robert had courted and eventually married Megan's sister, Sara, who had prepared the lovely spread for the funeral today. Robert had then moved to live at Sara's parents' farm in Tal-y-Cafn, and took over the running of it when her parents could no longer manage.

Hugh knew that seeing Robert's happy family together at the funeral today had definitely unsettled Lettie, rubbing fresh salt into that open wound of hers which never seemed to heal. No doubt this would account for her bad mood tonight.

As Hugh slowly ate his supper in the oppressive silence which hung between them, he ruminated that if this was all his life would now amount to, it wasn't a happy prospect. Just him and Lettie, day after day, night after barren night. She didn't want him near her now. He had noticed a new sharpness in her towards him recently, when there was no one else about. Was her inability to conceive eating away inside her? Did she blame him that they were childless?

He had also noticed more recently that she liked to talk and flirt with other farmers when they called by, especially that rogue from Bryn Uchaf, who endlessly flattered her. She cheered up when they were around but returned to her usual dour, miserable self once they had left.

When he talked to her, he would sometimes notice a faraway look on her face, as if she was only half listening to him – imagining she was somewhere else? – living a different, better life? – maybe with another man? Well, there was nothing to be done; it is what it is, he thought. The good Lord decides and directs our lives – we must live by his forbearance. He sighed, then rose.

'I'll go out and check the animals once more before I turn in for the night,' he said, picking up a lantern.

He stepped out of the front door before walking around to the farm buildings at the side. The frontage of Llan Farm, once a freestanding building, had gradually become part of the High Street. As he came out, onto the street, he looked down and saw the men coming out of the nearest public house at closing time. But his family, being teetotallers, did not frequent the gossipy Bee public house; most of their socialising and catching up was done in church on the Sabbath day.

Being the eldest son, Hugh had taken over the running of Llan Farm from Efan a while ago, when his father had become infirm. Today, however, on the evening of his father's funeral, he did not rejoice in being the new owner of Llan Farm. Instead, he felt the loss of his father more keenly than ever and while outside in the yard, gave way to the tears which he had been holding back all day. He missed his father's solid, comforting presence around the place and missed hearing his voice calling out across the farmyard to his old faithful sheepdog, Taff. His absence, plus the evening silence, was deafening and unnerving. Hugh knew then what it was like to feel utterly abandoned.

When Hugh finally went back into the farmhouse kitchen, the supper table had been cleared and was set for breakfast. Lettie had already gone to bed. He knew she had needed comforting tonight – but he did not know the words to say. She was probably beyond comforting by him anyway and would in all likelihood, in her misery, have pushed him away. Well, it was just the two of them now. They would just have to learn to rub along together for the rest of their lives.

The farm was running smoothly to be fair – and paying well. There was no mortgage or rent to pay; they had not had to go through the tough years Efan had before he inherited the farm.

No, he decided, all he could do was to carry on and build on Efan's legacy – but for whom, he did not know. He picked up the drink of milk Lettie had left for him, keeping warm on the corner of the range, then sat down in his rocking chair to drink it.

Hugh had recently added the names and birthdates of Robert's twins, Euryn and Mabli, in the old family Bible and had recorded Efan's death in this year of 1894. He thought he should probably hand it over to Robert's family now, if he was never to begat children. He continued to ruminate. He thought that maybe Euryn, the twin boy, could eventually run Llan Farm when he grew up – but then who would run Robert's Tal-y-Cafn farm? Or maybe, if Thomas had any sons, they could come over to Wales to farm it, or maybe even Thomas himself would return to help him run it. So many maybes but no proper solutions to be found anywhere.

* * *

Farm life continued for the next few years, as Hugh became increasingly concerned about Lettie. Given her bizarre behaviour, he believed at times that she was becoming quite unstable. She continued to look after him and manage the dairy side of the farm but there was just something about her demeanour he could not quite put his finger on.

But one thing was certain. Each evening, just before turning in, she always left a drink of hot milk for him on the stove. She knew that this helped him sleep, and Hugh believed it was the one small act of kindness she still showed him. So every evening, after he had banked up the range, he picked up his cup and sat in his rocking chair by the stove, while he planned what he needed to do the next day. It didn't taste quite the same as it used to – but he guessed it must be the sugar she told him she was now putting in and he did not dare tell her he preferred it without.

Hugh often mused on the different paths he and his siblings had taken in life. He thought that even though Thomas' choice of a farming life was the same as his, it was in a very different, often harsher, often snowbound environment. Hugh did not like the idea of the extremes of temperature they experienced in Canada and of being so far away from anybody. He wondered what it would be like if he had to endure that sort of isolation and solitude with Lettie. The thought made him shudder.

Then he thought about poor Mary Ellen, widowed young, then losing her boy within the year; it must have been very hard for her. Perhaps her son could have been a farmer. He also wondered if she would ever marry again – she was still a fine-looking woman – there was no reason not to. But it seemed that Matthew, her husband, would take a lot of living up to.

They had sounded very happy together – not like him and Lettie. She had been a pretty little thing when they married – but life and a general dissatisfaction with her lot, had taken their toll on her, turning her bitter. He was even beginning to suspect that she was hankering after another man; maybe she had already met one and was secretly seeing him. But he felt powerless to confront her about this, given how unstable she seemed.

He wondered if he even had the strength to confront her. He seemed to feel weak for much of the time now, which was disconcerting for someone who had always been as strong as an ox. He hadn't been feeling at all well recently, which he thought was probably making him think these distrustful thoughts. Maybe he was sickening for something. Some days he just couldn't quite get his brain to think clearly – it was as if a fog crept in over it, slowly and stealthily, like a river mist stealing in over an unsuspecting riverbank.

He was also vomiting occasionally and suffered with stomach cramps and diarrhoea. He did not tell Lettie, in case she thought he was just making a fuss, but then again, he wouldn't have expected any sympathy from her anyway, the way she was with him these days.

People commented that he hadn't looked at all well for a while – but nobody seemed to know quite what was wrong with him. He had taken on a greyish pallor and seemed to have been getting weaker by the month. But then the appalling accident happened. As he was trying to tether a bull in the yard, it suddenly turned on him. He was too weak to protect himself – a thing he would normally have been able to do. As he pulled at the bull's tether, he lost his balance and fell over – then the bull trampled all over him, causing appalling injuries.

Unconscious, he was quickly carried into the house by the farm hands. He was placed on a bed and the local doctor summoned. Lettie had already carefully washed his injuries by the time the doctor arrived.

'It's not looking good, to be honest, Mrs Jones,' he told her. 'He's lost a great deal of blood. Last time I saw Hugh, which I suppose must be quite a while ago now, he seemed to be in rude health. I don't understand why he couldn't handle that bull. He was always as strong as a horse himself. We'll just have to wait and see if he comes round or not.'

During the small hours of the night, Hugh succumbed to his injuries; he was too weak to fight. Maybe he didn't have enough to live for. He passed away quietly, without ever recovering consciousness. His sister-in-law, Sara, who had come over to help Lettie nurse him, noticed that Lettie hardly seemed affected and certainly did not cry for him.

The family and the whole village were shocked by this sudden turn of events, but these things did occasionally happen in farming life. They all agreed that it could certainly be a very dangerous occupation.

The next week, an article appeared in the local newspaper telling of Hugh's passing.

Then, when Lettie was finally on her own, she crept out at dusk one night to bury a tin in a remote part of the grounds.

It was labelled 'Arsenic.'

Chapter 8

Friday has come around once more and after a hectic week I need to unwind. I accept Ruth's offer to join her team at the Promenade Bar and amble up to the bar to get the first round.

'What the heck are you doing here?' I say, shocked – but enormously pleased.

'Good to see you too,' Alys responds jokingly. 'I work here three nights a week now in between studying.'

It's my turn to be caught off-guard and I am momentarily lost for words but recover my composure.

'Three vodka and tonics, a rum with lime and half of bitter, please.'

'Certainly, Sir. Coming right up – I'll bring them over if you like.'

Due to the unexpected feeling of joy at seeing Alys, I am somewhat gung-ho and have a bit more to drink than I normally would. This loosens my usual inhibitions and seems to give me the courage to go over to Alys in the bar, just before closing time.

'How are you getting back to your digs tonight? Do you want to share a taxi?'

'I'd planned to walk; I usually do.'

'Let me walk with you then. That way, I'll know you get back safely.'

We walk along the shore, in the balmy air of a summer's evening to the sound of small insistent waves coming in off a very calm sea. As we walk, I tell her the story of the large Bible I had bought and how I am becoming obsessed with researching the people in the family tree within it.

'That's fascinating, I'd love to see it.'

'There was a box of photos with it – and I think a girl in one of the photos looks just like you.'

Alys smiles.

As we reach her digs, I catch her hand. 'Alys…..'

'Thanks for walking me home,' she says.

As she turns to plant a polite goodbye kiss on my cheek, I hold her face in both my hands, then kiss her very gently on her lips.

It was her turn to be surprised.

'I had the distinct impression you didn't like me very much last time we met.'

'Come over Sunday afternoon, about three o'clock. I'll show you the Bible and I'll toast you some crumpets! Here's my address.'

'Ok then, crumpets sound good. G'night.'

Walking home, I feel exhilarated. Am I falling in love? Or is it the alcohol skewing my senses? Our relationship has definitely moved up a gear and I wonder where it will all lead. I feel excited at the prospect.

On Sunday, the doorbell rings on the dot of three – and I let Alys into my flat and hopefully into my life.

*　*　*

The following weekend, I visit the Local Records Office and trawl through the old censuses. I discover from the 1851 census that Llan Farm was then forty-seven acres. This census also concluded that two-thirds of all farms in Great Britain were under one hundred acres.

Once home, I look up the definition of primogeniture, which was alive and well in the time of Efan's adult children. The definition states 'the right of succession belonging to the first-born legitimate child, to inherit his parents' main estate.' This was the governing rule in the absence of a valid Will until the law was changed in 1925.

When I think about how this would have impacted on Efan and his adult children, I realise that Hugh would automatically have inherited the farm. I know that the rationale for this was that if farms were split up between many siblings, they would gradually become smaller and smaller – and would no longer be viable.

Then I consider the alternative options of earning a living available to Hugh's male siblings. Once they reached the age of about fourteen, the second and any subsequent sons might be sent out to other farms to work or go into service. If they were lucky enough to get an apprenticeship, they might learn a trade. Other options would be to take the King's Shilling, or to enter the church.

When I had arranged to look again at the church records, I found that in 1884, Robert, the brother of Hugh and Thomas, had married a

Sara Lewis. Her address was recorded as Cae Isaf, Tal-y-Cafn, which is not too far from Eglwysbach. By looking up Cae Isaf in the 1881 census, I found that it was a fifty-acre farm and that there were no male children. This makes me realise that another option for a male sibling would be to marry the daughter of a farmer who did not have a son to inherit his farm. I assume that this was the case with Robert.

* * *

Robert's Story

'I know Mabli can do no wrong in your eyes, but she really is getting out of hand,' said Sara. 'You need to give her a good talking to; she's very *penderfynol* – thinks she can do as she pleases. You've not been strict enough with her. She could have done with the *gwialen fedw* now and again when she was younger.'

Robert knew he had been too soft on her but could not bear the thought of beating his young daughter.

'We'll just have to keep a closer eye on her.'

He turned to her twin, Euryn.

'Do you know what she gets up to?'

Euryn was the quieter twin, while Mabli was extrovert and outgoing. He shook his head sullenly, having been sworn to secrecy by Mabli.

Robert had sent Mabli to work with Lettie at Llan Farm to help out, following Hugh's sudden death. Sara was hoping that Lettie could straighten her out. But after a few months, they were getting reports that she kept going missing when she was supposed to be working.

Little did her parents know that Mabli, aged fourteen, was already besotted with a young lad called Jared who she had been meeting in secret for a while. Because Llan Farm was situated in the village itself, it was relatively easy for her to slip away from the farmhouse to meet him, as he lived literally two doors down, in Ty Mawr Llan.

Originally, Llan Farm, Ty Mawr Llan and Llan shop had all been owned by the same family but over time, these three properties had gradually been sold off individually and were now separate entities.

Ty Mawr Llan, a small manor house, stood set back in a large garden, in between the shop and the farm. It had stood empty for decades after the previous owners had suddenly abandoned it. Rumour had it they had sailed off to America. The family, which had consisted of two daughters and their parents, was relatively wealthy. No one knew the reason why they suddenly upped sticks and left, just that the furniture was covered with sheets, the house boarded up and the staff instantly dismissed, leaving it empty. But one day, decades later, it was suddenly opened up again and made habitable by local builders. A new family had moved in about a year before Mabli was sent to work at Llan Farm.

It was easy for Mabli to walk unseen along the back, high-hedged track past the farm and up to an unused barn. The boy, who she had first met a few months earlier while out on a walk, was back again from his boarding school and had left a note for her under a stone by the barn, which they used to communicate. To her, he seemed exciting and exotic – very different from her brother and the other village boys, who she considered to be dull and uninteresting.

'Did you learn anything at your school this time then?'

'This and that', he said, as he lit up a cheroot and blew the smoke in her direction. 'You ever tried it?' he asked, handing it to her.

'My father sometimes smokes a pot pipe; is it like that?' she giggled, as she took it off him. She inhaled the smoke then started choking violently. Embarrassed and red in the face, she waited until the coughing subsided, then handed it back to him.

'You can keep it!'

'You have to learn how to do it properly!' he replied, laughing at her undignified reaction to it. 'What have you been up to then?'

'Just the usual wearisome stuff: milking, butter churning, cheesemaking, sewing, bread making, baking…...'

'I'd like to try one of your pies,' he said with a smile and a twinkle in his eye. She felt a flush of blood rise up in her face, not really understanding what he was insinuating but guessing it was not anything that her mother would approve of. Then as the penny dropped, she blushed furiously.

'Here, I have a little geegaw for you,' he said, as he dug into the inner pocket of his jacket.

She had no idea what a geegaw was but loved hearing the

American drawl in his voice and had never received a gift from him before.

'What is it then?' she said impatiently, clamouring to see.

'First, you have to give me a kiss,' he said.

Having never been kissed before either, she just stood motionless, her arms down by her sides. His face came slowly towards her, touching her lips lightly with his. Closing her eyes, she felt a responding sensation deep inside, as he began to kiss her more determinedly. Gently forcing her lips apart, his tongue probed in her mouth, as he groaned with pleasure. Mabli, not really understanding what was happening, drew back, shocked but not displeased.

Embarrassed but recovering herself, she asked, 'Where's this geegaw then?'

He handed over a tiny silver trinket box. It had a hinged top and the inside was lined in a purple crushed velvet.

'Thank you. It's really beautiful,' she said, lifting the little lid to peep inside.

'Not as beautiful as you though,' he said, as he lunged for her again. They both fell down onto the soft straw laughing – the geegaw forgotten.

Later, her told her how his father had learned that he had inherited a house in North Wales, so the family decided to sell up and move there. He said he thought his grandmother was from this part of the world originally but didn't know too much of the detail, as the subject was taboo. Then he pulled some letters out of his inner pocket. He said he had found them stuffed in the back of one of the drawers in his dressing table. The paper was yellowed with age along the folded edges and the ink was faded but still legible. It was obvious that he had not made any connection with them to his family, nor probably even read them. The letters read:

Ty Mawr Llan
February 19th, 1819

My Dearest Tomos
My father has finally discovered that I am with child. He greatly admonished me and I am locked in my room permanently. I

have been forbidden from seeing you ever again. They tell me that as soon as the baby is born, they will take it to some woodfolk to be reared.

Then I am told we will leave here as soon as berths become available on a ship to America. I fear I may not see you again and cannot bear the thought of that and I cannot tell you where I will be for you to write to me.

Yours forever lovingly
Dorothy

* * *

Ty Mawr Llan
March 28th, 1819

My Dearest Tomos

I write this last letter to you in the small, darkest hours of the morning to tell you our son was born this last evening after a long labour. He is perfect. I have named him Efan.

Although I have begged him, my father refuses to let me keep him and has arranged for him to be taken away in the morning. Therefore I only have a few precious hours left with him. I watch him as he sleeps, knowing we will soon be separated forever. This makes me heartbreakingly sad when I think of him crying out for me, his mother – and I am no longer there to comfort nor feed him.

I will try to get this letter to you, although the household staff have all been warned by my father not to deliver anything from me. But they do not realise that they will soon be dismissed anyway and should bear no loyalty to him. He will not keep on any staff who were tainted by what he calls 'this torrid affair.'

He has booked sea passages to America and I must accompany him. I have no choice in the matter, as I do not have any independent financial means of my own and I know you do not have the means to support us. It seems our future together has been decided by others.

 Always remember that I love you, and our son, deeply. I will refuse to let him arrange a marriage for me. I expect you will stay on at Llan Farm, so I will try to write there but I expect my father will thwart my every effort to do so, as he is extremely angry with me.

Yours, my love, forever
Dorothy

 A few hours later, Dorothy had given the letter to her maid to deliver by hand, but as with the first one, the maid was too afraid to cross her father. She put it in the back of the dressing table drawer with the first one, until she decided what she should to do about it – not knowing that she had irrevocably changed the lives of three people and their chance of happiness forever. However, years later, the maid told Tomos where the baby was taken and that she regretted not giving him the letters from Dorothy.

 'Can I keep those letters?' asked Mabli, intrigued by their content and the beautiful old-fashioned copperplate writing, while having absolutely no notion of their significance to her family.

 'Of course,' he said, nonchalantly tossing the other one over to her. 'They are no use to me,' not realising that they were written by his own great-grandmother.

 Jared and Mabli met regularly, until one day as they lay there, it dawned on him that her waist was thickening. Next thing she knew, his house was completely boarded up; the family had left to return to live in America. It seemed to be a family trait, to run away, to avoid facing their responsibilities. Unknown to them, history had repeated itself.

 At about the same time, Mabli began vomiting in the mornings. Having dismissed it initially as an upset stomach, she suddenly realised that she may be with child and was frankly terrified. She knew she couldn't tell Lettie and had no one else to talk to about it. In any case, she had thought for a while that Lettie was a bit odd and irrational and not someone she could confide in. Sometimes she heard her talking to herself, or rather she seemed to be talking to somebody that nobody else could see or hear.

A few weeks later, as Mabli was preparing to carry the bed sheets down for washing, she paused on the landing on hearing an unfamiliar man's voice downstairs. It seemed that Lettie and the man were having what sounded like an urgent whispered conversation in the parlour. Snatches of it drifted up to Mabli.

'…can buy the whole lot off you…….furniture…….I have money. We…….get married…..children need a mother……need a woman in the house.'

'Shush, keep your voice down, she's upstairs, she might hear…. Hugh……only dead…….few months, people…...be shocked,' replied Lettie.

'….. get used to the idea……. Why..…care what those old busybodies think….?'

But what the farmer didn't know, was how she'd helped him on his way.

'Robert's family…….very angry with me…….sell …..without telling them.'

'……don't tell them until..…..signed and sealed. You'll be gone by the time they find out…….won't be able to stop the sale. You own it, don't you? ….up to you what you do…….'

It dawned on Mabli that Lettie was secretly planning to sell Llan Farm and all the contents to this man. She couldn't imagine any man wanting to roll in the hay with stick-thin, dour-faced Lettie. But Mabli knew then that she had no future there, so a month or so later, she started walking back to her home in Tal-y-Cafn. Given her condition, she was exhausted by the time she got there.

She told her parents she had left her employment with Lettie. They were so angry and exasperated with her that they immediately sent her to her room without even asking her why she had left.

It was not too long after, that her mother also became aware that Mabli was with child. Her parents were obviously appalled.

'Think of the shame you have brought on our family with your wanton ways,' said Sara, visibly shaken and crying.

'Who is the father?' shouted Robert. 'By God, he will do the right thing by you if I have to drag him there kicking and screaming.'

Mabli infuriated him even more by just sitting there and saying nothing at all.

She never did disclose who the father of her baby was. She knew in her heart that he wouldn't be marrying her anyway – he had already left the country.

* * *

A few weeks later, Robert came home visibly furious, after being at the local farmers' market and getting into conversation with one of his neighbours.

'Shame Llan Farm's been sold to Bryn Uchaf,' the neighbour remarked. 'I thought one of you brothers could have taken it on.'

Robert had looked at the man in shock. Registering what was being said, he quickly rushed off home to tell Sara.

Sara was in the outhouse, boiling bedsheets. She had called Mabli down to help her lift them up to the mangle, as they were heavy with water. She was beginning to feel her age now and knew she was no longer the pretty woman that Robert had fallen for all those years ago.

Robert rushed up to tell them the bad news.

'Lettie has sold the farm and moved out. I can't believe it. Why would she do that without telling us?'

'I thought she might do,' said Mabli casually. 'I overheard her talking to that farmer from Bryn Uchaf. He was wanting her to sell it to him.'

Understandably shocked and angry, they both turned to her.

'Why didn't you tell us sooner, for goodness sake?' Robert asked. 'We could have done something to stop it.'

'Well, you weren't speaking to me at the time, if you remember, so how could I? You sent me straight to my room,' she retorted sulkily, realising now, on seeing how angry her parents were, that she should probably have made some sort of an effort to tell them.

'I despair of you, really I do,' said Sara, as she rolled her eyes at her husband.

'It's a shame she sold it to that man,' Robert said, changing the subject back to the shocking news. 'But with Hugh gone, Lettie did say she wasn't managing well on her own any more, even with Mabli's help. Hugh left everything to her in his Will, so she was within her rights to sell it to anybody she wanted to – but I wish she'd consulted with me first.'

'We could have looked at different possibilities,' Robert went on. 'I might have bought the land off her and she could have stayed on in the farmhouse. Thomas might even have come back from Canada to farm it. If only Thomas had stayed to farm with Hugh, this would never have happened. It's just a shame it's not been kept in the family, given that it was gifted to Father by his mysterious benefactor. I'm sure Efan would have preferred one of his sons to take it over, rather than have it sold off to a stranger. Damn it!'

Sara glared at him disapprovingly for swearing, as he continued.

'We all thought a lot of the old place – it was our childhood home. We could even have hung on to it until Euryn was old enough to farm it. Why didn't she say something to us about her plans at the funeral? Maybe she didn't want us to know……'

'Well,' said Sara, 'perhaps she thought she was preventing arguments if she did it this way. Anyway, what's done is done. There is nothing we can do about it now. Mrs Jones, Post, seemed to think she'd seen her talking to that scoundrel widower from Bryn Uchaf a few times over the last year. Maybe he wants her to raise his four children – Lettie was always desperate to have her own. Maybe this is the nearest she'll get to it; an answer to her prayers.'

'In truth,' she continued, 'we don't actually know if she has sold it to him, nor if she's living with him. Maybe it's just gossip. Nobody has seen hide nor hair of her.' Sara sighed. 'Odd though that she didn't say anything – just quietly sold the farm and all the furniture – then just disappeared into thin air. I would have liked to have a keepsake to remind me of your mam and dad. Maybe the parlour dresser or something,' she said, longingly remembering what a fine specimen it was.

'Lettie was peculiar anyway, always talking to herself or her imaginary friend,' added Mabli waspishly.

'Well, she didn't do a very good job of looking after you, did she? She must have let you run wild.' Turning to Robert, Sara added, 'Mabli's time is coming soon. What are we going to do about her? We can't hide her away upstairs forever.'

'We'll send her to Mary Ellen in Capelulo to have it. Then we'll have to find a family for it – or take it to the foundling hospital. Mabli can stay there and work for Mary Ellen in the tea-rooms. No one will know her there – certainly no one will want to know her if she stays here. We'll just say she's gone away to work in service.'

'Don't I have any say in the decision?' asked Mabli.

Both parents turned to look at her with complete disdain and contempt.

'If Lettie has taken up with that crook from Bryn Uchaf and sold it to him,' Robert said after a short pause, 'doesn't she realise that if she marries him, the money he paid her for the farm will be his anyway. She would have been better off renting it to a tenant. Silly gullible woman.'

'I'm going to go over there this afternoon to see for myself what's been going on,' he added as he got up.

When Robert arrived at the farm, he found the front door locked but he knew there were other ways into the farmhouse at the back. He went forlornly from room to empty room, which evoked memories of his childhood and young adulthood. He was saddened to see his former home stripped bare, denuded of the furniture which had made it their home.

Entering the parlour, a seldom-used musty room, he noticed a pile of dusty old books and legal-looking papers on the window ledge – obviously not considered good enough to sell or for Lettie to take with her. On closer inspection, along with a few religious books, he recognised their old family Bible with a sheath of old paperwork. Obviously, Jones family and Llan Farm documents were of no use to Lettie now. Deferentially, he picked them all up and cradling his beloved family's history to his chest, he walked away from his birthplace, knowing it would be for the last time. The thought made him tearful and sad beyond words.

His father, Efan, would be turning in his grave if he could see the place he had worked so hard to establish and keep, now empty and abandoned by the family he had raised there.

* * *

Taking clean laundry up to Mabli's room a few days later, Sara found Dorothy's letters carelessly tossed on her dressing table, as well as a little silver trinket box. Curious, she opened the letters and read them. She soon became aware of the significance of the contents and was shocked, hurrying downstairs to show them to Robert.

'You realise what this means, don't you?' he said slowly, as the enormity of what he had just read began to dawn on him.

'The woman who wrote these letters must be Efan's mother, Dorothy – and Old Tom was his father.'

'This also means Tom actually owned Llan Farm before my father, Efan,' Robert mused. 'He must have always known Efan was his son but had never told him; that's why Tom initially gave my father the tenancy, when the work got too much for him. He must have wanted him there all along. So Tom left the farm to him when he died but even then, kept his identity secret from Efan. That must be the reason why he stayed on the farm in his own accommodation, so he could be close to Efan.'

'I wonder why Tom never felt he could tell him,' Robert pondered. 'Perhaps initially he was protecting the identify of Efan's mother, Dorothy, but then later it became too difficult to break the habit of secrecy. Or maybe he felt he'd deceived Efan for too long – that if he was to tell him, Efan would be very angry with him; that he might even lose him,'

'So – Old Tom was our grandfather and Dorothy from Ty Mawr Llan was our grandmother,' Robert repeated deliberately, as this revelation gradually sank in. 'I wonder who owned Llan Farm before Old Tom. Maybe even his father did.'

'They were obviously forbidden to marry by Dorothy's father,' Robert continued sombrely. 'Perhaps Tom's father also disapproved of the union. It seems that although they both wanted to marry and were genuinely fond of each other, they were prevented from realising their hearts' desire.'

'It seems our family has had a very long history at the farm and now suddenly Lettie has sold it' – clicking his fingers – 'just like that. Without even a thought for our heritage and inheritance,' he added angrily.

'It seems like children born out of wedlock is a Jones family trait,' Sara remarked disdainfully. 'I would keep quiet about it if I were you, it's nothing to be proud of.'

With that, she got up to pull a fresh loaf out of the bread oven, leaving Robert annoyed at her thoughtless dig against his family.

He sighed deeply, then added, 'I will write to Thomas to tell him everything.'

'I wonder if my younger brother was named after Old Tom?' he speculated, as a parting thought.

Chapter 9

Alys and I have started to meet up regularly on her nights off from work. At weekends, we tend to go for long rambling walks along the beautifully rugged Caerneddau hills, often coming across the wild ponies who live up there. We talk endlessly about all sorts of things and the time seems to fly by whenever I am in her company.

If the weather prevents walking, I spend time researching the names in the old Bible while she studies. It occurs to me that the names of Robert and Sara's twins, Euryn and Mabli, are unusual, which is helpful to a family researcher. I notice that in the family tree, Mabli has a dotted line leading down to a daughter, Rebecca.

'This means that her child was illegitimate,' I explain to Alys.

'Wooo…… skeleton in the cupboard alert!' declares Alys. 'But do the sums – she was only fifteen years old when she had her. I wonder what the story was there?'

'The surprising thing is that this entry was even written in at all,' I say, 'given the social shame it would have caused at that time in history, with all their religious taboos. It does look to have been written in different handwriting though, maybe added in a later period, when it could no longer upset the sensibilities of the previous generations.'

* * *

Mabli's Story

Mabli's parents were incensed that she had sinned and thereby brought shame on the family. Robert had not followed his father's Anglican religion, as Sara's family were big chapel people, where such immoral behaviour was not to be condoned, nor ever forgiven. Consequently, Mabli had been mostly locked in her bedroom on their isolated farm, so that neighbours would not find out about her condition.

Mabli was a very spirited girl. She was enthralled by her Uncle Thomas' adventures. She admired the way he had been converted to

Methodism by the travelling preacher and had gone to Patagonia as a pioneer to farm. Mabli also had a certain admiration for Megan, who had run away with him on that fateful voyage. She found out about these juicy bits of gossip by eavesdropping – pressing her ear to the gaps in the floorboards of her bedroom. Listening in to snatches of her parents' conversations in the kitchen below was her way of relieving the boredom.

She was only allowed downstairs for meals or if they needed her to help with anything. Sometimes, when she heard her brother on the stairs and landing, she would call out to him and he would come to her door. She would press both her hands flat against the inside of the door, imagining that she was pressing her palms against those of her brother on the other side.

'I can't bear to be in this room any longer, Euryn,' she whispered. 'Please help me get out or I will go mad like Aunty Lettie,' she desperately implored him.

'I want to help but I can't do that, Mab. They'd punish me and I'd never be forgiven if something bad happened to you.'

Later that evening, wallowing in her pit of despondency, she suddenly remembered there was a fixed roof ladder to the side of her bedroom window. She reasoned that if she could somehow climb out of her window and onto that, she would be able to climb up to the ridge of the roof. From there, she could clamber along to the lean-to barn's roof, then drop down onto the haybales. It would be risky – but worth a try. She decided that the best time to try this was just before dawn when her parents went downstairs to light the fire. Then they would be out in the cowshed milking for about an hour, so wouldn't hear her rattling about on the roof.

Very early next morning, she placed a chair under her bedroom door-knob, then bundled her belongings in a shawl and tied it onto her back. Carefully, she slid open the sash window, which thankfully didn't make a noise. It was now or never, she thought, taking a deep breath. She would have to be as quiet as she could, in case they heard her.

A fine, misty rain was falling, so she needed to be extra careful not to slip on the wet slates. Tying her long skirt high around her waist, she carefully let herself backwards out of the window onto the deep stone window-sill. Then she reached over, grabbed the fixed ladder and carefully made her way along onto it. She found this difficult with her expanded waistline getting in the way but persevered. She then climbed up the ladder and onto the ridge of the house roof, before moving slowly sideways across to the barn roof. After pausing for breath, she carefully slid her way down the tiles to the barn roof, then dropped silently onto the hay, which was stacked inside.

Freedom at last!

Or so she thought. But freedom was to come at a deadly price.

Next, she had to carefully plan the best time to leave the cover of the barn. The dogs would soon make their way to the back door to wait for breakfast scraps, so would not be guarding the farmyard. As they knew her, they probably would not bark anyway. She waited until everyone had gone in to have breakfast after milking, then quietly crept away unseen along the side of the barn. Finally, she was out of sight of the farm and walked up the farm track.

At the end of the track, without a backward glance, she turned due west onto the narrow, steep, grass-centred public road. Just then the sun rose – it felt so good to be free and to feel the sun's warmth on her back.

Thankfully there was not a soul about at that time of the morning. After walking up this road for about ten minutes, she looked right over the hedge below towards the beautiful estuary of the Afon Conwy. It was now low tide. She saw both the free-flowing main river channel and the smaller snakelike tributaries winding their way through the river's mud flats out to the sea. Soon, the tide would flow swiftly back in, filling the mud flats once more. She knew the ways of this river; the farm on which she had grown up lay alongside its banks, where her father grazed his salt marsh lambs.

Twenty minutes later, she had walked as far as the staggered junction by Y Gwesty Groes, so turned right onto the main road leading to Conwy. After walking up the steepish hill for about ten minutes, she heard the clippity-clop of a slow, laborious work horse coming up behind her. Turning around, she saw what she guessed was a miller's boy, on his way with his cartload to the Gyffin flour mill.

'Ti eisiau reid i Gyffin, blodyn?' called out the carter with a cheeky smile.

'Oes, diolch,' she said, thankfully accepting his offer of a ride, which would take her to about halfway on her journey.

She had decided to go to her Aunty Mary Ellen's tea-rooms in Capelulo. She remembered that she had always been kind-hearted towards her, even when the others had scolded her. Mabli knew Mary Ellen had had her share of suffering and loss in her life, so would not turn her away.

'Where you going then?'

'That's for me to know and you to mind your own beeswax,' she replied tartly, thinking it best to show that she would not be messed about with.

'No need to be like that is there? Ungrateful wench,' he mumbled sullenly, having thought the boredom of his journey was going to be relieved by some friendly company.

They travelled in silence, with him giving her the occasional sideways glance, until they finally reached the bottom of Gyffin Hill.

As she tried to alight, he grabbed her by her upper arm and pulled her back.

'Aren't I going to get a little kiss as a reward then?'

'Let go of me, you brute,' she shouted.

But he held on to her arm and tried to pull her face towards him.

'Oi, let her go, you bully, she's just a child,' yelled a nearby, elderly man sitting outside a shop, sucking on his clay pipe.

'Oh, I don't think so, old man; more like 'with child.' She's got quite a swollen belly on her, that one.' Nevertheless, he was shamed into letting go of her arm.

Mabli jumped down as soon as she could.

'She's not worth the trouble anyway. Someone else has been there before me,' he shouted spitefully, as he turned his cart to the left and trundled off towards the mill.

Stunned at his callousness, Mabli gave the elderly man an embarrassed smile of thanks, then shyly asked him for directions to Capelulo.

'Follow that road up the hill, all the way to the top,' he said, pointing. 'Then turn left to get onto Ffordd Bwlch Sychnant, which will take you to Capelulo.'

'Take no heed of that oaf,' he added kindly, 'just get yourself going, girl.'

She set off up the hill opposite the one she had just descended, feeling physically rested after the ride but emotionally drained from the lad's abuse of her. She had not realised that her condition showed quite so much. Subconsciously, she wrapped her cloak more tightly, as if to hide the fact and protect herself.

Within half an hour, she had passed a couple of isolated farms, then finally reached a place where the road ran through the high stone walls of an estate which bounded a pine forest. Surely, she thought, it couldn't be too much further now? She was hot and exhausted. The climb up had taken it out of her and she was beginning to feel drained, her energy dissipating by the minute.

As she sat down on a large smooth boulder at the side of the road near to the walls to rest, she started to feel mild cramps in her abdomen, which she thought must be a stitch from all the walking. Looking behind at the way she had come, she thought she briefly glimpsed a figure further back, then dismissed it as her imagination, as she could no longer see it.

Somewhat rested, she set off once more, telling herself that it couldn't possibly be much further now. Behind the walls, amongst the undergrowth of the tall pine trees, she could hear tiny creatures scurrying about amongst the rotten tree trunks which lay on the ground, disturbing the brittle brown leaves which still lay there from last autumn. Then she heard the earnestly-beautiful, joyfully-melodic singing of a blackbird on a nearby branch, which made her smile.

She set off again. After about two hundred yards, as she passed the main gated entrance into the estate, she became aware of a different sound. Suddenly, she heard human footsteps echoing between the walls behind her and became apprehensive. It must be the figure she had seen earlier, who could have been hiding from her. The sound of hobnail boots grew louder and seemed to be gaining on her – but she couldn't see who it was, around the bends in the road.

With her confidence still shaken by the earlier incident with the carter, she asked herself how on earth she could have been so foolish as to set off on such a journey alone, in her condition. She now longed for the safe, cosy kitchen of her home. Even the dreary solitude of her bedroom seemed preferable at this moment. There was brave, then there was foolhardy, as her mother would say.

She thought she must soon be out of these claustrophobic walls. As she rounded the last bend, she saw a small, arched pedestrian gateway in the estate wall on her right. Although she could still hear the footsteps, she couldn't see anybody when she turned around to look. She tried to assure herself that she would soon be out of these oppressive walls.

But suddenly, she grew terrified – almost paralysed with fear – as the footsteps grew louder and gained on her. She tried to break into a run but a sharp stitch in her side prevented her. She wished her twin brother, Euryn, was there with her now to protect her. Suddenly he didn't seem so dull after all, just caring and dependable. She needed him now, like she never had before.

Finally, she saw the sky lighten as the high walls and the tall trees ended and the road began dropping steeply downwards. This gave her hope that she was safely out in the open again.

But the sound of the hob-nailed boots became a run. On turning around, Mabli saw a terrifyingly large, dirty, tramp-like man gaining on her, just as she reached the open top of the Pass. She tried to run downhill away from him but an excruciatingly sharp, painful cramp in her groin sapped her strength completely, causing her to collapse in a heap on the road. As she did so, he caught up with her and towering over her, gurned menacingly down at her, showing his rotted teeth.

'Mam, Mam, where are you?' Mabli screamed out hysterically. 'I need you. Help! Help me somebody.'

The man clouted her hard across the face and told her to stop screaming. An angry blue welt rose instantly on her left cheek. Then he quickly grabbed an arm, pinning it to the ground above her head, so she could not move. Putting his knee on her other arm, he ripped at her pantaloons. As she writhed to get away, he hit her again across her face so hard, that splatters of fresh blood and teeth flew sideways onto the track. He grunted and groaned as he lay on top of her. The stabbing pains as he entered her, together with the already horrific force of the cramps she was enduring, was far too much for her small frame to endure and her suffering was so overwhelming, that mercifully, she passed out of consciousness.

'Oi, you, get off her, you brute!' shouted Olwen, waving her stick in the air. The black-clad owner of the nearby Murddyn Potas was running down the path on top of the ridge to the left.

'Help, somebody help!' she shouted, the sound of her voice bouncing urgently back and forth among the otherwise silent mountains on both sides of the Pass.

On reaching them, she began to beat the man on his back with her stick. He rose and grabbed it. Snapping the stick in half on his knee, he threw it to the ground, then pushed her away by her shoulder. Satiated, he tucked in his shirt, then heartlessly kicked Mabli hard in her rib cage with his steel-capped boot.

'Whore,' he shouted. He spat at her as she lay helpless on the road, then ran quickly away towards the shelter of the pine-treed area behind.

'There, there, he's gone now,' Olwen told the semi-conscious, delirious girl, tenderly holding her hand, before Mabli passed out again. She saw that Mabli's face and clothes were soaked in blood and soon realised that she was with child and probably in labour.

'Help! Somebody help us, please,' she desperately shouted again towards her house close by. Olwen held both of Mabli's hands, trying to comfort her.

As she started to gain consciousness once more, Mabli screamed.

'Ssh, shush, quiet now,' Olwen said to her. 'You're safe now. He's gone. What's your name, girl?'

'Mabli…..Mary Ellen…..tea-rooms………' she managed to whisper before another excruciating cramp built up and she fell into unconsciousness once more.

'Help, somebody, help! This girl's very badly injured,' her voice echoing around the rocks opposite once more.

Finally alerted by the shouting, a waif appeared on the same path, running urgently down towards Olwen.

'Quick, run down to the tea-rooms and tell Mary Ellen that Mabli has been attacked.'

Despite the chill wind which funnelled up the pass, Olwen removed her cloak and covered Mabli, in an effort to both protect her dignity and make her as comfortable as possible. But she could see she was in a very bad way and visibly shivering violently with shock. She looked like her time had come but she was not yet full term. It was possible she could be losing the baby due to the brutal attack on her.

The longest ten minutes of Olwen's life followed, as they waited for Mary Ellen to arrive.

'Quick! Someone's been attacked up the pass,' the waif told Mary Ellen, having forgotten Mabli's name. 'You have to take a wagon for her.'

A supplier, who had been delivering flour to Mary Ellen's, was about to leave the tea-rooms.

'Quick, turn the wagon around,' she shouted to him. 'We need to go up the Pass to pick up someone who is badly injured.'

'Jump up then, let's go,' the man said without hesitation.

'I would have tried to take her home,' Olwen said to Mary Ellen as she arrived at the scene, 'but she said your name. Anyway, I don't think I could have lifted and carried her up the hill to my house by myself.'

'What happened?'

'When I got here, I saw this tramp lying on top of her, violating her. She told me her name was Mabli, I think. I'm not sure…...'

Mary Ellen was shocked to recognise Mabli.

'You did the right thing, Olwen, thank you. I will take care of her now.'

Mabli then let out a further bloodcurdling scream of pain and passed out again, having just seen the floating face of Mary Ellen looking tenderly at her.

'What have you been up to, Mabli *bach*? This is more than an attack by that man. Come on, let's get you home, see what we can do for you.'

They lifted Mabli gently onto the cart. Mary Ellen sat next to her, cradling her head on her lap, stroking her face gently and pushing her blood-stained hair away from her swollen mouth, eyes and face. As the cart drove carefully back down the Pass to the village, Mary Ellen wondered if Robert knew where Mabli was. Maybe she should send word to Tal-y-Cafn to tell them, to stop them worrying. When they found out what had happened, they would be mortified. Maybe best not to tell them about the attack by the vagrant – but how would she explain the bruising on her face?

With the help of the carter, Mary Ellen and Sammy managed to get Mabli onto a bed. Sammy then took the carter downstairs and offered him something for his trouble. Although he would not hear of it, he accepted a cup of sweet tea for the shock.

Mary Ellen gingerly removed Mabli's clothing and washed her as gently as she could, given that the cramps were now getting stronger and more frequent. She gently slipped a cotton nightdress over her head, then mopped her tacky forehead with lavender water.

'I think we'd better fetch the doctor,' she said to Sammy when she returned to the bedroom. 'She's still losing a lot of blood, even though we've propped her legs up. She's writhing too much to keep them up there. The bed is already saturated. Poor mite, to be going through all this and she's only just fifteen.'

An hour later, the local doctor was there.

'It's not looking very hopeful I'm afraid,' he said sombrely, after examining Mabli. 'The internal injury is quite significant; the birth canal skin is badly torn. I'm not sure that we can save either the mother or the baby. All I can say is do what you can to make her as comfortable as possible. The fate of both is in your hands and the lap of the gods.'

* * *

Earlier, when Sara had gone upstairs to fetch Mabli for her breakfast, she found her door was jammed. She forced it open, only to discover her gone and the curtains billowing in the wind outside the window. The silly girl had risked her life and limb to get away, Sara thought.

'She's gone, Robert,' she shouted, as she ran across the farmyard, scattering the geese. 'She climbed out through the bedroom window,' she added as she reached the barn where Mabli would have dropped down.

Despite searching everywhere, Mabli was nowhere to be found on the farm.

'I think she's probably walked to Mary Ellen's,' Euryn volunteered. 'I'll get the trap ready.'

'Did you know she had planned this?' Robert shouted at him.

'I had no idea. I would have told you if I'd known. I told her I couldn't help her when she asked me to. But she was desperate to get out of that room.'

The three of them had soon climbed up onto the trap and were on their way, leaving the farm hands in charge of the animals.

'The doctor has warned that she may not survive,' Mary Ellen warned them when they arrived, before going upstairs to see their daughter.

Both parents shook their heads sadly. But they believed she had brought it all on herself, while having no real understanding that their draconian regime had also contributed to the current, sad situation.

Euryn, who was quietly told by Mary Ellen about the attacker, was white with rage and shock. He freed the horse from the cart and immediately rode off up the Pass to avenge his sister. But search as he might, he found nothing. The criminal had made sure he was already miles away. Euryn realised that the man was unlikely to be hanging around there to be caught. But by looking for him, he felt that at least he was doing something and was glad to be away from the blood-curdling screams of his sister.

Finally, a tiny pre-term baby girl was delivered, barely alive. Mary Ellen cut the cord and cleared out the baby's airways. She smacked her to make her breathe, then wrapped her tightly in a soft white cotton sheet.

Mabli was weak, grey and exhausted by both ordeals and still losing blood. When Mary Ellen finally brought the cleaned-up tiny baby to Mabli to suckle, she realised that she had quietly passed away.

Her distraught mother, Sara, who had been by her side, was now beside herself with guilt and grief but did not offer to take their daughter's body home with them. They did not want her buried in Eglwysbach churchyard, as that would have raised questions amongst the chapel congregation about the circumstances of her death. She would not allow Mabli to be buried there because she felt Mabli had acted shamefully against the will of God and broken his Commandments.

She also refused to take the baby, their granddaughter, home with them. Instead, she asked Mary Ellen to see to it that Mabli got a good

Christian burial locally. Mary Ellen agreed on condition that she be allowed to keep the baby.

Rebecca was born in February 1907. Mary Ellen would not hear of her being farmed out to foster parents, nor did she consider sending her to the foundling hospital, as Sara had initially insisted. In Mary Ellen's estimation, this tiny precious scrap of humanity, whose life still hung in the balance, was worth fighting for. She was determined to give her the best chance of survival. She asked Sammy to go and fetch some goat's milk, then slowly squeezed drops of the milk from a gauze pad into the baby's mouth.

Knowing how precious life was, having lost her beloved husband and son, she had demanded of Sara that she be allowed to keep Rebecca and in the end Sara agreed. No one had any idea who had fathered the child, so they could neither inform nor confront him.

Mary Ellen poured all her love into this essentially-orphaned baby, who was utterly adorable. The entire household began to revolve around her and her routine. True, she had lost her mother and would never know her father, but instead she had three surrogate mothers – Mary Ellen, Jane and Sammy, who took it in turns to be with her around the clock.

Although Robert now had possession of the old family Bible after rescuing it from Llan Farm, Sara felt it was not proper to record her daughter Mabli's death or the illegitimate birth of her granddaughter, Rebecca.

Mary Ellen felt no such misgivings – only pride at such a blessing. She purchased a plot in the cemetery at St. Gwynan's and buried Mabli there. It was close to the small side gate of the cemetery, where her beloved Matthew and her little boy were buried. She had already requested that she be buried there with them when her time came.

* * *

Many years later, when Mary Ellen finally became old and frail, she no longer worked in the tea-rooms. Most days she sat in her bedroom looking out onto the goings-on in the sleepy village below, which usually weren't very much. Sammy, only a few years younger herself, cared for Mary Ellen. She had never left her side since

Matthew had brought her up to North Wales on his cart. Mary Ellen's daughter, Jane, had taken over the running of the tea-rooms, with the help of a village girl. Meanwhile, Rebecca had left them to get married.

The tour parties in the cream and red charabancs of earlier decades now came in the Red and Cream Line motorised coaches from Llandudno. The tea-rooms also catered for hill-walkers and those out for drives in the countryside, many in open-topped cars. All this change had become quite normal. However, an American visitor was certainly out of the ordinary in that setting.

'There's an American gentleman downstairs asking to speak to you,' said Mary Ellen's daughter, Jane, having gone upstairs to tell her.

'What about?'

'He said he wants to talk to you about Mabli.'

Jane was reluctant to even mention Mabli's name. She knew that her mother would get upset, as the subject still brought back painful memories for her.

'Do you feel up to it? You don't have to speak to him if you don't want to. I can send him away.'

'Put him in the parlour, I'll be down as soon as I can manage. Give him a tray of tea and a cake or something to eat while he waits,' Mary Ellen replied, thinking that people don't come all the way from America just to make small talk.

Mary Ellen slowly got ready to go downstairs. She looked in the mirror, hardly recognising the face now looking back at her. Where had the face of the Mary Ellen who had fallen in love with Matthew gone? It had slowly changed after the death of her husband. Her laughter lines had turned to frown lines as there was little to smile about since he had left her.

She checked her plain grey box-pleated skirt was straight then put on her maroon cardigan. She went over to her jewellery box and picked one of the brooches Matthew had given her and pinned it to the neck of her fine satin blouse. She wondered if Matthew would even recognise her now when they finally met again in heaven. It was 1935. The woman she no longer recognised in the mirror was now aged eighty-five and had been widowed for nearly sixty years.

Having lost Matthew and her son, she had poured all her love into Rebecca when she had become responsible for her after she was rejected by Sara. For a while, the love she got from her had filled that empty hole. But now, what did she have to live for? She was tired of this world. She'd had enough of pain and suffering and of waiting to leave.

As she prepared to go down, she speculated as to what on earth this visit could be about. She knew of no American. She looked around her cosy room and was reluctant to leave it to face any more upset.

Gazing around her quiet sanctuary, her eyes fell fondly onto the bed she had shared with her beloved Matthew, then across to the mahogany dressing table with the silver-framed photograph of them both standing proudly outside Bodhyfrydle. She ran her finger fondly along the top of the silver frame. None of this was fair, she thought, as she stroked his face. He had not aged at all – whilst she had.

On each side of the photograph was a cut-glass candlestick, standing on their crocheted lace squares. At the front in the centre was the shallow cut-glass tray which held her silver-initialled, ebony-backed hairbrush and comb. Next to this was her compact green jade-handled manicure set and her little brass-clasped hand Bible.

That made her recall the big family Bible that her father had written all their names in when they were children. She wondered if Robert had kept it up to date after rescuing it from Llan Farm. She doubted it – he was never a writer and would not have wanted to enter Rebecca's name in it.

Euryn had now taken over the running of their farm. She had not visited there for years, nor had she heard much from Thomas in Canada recently. She wondered what his life was like now; was it better than hers? Last time they saw each other was just before he left for Canada.

Drawing back the net curtains, she noticed a fancy motor car parked in front of her wrought-iron gate, with a chauffeur wearing a peaked cap sitting in the driver's seat. She wondered what connection this American man had with Mabli. Well, there's only one way to find out she thought, as she reached for her ivory-handled walking stick. Turning the small brass door-knob, she gently opened the bedroom door and made her way slowly down the stairs.

A tall, handsome, distinguished-looking man, rose as she entered the room. He cradled her elbow as she shuffled her way across the room onto an upright winged armchair. She was glad Jane had thought to light a fire. The sun was too low in the sky at this time of year to warm the front rooms of the house, blocked out as it was by the steep hills surrounding it.

'My name is Jared Knox,' he started. 'As you can hear, I'm an American, although as a young boy, I once lived in Eglwysbach.'

Mary Ellen's eyes widened, suddenly interested.

'Where and when did you live there?'

'When I was a young man, my parents inherited Ty Mawr Llan and we moved from America to live there for a short while. I went there yesterday and found that your family is sadly no longer living in Llan Farm. Someone told me that your brother, Robert, farmed in Tal-y-Cafn and gave me the name of his farm, so I went there. His son, Euryn, Mabli's twin, thought you'd know more about her, so here I am.'

'He would have found it much too difficult to talk about the tragedy which befell her.'

It was Jared's turn for his eyes to open wide in surprise at this – he had obviously been hoping to find Mabli alive and well, living in the area.

She shook her head sadly.

'It was all a long time ago now – but I still remember the events clearly.'

He took a gulp of his tea, as if to fortify himself for bad news.

'Llan Farm was sold after the death of my brother, Hugh. His wife, Lettie, did not want to carry on with it even though Mabli had been working there to help her out.'

'Yes, that's when I met Mabli.'

'Mabli realised that Lettie was intending to sell the farm, so she made her way home to her parents,' Mary Ellen continued, looking into the distant past. 'They were very angry with her when it dawned on them that she was carrying a child.'

'You see, she was only fourteen then,' she added, looking up at him.

Jared shuffled uncomfortably.

'I suspect that it was my child she was carrying,' he said in a low voice, looking shamefaced.

'You? You were the father?' asked Mary Ellen angrily. 'She never told a single soul.'

'I wanted to stay to help her but when I told my father about it, he made us all leave the village almost immediately to return to America, as he could not face the scandal.'

'Do you realise you caused her death?' responded Mary Ellen ruthlessly, as she looked directly at him with her rheumy eyes.

'She was tired of being locked up at home to hide her shame from the neighbours. So she left the farm early one morning and was making her way over to me here in Capelulo on foot. She had reached the top of the Pass when she was violently assaulted by a tramp. Her birth cramps had just started, so she couldn't run from him. He inflicted severe internal injuries on her, just as she went into labour. I was called to fetch her with a cart. We brought her back here and a few hours later, her tiny daughter was born – but Mabli had lost too much blood.'

'A daughter, you say?'

'Yes – Rebecca – but at the cost of Mabli's life. She died giving birth at the tender age of just fifteen. A life hardly lived.'

Jared bowed his head in his hands, shocked and ashamed by what he had just been told. It took him a while to recover himself and when he did look up, his face was pained and ashen. He now wished he'd never come here. He had come hoping to find a happy ending, not news which was to disturb his peace of mind for the rest of his days.

'Oh my God,' he mumbled. 'I never knew.'

'And you never bothered to find out until now. Seems you had your fun, then disappeared.'

'How can I make it up?'

'You can't.' Mary Ellen felt no pity for him and part of her was glad to be able to punish him with her harsh words.

'Can I meet Rebecca?'

'That's entirely up to her. She's a married woman; she will make up her own mind.'

'How can I get in touch with her?'

'You can't. I will tell her about you and ask her whether she wishes to meet you or not. If she does, you can meet her here. I don't want you upsetting her. She doesn't know all the violent circumstances of her birth and she must never know. You can write to me in one week's time. Meanwhile, I will find out what she wants to do. Then I will reply to your letter, to let you know what she decides.'

'If there's any way I can make her life easier? I have plenty of money.'

'I doubt that would interest her. She is already financially comfortable, has a loving husband and a young daughter.'

'She has a daughter? I have a granddaughter as well?' What's her name?'

'Lowri.'

'Let me pay for her education.'

Undeterred and insensitive, Jared continued, even after Mary Ellen's look of utter disdain.

'I have grown-up children but my wife, who was always delicate, died a year ago. I don't want to brag – but I have done well in industry and am very wealthy.'

'I lost my husband, Matthew, very young, then our son slipped and died in the river below, a year later,' Mary Ellen said quietly, her eyes swimming with uncharacteristic tears of self-pity.

'I'm so sorry to hear that. You had to bear all that and then the tragic death of Mabli.'

Mary Ellen did not know how to respond to this, so after a long, painful silence, Jared continued.

'I was always aware I'd treated Mabli badly. I was a young, irresponsible lad – we were both still children really. But I felt I had no choice than to do as my father told me and leave for America. I have often thought of her and have wanted to make amends for years. I was very fond of her, you know; she was quite a character.'

'Well, she's not here, so you can't. Give your guilt money to charity instead, we don't need it. There's a home for waifs and strays at the top of the Pass. The former owner, Olwen, was the one who found and helped Mabli on the day she was attacked. She beat the attacker off with her stick – but it was all too late. Give your money to the foundlings they look after there. Pay for their education.'

'I'll give it some consideration,' Jared replied.

After a long, thoughtful pause, he concluded he had done what he had come here to do, so rose to his feet.

'I'll say good day to you then, Mary Ellen. Thank you for the refreshments. Thank you for having the courtesy of seeing me and telling me what happened to Mabli. As I say, it's the one big regret of my life.'

As he left, he gave her a business card.

'In case one of your family should ever want to get in touch.'

Did Jared ever get his wish to meet Rebecca? Maybe not – but instead of the children's home, he left her a great deal of money in his Will.

* * *

Barely two weeks after Jared's visit, Mary Ellen received a second visitor – her brother Robert's son, Euryn, twin of the late Mabli. By contrast, he had travelled by horseback over the mountains from Tal-y-Cafn.

This visitor was a bit more welcome. Again, she asked him to be taken to the parlour and given something to eat as she slowly got herself dressed and made her way downstairs.

'*Wyt ti'n cadw'n dda?*' she said as she entered.

Euryn, shocked to see her so aged, rushed to help her into the upright chair.

'*Iawn, diolch.*'

As Mary Ellen looked at him, she saw a typical-looking, prosperous farmer. His face was florid and weathered. She noticed he was wearing his best clothes for the occasion: a fine blended green wool jacket, checked shirt, brown corduroy trousers and shiny brown brogues.

'I believe you had an American visitor recently. I knew he must have been connected to Mabli somehow, as he seemed determined to find her. I hope you didn't mind me sending him to you – I couldn't face talking to him about what happened.'

Mary Ellen thought it was just as well that Euryn had not realised that the American had fathered Mabli's child, as he may very well have reacted badly, even violently.

'But what I really want to talk to you about, Aunty Mary Ellen, is what I should do with the farm. As you know I'm a *'hen lanc'* – never met the right woman, I suppose, so have no children – that I know about anyway!' he said, laughing at his own joke.

Mary Ellen gave him a withering look at his bad taste. Undeterred, he swallowed hard and carried on; he was not going to be put off his mission.

'As I've no children of my own, I have been wondering about who should inherit the Tal-y-Cafn farm. There is no one on my mam, Sara's side left. Of course, the farm had belonged initially to her family, then her sister Megan had died young. Uncle Thomas, who went to Patagonia, then Canada had no children. Your lad, Matthew junior, died young, and Uncle Hugh and Lettie had no children. Mabli is dead of course, but at least she had Rebecca.'

'When I think about it,' Euryn reflected, 'out of all my father's surviving siblings, the only one keeping the bloodline going now is Rebecca's daughter, Lowri. What a sorry lot we are, eh? So, I have decided to leave the farm in Tal-y-Cafn to Lowri. She can either let it to a tenant or sell it. So that's why I'm here, to let you know that I have written my Will, stating that she should inherit it.'

Mary Ellen nodded her snowy white head in agreement – but goodness knows what Lowri will do with a farm, she thought, and a substantial one at that.

'The other thing is, I've brought the old family Bible with me, the one with the family tree in it.' Euryn pulled it out of the saddle bag he had brought in with him.

'There is a box of old photographs and certificates here too; not sure what they all are. They'll be safer here and you can give them to Rebecca if Jane doesn't want them.'

Mary Ellen shook her head from side to side. She already had enough memories floating about in her old head, she did not need to be bombarded with any more. Well, she thought, she didn't have to look at it if she didn't want to, did she?

Undeterred by her luke-warm reaction, Euryn determinedly placed the Bible on a gateleg table in the parlour, as if to say she had no choice but to accept it as he would not be taking it back with him.

'I'll leave this here then.......oh, and there's a little silver trinket box I found in Mabli's dressing-table drawer – Rebecca might like it. And a couple of very old folded up notes – don't know what they are – haven't read them.'

Mary Ellen suspected that this was because his eyesight was not too good.

Later, after he had left, Mary Ellen wrote Rebecca's name in the Bible, as daughter to Mabli, as well as recording the date of Mabli's death. Next, she entered Rebecca's husband, Richard and their daughter, Lowri.

Then it occurred to her that apart from Euryn, she was the only one left who knew what had befallen Mabli, although she had told Rebecca years before some of what happened.

'Maybe if I was to sit down and write what I remember,' she thought, 'it might all stop swirling around in my head, as it has done for years. But I won't mention the ghost that is said to haunt the top of the Pass every year on the anniversary of Mabli's death; a ghost which throws itself into the path of moving vehicles as they drive down the Pass so that when they arrive at the village hostelry, they demand a glass of brandy to steady their nerves.'

Luckily, given it was summer, her arthritis was not too bad – but her handwriting had become quite shaky. Nevertheless, she began:

To whom it may concern:

I am Mary Ellen Rowlands, widow of Matthew, mother of Jane and the deceased Matthew junior. I am great-aunt to Rebecca, whose mother was my brother Robert's twin daughter, Mabli, and am great-great-aunt to her daughter, Lowri.

At the tender age of fourteen, Mabli found herself with child and abandoned by its father, Jared Knox, an American. Her father Robert was very angry with her and kept her locked in her room. She was a very beautiful, spirited girl and escaped out of her locked bedroom through the window, then climbed across the roof to the barn where she dropped down onto the hay. She had decided to walk from their farm in Tal-y-Cafn to see me in Capelulo. At the top of the Pass, already in labour, she was violently attacked by a vagrant, who left her half dead. She was brought down to Bodhyfrydle - but we failed to save her life. She had lost too much blood, but we managed to save her daughter, Rebecca, who was then brought up by me. Rebecca married builder, Richard Griffiths. They have one daughter, Lowri.

Mary Ellen Rowlands

When she had finished writing, she thought that hopefully, this note would serve as a link from the people in the Bible family tree to today's family. She knew Rebecca would never look at it anyway, so had no concern on that score. But maybe Lowri or her descendants would be interested someday.

Tired from all the effort and somewhat emotionally drained, she fashioned a sleeve from some white card by partially gluing it along the edges onto the inside of the back cover of the Bible. When the ink and glue had dried properly, she tucked her note and the business card Jared had given her, inside the sleeve.

After she had done that, she saw the little silver trinket box that Euryn had left on the table. Picking it up to examine it, she wondered where it had come from. It was a pretty little thing with a purple velvet lining. Little did she know that if it had been there a few weeks earlier, Jared could have told her.

Opening it, she saw two folded-up notes. She pulled one out and opened the folds carefully, as the paper was quite old. What beautiful writing, she thought. When she read the contents of the note, however, she realised just as Robert had done, that Old Tom had actually been her grandfather. She picked up a pencil and faintly wrote his name up above her father, Efan's name in the Bible. Another shock to deal with, she thought.

She didn't read the second note but pushed them both firmly inside the bottom of the Bible's new sleeve, then went to lie down, hopefully to fall into the unconscious bliss of a deep sleep.

Mary Ellen died in 1938 at the grand old age of 88. She left the tea-rooms to her daughter, Jane, who carried on running them until she finally passed away. Jane in turn left the tea-rooms in trust for Rebecca's granddaughter.

Euryn never married and died in 1948.

Chapter 10

I know that Mary Ellen lived in Capelulo and her marriage certificate cites St. Gwynan's Church, so I decide that the cemetery next to the church might be worth a visit to see if I can find her grave.

When I get there, I realise that it is quite a big cemetery, so decide to take my time and methodically go along the rows, as I don't want to risk missing anything. Again, I am fascinated by some of the detail I read on the headstones and could easily go off at a tangent but make myself stay focused.

I notice that some of the graves in the deserted cemetery have completely or partially collapsed or are sinking. Some have had wooden stakes put in to hold up the headstones. Many are overgrown with bramble but some have obviously been lovingly tended and have fresh flowers in the vases. After about an hour and half, I finally come across a black polished granite headstone with gold lettering which reads:

Matthew Rowlands of Bodhyfrydle
died tragically in 1877 aged 29 years
Beloved husband of Mary Ellen
Also their son Matthew who died tragically in 1878
Safe in the hands of God
Also buried here is Mary Ellen
who died in 1938 aged 88 years

Well, finally my perseverance is paying off. I have actually found Mary Ellen's family grave. What a gratifying moment! I take a photograph to cross check with the dates in the Bible family tree and to put in my reference file. The grave itself is a bit unkempt but sound and I spend some time just tidying it up a little.

As I prepare to leave, I turn to head for the kissing gate near the little path which runs alongside the cemetery. Unable to switch off from reading the inscriptions, a name on a small white marble headstone suddenly catches my eye:

Mabli Jones
died tragically in 1907, aged 15 years
Daughter of Robert and Sara Jones
Fferm Cae Isaf, Tal-y Cafn

I wonder what the tragedy was which befell Mabli and why she was buried here.

* * *

I look again at the photo of the couple outside the tea-rooms and compare it with another black and white photo of a young girl with an older lady. This lady looks like an older version of the woman in that happy couple. She is still beautiful despite her years but there is a deep unfathomable sorrow etched there in her face.

I am always fascinated with the social lives of those who have lived before us, so much so that I have recently joined a local Historical Society which meets once a month. Some of the members have an excellent knowledge of local history, so at the next meeting, I take the photo of the couple outside the tea-rooms with me.

'Do any of you recognise this building?' I ask, showing the photograph to a small, pre-talk group.

They say it looks very familiar but cannot quite place it. They suggest that I show it to local historian, Mr. Davies.

'Oh yes, I recognise it. That building is in the village of Capelulo. It used to be tea-rooms. Looks to me like that photo was probably taken in the nineteen-twenties. Best go and speak to Lily Ann Edwards up at Nant Uchaf – she has lived there all her life. She's pretty old now but her memory is excellent. She might know a bit more about who lived in the house in the nineteen-twenties.'

I thank him profusely and decide I will go to the village at the weekend to look for the house and to try and speak to Lily Ann.

* * *

Lily Ann is quite the village character.

'I used to sell sweets and pop here on a little stall outside the cottage, to the people who walked past on their way up the Fairy

Glen,' she tells me. 'You wouldn't think to look at me now, but I was quite a beauty in my youth, you know – but I lost my heart to a young man who sadly let me down. I never quite got over that,' pensively looking down and fiddling with her hands.

She is dressed in clothes that have not seen a good wash for months; they give off an air of staleness. Her woollen, fingerless gloves are grubby, her nails black, her stumpy teeth rotten and she wears rough workman's boots on her feet. Her iron-grey hair, probably once black, is pinned up in a messy bun on top of her head but many stray tendrils have escaped their captivity and are dangling untidily around her face. But her eyes are young, a kindly periwinkle-blue, while her heart is gold – and she seems glad to talk to me of the past.

I don't know quite how to respond to the unsolicited information about the lost beau, so change the subject by asking her about the former occupants of the tea-rooms.

'Oh yes, I remember when I was a young girl, Bodhyfrydle was a tea-room then. We didn't go there, mind, didn't have two ha'pennies to rub together, us. I remember Mother telling me that the assistant housekeeper from Pendyffryn Hall had bought it from the man who had lost his wife suddenly. It was a post office before then as I recall. But she wasn't destined to be happy there. It was all quite tragic really. A few years after they moved here, she lost her husband very young, then her little boy soon after. Both fell in the river and died, that's why Mother always warned me never to play near it. The tea-rooms were very popular though – people came here in the posh charabancs to walk up the Glen, then went there for afternoon tea.'

'Can you remember her name, Mrs. Edwards?'

'Oh, I'm not Mrs., young man, just call me Lily Ann. Everybody else does. Now let me think. Oh yes…. Mrs. Rowlands comes to mind; I think that was the owner's name. I used to play sometimes with Rebecca who lived there. I don't think she was her daughter though – her orphaned niece, as I recall.'

'Thank you…..Lily Ann, you've been a great help.'

Now that she has told me about somebody from Pendyffryn Hall buying it, I have the link to the staff photo there. I am now convinced that the maid in that photo and the woman in the photo of the couple standing proudly outside the tea-rooms are both Mary Ellen, daughter of Efan, of Llan Farm. The man standing next to her must be her husband, Matthew Rowlands.

When I return home, I look again at the two photos of Mary Ellen. How strange – there is a look of Alys around Mary Ellen's eyes. Here I go again! My mind always drifts back to thinking about Alys. I think I am becoming infatuated by her. She has a way of getting into my head, as well as quietly slipping into my heart. This thinking happens far more often than is healthy for me these days as I obsessively see her in everything.

Then I find two more photos that appear to be also of Mary Ellen, but older. In one of them, there is a baby in an old-fashioned pram in the background. In the other, Mary Ellen is holding the hand of a young girl. Maybe this is the Rebecca who Lily Ann mentioned playing with as a child.

* * *

Rebecca's Story

Rebecca had an idyllic homelife with her three mothers and was popular with the village children with whom she mixed well, as children do. Their outdoor surroundings were their playground; they had the heady freedom of having many exciting places to play. They liked to build dens, climb hills, play hopscotch, conkers, catch stick insects in the river and dam small streams. Occasionally they managed to tickle a brown trout. When Rebecca was not at school, she also liked to help out in the tearooms where Mary Ellen taught her to bake the wonderful cakes they produced for their customers

But it was a very different story for her at school. Having a very strong sense of what was right and wrong, she did not always fit in with the other pupils, nor did she agree with how some things were done at school where she attended in the vestry of Glanrafon chapel, which bounded the church cemetery. Due to being a good, able and conscientious pupil, she attracted the ire of some of the less able boys, who tormented her and called her a 'Miss Goody Two Shoes.'

She was also better dressed than most of the other children – because Mary Ellen, always frugal, was very good at making her nice clothes. While the other girls played in one corner with their cloth or wooden dolls and the boys kicked a ball around the schoolyard, she often stood on her own against the wall, waiting for break to be over so she could get back to the relative safety of the classroom.

One particular boy, Eifion, bullied her mercilessly and teased her for not having a mother or a father.

'You're a bastard, did you know that? Illegitimate. Nobody wanted you around except your potty old Nain,' he would say, taunting her mercilessly in the playground and getting the other boys to join in.

He often tripped her up as she walked past him. He would slyly knock over the ink pot onto her schoolwork when the teacher turned her back to write on the blackboard or knock her elbow as she was carefully writing. Sometimes he would thump her in her upper arm as he walked past, with his middle knuckle sticking out, giving her a dead arm. The only time she got any respite from him was when the pupils were split up to do the practical classes: needlework and cooking for the girls; woodwork and PT for the boys.

One friend she did have was Lily Ann, who lived up the Nant. Lily Ann did not always attend school but on the days she did, they would walk to and from school together. Lily Ann was kind to most people and would often stand up to the bully for her.

Despite Rebecca being an ideal pupil who achieved her Qualifying Certificate, she decided not to stay on any longer at school. She enjoyed her schoolwork, apart from the bullying of course, but there was one other thing she strongly disagreed with. The pupils were not allowed to speak Welsh at school and if they inadvertently did, the teacher would hang a wooden paddle with the words 'Welsh Not' round their necks. This punishment was to shame them for speaking their native language. They had to keep wearing it until another pupil spoke in Welsh, then they could pass it on to them to wear instead. The pupil left wearing it at the end of the week would be severely beaten by the teacher with the wooden paddle.

When Rebecca was given it, she tended to keep it, as she could not bear to pass it on to the younger pupils to see them humiliated and hurt. Consequently, she came in for a lot of punishment because she was usually the last one left wearing it. The rationale for this policy of the Education Department was to make the pupils proficient in English. Rebecca, however, was competent in both languages, so not only was it unnecessarily harsh but also there was little point giving it to her. Her refusal to comply made the teachers eventually realise that it was not having the desired effect and they no longer used it on her.

The use of this form of punishment gradually started to wane, as did many of the previous norms by which people had lived their lives at that time. Thankfully, things slowly began to change. During and after the First World War, women had done the jobs of the men while they were away fighting and many were reluctant to give up this new independence and wage-earning ability.

Although plenty of men had initially volunteered to join the Army at the beginning of the war, the Military Service Act was introduced in 1916, which imposed a compulsory call-up. There were of course some exceptions, such as poor health, bad eyesight, or being involved in the production of food. But those who did join up left a shortage of workers in a number of workplaces. This was the case with the Capelulo village grocery shop.

By 1918, it was clear that the previous worker was not going to return to his job, so Mary Ellen suggested to the owners that they take on Rebecca. Their flour, sugar, tea and other dried goods were usually delivered in large sacks. These had to be weighed and decanted into smaller brown paper bags, then labelled. She was also required to measure and bag dried foods such as beans, lentils, peas, dried fruit and round rice. Butter and cheeses needed cutting into blocks with a fine wire, then wrapping in greaseproof paper. She also did local deliveries on the grocer boy's bicycle once a week.

Initially, Rebecca worked in the shop after school and at weekends but later became a full-time member of staff. There was now less trade at the tea-rooms, so they could cope without her. She was glad to leave school – and the bully – behind.

Rebecca became friendly with the children of the next-door Glyn Chapel, who had recently moved into the caretaker's accommodation below the chapel. She started attending Sunday School classes with them, joined the chapel choir and belonged to the Band of Hope.

Over time, she grew fond of the son, Roly, who later worked in the new bakery which had been built behind the shop by the local builder, Richard Griffiths. The bakery supplied all the bread to the village shop and other customers.

One of the benefits for Rebecca of working in the shop was that she was allowed to have some of the prized, tightly-woven, empty flour sacks. Once washed, these were put to a multitude of good uses by Mary Ellen, such as making clothes, toys, quilts, curtains, pillowcases, undergarments, nappies and dishcloths. The manufacturers became aware of this and began putting patterns on them, to encourage more women to recognise their brand.

Mary Ellen had proudly watched as baby Rebecca grew up over the years to become a lovely young woman, who was far more sensible and less impulsive than her mother, Mabli.

In the village shop, Rebecca looked the part of an efficient shop assistant, behind the thick wooden countertop, with her black taffeta skirt hemmed to just show off her pretty ankles. Her white bordelaise anglaise blouse with its cuffed full-length sleeves and high round neckline topped off the outfit. Her dark hair was usually tied back with a black velvet ribbon, or piled high on top of her head as she got older. To protect her clothes, she wore a voluminous square-fronted white starched apron, which she tied into a neat bow at the back. She was very popular with the customers, who liked to pass the time of day with her – but she never gossiped about anybody; she had learned at school what a cruel tongue could do to a person.

Rebecca loved her job in the shop and liked dealing with the suppliers. One particular favourite, who flirted outrageously with her, was Johnny Onion. He cycled over from Brittany every year, ladened with strings of pink onions on his bike.

Rebecca had been told the story that about a hundred years earlier, a Breton farmer decided it would be quicker to sail to Plymouth to sell his onions than face a long road journey to Paris. He was so successful that more and more 'Onion Johnnies' joined him each year – selling everywhere but particularly in Wales, where there was an affinity due to the similarity of their languages.

Rebecca and Roly had been close from when they first met and had decided while still youngsters that they would one day marry each other. Later, Roly was taken on as a gamekeeper on the Glyn Estate, whose land abutted the curtilage of the chapel. But even though gamekeeping was more the outdoor type of job which Roly craved after the heat of the bakery ovens, he never seemed to quite settle into it. He was a restless spirit.

Then one day, out of the blue, Rebecca was devastated to be told by his sister, Grace, that Roly had suddenly upped sticks and joined the Merchant Navy. She said their mother was distraught, whilst Rebecca was left feeling abandoned and jilted by him. For a while, she was beside herself with grief and anger. With the promise of a life with him gone, her already fragile confidence was shattered – and she soon became withdrawn and despondent.

But life and work carried on. After about three years, she realised that Richard, the builder, was calling in the shop far more often than was really necessary. He had heard the rumour that she had been let down once before. He was very shy around women generally and was still single but he eventually plucked up courage.

'Rebecca – is it alright if I call you Rebecca?' he asked, while twisting his flat cap.

She nodded encouragingly.

'Would you like me to take you to this village dance?' as he pointed to the poster which was advertising it in the shop window.

'I'd like that very much,' she replied and was rewarded with a massive happy grin.

'Right then,' he said, not quite believing his luck, 'I'll pick you up by your gate at seven o'clock tomorrow evening.'

After that, they courted for about two years before he finally asked her to marry him. Richard was quite a bit older than her – but they were very fond of each other and comfortable together. He was a very hard worker and during their engagement, he started building them a large house on a plot he'd purchased on the edge of Glan-y-Coed Park. When they did go out, it was generally to a local dance. They both enjoyed ballroom dancing and became very proficient.

Richard's business flourished and expanded. He went on to build many of the fashionable grand period residences during the time when Penmaenmawr was popular as a tourist destination.

Despite wanting more, they only had one child, Lowri, in 1928.

* * *

In 1948, Rebecca was surprised to receive a letter from America:

> *Conrad and Sons*
> *Attorneys at Law*
> *Wills, Trusts, Estates*
> *Main Street, Connecticut*
> *USA*

Dear Miss Rowlands

I write to inform you that your father, Jared Knox, has bequeathed to you the sum of $750,000 from his estate.

He has also left you a property in the Parish of Eglwysbach, called Ty Mawr Llan.

Please advise us at the above address as to which account we can remit the aforementioned sum.

Please also advise us of the name and address of your solicitors so that we can arrange for the conveyance of the said property.

Yours truly
Jessie Conrad
Senior Partner

Although she had never met him, Rebecca was sad to hear of her father's death. She had learned about him from Mary Ellen when he had paid her a visit. At that time, Rebecca had declined the opportunity to meet him but later, having reflected on it, had regretted what was probably the only impulsive decision she had made in her entire life. Perhaps it was her lack of confidence at the time which had clouded her judgement.

However, she was more than pleased to receive the money, the amount of which was increased by the proceeds of Ty Mawr Llan, which she decided to sell.

Sadly, Rebecca didn't have much time to enjoy her inheritance.

Once Lowri was old enough to be left at home in the evenings, Rebecca and Richard started to enter dancing competitions far and wide and won many silver cups due to their dedication and style. They presented as a very handsome couple.

One of their favourite venues was Payne's Majestic Ballroom on Mostyn Street in Llandudno. They would go there regularly for dinner, then dance the night away on the wonderfully sprung dance floor until the band stopped playing at 11 o'clock.

'They've got the Cliff Gwilliams Band playing tonight. Should be good,' said Richard to Rebecca while she sat at her dressing table putting on her jewellery, spraying her eau de toilette and checking her hair.

'That's good,' Rebecca replied, 'he likes to play lots of Foxtrot tunes, so we can practice our dance moves for the competition in Bangor next week.'

'There. I'm ready,' she said, as she finished off powdering her nose with her powder puff compact, which she slipped into her black patent leather handbag for later. Standing up, she looked lovely in her favourite polka dot dance frock with its full flared skirt, which showed off her slim waistline, with white shoes and gloves.

They liked to eat dinner up on the Balcony Café, where they watched people coming and going on the dancefloor below, before themselves joining in with the dancers who moved in a circular movement around the edge of the ballroom.

Come the night of the competition the following week, they were both getting ready to go out.

'You look pretty as a picture, Rebecca.'

Richard was always proud to lead her onto the dance floor with a flourish. But tonight, she looked exceptionally stunning in one of her competition dresses, of pink tulle, with its sequinned bodice and many layers of lace petticoats.

He didn't look too shabby himself, in his black dinner jacket. His work as a builder had helped him to keep his well-proportioned body in shape.

'Don't forget your patent leather dance shoes,' said Rebecca.

'Already got them in the car,' he replied. 'Let's go or we'll be late.'

Dusk was falling as they made their way down the drive of Glan-y-Coed Park in their Sunbeam Talbot, to which they had treated themselves out of Rebecca's inheritance. Richard drove carefully down Glanrafon Road towards the Ship Inn. He turned left at the T-junction in the direction of Llanfairfechan. This was the main A5 road to Holyhead.

As they exited the Pen-y-Clip tunnel road, which had been built to replace the old road higher up the mountain, Rebecca said,

'I wonder who will be competing tonight in the…………'

* * *

'I was walking from Llanfairfechan towards Penmaenmawr when I heard a very loud cracking sound coming from above on the mountain. I looked up and saw this massive boulder starting to fall. It began hurtling and bouncing down the mountain towards the road below. I could see the lights of a car coming towards me and thought it might hit it. I waved my arms to try to warn them, but it was hopeless. I was too late. It was as if it all happened before my eyes in slow motion, as I saw the boulder finally bounce onto the roof of the car. There was a terrible, terrible sound of metal being crushed as it landed.'

The workman was telling the local newspaper reporter who had soon arrived at the scene, what he had witnessed. It was clear to the reporter that the man was completely traumatised. He was in shock and still visibly shaking as he was speaking to him.

The driver of the first car to arrive on the scene had soon realised that the occupants were beyond help, so continued driving straight to the nearest red telephone box to call 999 to alert them about the accident. The police and an ambulance were immediately despatched, followed by a doctor.

'They would both have been killed instantly,' the doctor later reported. 'There was nothing I could do when I arrived there. It was an horrific scene.' It had affected him so much that he had turned away and vomited; he felt sorry for the police and other workmen who would have to clear it all away.

That same evening, as Rebecca and Richard's daughter, Lowri, was busy clearing up in the kitchen, she saw the headlights of a car pull up outside the house. Curious, she had reached the hall, when there was a knock on her front door, which she opened to find a policeman standing there.

'Good evening, Mrs. Jones. May I come in please?'

He knew Lowri personally and she wondered at his formality. He removed his police helmet and tucked it under his arm.

'I am here in my official capacity,' he said gravely.

Once he had been shown into the sitting room he shuffled uncomfortably, declining the seat he was offered. This was one part of the job he did not relish.

'I regret to have to inform you that both your parents are dead.'

Lowri's hand flew up to her mouth. The shock she felt was profound, palpable. Her legs suddenly felt weak, as she collapsed down on the nearest sofa.

'What….what happened?' she asked tearfully, as her husband, Edward came into the room and put his arm around her shoulders protectively.

'Earlier this evening, they were driving along Pen-y-Clip in the direction of Llanfairfechan, when an extremely large boulder fell onto the top of their car. I'm sorry to tell you they were both killed instantly.'

Lowri was beside herself and hysterical with grief.

'They were both far too young to die, they were devoted to each other,' Lowri reflected to Edward later when she had become more coherent. 'They loved their dancing. What am I going to do without them?'

Edward, was a great comfort to her in her bereavement.

As her parents' only child, Lowri inherited their house and eventually decided with Edward to move their family into it. It was comforting to be surrounded by her mother's things in the house her father had built.

The report in the local newspaper suggested that the accident had resulted from a recent storm, which had brought in heavy rain and high winds. These had combined to cause the large boulder to become dislodged and fall.

At the subsequent Inquest, a verdict of Accidental Death was returned on Rebecca and Richard. The coroner recommended that action should be taken to prevent any repetition of this type of accident at this location.

In view of this and also the fact that the area had a history of rockfalls over the years, the local council decided to commission an extensive programme of building check-fences. When completed, they had secured any loose and overhanding rocks, preventing them falling onto the road below in the future.

Chapter 11

Alys is studying at her aunt's house this afternoon and won't be here for hours yet. It's a beautiful day for a trip up the Conwy Valley, so I decide to drive to Eglwysbach. I find Llan Farm easily and stand in the High Street looking at it. I think how strange it is to have a farm frontage onto a high street – but I suppose the other buildings were erected later, as the village grew.

I notice that there is a deserted manor-type house close by, with the name Ty Mawr Llan at the entrance. I imagine that the farm had probably serviced this house originally.

I have recently searched parish records for proof of where Efan was born and who his parents were, but without success. There is an entry in the district of an Efan Jones, an illegitimate child, but because it is such a common name, it is inconclusive. It could be anybody, as neither parent was recorded for him.

I decide to walk along to St Martin's churchyard to see what I can dig up there – pardoning my own macabre pun. I plan to look for the graves of the Jones Bible family, who had farmed at Llan Farm around 1850.

Presently, after going up and down the rows of graves, I come across the Sexton, who is busy digging a fresh grave.

'Excuse me. I wonder if you could help? I'm looking for the graves of a Jones family who had lived at Llan Farm in the eighteen-hundreds.'

Glad of a break from his digging, he raises his arm to wipe the sweat from his forehead onto his sleeve.

'I know that there is a children's one just over there – that small headstone by the wall' he says, pointing me in the right direction.

I find it. It is a simple rounded granite headstone engraved:

In memory of
William Kyffin Jones of Llan Farm
died tragically in 1855 aged seven years
*Here also lieth his younger brother **William Jones***
who died aged six in 1864

Safe in God's hands forever

I remember seeing the first-born William on the family tree. He had definitely died aged seven, and then another William had been born later, who died aged six. Brothers – this is most definitely the Bible family. The first-born and the last-born of Efan and Myfanwy's children – these dates correspond. Maybe there are more family members buried nearby. Then my eye is caught by a tall purple slate headstone which is inscribed:

> **Hedd Perfaith Hedd**
> **Buried below is Robert Jones who died in 1918**
> **and his wife Sara who died in 1920**
> **Also their son, Euryn, who died in 1948 aged 56**
> **twin brother of Mabli**

This must be the family of Efan's son, Robert.

Next to Robert's family grave is an older, taller purple slate headstone with a carving of a wheatsheaf on the top, which I believe is a symbol of resurrection after death. As I read it, it dawns on me that I have at last found Efan's grave. In fact, a relative cluster of graves, once more pardoning my own pun.

> **Here lies Myfanwy Jones**
> **who departed this earth 1865**
> **Beloved wife of Efan Jones of Llan Farm**
> **also buried below, who died in 1894**

Well, well, well! What a triumphal moment!

I have found the family's graves at last. Three graves belonging to the same family, the family of Efan Jones who started the family tree. Well, I never…..

What a discovery! What jubilation! I feel elated. I want to tell Alys straight away. Yes – his wife's name was Myfanwy and they had a son called Robert. I take photographs of each grave, so I can cross check dates when I get back.

Driving back, I divert to Capelulo to see if I can find

Bodhyfrydle, as I didn't have the time when I was there before, speaking to Lily Ann. I have discovered that Bodhyfrydle is a common house name in Wales, meaning 'pleasant place.'

I park the car and start walking up the road.

And then I recognise it – in all its glory! Bathed in sunshine. This is indeed the very same property as in the black and white photograph, with the handsome couple standing outside the glazed porch.

I take a photograph of it, before getting in my car and driving home to cross-check all the details I have uncovered this afternoon.

Once home, I get the Bible out to check the dates with the graves. Looking at the family tree, it occurs to me that I have not devoted much time to the more recent names. My attention is drawn to Lowri, which I consider an unusual name.

When I ask one of my Welsh-speaking colleagues about the name, she tells me that it means 'Laurel.'

* * *

Lowri's Story – Part 1

'I see that Brief Encounter is on at the Crescent Cinema. Do you fancy going to see it on Saturday?'

Edward was a few years older than Lowri but she had been drawn to him from the first time they met for his gentle ways and good looks. They had been courting for about a year or so now and she was quite smitten with him.

Edward had returned from the War about a year earlier in 1944, having been invalided out of the army due to trauma. However, with rest and recuperation he had gradually been getting better, so much so that he had recently been promoted to Manager at the local bank where he worked. He now felt he had some status. Something to offer.

They had first met at the village dance hall. Lowri had been longing for Edward to ask her out, as he was quite a catch in his Fair Isle pullover, grey flannels and tan brogues. When he did finally ask her to dance, she was quite impressed with his dancing.

'When did you learn to dance so well then?' she asked him, as they waltzed around the floor.

'Oh, I used to take my mother to the Old Time Dancing evenings, upstairs in the Young Men's Institute before war broke out and I suppose you don't easily forget the routines. I also used to go there to hear the excellent lectures they put on.'

After that, they started going out as a couple and several months passed by contentedly. Now they were going to see Brief Encounter at the Crescent Cinema, which was not far away from the Institute in the village.

The lights came up at the end of the performance and people stood for the National Anthem, before starting to shuffle slowly out of the cinema.

'Listen,' said Edward. 'There's something I've been meaning to ask you. Can I come over to your house tomorrow afternoon? Will your father be in?'

'Yes, of course; it's Saturday, come for tea at three. I'll make us some scones.'

'You certainly know the way to this man's heart,' he replied.

'I certainly hope so,' she said under her breath, as they exited the main foyer.

They eventually married in 1947. Their twin daughters were born three years later. Lowri never discussed the tragic deaths of her parents with the twins.

* * *

'Ellen and Gwenda, come on,' said Lowri. 'What's the hold-up now?'

'I'm looking for my fishing net so I can catch tiddlers in the rock pools,' Gwenda replied.

'It's under the stairs. Do hurry up, we'll never get there at this rate. The tide will be too far out for you to swim soon.'

The ladened little party of three finally set off from Glan-y-Coed Park. They took a shortcut between the fields onto Glanrafon Road, then walked towards the Ship Inn on the A5. Mid-morning, there wasn't much traffic about, so they easily crossed the road, then went through the rounded little corrugated-iron-roofed tunnel under the railway line onto the beach.

To the accompaniment of 'oohs' and 'aahs,' they walked carefully but painfully in their plimsolls across a swathe of blue, purple and grey granite pebbles, weathered smooth by the sea and millennia of tempestuous north-westerly storms.

When they finally reached the soft, rich-brown demerara-like sand, it was balm to their soles, after the relentless hardness of the pebbles.

Dropping their towels, buckets and spades where they stood, the girls hopped as they threw off their shorts, then dashed ahead into the crashing waves. Their elasticated, ruched swimsuits with the sweetheart necklines were instantly soaked.

Lowri had brought the small woven picnic basket and a Welsh tapestry rug to sit on. She propped up her white broderie anglaise sun parasol and looked a picture in her French-blue polka-dot sundress as she read her book and listened to the sound of the waves, which she found endlessly relaxing.

Intermittently, she looked up as the girls frolicked and swam about, splashing each other. Both swam like otters, so she did not need to worry about them on this safe, isolated bit of beach. But it would be a different story in the bay just around the nearby headland, notorious for its sudden rip tides and soft sinking sands.

Weather permitting, summer holidays from school were more often than not spent on this beach; an important part of the idyllic pattern of their privileged childhood.

'Come in now, you two,' she shouted, waving both arms. 'Dry off a bit, then you can have something to eat.'

As they reached the shoreline, she handed them each a beach towel, which they quickly wrapped around themselves. They then sat on their towels, leaving the sun and wind to finish off drying their nylon costumes.

Lowri set out the fishpaste sandwiches, Madeira cake and the bottle of homemade lemonade on the blanket and they were soon tucking in, ravenous after their swim.

Even though they were her own children, Lowri still thought they were lovely girls, who until recently, had got on well together. Lately though, she noticed there was an edge to Gwenda, who seemed to be becoming jealous of her sister, Ellen. They were non-identical twins, with completely different personalities and characters. Ellen was popular, amenable to everybody and artistically talented. Gwenda on the other hand seemed socially awkward, lumpy, often grumpy, but with a good aptitude for arithmetic.

Lowri really couldn't understand it. She felt she had treated them both equally – but Gwenda always seemed to think her sister was the favourite and was frequently heard to bemoan, 'That's not fair.'

'Mmm, these are good,' said Ellen.

'Well, don't eat them all. I want some more,' retorted Gwenda.

'I'm not……'

'Now now girls, that's enough, there's plenty for everybody. When you finish eating, why don't you build a sandcastle? The tide's gone out a bit already.'

The next hour was spent building a replica of what they said was Conwy Castle. Then they dug a channel running in to it from the sea, to form a moat. Soon, it was time to go home.

'Come on, let's pack up. Your father will be home soon and I have to make tea.'

Their house had been left to Lowri after the tragic death of her parents. It was large enough for the twins to play inside or out – so they did not need to go far from home. They spent many hours playing in the well-kept gardens, or up in the cedar tree-house their father had built for them, where they read, played lookout or sea pirates.

Ellen would sometimes walk up to the tea-rooms with Lowri on Sunday afternoons. Gwenda thought it was boring there, so stayed home with her father who set her little sums to do.

On their walk up there, they would meet and chat with some members of the Glyn Chapel congregation, on their way back home from their afternoon service. Lowri knew most of them – but she still attended St Gwynan's Church, where she was married. She knew the original church had been re-built in 1889 and her favourite part was the window of three leaded lights in a square frame. She also liked entering through the lychgate with its quaint little tiled roof and would often shelter there from a squall of rain, as she waited for the *Bws Bach Hên Bentre* to take her down to Pant-yr-Afon to shop.

Once, when they were seated at one of the tables in the garden of the tea-rooms, Lowri had cast her eyes across the front of the house.

'You might even live here one day,' she had mused whimsically.

'But I want to live with you!' Ellen exclaimed, not understanding what she meant.

At this, Lowri smiled fondly at her.

The place brought back happy memories for Lowri from when she was a girl, and Rebecca would take her there. In an unguarded moment, Rebecca had told Lowri the sanitised version of the story of their connection to the place, which she had learnt from Mary Ellen after the visit of an American gent.

'I was born up there in that bedroom – but I nearly died,' Rebecca had said mysteriously. 'It was all very tragic apparently. My mother had got herself into trouble with a young American.'

'Years later,' Rebecca continued after a pause, 'the American turned up looking for my mother, claiming to be my father. I could have met him but thought, what's the point? He wasn't in my life when I needed him. But later he left me a very nice little legacy in his Will. Maybe I should have met him. But I was married by then and was quite comfortable anyway, thank you. My only regret in life is that you were my only child, Lowri. I would have liked you to have siblings.'

* * *

At the back of their house in Glan-y-Coed Park, was a red-bricked, walled garden. Ellen liked to go there to escape her annoying sister, who somehow always managed to create tension. She let herself in through the faded green, metal-barred gate, which protected the garden. It had, what she thought of as a row of pointed spears reaching for the sky, standing guard over the garden. All they needed for defence was some magical propulsion to make them fire at the oncoming enemy.

The garden grew a variety of long-established soft fruits and trees. Along the south-facing wall in full sun were bushes of raspberries, gooseberries and cranberries. Trained along the back wall were fruit trees: Cox's apples, Bramleys, Conference pears and quince. In the corner was an ancient Victoria plum tree.

In the centre of the garden was the old, ornate greenhouse, built by her grandfather. Here, seedlings were sown and copious amounts of tomatoes grew. In the middle of the greenhouse was the large, gnarled old trunk of a vine, whose branches now grew out through an open window in the roof, allowing hot air to escape. All around the greenhouse outside were neat rows of raised vegetable beds, which grew salad vegetables, onions, spinach, cabbages, cauliflowers, leeks, carrots and potatoes.

There were also beds of dahlias, gypsophila, chrysanthemums and carnations, grown to supply the house and for when it was Lowri's turn to provide flowers for the church altar. Beautifully scented tea roses and standard rose bushes grew along the side of the drive up to the house, flanked by the immaculately rolling lawns.

Lowri generally bought her dry groceries from the Co-op, up by the Horeb Chapel, while the boy from Uncle Ned's bakery next door delivered her bread. Occasionally, she would order the ha'penny iced buns as a tea-time treat but generally, did all her own baking.

Lowri spent hours tending the garden, which was her pride and joy. It supplied all the family's seasonal fruit and vegetables for most of the year. Every Friday, Happy Charlie would come and tend the lawns, borders, shrubs and do the heavy digging. Ellen would plonk herself up on the seedling table in the greenhouse as he worked there. She loved talking to him. He in turn, loved her innocent, uncomplicated chatter and was endlessly patient with her.

In the garden, Ellen knew there were secret places where fairies sheltered underneath the larger leaves, such as rhubarb. They rarely showed themselves to humans – but she knew they were there, as she often saw the silver dust which they sprinkled from their wands.

'This is a secret,' she told Happy Charlie. 'You mustn't tell anybody – but there are fairies in this garden. I have seen their silver dust on the plants.'

He didn't have the heart to tell her that these were snail trails.

'Why do you walk here?' Ellen asked, ever curious. 'Why don't you come on a bike? It would be quicker.'

'Well,' he said, foot up on a raised bed frame, twirling his moustaches, 'it's like this: I could ride down the Pass and get here very quickly but it would be very hard to push the bike all the way back up the Pass going home, when I am tired at the end of the day.'

'Oh, I see. Do you have a beautiful home like me?'

'Oh yes, it's very quiet and peaceful up there and the view over the Conwy Bay to the Great Orme is magnificent.'

She did not understand that he actually lived in an abandoned, dusty old quarry building out of choice; he preferred to be on his own when he had his attacks, having suffered shell shock during the war. He did not need to live there, as rumour had it that he came from a very wealthy family but had walked away from them all.

'Mammy's making us shepherd's pie for lunch – she asked me to get some pea pods from you when you have a moment.' Most of the locals knew his situation and fed him well on the days he worked in their gardens.

'I'll pick you some now, sweet pea.'

'Why did you plant marigolds with the tomatoes?' she asked as she watched him.

'Because they keep the bugs away.'

Seemingly satisfied with his answers, she went back to what she was doing.

She had been sketching him as he worked. The likeness she captured of him was impressive. She drew the magnificent moustaches covering most of his face and the crinkles around his eyes when he smiled. His collarless shirt, the red kerchief round his neck and the thick twine which held up his brown corduroy trousers, were all replicated accurately.

'There, it's finished,' she declared with a flourish, dropping daintily down from the table in her prettily smocked summer dress.

'What do you think – do you like it?' she said, carefully tearing the sketch from the pad. 'You can have it if you like.'

He paused to examine the sketch.

'I do like it, very much, and I think you are a very talented little girl,' he said, as he handed her a bowl of pea pods in exchange.

***

The girls were growing up rapidly. When they awoke on Boxing Day in 1962, they sensed an eerily silent stillness outside and a strange broody-like morning light.

Ellen drew back the drapes to look out the window.

'It's snowing! Whoopee!' twelve-year old Ellen shouted excitedly. 'Come on lazy bones, get up. We can go sledging.'

They were outside soon after breakfast, togged up in their warm hooded gaberdine mackintoshes, balaclava hats, hand-knitted scarves, gloves and black Dunlop wellington boots.

Their father could not get his car out of the drive to go to work. He had already been to the garage to brush the cobwebs off the old sledges and had put wax along the runners.

'Do you like our snowman, Daddy?' they shouted as he brought out their sledges.

It had a carrot for a nose, coal for eyes and twigs for fingers.

They spent a couple of hours sledging down the drive, until they could no longer feel their fingers and toes. Then Lowri called them in to change out of their wet clothes to have a drink of hot beef tea to thaw out.

By the end of the week, the novelty of the snow had worn off. The freezing weather continued for week upon seemingly endless week and the snow stayed piled up on the roadsides until March. Trapped indoors, the sisters soon began to bicker with each other.

In the evenings, the family sat by the open log fire, listening to the Home Service on the wireless. They heard daily reports that rivers and lakes had frozen solid, of ice boulders on the beaches and even ice floes in the sea. Blizzards caused main and side roads to block, whilst snowploughs could not get through to clear them. Home and shop deliveries were impossible. Telephone lines were down, due to the weight of the icicles which clung to them. Power cuts became normal, candles and oil lamps were used and household pipes froze solid, then burst on thawing.

In mid-January, the coldest day since 1814 was recorded at minus eight degrees Fahrenheit. Drivers had to put chains on the tyres of their cars and extra anti-freeze in the radiators. Sheep had to be dug out of the large snow drifts against the stone walls on the golf course, where they had initially gone for shelter – and many small birds died, unable to get food from the frozen ponds and ground.

Luckily, Lowri had ordered in plenty of coal and Happy Charlie had logged a scrub oak tree, which had come down in a previous storm. She wondered how he was coping up in his stone outbuilding and hoped that he had managed to get himself to the barn at Pen Pyra Farm to keep warm, before the snow had got too deep.

They had plenty of potatoes stored in the sheds and brought them inside before the intense cold could turn them black. Fortunately, Lowri had a good stock of bread flour and fresh yeast and their half a dozen chickens continued to lay despite the cold. They survived, as most did at that time, mainly on tinned food such as spam, corned beef and peaches. Finally, at the end of March, the weather started to improve, bringing a welcome respite.

* * *

Both girls did well at school. Ellen was pretty and popular with everybody. She had plenty of friends, whilst Gwenda's friends were a close-knit circle, whom she ruled with an iron rod.

Unfortunately, their idyllic domestic lifestyle would soon be shattered. Without any warning, Lowri's husband Edward collapsed one day at work from a heart attack and died. This came as a terrible shock to them all as he had always 'been there.'

'What are we going to do without him?' wailed Ellen, after a well-attended funeral.

'We'll be alright, we are well-provided for, so we don't need to worry,' replied Lowri.

When they left school, Gwenda trained as an accountant, while Ellen, with her ability to sketch an exact likeness of any person, went to art school.

Chapter 12

The next task I set myself is to find the Will of Jane, the daughter of Mary Ellen to discover who inherited the tearooms. The following weekend, Alys is studying at her aunt's house again, so I decide to drive down again to the National Library of Wales in Aberystwyth, where Welsh Wills are retained.

According to the family tree in the Bible, Jane died in 1964 and was unmarried, so presumably she was Jane Rowlands. I am gratified that this information proves to be correct. I discover from her Will that she left Bodhyfrydle Tea-Rooms in Capelulo in trust to an Ellen Jones.

* * *

Ellen's Story

Although Ellen had known Edwin Roberts right through school, they had become an 'item' in their teens, following her father's death, as if filling a void he'd left behind. They began spending every possible hour together after school, doing homework together, or just talking about everything and anything. Gwenda soon began to feel left out at their closeness.

Later, much to Gwenda's disgust, they embraced the hippy culture of that period. They grew their hair long, wore head bands and flowers in their hair, beads around their necks and dressed in colourful kaftans. They played their pop records on the red and white Dansette record player, repeatedly and very loudly for hours on end. Lowri had been cajoled into buying this on the pretext that she could play the LPs of musicals she was fond of – but she could never get near it when she wanted to.

They also listened to Radio Caroline, a 'pirate' radio station broadcasting from a ship moored off the Isle of Man. In the evenings, they tuned in to Radio Luxembourg. The music was all played at full volume, often driving Lowri into a different part of the house to get away from it. She was also persuaded to buy a Polaroid camera, which they all used to take photographs of each other.

'We want to get married Mam – in the Registry Office,' Ellen suddenly declared, which was strange in view of their alternative lifestyle choices. 'Is that alright?'

'What's the rush? You're still only sixteen.'

'But it's what we want, Mam. Please say yes – oh, and can we live here?'

There was no possibility of them owning or renting their own house on Edwin's trainee architect's salary. There was plenty of room for them in the house and having considered it, Lowri agreed, although there was a condition.

'You'll have to keep your music turned down though!'

Gwenda, however, was none too keen on having Edwin living there and accused him of being a prat and a sponger – although not to his face, of course. Seeing Gwenda's reaction to Edwin living with them, Lowri feared that the sibling rivalry was becoming even more intense and turning quite ugly.

'I hope he's going to pay his way here.' said Gwenda tartly.

'Do you pay your way? You could contribute something towards your keep,' retorted Ellen.

'But it's my home……' was Gwenda's indignant riposte.

* * *

Unbeknown to Lowri, Edwin had started experimenting with cannabis, which had become fashionable with their crowd. Ellen was not really that interested. She felt she didn't need it; her life was pretty good without it – but she tolerated his usage.

Lowri tried again to talk them out of a Registry Office marriage.

'It's what we both want, Mam. We don't need a lot of fuss,' said Ellen, before adding mischievously, 'I'm sure Gwenda will oblige you with a traditional wedding with all the trimmings, when she finally finds someone good enough for her.'

Ellen's disdain for her sister was increasing, probably influenced by Edwin, so she tended to keep out of her way. Consequently, Gwenda felt even more left out of things.

'He's just a freeloader, can't you see that?' Gwenda said to Ellen during a heated argument one day.

'I don't care; he's my freeloader. I'm happy with him – you're only jealous.'

'You must be mad – jealous of him?'

Jealous of somebody actually loving me!' Ellen screamed.

'Well, we all know that everybody loves you, don't we?'

Ellen had always been close to her Aunty Jane, who had never married. When she died in 1964, she had left the Bodhyfrydle Tea-Rooms in trust for Ellen, for when she reached the age of twenty-one. Jane wanted it kept in the family, as her mother would have done. She knew that Ellen would look after it, whereas Gwenda would probably sell it as soon as she could – she had never had any real interest in the place. Ellen, however, felt a real attachment to it and was hoping to move there with Edwin to live when she became of age. This bequest was another bone of contention and resentment for Gwenda, who felt she had been slighted. In the meantime, it was rented out as a going concern.

Soon after Ellen and Edwin married in 1966, they were ecstatic to learn that she was expecting. Barely seventeen, the pregnancy progressed well until Ellen woke early one morning from a nightmare and a premonition that something was terribly wrong. She was many weeks away from full term but on that fateful morning, she felt wet underneath, then realised she was lying on a blood-soaked sheet. Soon she felt a strong cramping pain, so strong that it caught her breath.

'Help!' she shouted hysterically at a sleeping Edwin. 'Look, blood! Awful pain!' as she doubled over, holding her belly.

'Oh my God, I'll go and get your Mam,' he cried, rubbing sleep from his eyes. 'Don't worry, it'll be OK,' knowing full well that it was far from it.

'No, don't leave me here on my own,' she pleaded, desperately grabbing for his arm. She was now quite lightheaded and feeling that she might pass out.

'I won't be long, hold on,' he said, instantly stressed and panicky.

'You should have called the doctor straight away,' Lowri scolded Edwin as she ran into the room in her quilted dressing gown and her hair in rollers.

'Quick, let's lift her legs higher, then you go and call him. I'll stay with her'.

Ellen was now drifting in and out of consciousness.

'Stay with us, Ellen *bach*,' said Lowri, putting her hand on Ellen's forehead, seriously worried. 'Hang on, the doctor's coming.'

'Call an ambulance!' she screamed at Edwin, as he reappeared after calling the doctor.

Gwenda woke, wondering what the noise and commotion was all about. She put her head round her sister's bedroom door.

'Go and get me some towels.' ordered Lowri.

Gwenda rolled her eyes. What an attention-seeker, she thought, unsympathetically. Serves her right for marrying that loser – but nevertheless did as she was told.

Twenty minutes later, the ambulance and doctor arrived at the same time.

'Please take her temperature and check her blood pressure, while I examine her,' the doctor said to the nurse from the ambulance.

'Her blood pressure is extremely low, Doctor,' the nurse informed him.

The doctor completed his examination, with Ellen now very obviously unconscious.

'I think the placenta has come away and is blocking the birth canal,' he said, before continuing more urgently. 'I'm afraid we may be losing her, she's lost too much blood already. Let's see if we can try to save the baby. I'll have to perform a caesarean section.'

'No, you must try to save Ellen first,' pleaded Lowri, not accepting his decision.

Tense moments followed as he went ahead anyway, carefully slicing open her abdomen with a scalpel, while Lowri winced and looked away.

'It's twins!' the doctor exclaimed, as Ellen lay there, ashen faced,

'Twins! We didn't know!' blurted out a shocked Edwin.

'I think she's gone,' said the nurse grimly, as she bent down to search for a pulse in her neck. The doctor looked over his glasses at Lowri, who sat there holding onto Ellen's hand as if to physically stop her from leaving her.

Lowri let out a primal howl of grief.

'Noooo…...don't leave us, *fy'n ghariad bach i*,' before collapsing and weeping inconsolably over Ellen's shoulder.

Even Gwenda suddenly seemed shocked, having thought Ellen had somehow been over-reacting all along.

The doctor, assisted by the ambulance personnel, lifted the two little babies out of Ellen's womb – one dead baby boy and a tiny little girl, barely alive. Once the cords were cut, they wrapped the tiny girl in a blanket and whisked her away to the ambulance to try to save her life.

The ambulance which had been called to save Ellen's life, was now transporting the surviving baby to Llandudno Hospital. Meanwhile, the doctor lay the stillborn baby boy down by Ellen's side, then grim-faced, covered both bodies with a red ambulance blanket.

Edwin, sitting on the other side from Lowri, was now sobbing hysterically, trying to hold onto Ellen's hand, beside himself with grief.

'See what you've done to my sister; you've killed her,' Gwenda spat venomously at him, adding to his unbearable pain.

'You useless excuse for a man,' she continued to scream at him, oblivious to his personal loss. 'Get out of this house! We never, ever want to see you again.'

Lowri, too drained to counter Gwenda's vitriol, was herself crying uncontrollably at the sudden awfulness of it all.

Shocked by what Gwenda had said, Edwin looked up abruptly. He was bewildered, hardly believing the events of the last couple of hours. Yesterday, everything was normal but now everything had changed, as if on fate's whim. The love of his life was gone – she now lay there, drained and lifeless.

The realisation of what this meant suddenly hit him. He could no longer hold her, speak to her, hear her voice, nor listen to her breathing as she slept next to him. She was gone from him for ever.

After kissing her very tenderly on the forehead, he left the room like a robot obeying an order, barely giving a thought to the surviving twin. He even started to believe Gwenda's assertion that he may have caused Ellen's death and felt all the guilt slowly seep into his shattered soul.

'Why should that baby live while the beautiful spirit and soul of my beloved Ellen has left me?' he thought. He asked himself whether or not he wanted to carry on living himself, if it meant being without her.

He walked forlornly and with round shoulders away from the house, carrying a small rucksack of his things.

'I need to get something stronger than cannabis to numb this awful pain inside of me,' he decided. 'My heart is slowly shattering into tiny little pieces. I need to escape from it. It's unbearable.'

He found himself a lodging room, then went straight out on the back streets to find his release.

Meanwhile, Gwenda tried to console her distraught mother – but she was beyond comforting. She had suddenly lost her little girl, as if a puff of wind had just carelessly blown her away, as the wind does to dandelion seeds. There one minute, gone the next, leaving the bare stalk behind. She had just floated away like the seed. Lowri felt bare and stripped of the one she had loved so deeply.

Once Lowri had exhausted herself with crying, an icy coldness began to creep inside her and wound its way heavily around her heart. Her whole life had changed in a heartbeat; there was only dying. Death had come suddenly.

She stood – and unable to cope with it all, walked trance-like up the stairs to her room and locked the door, leaving Gwenda and the doctor with the lifeless bodies of Ellen and the baby boy.

Now contrite, Gwenda wished she had been a little kinder to Ellen earlier, but unfortunately, this unfamiliar feeling was short-lived.

The doctor began to make arrangements for the bodies of Ellen and the baby boy to be removed to the mortuary. He filled in the Certificate of Cause of Death for Ellen and the Certificate of Stillbirth for the baby.

'Do you know if she had chosen a name for the dead boy?' he asked Gwenda.

'I think I heard them mention Alys Ellen for a girl's name – Ellen after her mother, of course, but also my great-aunt Mary Ellen. But I'm not sure about a boy's name.'

'What is his father's name? Maybe we could give the boy his father's name.'

'He doesn't deserve to be named after that murderer, Edwin,' Gwenda spat out vituperatively.

'Call him Edward, after my father. He will now be turning in his grave given what has happened to his favourite daughter.'

Her one moment of real contrition had quickly passed.

'She brought it all on herself, if you ask me,' she added heartlessly.

The doctor was shocked by this. But he knew that grief affected people in peculiar ways, so let it pass without response or rebuke.

Many hours later, Gwenda heard her mother begin to move about upstairs, before finally making her way down. She found only Gwenda there, seated at the kitchen table, her head in her hands.

'They've taken them both to the mortuary,' Gwenda told her flatly. 'The Vicar called to offer his condolences. He asked if you wanted him to call to see you, to talk about organising a funeral. Also, we had a call from the hospital to say the baby was still very poorly, in an incubator – but not expected to survive.'

Lowri did not respond.

'I've put the bloodied bed sheets to soak,' Gwenda continued, 'but I think they're beyond saving……'

'Put them on the garden bonfire for burning, or they'll always be here to remind us,' said Lowri uncharacteristically.

Apart from this one response, Gwenda could see that her mother wasn't thinking straight and not really taking in any information. She just stood there, wringing her hands.

'Let me make you something to eat, you've had nothing all day. You sit down, I'll heat you up a tin of chicken soup.'

Obediently, Lowri sat in the chair Gwenda had just vacated, too lost to know what else to do with herself. She pulled her cardigan tightly around herself for protection.

'You deal with it; my mind is befuddled,' she said, clearly incapable of conversation or decision-making. 'I can't think straight – my head is full of sorrow and regret.'

All she could see in her mind was the floating image of her daughter's ashen-faced body, lying in a pool of blood.

'What regret? You did nothing wrong.'

'Maybe if I'd made them wait to get married……she was so young…...'

***

Ellen's funeral took place a week later. St Gwynan's church was packed to the rafters with shocked and subdued local people, as well as Ellen's former school friends. She lay there in her open coffin, wearing a white linen summer dress and a beautiful garland of wildflowers in her hair. Her baby son had been placed next to her in the coffin with her arm around him. Members of the congregation, all dressed in black, filed silently past the coffin to pay their last respects, some with tears streaming down their faces at the sadness, unfairness and inequity of it all.

There was no sign of Edwin anywhere, although he must have known the funeral was taking place. Locally, people had been talking about nothing else for days and a funeral announcement had been put in the Daily Post. People in the congregation began to whisper amongst themselves, speculating as to why he wasn't there and commenting on how very disrespectful to her memory it was for him not to make an appearance. However, Gwenda was more than glad he was absent, whilst Lowri seemed too oblivious and dazed, in a sad world of her own.

Ellen's body was interred in a newly-dug grave in the cemetery ground next to the church. At about the same time this was happening, a local woman, wearing her apron and with her hair in metal curlers, suddenly ran screaming in panic from her lodging house.

'Help me! Help me!' she shouted. 'He's hanging from the bedroom beam – we need to cut him down. Maybe we can save him.'

A couple of men rushed up the stairs of the house but could see that Edwin had already been dead for a few hours and was way beyond resuscitation. Her next-door neighbour ran to the nearest red phone box at the end of the street and dialled 999.

In the meantime, a passing local coalman, well used to carrying dead weight, lifted him up, while his mate used his penknife to cut through the rope which was tied around his neck. They laid him gently on his bed, while the woman cried hysterically from the trauma of finding him. The coalman was shocked to notice that the tops of both the dressing table and chest of drawers were strewn with an array of drug paraphernalia and empty bottles of whisky.

The case was subsequently referred to the coroner, who duly recorded his verdict as:

'Death by Suicide, while the balance of his mind was disturbed.'

Although it was a few years since suicide had been decriminalised, it was still considered to be shameful for Edwin's widowed mother in the religious environment in which they lived. The 'unsound mind' element was ascribed to the drugs and alcohol found at the scene, which Edwin had used in his desperate need to escape his abject misery.

Since Ellen's death, he had been taking a toxic mixture of any drugs or alcohol he could lay his hands on, to escape the extreme pain of his unbearable loss. He could not face the world without his Ellen in it. Too wrapped up in his terrible grief, he had not been able to see that there was a little soul who desperately needed him – and for whom he was legally responsible. He could not climb up out of the pit of his misery and despair for long enough to make the mental leap needed to begin thinking about his critically-ill baby daughter. Had he done so, it may well have saved his own life. Instead, he selfishly chose to leave her an orphan, at the mercy of the world.

His weeping mother was the only mourner at his funeral – in contrast to the hundreds who had turned up to pay their respects to Ellen and her family. She was left to grieve the tragic loss of her only son, Edwin, alone.

Weeks later, his landlady finally steeled herself to enter his room to clean it. The police had long since cleared out and destroyed the drug paraphernalia. As she ran a long-handled feather duster under the bed, an envelope was swept out. Gingerly the landlady pulled out a folded sheet of paper, which read:

My Darling Ellen

Our lives together were only a few short, beautiful years – but during that time I knew what it was to be loved and to truly love another – you, my love. You made me feel like a whole person. I cannot face the rest of my life without you, as half a person. Neither can I bear this pain you have left me with. You were always the strong one and I miss your gentle, tolerant, loving presence.

Forgive me. I want only to be with you in heaven and hope we soon will be united in death. I know you might be angry with me for not visiting our baby daughter – but had she lived, I could not have borne to see you in her, reminding me of my devastating loss, every single day for the rest of my life.

Forgive me for being selfish.
Longing to be with you,
Yours for eternity
Edwin

The landlady was barely able to read this heartrending message without her throat painfully choking up. Tears welled up in her eyes, magnifying and distorting the beautifully written words. When she had finally composed herself, she called the doctor to tell him about the note. He requested that she bring the note to the surgery and instructed her not to discuss its contents with anyone.

When he had read the note, the doctor conferred with the coroner, who directed that the note was to be passed over to the possession of Edwin's mother, as his adult next of kin. In turn, Mrs. Roberts eventually passed it on to Lowri. She wanted her to understand the true depth of her son's love for Ellen. After that, both mothers had no further contact.

Chapter 13

We spend most weekends together now since our relationship moved onto the next level. I love being with Alys and believe she is good for me; she helps me to relax and stops me taking myself too seriously. Whereas I am staid, considered and work-driven, she is the exact opposite. She is fun, impulsive and caring – and lives in the moment. But there is also a serious, more responsible side to her which comes to the fore with her studies, at which she is very determined to succeed.

Weather permitting, we take long coastal or hill walks, discovering places we didn't even know existed. We both agree we are very lucky to live in such a beautiful part of the world. But the places themselves aren't that important to me – it is enough for me just to be with her.

It's a cold, rainy weekend afternoon, way too wet for even the most stalwart of walkers to be out. So once again, for relaxation, I am researching the people in the big Bible.

Alys is sitting by the fire working on her latest assignment.

'When you've finished looking at that old Bible, maybe you can do some research into my family history,' she pipes up. 'My Nain never did speak much about the family. I had the distinct feeling there may have been a few skeletons lurking about in their cupboards back then.'

'We can do that,' I reply enthusiastically, immediately picking up on the idea. 'What was your Nain's name?'

'Lowri,' Alys replies.

It occurs to me that as Lowri is not a common name, even in Wales, it is an interesting coincidence that there is a Lowri in the Bible family tree.

'What was her father's surname?'

'Griffiths. I know for sure she was born in Capelulo in 1928.'

I am suddenly taken aback. To confirm my suspicion, I take a look at the family tree, which verifies that Lowri was the daughter of Richard Griffiths and was born in 1928.

Oh, my goodness! Does this actually mean what I think it does?

The enormity of my discovery overwhelms me. Is Alys actually related to all these people? Are the people in the Bible family tree really her ancestors?

Thinking quickly, I decide not to say anything to Alys until I'm absolutely sure.

'That shouldn't be too difficult to trace,' I say to Alys. 'When I go to the Registry Office next week, I'll look her up.'

* * *

'There was a Conwy birth registered for a Lowri Ellen Griffiths in the last quarter of 1928,' I tell Alys a week later, 'so I bought a copy of her birth certificate. It shows her place of birth was Ty Glan-y-Coed, in the Parish of Dwygyfylchi. Her father and mother were Richard and Rebecca Griffiths. Her father's occupation was Master Builder.'

'Oh, so she was actually born in our old house,' remarks Alys. 'I remember there was a foundation stone with RG 1925 carved on it by the front door. He must have built the house.'

* * *

Lowri's Story – Part 2

'I suppose we'd better go and see this baby then, we're probably responsible for it now,' said Gwenda unenthusiastically to Lowri at breakfast – while secretly thinking, 'Do we really want another cuckoo in the nest?'

Now, with her sister not around, she was feeling more valued and important to her mother – and quite liked it. She would endeavour to persuade her to have the baby adopted, that is, if it managed to miraculously survive. She couldn't bear the thought of the disruption a baby would cause, once again taking away the focus of attention from her.

'I suppose you are right; I'd better get the car out of the garage to make our way over to Llandudno Hospital.'

It was a cool, rainy, autumnal day when they set off in the Morris Traveller. Multi-coloured leaves were being picked up by the blustery wind, then randomly tossed and blown about all over the place. Rain occasionally lashed across the car windscreen and large puddles gathered at the kerbsides, ready to soak unsuspecting pedestrians as the cars sped by.

When they finally reached the quiet sanctuary of the Maternity Unit, they were directed by Reception staff to the Incubation ward. A woman was standing next to an incubator which was labelled 'Baby Roberts'. She was seemingly discussing the baby with the immaculately-presented staff nurse.

'Ah, good morning,' said the woman. 'Are you the baby's grandmother?'

'Yes, I am,' said Lowri, guardedly, 'and who are you, may I ask?'

'Sorry, I should have introduced myself. I am Gwen from Caernarfonshire Children's Social Services. The hospital made a referral to us regarding the baby, so I am here to make an assessment of the situation.'

Lowri looked down at the baby lying in the incubator. Tiny tubes were coming and going, in and out of everywhere, helping her to fight for her life. Suddenly, as if sensing Lowri's presence, the baby opened her eyes briefly and her little hands began to flex open and then close. At this, Lowri softened a little, remembering that Ellen had looked just like this as a baby – but had not been as tiny or as fragile.

'Oh!' exclaimed the staff nurse, 'she likes you; it's the first time we've had that response from her.'

That seemed to have been the pivotal moment in which the bond between Lowri and the baby was irrevocably sealed. She turned to Gwenda, who during their drive to the hospital had been trying to persuade her to get the baby adopted.

'A young family could give her a good life,' she had said. 'A baby would be a lot of work for you.'

'She's coming home with us when she's well enough,' Lowri now insisted. 'There'll be no adoption or fostering. She's family, our flesh and blood and we'll care for her somehow, poor little mite,' turning back to look at her.

Gwenda scowled sulkily at the thought of this.

'She's not quite out of the woods yet,' the nurse warned, 'but the vital signs are slowly improving.'

'We call her Baby Roberts,' she continued, 'Do you have a name for her?'

'Alys,' said Gwenda sullenly, not at all happy with the direction things were now moving in. 'Alys Ellen. It's on her birth certificate.'

Lowri then got the distinct impression that Gwenda's previous resentment of her sister, Ellen, had subtly and imperceptibly transferred to her sister's baby. She was concerned when she realised this but did not feel able to counter Gwenda's irrationality.

'That's a pretty name, I think it suits her,' said Gwen, distracting her.

The baby opened her eyes again, as if acknowledging this. Lowri put her little finger in through the hole in the side of the incubator to stroke Alys's tiny hand – which instantly grabbed it as if to say, 'Save me, let me hold on to you, don't let me go.'

Lowri now had absolutely no intention of letting her go.

Over the next few weeks, Lowri visited Alys every day. She sat by her side for hours, willing and praying for her to pull through. She talked to her about her mother, Ellen: how beautiful she was inside and out; how clever she was at drawing people; how she would have stayed to look after her if only she could have…… She often cried openly as she talked to her, and this seemed to be helping Lowri to work through her own raw grief.

Finally, the day came when she was rewarded. Sister told her that baby Alys was finally well enough to be taken home the next day. There was then an urgent rush to prepare. The old baby cot was brought down from the attic. Milk formula, feeding bottles, towelling nappies, safety pins, talcum powder, zinc ointment, dummies and baby clothes were bought. Lowri made baby cot sheets out of an old single candy-stripe flannelette sheet and decided Alys was still tiny enough to be carefully bathed in the white enamel washing-up bowl for now.

Lowri gradually became obsessed with her granddaughter; her very reason to live. She had her cot next to her bed for when she needed a feed at night and nothing was too much trouble.

Gwenda, on the other hand, was feeling totally pushed out again. She had closed her heart completely to the baby and was furiously seething inside. Although somewhere deep down she knew that her mother had done the right thing, she was reluctant to help, having had her nose put out of joint once more by the recent turn of events. Lowri instinctively knew how Gwenda would be thinking and was not surprised at her rejection of the baby.

Lowri felt she needed to be vigilant in watching Alys' every waking moment to prevent any harm befalling her, in case she suddenly slipped away from her – as her lovely daughter Ellen had done.

Their bond grew stronger still, as the months, the milestones, then the years began to slip by.

When Alys was about three, Lowri received a rather important-looking letter from a solicitor, addressed to Ellen. She quietly slipped it into the pocket of her summer dress to read later in the privacy of her room. It read:

Cecil Jones, Solicitors
Castle Street
Conwy

1st June 1971

Dear Miss Jones

As trustees of the property of Bodyhyfrydle, in the hamlet of Capelulo, we are writing to you because you will become twenty-one years of age on 19th June 1971. Therefore, the ownership of this property, having been left in trust for you by the late Miss Jane Rowlands, of Bodhyfrydle, Capelulo in 1964, will be transferred into your ownership on that date.

The property has been tenanted by the same family for many years and they are happy for that to continue, if that is your wish. The monthly rental has been put into the trust fund and has been carefully invested.

We look forward to receiving your instructions regarding this matter.

Your obedient servant
Ieuan Cadwalader Jones

The letter fell from Lowri's hand. The unsettling shock of receiving information regarding her dead daughter as if she was still alive and whose twenty-first birthday she should now be celebrating, caused her to cry. The grief was always just under the surface, no matter how brave a face she put on. She did not blame the solicitor, he was not to know – but the bitter tears of what might have been, sprung up once more, as they had done intermittently over the long grieving years.

She had all but forgotten about the Bodhyfrydle Trust, obsessed as she was with Alys. The current tenants were paying rent to the Trust, which managed the fund and a statement of the account was attached. This had slowly accumulated to a very tidy sum and had, as they claimed, been invested wisely.

Yet another thing to have to deal with, she thought. She would have to write to them to inform them of Ellen's passing and tell them that she had had a daughter. She would ask for a new Trust to be set up for the benefit of Alys and ask them to continue to manage the property until Alys became twenty-one years old.

This letter reminded her that Gwenda's twenty-first birthday was also coming up soon and that she needed to make plans for that. Gwenda was getting married in a few months' time, so maybe she would rather have some money towards that occasion. She would ask her tomorrow.

* * *

After this, the years slipped by almost unnoticed and before Lowri knew it, Alys was a teenager. She was doing well at school and had inherited her mother's artistic talent. She and Lowri were still very close, always content and comfortable in each other's company.

Although Lowri already had an accountant to manage her portfolio, she felt she was getting too old to have to make decisions about investments and such now. In this vein, she began thinking about her own mortality and decided it was high time for her to write her Will. Her main concern was Alys, bless her. Lowri was determined that after her death, Alys would still be secure, so she contacted her solicitor to make an appointment to draw up her Will.

Gwenda was already settled and was well provided for, so Lowri did not worry too much about her. Money would be more useful to her than property. Lowri thought about her lovely jewellery, her beautiful antique furniture and the old family Bible – who would best care for those? Lowri remembered that ever since Alys was a little girl, she had loved to go through the jewellery box pieces with her. Lowri had patiently explained the significance of each piece and who had owned it before her. She also had a small silver trinket box lined with faded purple velvet which she let Alys play with. She wasn't sure where that had come from – but it had been passed on to her by Jane, along with the old Bible.

Gwenda had never shown the same interest in any of it. Lowri believed that she would think all her lovely furniture was too old fashioned. She seemed to be into this modern painted ply stuff, as was fashionable at the time, and moquette settees which Lowri thought would soon become snagged and shabby in no time at all.

But she told herself not to worry. Alys would be sure to keep the house, its memories and its precious contents safe. Little did she realise how differently things would actually turn out.

* * *

As Lowri aged, their caring roles reversed. Alys became her grandmother's main carer, a role she had been happy to take on, as Lowri's heart condition had been getting steadily worse. She now struggled to get up the stairs and needed to rest a great deal. Gwenda was married, had a daughter and her own home locally. She was secretly relieved that Alys was looking after her mother, as it saved her from having to do so. At least she was useful for that. She occasionally visited her mother but Lowri now sensed it was more out of duty than for love – she wondered if it had ever been for love. They certainly weren't close.

A year or so later, during one of Gwenda's duty visits, she asked her mother if she had written a Will yet, given her failing health.

'Oh yes, I've taken care of all that,' she said, looking at Gwenda over her half-rimmed glasses. 'I've made you an executor and I want you to make sure that Alys is well looked after when I'm gone.'

Gwenda's self-regarding interpretation of that was probably 'you'll inherit everything but make sure Alys has somewhere to live.'

Gwenda had to be satisfied with that for now. She did not have the temerity to ask her mother what was in the Will, or where she kept it, as her mother was a very private person when it came to such matters. She did have a couple of ideas though as to where it might be – but in the event, she was completely wrong and utterly frustrated when she could not find it.

One morning, Alys took the usual cup of tea up to Lowri's bedroom where she found her sleeping peacefully in her winceyette pyjamas, with her greying hair in curlers – maybe, Alys thought, suddenly anxious, a little too peacefully.

'Wake up, Nain, I've got a *panad* for you.'

But Lowri did not stir, so Alys put the cup down, then gently shook her Nain's shoulder to wake her. Seeing she was totally unresponsive, the awful realisation struck her. She was dead. She must have passed away in her sleep, sometime during the night.

Alys broke down in tears over the bed, hardly believing her precious Nain had gone. She had always been there all her life – but no more. She felt an acute sense of abandonment – she had been left totally on her own once more. She carefully removed the curlers from her Nain's hair and gently brushed it, as the tears streamed down her face.

Heartbroken, she called Gwenda, who came straight over to the house – but not to comfort Alys, nor to grieve – she seemed almost excited. She had another mission in mind.

Seemingly unaffected, she drew the bedsheet up over her mother's face.

'Why don't you go downstairs and phone the doctor's surgery to let them know?' she suggested. 'Then put the kettle on so we can have some breakfast. There's nothing much we can do for now.'

Alys thought that as Gwenda was Lowri's adult daughter, she should be the one phoning the doctor. However, she did not say anything but did as Gwenda had asked her.

Once Alys had left the room, Gwenda quickly walked over to her mother's little writing bureau and started rifling through for the Will. She became crosser by the minute, because it clearly wasn't where she had expected it to be. She then started cursing under her breath as she rummaged through each section again. She couldn't think of where else to look. But she was careful and calculating enough to leave everything as tidy as she'd found it.

Finally, Alys called her to have some breakfast, so she went downstairs.

'Do you know where Mam kept her Will?' Gwenda asked tentatively.

'I don't know, I have no idea,' Alys replied, shocked that she could even ask such a question at this time, with her Nain not yet quite cold.

'Did she tell you what was in it?'

'No, only to say I'd be well looked after and that I could stay here.'

'She might have said that in passing – but we don't really know for sure, do we?' said Gwenda, in a hugely doubt-inducing way.

'She wouldn't say it and not mean it….'

'Well, we need to find it soon, so we can sort things out legally.'

'Shouldn't we be thinking about arranging a funeral first?' asked Alys.

'Yes, of course, you're right,' Gwenda replied sweetly, although in reality, seething with frustration. 'Let's get on to the Vicar and sort it out.'

A week later, after the funeral, Gwenda turned up at the house.

'I've come to have a look for the Will. I'll go upstairs to Mam's room to look there again.'

'Why? Have you looked there already?'

Gwenda realised her slip-up and mumbled something about having had a quick look a while ago.

'Well, that must have been on the day Nain died,' Alys thought suspiciously, 'because she hasn't been here since, except for when the cortege left to go to the cemetery. What a callous cow she is.'

A while later, Gwenda came down the stairs waving an envelope.

'I've found it. It was where I thought it would be all along,' she said, tucking it into her handbag. 'I'll take it down to her solicitor this afternoon. He should be the one to officially open it,' she added, as she walked towards the front door.

A few days later, Alys received a letter in the post. She slit open the envelope and as she began to read, she sank onto the nearest kitchen chair in utter disbelief:

Dear Alys

Following the death of my mother, Lowri, I have to inform you that I have been made executor of her Will and that she has naturally left the house and all its contents to me, her only daughter.

I would appreciate it if you could <u>vacate the property by the end of today</u>, so that I can begin to make arrangements for the clearance of the contents and for the house to be put on the market.

You can choose something small as a memento to take with you if you like. Please leave your housekey on the kitchen table.

Your aunt

Gwenda Pritchard

P.S. I suppose you could stay at my house for a short while if you really had to until you make other more suitable arrangements.

Alys was stunned.

'What?' she thought. 'How can she do that? It's been in the family for sixty years. My great-grandfather built it.'

Horrified, Alys read the letter again.

'Clearance! What about all Nain's things? She's getting rid of everything?'

Alys felt that the proverbial rug had been pulled out from under her.

Gathering her wits about her, she thought she'd better go and pack but knew she had nowhere else to live. Finally, she broke down at the unfairness of it all, giving way to the tears which had been threatening since she first read the letter. Why would her Nain tell her she was leaving her the house and then not do so?

Had Alys only known, Gwenda would have had to obtain probate before she could do this. But Alys was young and naïve. She was still grieving and in shock, so did not think to question her aunt's actions.

After wandering through each of the rooms as if to say goodbye to them and the happy memories they held, she sat down at her Nain's dressing table. She pulled forward her beautiful ebony jewellery box. Lowri had told Alys that her husband, Edward, had bought it for her on their first wedding anniversary. It had a multitude of little red velvet-lined compartments which held her various pieces. Alys thought that as much as she'd like to, she couldn't take it as it was too bulky and heavy. Anyway, could she guarantee the safety of its contents where she was going? No, she was resigned to the fact that she would have to travel light from now on.

Gently going through the pieces one by one, she remembered the occasions when her Nain had worn a particular piece. Beautiful memories. She had shown her those which had belonged to her mother, Rebecca and those to her great-aunty, Mary Ellen. They were mainly Victorian, mostly rose gold. She cried again, thinking that her cousin Lena would probably get them but in all probability, wouldn't even want them. Gwenda certainly wouldn't – and Lena only liked modern tat, not wonderful pieces like these, which held real sentimental memories. The only piece she took was her Nain's rose gold wedding ring, which she placed on the fourth finger of her right hand.

Alys found a small weekend case in the attic and filled it with as many of her things as she could, putting the rest of what she could carry into her rucksack. She walked downstairs for the last time and placed her housekey on the breakfast table. She gently closed the door and made her way down the drive, through the beautiful gardens, with absolutely no idea where she was heading.

She walked down Chestnut Avenue, then turned right onto Old Mill Road, passing the beautiful, shuttered house they had always called Hickory House. She was glad there was nobody about to see her. Had she turned left, she would have passed along what was known locally as Millionaire's Avenue, leading to Glyn Terrace, with its ancient little bridge over the river.

As she neared the church, she remembered how as a child, she used to call in to Bert Llan's Dairy to buy a quarter-pint bottle of orange juice. She remembered hearing the clunking of glass bottles moving along the conveyer belt, as they were filled with fresh milk or orange juice, before being capped with a silver foil top for ordinary milk, or a gold top if it was full cream milk. She couldn't quite remember the colour for the orange juice top though. Maybe it was blue. She remembered at Christmas time the silver caps had green holly leaves with red berries and if she asked nicely, they would let her have the strips that the tops were cut out from, to use to decorate her

Christmas tree.

Oh, how she wished she could go back to those days, when everything was safe and predictable, instead of now, when she was facing the harsh reality of her awful situation, when even the next few hours were unknown.

She bore right at the church, passing the lychgate, then followed the high wall and curve of the road down to the tall ornate black wrought-iron cemetery gates. She entered and sat down on the newly mown grass next to the fresh grave of her Nain, who had been buried with her husband, Edward. The funeral flowers were not yet dead – but Alys's life as she had known it, was.

She made her way down to the grave of her mother, Ellen, and her baby twin brother, Edward. She remembered coming here when she was younger with Lowri on Sundays. They would put flowers on the grave before walking up to the tea-rooms in Capelulo – their Sunday treat. Later, when Lowri became unable to walk far, Alys would come on her own to spend time here, just to be near them and to think.

It was such a lovely headstone, white marble, with an angel holding a baby cherub, which depicted her mother and baby brother. She sat there for a while, wondering how very different her life might have been had they both lived. She wondered where her father had been buried; she hadn't been told and had not liked to ask. She had always felt that a part of her was missing. Was it her dead twin brother, her other half? Would he have been the quieter or more outgoing twin?

'Why did you all have to leave me on my own?' she said out loud to nobody in particular, as tears of self-pity welled up once more. 'Now I have lost Nain, I'm totally alone again.'

She got no answers from the long-dead in the cemetery, so pulled herself up off the damp grass. Picking up her belongings and leaving the cemetery, she made her way towards the old Glanrafon School Hall, where they used to practise the Morris Dancing routines for the local carnivals. She remembered feeling special then, in her short silky flared skirt, the white pumps with Morris bells threaded through the shoelaces, a pillbox hat worn at an angle and the two-coloured crepe paper hand streamers.

As she reminisced, a large green Crossville bus came hurtling around the bend, forcing her into the hedge. 'Idiot!' she shouted after it, as she brushed herself off.

She then passed Pendyffryn Farm and wondered if they needed live-in staff for the summer camping site. Maybe she could live in a tent there until she sorted things out – but her mood was so riddled with despondency, she did not even venture to ask.

She carried on walking down towards the A5, with lush green fields on both sides of her and the cattle grid just ahead. She told herself she'd decide when she got to the T-junction whether to go left or right, such was the current capriciousness of her life. But when she did reach the main road, she looked across it and saw the Ship Inn and next to it, the little tunnel under the railway line leading to Ship Shore. She remembered the countless happy summer days spent there with her Nain. So she headed there instead and sat down on the hard beach pebbles.

'Why has this happened to me?' she mentally beseeched her Nain. 'Look at me, homeless, sitting on the beach like some tramp, when you told me I'd always be safe.'

This triggered more bitter tears of anger and grief. Wracking sobs overwhelmed her as she keenly felt the loss of her Nain, her home and her life as she'd known it, until she was finally drained and her eyes stung, as if salty seawater had accidently entered them.

Alys sat there on the beach for hours looking out to sea, playing over and over in her mind the moving images of the carefree days she had spent there as a child and young adolescent, swimming and building sandcastles – carefree days of seemingly endless sunshine.

Suddenly hungry, she remembered she had put a sandwich in her bag earlier. So, sitting with her back to the wooden breakwater, she ate without even tasting it. She tried to think of what on earth was she to do? She had no other relatives – not that she knew of anyway – who could help her. They were such a very small family, which she suddenly wished was big; she only had Gwenda, who hated her. She could not understand why she was like she was with her; what had she ever done to her? It was as if her very existence annoyed her.

She really didn't want to live with Gwenda if she could possibly avoid it. She did not want to be where she was not wanted. She had her pride. She knew there were property agencies which could help her find somewhere to live; but she had no deposit. She guessed that as she was now eighteen, she no longer met social services' criteria as a child needing help.

As the tide turned, a sudden breeze sprang up, so she pulled her duffle coat more tightly around herself. Next thing she knew, she woke to the sound of small pebbles being forced forward, then sucked back by powerful waves. She felt just like those pebbles, powerless against the strong forces surrounding her, pushing her forward, then dragging her back again. Endlessly.

Dusk began to fall. Sleep had brought some relief from her nightmare situation, but the reality was still there when she awoke. She knew she wouldn't sleep again for hours, so picked up her case and rucksack and started walking westwards along the beach, towards the gentle evening sun which warmed her face. The tide was now too far in for her to walk the other way around the headland to Conwy. As she walked along the beach, she spotted trains passing nearby, full of people who actually knew where they were going – unlike her.

As she made her way over the stones, the sun began to slowly sink behind the Penmon lighthouse, between Llanddona and Puffin Island. It was turning the sky into a cornucopia of kaleidoscopic streaks of magnificent colours. But she was too wrapped up in her own misery to notice this utter beauty right in front of her. Her mind was elsewhere.

As she walked towards the Pen beach tunnel, she saw a girl she knew from school sitting in a beach shelter with her boyfriend, deep in conversation. When she recognised Alys coming towards her, she waved then ran up towards her.

'What's wrong, Alys? Why are you walking on your own on the beach with a suitcase?'

'My aunt has thrown me out of the house; she's going to sell it. I've got nowhere to live now,' she replied, finding it hard not to burst into tears again, at her friend's obvious sympathy.

'That's bloody awful. You can come and stay with me until you get sorted.'

'I was half thinking of sleeping in one of the beach shelters.'

'You can't stay out here on your own, it's not safe,' she replied, appalled at the very idea.

'Shouldn't you ask your mother first, Jackie?'

'She won't mind. You can sleep on my bedroom floor. Not quite what you're used to though,' she said teasingly, trying to cheer Alys up a bit.

'Come on,' said Jackie, taking the case off her.

Jackie linked her other arm with Alys' and they started walking towards the pedestrian tunnel, leaving her bewildered boyfriend sitting open-mouthed in the shelter, wondering what on earth had just happened.

'You look shattered, poor thing. We'll make a nice cup of tea, then you can tell me everything…….'

In this way, Alys became involved with a group of girls, some of whom she did not like very much. She liked Jackie though; she and her mother were very kind to her – but in time, she began to feel she could not continue to impose on their hospitality indefinitely. It had only ever been a stop-gap. Besides, sleeping on the floor was very uncomfortable and she often woke exhausted. She came to the sorry conclusion that she would have to swallow her pride and go to stay in her Aunt's house for a while.

'Oh, it's you!' said her unenthusiastic cousin, Lena, on opening their front door.

'Can I come in then?'

'Suppose. Mam isn't home from work yet though and I'm doing my homework,' she said in a do-not-disturb-me sort of tone. She was a few years younger than Alys and seemed strangely reluctant to have eye contact. Had her mother turned her against Alys? Or did she feel that her mother had been unkind to make her leave their Nain's house? It was hard to tell.

'I'll wait in the kitchen then,' thinking what a miserable girl Lena was becoming.

'Oh, it's you,' said Gwenda, as she came in a short while later, echoing her daughter's reaction. 'What can I do for you?'

'Give me a roof over my head would be a good start.'

'We heard you'd got fixed up with a friend.'

'I can't stay at her place forever. I need somewhere to stay to get back on my feet. Can't do anything without a permanent address these days,' Alys said in justification, adding, 'I want to enrol for a course so I can get some qualifications, if my A-levels are good enough for me to do the one I fancy.'

'Drawing, is it?' Gwenda asked disinterestedly.

'No, social work. Looking after Nain made me realise I needed a recognised qualification to be able to practise.'

'Oh my – making yourself sound like a lawyer now?'

'So, can I stay here or not?' Alys persisted, impatient at the barb.

'I suppose so – but you'll have to pull your weight with the housekeeping.'

'When have I ever not?' Alys retorted, rolling her eyes.

* * *

Things were stable for a while but the atmosphere at home was uncomfortable and strained to say the least, so Alys kept out of the family's way as much as she could. Occasionally, she saw Jackie and her wider circle of friends but mainly stayed in during the week. She studied for her A-Levels up in the little boxroom that Gwenda had allotted her from her great big house.

Then late one Saturday afternoon, as a break from studying, she met up with the group at the far end of the beach. Some were already drinking cheap cider and becoming quite loud. After a while, they began picking on a young lad with obvious learning difficulties, which made Alys feel very uncomfortable. He was taking it all in good spirits, thinking they really liked him and were just having fun. He was glad of the attention initially – but he did not realise they were really mocking him. Then they started spinning him around, making him dizzy.

Alys wanted to tell them to stop but knew if she did, they would turn on her.

'I'm off,' she said to nobody in particular – but within earshot of most. Then, by way of explanation, 'I've got an exam to prepare for on Monday.'

As she started walking away, she heard a girl's voice that she recognised as Sylvia's.

'Doesn't half fancy herself, that one.'

This left Alys thinking that she really did need to make herself some new friends.

When Alys let herself in by the front door, she noticed Lena was working in the kitchen, although she didn't look up, nor acknowledge her arrival. Alys made her way up the stairs to the bathroom and ran herself a bath, after which she went up to her room to settle down to her studying.

The bath had soothed her. She felt cleansed after being in the company of those girls, some of whom were drinking the cheap cider and tormenting their victim. She now felt a twinge of guilt as she knew she should have said something to stop them abusing him.

'What sort of social worker will I make if I can't stick up for the vulnerable?' she asked herself critically. Despite knowing full well that if she had, they would have turned on her, she was still ashamed of what she now saw was her cowardice.

Chapter 14

I decide to visit the Registry Office again to try to search for Lowri's marriage in the register. Sure enough, we find the record of her marriage to Edward Jones in 1947.

I think it might be interesting to see the Will of Lowri's mother, Rebecca, so I pay another visit to the National Library of Wales in Aberystwyth. Searching the records, I eventually find the Will of a Rebecca Griffiths, who died in 1952. I see that she was a very wealthy woman and had left everything to her daughter, Lowri.

I would now like to find Rebecca's birth certificate, so I can work backwards up the family tree, as Alys wants to do – but she doesn't seem too keen to talk about the more recent generation.

When I show her the will, Alys is shocked.

'I never knew my Nain was that wealthy!' she exclaims. 'Where's all that money now?'

I, on the other hand, wonder where that money had initially come from. Surely not from a builder's business, even if he was a very successful one. I think that it is all a bit suspicious but say nothing to Alys.

Unbeknown to Alys, I am working on a theory which may explain why Lena lied to the police about Alys not being in on the evening of the assault. I consider all the pieces of information I now have, which leaves me with a number of questions.

What if Lowri's money was the motive? Lots of money. Rebecca's Will is a clear indication of where Lowri's money originally came from. Of course, people can easily spend a fortune during their lifetime but what would Lowri have spent it on? She was widowed about twenty years ago and since then, only had Alys living with her after Alys' aunt had left to get married. From what Alys said about her, Lowri sounded fairly frugal and did not seem to have led an extravagant lifestyle. She had a lovely house, which she had told Alys she would leave to her in her Will. So why didn't that happen?

Alys said that Gwenda had married well to a local solicitor – she had her own house, a good job and was financially sound. She liked the good things in life: foreign travel, good food, expensive clothes.

And she had her daughter, Lena, Alys' first cousin.

Later, when I bring up the subject of Gwenda again, Alys holds back a bit as she knows the subject will inevitably get round to her mother, Ellen, then her father, Edwin, who she still seems reluctant to discuss with me.

As it stands, all I know is that Ellen married her teenage sweetheart, Edwin, then died giving birth to Alys in 1967.

On one of our many walks, Alys finally opens up to me about what she knows about her parents, which in fact, turns out to be only a small fraction of the full story.

* * *

The following weekend, while Alys is studying in her little room at her Aunt's house, I am continuing with my research. As I turn around quickly to reach for my reference file, I clumsily knock the Bible over with my elbow. Although I try, I fail to catch it before it falls onto the floor.

Horrified that I may have damaged the spine, I stoop down to gently pick it up. It has landed upside down with just its back cover wide open. I haven't previously looked at the back page, or any other section for that matter, having been totally engrossed with and focused on the family tree written inside the front cover. I see that there is a piece of thin card stuck onto the inside of the back cover with glue that is cracking and yellowed with age. This forms a sort of sleeve and there appears to be some papers tucked inside it.

Hoping I haven't damaged it, I gently lift the Bible up off the floor and lay it back onto the table to study this newly intriguing back cover. Tentatively, I pull out a folded sheet of paper from behind the sleeve. Written on it is:

To whom it may concern by Edwin Roberts.

Oh my gosh! This is Alys' father's name. This now absolutely convinces me that the Bible family is actually Alys' family.

Tucked in above it is another longish document which I gently slide out from the sleeve. It is entitled:

Last Will and Testament of Lowri Jones

I am in absolute shock. I feel my legs go wobbly, so I sit. I hold these two documents, one in each hand, as I consider the immensity of this discovery. One may be of enormous significance to Alys, while the other will reveal the truth of who was meant to be the beneficiary of her Nain's Will.

Then I notice there is another document in the sleeve. I remove it to find it is a letter from an American lawyer informing Rebecca Griffiths that she is a beneficiary in the Will of a Jared Knox. He not only left her an enormous amount of money but also a house called Ty Mawr Llan in Eglwysbach.

So, Alys' Nain, Lowri, is the daughter of Rebecca, who is somehow connected to an American man, who seems to have links to Eglwysbach, where Mary Ellen's family originated.

At this point, there are far too many unanswered questions buzzing around in my brain. I just need to get all these jigsaw pieces to fall into place. A suspicion slowly begins to form that there may have been some foul play regarding Lowri's Will. If Rebecca's substantial wealth had been passed on to Lowri, I can certainly see a motive for someone to tamper with her Will.

Opening up Lowri's Will, I settle to read its contents:

<pre>
            Last Will and Testament
                of Lowri Jones
             Dated: 7th July 1981
</pre>

```
    I, Lowri Jones of Ty Glan-y-Coed, being of sound
mind, make this my last Will and Testament.
    I appoint my daughter Gwenda Pritchard of Derwen
Deg, Penmaenmawr to be the Executor of my estate.
    I bequeath my property, known as Ty Glan-y-Coed,
with all its contents, including my jewellery, solely
to my granddaughter, Alys Roberts, to be held in trust
until she attains the age of eighteen if she has not
already done so. I appoint my good friend, Edith
Parry, the headmistress of Wimborne School for Girls,
to be Trustee and guardian.
    Also I leave Fferm Cae Isaf in Tal-y-Cafn to Alys
Roberts to be held in trust until she attains the age
of eighteen if she has not already done so. This
property was left to me by my Uncle Euryn, twin
brother of Mabli, who was Rebecca's mother and Alys'
great-great-grandmother.
    The property known as Bodhyfrydle in Capelulo,
```

together with its rental income, is already held in trust for Alys until she attains the age of twenty-one, which I arranged following the untimely death of her mother, my daughter, Ellen.

All of my other investments and savings are to be shared equally between my granddaughter Alys and my daughter, Gwenda Pritchard, of Derwen Deg, Penmaenmawr.

Signed: *Lowri Jones*

Witness: *Ieuan Cadwalader Jones*
Solicitor
7/7/81

Witness: *Rhys Hughes*
Articled Clerk
7/7/81

Well, there it all is in black and white. It was definitely Lowri's intention that the house was to go to Alys – unless of course Lowri wrote a later Will. In addition to this, she should have inherited the Tal-y-Cafn farm, as well as half of all Lowri's investments and savings, which may amount to a great deal. She should also become the owner of the Bodhyfrydle property and its accrued rent in the Trust fund when she becomes twenty-one. In view of all this, I find it absolutely preposterous that she is currently homeless.

A shocking thought then occurs to me. What if not preventing Alys from being arrested for the offence created a serendipitous advantage to get her out of the way for a few years, while some financial skulduggery went on? What if Lena was coerced into lying to say Alys wasn't at home at the time of the offence, leaving her without an alibi?

Even more outrageously, what if Gwenda did not actually find the original Will, but decided to produce one herself? She was the executor of Lowri's Will. She may also have seen bank statements which revealed how much money there was in Lowri's bank accounts.

Perhaps if she had just fraudulently bequeathed those accounts to herself and let Alys have the house as Lowri planned, nobody would have been any the wiser. But it seems she was greedy. If she has produced a fraudulent Will, she will be in very serious trouble, as forgery is a criminal offence under the Fraud Act. This is all conjecture of course, but my theory could be correct.

I urgently need to have sight of Lowri's legally accepted Will, which left nothing to Alys, so will order a copy from the Probate Office.

I still need to do a bit of sorting out of my theory before I approach Alys with this new information – she may even be able to fill in some missing gaps. There is absolutely no doubt that Lowri was very wealthy, which further confirms my suspicion that the investments and savings mentioned in Lowri's Will may have been a considerable amount. But where has all that wealth gone?

Now I know that the family tree in the Bible is definitely linked to Alys, I sit there, flabbergasted. I feel paralysed as to what to do next. The potential implications of the information contained in these documents I've just discovered are enormous. The possible fallout from the reading of them may be lifechanging. I try to calm down and think logically, strategically.

I already suspect that the document written by Edwin may have a huge emotional impact on Alys. It feels as if I will be intruding by reading it, so I put that to one side for now.

I guess Lowri had put the Will where she considered to be the most sacred of safe places; it had obviously never occurred to Gwenda to look in there even if she had seen the Bible in the drawer as she rummaged. Had she found the Will, she would most likely have destroyed it, given its contents. The Bible must have been taken along with everything else when the house clearance took place. Maybe she thinks that if the Will had been in the house somewhere, it would either have been found by now or lost and destroyed during the house clearance. Whatever the reason, it is very clear to me that Alys was meant to be very well provided for.

I feel beyond furious that Gwenda has been so deceitful, so I am now all the more determined to prove the legally accepted Will is fraudulent. If I have anything to do with it, Gwenda will get her comeuppance, which is no more than she deserves. I do however feel a small amount of sympathy for her daughter Lena, who I suspect has been coerced into being involved by her domineering mother.

I am bursting to share this new information with Alys but will not do so until I am absolutely sure of my facts. I know that she is busy studying at her aunt's, so I don't want her to be unnecessarily distracted.

I persuade myself that I also need to read the note written by Alys' father, Edwin, to prepare myself for any possible fallout when I show it to Alys. I procrastinate by completing various unnecessary domestic tasks, until eventually, I steel myself to look at it.

Reading it, I find it both extremely painful and touching. I feel myself choking up. What an absolute tragedy. I know that it will be very difficult for Alys to read this and to actually comprehend his extreme actions, which left her both abandoned and orphaned. I dread having to disclose the letter to Alys. Revealing it to her will take careful timing and infinite support and empathy.

On a personal level, I am also anxious that if and when Alys receives what is rightfully hers, it may adversely affect our relationship. She is potentially a very wealthy young woman and I hope that this will not change her feelings towards me. Maybe my usefulness to her will be over, my role in her life complete, my purpose fulfilled, and that she will move on from me. I pray this is not the case, as I cannot now imagine nor bear the thought of being without Alys in my life.

Who would have thought that this old Bible, which I just happened to pick up at an auction, would hold all these long-ago secrets, then go on to solve all the current day mysteries I have been pondering for so long? Thank goodness I was duty solicitor on the day of Alys' police interview, causing our paths to originally cross.

These factors threw us together. Was it all just coincidence? This then got me thinking on a more philosophical level. Is everything in life actually preordained and not purely coincidental as most would have us believe? Are our lives already mapped out before we are born? Does fate play a part? Curious, I look up the definition of fate which reads:

'The development of events outside a person's control, regarded as

predetermined by a supernatural power.'

This is all far too mind blowing for me to continue to contemplate but it does throw up some considerations. Was it also mere coincidence that the prison van was held up by traffic that day, putting the case back until later, causing me to walk into town to buy a sandwich; then the sudden deluge which drove me into the auction room, where I came across the old Bible? I thank God for the rain which fell that day.

Was it all purely a string of circumstantial coincidences – or were these circumstances pre-planned by a higher power as I read in the definition of fate? Were all my actions guided by something much bigger than we mere mortals? I shudder as I contemplate this.

* * *

From the Will I found in the back of the Bible, I now have the name of Lowri's solicitor. If I can contact Ieuan Cadwalader Jones, he could prove to be a useful witness. He may have a copy of her will as well as holding the original documentation regarding the Trust Fund for the Bodhyfrydle property.

When I enquire, I find out from a colleague that Mr. Jones had died in 1982; a potentially useful lead lost.

As soon as I receive the copy of Lowri's Will from the Probate Office, I can compare the contents – and Lowri's signature. I conclude that I must see it first before I do anything else, so will just have to wait patiently until it arrives.

* * *

Alys continues to live in her aunt's box room, even though I have asked her many times to move in with me permanently. She says she doesn't want to be beholden – whatever that means. She seems to want to make it by her own endeavours; I suppose she values her independence. But I believe she should get out of that toxic atmosphere as soon as possible. Seems to me that they use her as a skivvy, but then again, she feels compelled to justify her keep there.

Earlier today, her aunt Gwenda left her a note telling her to make a large lasagne, as she had friends coming over later for supper. Alys was busy finishing it off when Gwenda's husband arrived home early, a little the worse for wear, as he'd been to a colleague's leaving do. He came up to Alys as she was grating parmesan cheese on the top and put his arm around her shoulder. This made her feel very uncomfortable, so she side-stepped away from him. Then as he leaned over and tried to nuzzle at her neck, she got a waft of his alcoholic breath.

'Get off me!' she shouted.

'Come on, just a little peck,' as he lunged at her face.

'What the hell's going on here?' shouted a furious Gwenda, on entering the kitchen.

'You little harlot, you're no better than your mother. I should never have taken you in. Pack your bags and get out of here right now – and don't ever come back,' she screamed hysterically at the top of her voice. Alys thought that she seemed a little unstable and out of control, noticing the spittle which was being forced out with her words.

Alys also told me later that at that moment, she felt the same intense sense of injustice she had experienced at being accused of committing the offence. Talk about blaming the victim. But evidently Gwenda was blinkered; seeing only what she wanted to see, believing what she wanted to believe. She obviously couldn't blame him, so once more, Alys was the scapegoat.

'With pleasure,' Alys said, untying and flinging her apron on the floor, 'and by the way, I wouldn't touch him with a bargepole. You're welcome to him.'

Absolutely furious, Alys stomped up the stairs to her boxroom. She could hear a ferocious argument going on in the kitchen below. It was still raging when she slammed the front door and left the house behind her for the last time. She felt glad to be finally leaving – a weight off her shoulders. She knew she had never been welcome there. She walked down the drive from the house carrying her suitcase and rucksack, homeless once more – but with the comforting thought that at least this time, she did actually have somewhere and someone to go to. Me.

When she arrives at mine a while later, she relates what had happened. I can see that she is deeply upset by what Gwenda has said about her mother; always a sensitive subject. But I tell her – and she acknowledges now – that Gwenda knows exactly how to hurt her. In recognising this, she has decided not to let her win this time – she refuses to internalise the cruel and untrue barb.

I am inordinately pleased that Alys is here at last to stay. It feels so right – and I am happy that she has finally turned to me. If this is what it took to get her here, then I am glad they argued.

'Do you still have the note Gwenda wrote you?' I casually ask her later.

'Probably screwed up in my pocket somewhere,' she replies, giving me a look as if to say 'what a curious question.'

'I had to go and buy some of the ingredients,' she continues. 'What do you want it for?' as she rummages about in her coat pockets.

'Just humour me, I'll tell you later,' I say, as she plonks the screwed-up note on the table.

*　*　*

The copy of the Will from the Probate Office arrives on Friday. I'm glad Alys is out as I read the contents:

```
                Last Will and Testament
                          of
                      Lowri Jones
                Dated: 13th May, 1983

    I, Lowri Jones of Ty Glan-y-Coed, Dwygyfylchi,
being of sound mind, revoke all previous Wills and
make this my last Will and Testament.
    I appoint my daughter, Gwenda Pritchard of Derwen
Deg, Penmaenmawr to be the Executor of my Estate.
    I bequeath my house and contents, in Glan-y-Coed
Park, together with all my investments and savings, to
my only daughter, Gwenda Pritchard, of Derwen Deg,
Penmaenmawr.


  Signed:      Lowri Jones
  Witness:     Richard Owens
               Personal Assistant
               13/5/83
```

Witness: Glynne Williams
Secretary
13/5/83

So all of Lowri's belongings are being left to Gwenda. No mention of Alys.

Well, the date is later than the Will I found in the back of the Bible. Perhaps this is a genuine Will that Lowri made, superseding the one I found.

I study the signatures and although very similar, they do not look quite the same. However, I do appreciate that there can be variations in people's signatures.

Next day, I contact Hefin, a forensic handwriting analyst I have worked with on a previous case, and we agree to meet.

'So here are the two Wills, and the note that I mentioned about making a lasagne, written by the aunt,' I say as I hand them to him.

'The 1981 Will is the one we found in an old family Bible. This 1983 one is a copy I obtained from the Probate Office.'

'Mmm. On the face of it they both look genuine enough – but would you mind if I take them with me, so I can study them more thoroughly?'

It is a week before he gets back to me. The wait is excruciating but the news is positive.

'What we look at mainly in determining if a signature has been copied is to see if the signature has been written slowly, stopping and starting. This appears to be the case with the signature on the later Will, which doesn't flow naturally. Therefore, judging on the signature alone, I would deduce that the 1981 Will was signed by Lowri but the signature on the 1983 Will is a forgery.'

'But what about the signatures of the witnesses?' I ask.

'I was coming to that. On the later Will, there is strong evidence that they have both been written by the same person who wrote Lowri's signature, although of course the writing has been disguised to look as if it had been signed by someone else. I have explained this and some other anomalies in more detail in my report, which I am quite happy for you to show the police to help in their enquiries.'

'Is there anything else?'

'Well, the paper used for the documents has different watermarks, which denote the trademark of the paper mill. Solicitors' and other professionals' offices tend to be consistent in the brand of stationery they use, so this could indicate from whose office the document originated.'

'I also showed the Wills to a colleague who is an expert in typewritten documents,' Hefin continues after a pause. 'He believes the later Will was typed on a traditional Remington Rand typewriter. Because all such typewriters have their own little tell-tale irregularities in the characters, he would be able to identify the machine it was typed on if it could be found. For example, you can see here that the bottom of the letter f is raised slightly higher than the other letters. Just out of interest, did you know that Remington started off by making rifles in New York in 1816. They only started producing typewriters in 1868.'

'That's all well and good but we need to focus on finding this particular typewriter, which I suspect is possibly located in Gwenda's office, or her husband's. If the police decide to investigate, they will have to obtain warrants to search their premises. On the face of it, this appears to be a case of forgery because of the value involved. We just need to prove it. We now need to report our suspicions to the police, outlining all our evidence as well as any other useful information.'

Continuing, I reflect, 'One would also have thought that Alys, as a juvenile dependent, should have been considered by the Probate official at the time they were processing the Will. This doesn't appear to have been the case but perhaps they were totally unaware of Alys' existence.'

'Can we, or the police, call you as an expert witness if the case proceeds to court?' I ask.

'Of course.'

'I've looked into the likely outcome of the case. Offences under The Fraud Act can carry up to a ten-year sentence, but most likely it would be two to seven years, perhaps less. They would consider a range of factors, both aggravating and mitigating.

'What would be regarded as aggravating factors?' Hefin asks.

'The court will look at whether Gwenda made or supplied articles for use in the fraud, which we believe she did by writing a false Will. They will consider whether the fraud was sophisticated and professionally planned. Also, the value of the fraud, which being in the hundreds of thousands of pounds, could carry a three to five-year sentence. They will consider if there was high culpability and motivation. They will also look at the impact on the victim, such as vulnerability or targeting, which most definitely applies in Alys' case. Also, the aunt's abuse of power as executor of the Will should certainly be considered.'

'What about mitigating factors?'

'Mitigating factors could be an early admittance of guilt at police interview, the fact that she has no previous convictions and whether she is mentally unstable.'

'Will you be able to get back what Alys is owed?' Hefin asks.

'The court could make a Confiscation or Restitution Order to recover it. It's often difficult to enforce though if the property has already been sold. New owners may not want to part with it. If the daughter still has the jewellery and not already sold it, that could be retrieved more easily, but the furniture may be harder to trace and recover.'

I now finally have the means to start building up a case against Alys' aunt.

I know I will have to break all this to Alys over this weekend. I can't keep this knowledge to myself any longer; it's not mine to withhold. But I have delayed because I wanted to be very sure of the facts first. Well, I certainly am now.

I will have to choose my moment carefully, as things will probably become tense. Which news to break first though? Her father's note, Lowri's Will or the source of Rebecca's inheritance? I will let her decide. My guess would be her father's note, which I'm certain will distress her, although I really don't know how she will react. Her defensiveness and feelings of rejection, always close to the surface at the best of times, will reappear; I will have to manage the fall-out carefully. All I can do is be there when she needs me – and she will definitely need me.

Edwin's note will upset her and make her immensely sad. By contrast, when she reads the Will, it will evoke another emotion –

extreme anger towards her aunt.

Next day, after supper, I take her hand and lead her to the sofa.

'Alys, I have something I want to talk to you about.'

'Oh no, you don't like how I load the dishwasher!' she jokes.

'It's far more important than that.' I say seriously, while wishing it was only that mundane.

She casts me a worried look.

Swallowing hard and metaphorically grabbing my courage with both hands, I begin.

'The other day, I knocked over the old Bible. It fell onto the floor and landed with the back cover open.' I hear a sharp intake of breath. 'No, don't worry, I haven't broken it. But when I bent down to pick it up, I saw the back cover had a pasted-on section and behind it were some documents. One was Lowri's original Will, another was a note written by your father, Edwin, just before his death.'

'My father? Oh my good grief!'

She looks horrified as her hands go straight up to cover her mouth. Nevertheless, I plough on.

'I believe the family tree on the front cover is yours. I think the Bible I picked up in the auction came from Lowri's house.'

She sits there opened-mouthed.

'God, what makes you think that?' she says after a long pause. 'I never saw that Bible there, anywhere. It must have been in a cupboard or drawer in my Nain's bedroom.'

'Your Nain's name, her year of birth and her parents correspond exactly with an entry in the family tree. Then, your Nain's Will and the note written by your father were inside the back cover.'

I pause to let Alys take this in before continuing.

'Also,' I continue, 'when I went to Capelulo and saw the property, Bodhyfrydle, which is mentioned in your Nain's original Will, I recognised it from the black and white photograph of the tea-rooms in the bundle of photos. So there is also evidence of a link from those photos to your Nain.'

I sit and wait for her to absorb this absolutely life-changing information. She rises and paces up and down the room, then she sits down on the window seat. She looks outwards into the dark wet night, hearing only the relentless wind tugging at the window, as if she is searching for answers out there. Eventually, she turns towards me.

'But what about the Will?'

'I've had my suspicions about the validity of the Will for a while and about Gwenda's irrational hatred of you. I think Lena was told to lie about you not being in the house on the day of the offence, so you would be locked away while the deception was going on. But most of all, it was about your unwavering insistence that Lowri had said she intended to leave the house to you. All of this indicated to me that there was something amiss somewhere. Originally, I suspected that the original Will had been destroyed or perhaps Gwenda couldn't find it. Either way, I believe she decided to produce a forged one.'

I wait to allow Alys to process this information before continuing.

'I also discovered, from another letter stuffed in the folder, that Lowri's mother, Rebecca, inherited a very large amount of money from her father. He was an American who had links with Eglwysbach. Because there is a great deal of money involved, Gwenda's motive was probably financial – pure greed. Maybe her solicitor husband helped her, so she could inherit everything – but that is just sheer speculation on my part and I may be unfairly implicating him. My assumption is that Gwenda probably thinks that as she was her mother's only living child, she should be entitled to inherit everything, despite Lowri's wishes.'

I pause again to let all that sink in.

'But I needed proof of my theory, so I ordered a copy of the Will from the Probate Office. The bequests in it are completely different from the Will that I found in the back of the Bible. Crucially, I now have some evidence suggesting that the Will accepted by the Probate Office is a forgery.'

Alys takes all this in and slowly nods her head in agreement, as I reveal the information.

'I suppose it all does makes sense when you think about it.'

Then I quietly ask the crucial question.

'Which one do you want to read first?'

She takes in a deep breath.

'Oh – I think my father's note,' she replies. 'It may clear up a few things for me that I have always wondered about.'

I knew she would choose this one and I now ache to be able to save her from the hurt she will inevitably feel – but I am powerless to protect her from it. She will have to digest it, then experience the pain which reading his words will give her. I tell her to come and sit down by me.

She takes in another deep breath and begins to read. I watch as the colour slowly drains from her face. Then her fingers, as if suddenly paralysed, drop the note, which flutters down to her lap. Her face begins to crumple as she struggles to control the threatening tears.

'Just let it go,' I say, as I wrap my arms around her, helpless to protect her from this onslaught of emotion she is suffering inside. These feelings are attacking her deep down in her soul – while I am on the outside. I feel inadequate, as I am unable to shield her from them. Then finally, the dam of pure, raw emotion finally breaks. Years of hurt feelings of real and imagined rejection are finally given vent.

Later, totally drained and emotionally exhausted, Alys lays her head on my knee. I gently run my finger over the contours of her beautiful face.

Then, I surprise even myself.

'Alys, I do love you.' I say softly.

She smiles a little at that.

She is desperately trying to rationalise what her father had done.

'His love for my mother must have been incredibly strong to do that,' she says presently, 'so I know for sure that I was conceived in love. I can also sort of understand that I could have been a constant reminder of his loss, had he raised me. I'm just so grateful though that my Nain took me home from the hospital and looked after me, otherwise who knows where I could have ended up.'

Alys continues justifying her father's actions before moving on.

'Right. Let's look at the original Will now.'

'So she did keep her promise after all,' Alys smilingly reflects after we read it. 'She did leave the house, furniture and her jewellery to me – and all her savings were to be divided between Gwenda and me.

What a devious cow Gwenda is! There's also a farm in Tal-y-Cafn; I never even knew about that. But I do have a sort of vague memory of walking to a tea-room somewhere with my Nain when I was little – I suppose it could have been Bodhyfrydle. Maybe she decided not to talk about it as it would have reopened her fragile, hardly-healed wounds about my mother, which would have been painful for both of us.'

'Originally, Bodhyfrydle belonged to Mary Ellen,' I point out. 'See, here she is on the family tree, also here in this black and white photo. Can you see her resemblance to you?'

Alys smiles and nods as she looks at the photo, before I continue.

'Mary Ellen was the only daughter of Efan, who started the tree. She left the property to her daughter, Jane, who later left it in trust to your mother Ellen. When she died, Lowri arranged for you to become the beneficiary of the Trust fund.'

'Who would have thought this old Bible would hold all these family secrets?' Alys remarks.

'I just wish we knew more about these tragedies,' I contemplate. 'There must have been heartbreaking stories in Mary Ellen's life but she took them all to her grave with her.'

Then as I idly flick through some of the pages of the Bible, I spot yet another small sheet of writing paper, tucked deep inside one of the centre pages.

'Hang on, what's this here?'

I quickly scan it.

'Seems it's yet another note from beyond the grave – written by Mary Ellen Rowlands. Well, well, fancy that. There's also an American business card for a Jared Knox.'

I pass the note to Alys, who reads it.

'It looks like this is an account of what happened to Mabli, the daughter of Mary Ellen's brother, Robert. The way she died was really tragic. It goes on to say Mary Ellen raised Mabli's orphaned daughter, Rebecca. So this Mabli must be my…… great-great grandmother, who died when she was only fifteen. Wow! Seems the American was the father.'

'This note says that Mabli walked from her home in Tal-y-Cafn,' I observe. 'That's where the farm in the genuine Will is located, so perhaps this farm originally belonged to her family and will now be yours when you're twenty-one.'

We are now completely engrossed in our discoveries and the jigsaw pieces are finally, slowly beginning to fall into place.

'I think we'd better have a look to see if there are any more notes hidden away somewhere!' I suggest.

By gently lifting the front of the sleeve which had held the other documents, we're able to see there are probably two more letters tucked in at the bottom of it. They look fairly fragile, so Alys' slim fingers very gingerly work them out so as not to rip them.

'This is a letter to Tomos. It's written in beautiful calligraphy by someone called Dorothy.' Alys passes it over to me, saying, 'Here, I'll let you read it.'

'Seems it's a letter telling Tomos that their baby has been born but that she's forbidden from keeping him,' I read. 'She says she's named him Efan.' Alys looks straight at me before I continue. 'It seems he is to be raised by someone else. Well, that's it! Tomos is our Efan's father and Dorothy is his mother.'

'Gosh. To think that all these people are my relatives and that we can go back that far! Isn't that wonderful? I have ancestors, I have a heritage and a past. These are my roots. I feel properly grounded now – I have belonging and finally know where I have come from.'

'You belong with me now,' I say to her – she then bends forward and kisses me softly on my lips.

'What do we do now?' Alys asks, feeling overwhelmed while trying to process all this new information. 'Where do we go from here?'

'We contest the Will. I have a friend who trained with me who is now a Wills and Probate solicitor. I will speak to him first about having the Will investigated for legitimacy. Then we should be able to file a Post Probate Decision, outlining our allegations about the legitimacy of the probate rule. Hopefully, we can get the current Will annulled through the civil court process.'

I then move on to the position of Alys' aunt.

'We will build up a case against Gwenda, then report her to the police, who will decide whether to investigate. We will pass on all the information we have collated to them. Perhaps I should also look into whether we could sue for the time you had to spend in custody on remand, wrongly accused. That would be a civil action. You shouldn't go anywhere near that family now, Alys.'

'They're the last people I want to see anyway. They all disgust me. I disown them. I wonder what made Gwenda do it? Greed obviously; jealous that my Nain had favoured me in her Will, but I think she's always hated me because of my mother. Remember, she said I was a harlot, just like my mother. And there was me thinking twins were supposed to be close.'

This is a statement rather than a question, so I do not respond. She needs to mull all this stuff over in her own good time, then let the pieces fall into place.

Alys rises as if in a daydream. Biting the nail on her little finger, she walks over to the window seat where the lashing, wind-driven rain is streaming down the window-panes. Maybe she seeks the answers to her complex family relationships out there. Maybe not. I leave her to her thoughts.

***

I believe we now have enough of a case to approach the police to ask them to investigate. I have had the documents back from Hefin, together with his report.

'Can you meet me later,' I say next morning to Alys, 'to go to the police station together to report the crime?'

Once my morning cases have appeared before the court, I will have an hour or so before I need to be back at the courthouse for the afternoon. At lunchtime, I walk around to the police station and sure enough, Alys is there waiting. She is both anxious and understandably, extremely nervous about what we are about to do. Taking her hand, we walk into the police station together.

'We'd like to report a crime,' I tell the noticeably bored Desk Sergeant.

'And what sort of crime would that be then?'

'We believe that a Will has been forged.'

'What is your name?'

'Gareth Morgan.'

He picks up the phone to call the Detective on Duty, who tells him he'll come through when he has finished what he is doing.

'Take a seat, he'll be with you shortly.'

I look towards the hard, grubby uninviting wooden benches which flank the waiting area with its grey, soulless walls and decide to remain standing. Alys is looking thoroughly uncomfortable and far too on edge to sit down. Not surprising really, considering her last experience with the law, not that very long ago.

Presently, the detective comes through.

'Mr. Morgan? Follow me please,' as he leads us through a labyrinth of corridors to one of the interviewing rooms.

'Right, what's this all about then?'

I give him an outline of the case, a list of the evidence we have so far and wait for his response. Taking notes as I talk, he nods occasionally to indicate he understands.

'Can you leave these documents with me so I can look into the matter?'

'Of course.'

'I'll be in touch in due course to let you know whether or not we decide to investigate.'

'Do you think there's a chance they might not investigate it then?' Alys asks, when we are outside.

'He didn't sound too enthusiastic, did he? – but then again, he's trained not to give anything away. Anyway, it's out of our control now. Come on, let's go around the corner for a coffee and some cake.'

I hate seeing Alys stressed like this, so I try to distract her from brooding, as she just picks at her cake.

'Let's go out to dinner tonight,' I suggest. 'We can go to the bar where you used to work first if you like.'

During dinner, we discuss the possibility of what will happen if she wins her case. Tentatively, I reveal my own niggling anxiety.

'Alys, I don't even know if you will still want to be with me when this is all over – when you are a wealthy woman. You can do whatever you want, go wherever you like, be with whoever you want……….'

As my sentence peters out, she smiles and takes my hand.

'Let's make plans for our future together, Gareth.'

This says it all – and my heart is overjoyed.

Chapter 15

I am informed that the police, having decided to investigate our complaint, obtained a warrant to search Gwenda's office and found the actual typewriter the forged Will had been typed on, tucked away in a dusty old cupboard. After gathering further evidence, they decided to go ahead with the prosecution, so the case is consequently being brought to court.

As we wait for Gwenda to take her place in the dock, we are both on pins at the thought of seeing her – even my stomach is doing somersaults and I don't even know her!

'All rise.'

The magistrate enters.

'Please be seated except for the defendant. You will remain standing while the charges are read out to you.'

'You, Gwenda Pritchard, are charged with Fraud by Misrepresentation,' the Clerk of the Court begins. 'How do you plead?'

'Not guilty!' she replies angrily. As she turns round to face the back of the court, seeking out Alys, she glares directly at her with pure, unadulterated hatred. There is a wild look in her eye and she appears dishevelled and almost unstable. She obviously blames Alys for everything that has happened to her, not her own greedy nature and long-festering hatred. Rather blame the scapegoated victim.

Gwenda points wildly at Alys.

'This is all her fault,' she shouts. 'I gave her a roof over her head when she was homeless– and this is how she repays me!'

No thought that it was her who made Alys homeless.

'Silence in court!' says the magistrate banging his gavel. 'One more outburst like that and I will clear the court.'

I heard Alys gasp. We hadn't expected Gwenda to be so brazen as to deny what we believe is indisputable. She obviously intends to fight this to the bitter end. I suppose she has nothing to lose now – but a guilty plea would have gone in her favour at sentencing.

The magistrate waits for things to settle down.

'In that case, given your plea and the fact the offence carries a potential sentence of more than a year, which is beyond the jurisdiction of this court, I will remit this matter to the Crown Court, where a trial date will be set. The application by the defence to extend community bail is granted.'

I think it's a pity they had not done the same for Alys when she had initially applied for bail but then again, this is deemed white-collar crime as no one was physically hurt.

The magistrate turns to the Clerk of the Court.

'Can we get a date for the Defendant to appear at Crown Court please?'

'Well, I didn't expect that, Alys,' I say, when we are out in the court foyer.

'What happens next?' she asks anxiously.

'First, the matter will be remitted to the Crown Court for a pre-trial review. She may not actually have to appear for that.'

'What will happen to her?' Alys asks apprehensively.

'Gwenda has been charged under the False Accounting Theft Act 1968, Section 17, which carries a possible seven-year maximum prison sentence. Aggravating factors considered at sentencing will be mainly the abuse of power as executor of her mother's Will; also, the sophisticated nature of the offence, given the significant planning involved and the fact she supplied articles – the forged will. They will also look at the coercion of her daughter, through intimidation and exploitation. A lesser culpability, that it is her first offence, would also be taken into consideration.'

At the weekend, needing some fresh air and to take our minds off the case, we decide to walk around Glan-y-Coed Park to see if anyone has moved into Ty Glan-y-Coed. We are shocked to see a developer's sign at the front gate and a planning application notice tied to a lamppost nearby, seeking permission to convert it into three flats. Knowing the site is empty, we walk up the track to the house and find all the windows boarded up.

'We should try to get the council to put a stay on the planning process by informing them the property is currently subject to litigation,' I say.

But Alys isn't taking in what I am saying; she just looks incredibly sad at seeing the house and the once beautiful gardens in this sorry neglected state, with weeds growing everywhere.

'They haven't done any work on it yet,' I say, trying to cheer her up. 'Maybe we can still save it. I'll take the developer's contact details on our way out and get in touch, as well as with the local planning department.'

* * *

Months pass while we wait for Gwenda's trial date. We are told that the pre-trial review has taken place with a decision to proceed. Finally, we receive notification that the trial is set for three weeks' time, in the Crown Court.

* * *

The day of the trial finally arrives. The defence solicitor stands.

'Your Honour, my client wishes to inform the court that she would like to change her plea to one of Guilty, on the grounds of diminished responsibility.'

'Oh, she's trying that old ploy is she? I whisper to Alys. 'Trying to get a reduced sentence or to get off completely.'

Subsequently, the trial is cancelled and the jury summarily dismissed. It is a huge let down. All that time, effort and money spent on trial preparation was for nothing. She should have pleaded guilty in the first instance instead of wasting the court's – and everybody else's time.

The court then orders a psychiatric assessment and a pre-sentence report, with a sentencing date set in four weeks' time.

'Why do you think Gwenda changed her plea?' Alys asks after we leave the court.

'I assume that as well as trying to reduce the sentence, she pleaded guilty because she doesn't want her dirty deeds aired in public by the witnesses' evidence, which would highlight her downright deceitfulness and her significant fall from grace.'

Whilst at the court, we hear through her defence solicitor that her husband has left the family home, taking Lena, their daughter with him to live with his mother. The police have decided not to charge Lena, given her age and the fact that she was probably coerced and has no previous convictions; also providing she was willing to turn

Queen's evidence. Once Gwenda was informed her daughter was going to testify against her, she knew the game was up.

*　*　*

Sentencing day arrives. The pre-sentencing report recommends Gwenda receives a three-year suspended sentence. An Order is made for her to repay the proceeds of the offences. That includes the income from the sale of the house and Alys' half of the investments. This is done by means of a Confiscation Order by the court, withdrawing the due amount from Gwenda's bank account then remitting it to Alys'.

A further Order is made for Lena to return Lowri's jewellery to Alys. Gwenda had been unable to breach the Cae Isaf Farm Trust or the Bodhyfrydle Trust. As Alys is eighteen, she now becomes the owner of Cae Isaf Farm and will automatically become the owner of Bodhyfrydle when she is twenty-one.

Because of her avaricious behaviour, Gwenda has now lost her husband, her daughter, her good name – and has recently been struck-off professionally.

Given her unstable behaviour, I warn Alys to always be wary in case she tries to seek revenge – as she now has nothing to lose. At least she will be monitored by the Probation Service whilst she serves the community Court Order and although the psychiatric report does not indicate she is a risk of harm to anyone, who knows what she will try to do? I believe her hatred is a very strong motivator, once it is funnelled in a particular direction.

Although Alys is finally cleared of absolutely everything, the fact that she had been accused of the offence makes her feel the stigma of it will always stay around, like a bad smell. But the whole experience has given her an insight into the justice system. She feels motivated to do something about the plight of those, particularly women, who are adversely affected through being incarcerated, rightly or wrongly, depending on your perspective.

Alys achieved the A-Level results she needed to enable her to study for a career in social work and is now on her way to getting the qualification she wants, despite all the peripheral distractions.

In the end, she has got most of what her Nain had intended her to have.

'Well Alys,' I venture tentatively, 'you are now a very wealthy young woman and Lowri's hope that you would be secure and looked after has come true. I only hope that you will now let me look after you.'

I am rewarded with a sweet smile.

'What do you intend to do next?' I ask.

'I want to get the house back from the developer.'

'I have already made enquiries with the new owner – he seems open to the idea.'

Together we approach him. After discussing the matter, he is happy to sell it back at his cost price plus some administration fees. He says he has lost interest in it anyway, as the planning delay caused by the court case had been costing him money. The conveyancing agreement is drawn up and agreed by the respective solicitors, with the property back in Alys's ownership and made good within the month. Alys is obviously delighted.

'I wonder if it's possible to retrieve some of the original house contents,' I muse. 'If they have not already sold, they might still be sitting there in the auction room. I'll ask the friendly admin person there – the one who gave me the bag to carry the old Bible – she should know where they went. Or maybe better still, we should just go and have a look ourselves; you might be able recognise some of them. It's also possible that an antiques dealer bought a job lot of the stuff at the auction, so there might be a possibility we could get it back from the dealer. Long shot but we could try.'

We decide to go to the auction room on Saturday morning when it is possible to view what is coming up for auction the following Wednesday. On walking down one of the aisles, Alys stops in her tracks in front of a lovely Welsh dresser with a set of blue and white pots on its shelves.

'That's my Nain's!' she exclaims. 'I'd know it anywhere. It's got a wonky middle drawer which doesn't open properly.'

When I come to think about it, I do remember noticing it that day I bought the Bible at the auction.

Sure enough, when she tries to open the drawer, it's stuck fast. Alys is very excited at this find and we approach the office to speak to the auctioneer. I explain that it has been subject to a court case and show him the Restoration Order. He then kindly agrees to arrange for it to be returned, charging just the delivery cost.

Later, when we get back home, I take out the box of photos.

'Last night, I looked at the photos again, this time the polaroid ones,' I tell Alys. 'I hadn't really looked closely at them before because I was focusing mainly on the people in the family tree. I could be wrong – but I think the ones that look like hippies could be of your mam and dad. If you like, we can get them enlarged. I think this is a good one.'

She takes it off me.

'I think I look like my mam,' she says, after looking at it. Turning to me, she adds, '– and I feel I know her somehow.'

Then she strokes her father's face with her forefinger.

'I know you would have loved and cared for me if you could have,' she says, 'but the trouble was you loved her too much.'

'You are the spitting image of her,' I tell her softly. 'We must explore some more of those photos, as we might be able to put some more faces to the names on the family tree.'

'Thank you, Gareth, for everything you've done for me,' Alys says, taking my hand. 'First, you defended me, then you discovered my complete family history and then you won back what was legally mine. I will be eternally grateful.'

'I don't want your gratitude – I want your love.'

'You already know you have that in bucketsful.'

* * *

In the end, justice is served. But Alys is not one to rest on her laurels. I have a feeling she will do something worthwhile with her fortune. This proves to be true when she tells me of her plans.

'Given my experience within the justice system, it's clear to me that there isn't much support for ex-prisoners to 'go straight' as they say, so I've decided that I'll convert Ty Glan-y-Coed into a halfway house for newly-released female prisoners, to help them get back on their feet, as well as those who need a community bail address as I did. They will be met at the prison gate and be transported to the house, where they can reside to serve the community part of their sentence. I want to support them to learn skills which will help them start their own businesses, such as gardening, cooking or cleaning. They could even become car mechanics, or painters and decorators if they wanted to. Training could be undertaken inside and outside of the house. We could even house those who just want to go to full-time college to get a qualification – but they will all have to do their share of the household tasks. It's really difficult for them to get employment when they have a criminal record, so this would be a way for them to earn an independent living. I may even consider giving the women capital loans to help them to start a small business.'

I sit there open-mouthed, as she continues.

'The other idea I had was to turn the farm in Tal-y-Cafn into an agricultural training farm. I could keep the existing tenants and negotiate with them to provide apprenticeship placements there, so the women could learn on the job. We could even consider opening a farm shop there where the women could work.'

'But first, I need to complete my course to get my qualification.'

I am astonished at how she has thought everything through and at the scope of her imagination.

'Well. I didn't expect any of that – you really have given it some thought, haven't you? Do you know, you never fail to surprise nor impress me, Alys Roberts. It's quite an ambitious plan, but if anyone can pull it off, you can,' I tell her, as she smiles at me. 'You will need to get permission for change of use for the house though – and there could well be some local opposition.'

'I'll deal with that when it happens. We will be very selective in our criteria for housing them. They would have to be highly motivated to change their lives. There would be a very thorough risk assessment process and rigid criteria for placements. I don't want anyone who is a risk to others or someone who might cause friction. I would like to work with the prison authorities to see if they have an in-house charity with which I can liaise to prepare for their release.'

'So they will be thoroughly vetted,' she continues, 'and we will work with them before and after release. There will also be very strict house rules and a complete ban on drugs and alcohol on the premises. I will possibly need to employ a live-in couple to run the house and supervise the women.'

Then, taking a very deep breath and swallowing hard, Alys completely floors me.

'I also want you to move with me to live in Bodhyfrydle when I inherit it at twenty-one. I really can't bear to sell it, given that it has been kept for me all these decades. It is a lovely house – and I can't imagine anyone I would rather share it with.'

'Oh, I can't do that.' I tease.

'Why on earth not?' she says, sounding mortified.

'Unless you agree to marry me first; I can't possibly be kept by a wealthy woman…….'

'I couldn't have done any of this without your belief in me and for that, I am truly, deeply – and will be eternally grateful,' she says, taking my hand. 'I think I knew we would be together from the first time I set eyes on you – and I was certain of it when you visited me in prison – when your heart first spoke to mine.'

'Yes, I think you must have cast a spell on me then,' I laugh. 'Can I assume that's a yes then?'

She smiles that bewitching smile she has.

'It's a yes from me! But in the meantime, I'm going to continue with my studies – eventually I'd like to do a PhD in Business Studies – I quite like this studying malarkey! Then I want to have lots of children; it's no fun being an only child.'

Jubilantly, we decide we will go out to celebrate all the wrongs having finally been put right – and the prospect of our future lives together.

Alys smiles to herself as she looks at the Bible. I can see that she wonders what her ancestors in the family tree would make of her and the recent ordeal she has been through. In her own way, she has overcome adversity, just as they had done in their time – she is a true survivor. She is also a pioneer in her way, with her scheme to help people make a new start in life.

'What about you, Gareth?' she asks. 'Do you have any plans?'

'Do you know, I really enjoyed researching your family tree, so much so that I have been thinking of doing ancestry research full-time. I might start my own business, offering my services to people trying to trace their own family histories. I seemed to enjoy doing that more than my legal work on some days; I feel I have become addicted to discovering people's long-lost relatives!'

* * *

Six months later, Alys is walking down the aisle towards me, alone, looking stunningly beautiful, as I wait for her at the altar in St Gwynan's Church. We exchange our vows and I slip her Nain's rose gold wedding ring onto her third finger, left hand – then softly kiss her lips after we are declared man and wife.

After the ceremony, we walk down to the cemetery and she lays her bouquet on her Nain's grave and the altar flowers on the grave of her mother and baby twin brother, Edward – before we go and celebrate our marriage.

'I think my Nain would have approved of you and would be very glad that I have found my soulmate,' Alys says.

A couple of days later, we drive up to Eglwysbach and lay some wedding flowers on the grave of Efan and his wife Myfanwy, acknowledging that this is where Alys' story began. We also lay a small bouquet on the grave of his father, Tomos, which is next to his.

'Been thinking,' said Alys when I had asked her where she would like to go on honeymoon, 'maybe we should travel to Patagonia to see where Thomas farmed, or Canada even.'

No Spanish or Greek islands for Alys then. She truly is an original.

* * *

Alys is reconciled with Lena, recognising it wasn't her fault – she just did what she was told by her domineering mother. Alys is grateful to have her Nain's jewellery back and vows never to be parted from it again. Mary Ellen's Welsh dresser is now safely stored away ready to go back into Bodhyfrydle where it belongs, as we do.

The halfway house is now well established and currently has three ex-prisoners helping the housekeeper and handyman couple to run the house. For some, it is the first proper home they have ever had; a new start in life, with proper support. Similarly, the farm tenants have agreed to take on apprentices at the farm and to work on a programme which will lead to an agricultural qualification. They are also considering diversifying by developing a local farm shop.

Most gratifying of all is watching Alys as she writes her name, then mine as her husband, in the family tree of the now revered old family Bible, which I innocuously picked up at auction and which has since become an integral part of our lives.

Epilogue

Five years have passed. Bodhyfrydle has been completely restored and we have already moved in and have begun the next stage of our lives together. The old family Bible sits on its own newly-acquired preacher's plinth in the sitting room, acknowledging its importance in our coming together – that, and the little bit of help we had from fate, of course.

Next to it is Mary Ellen's Welsh dresser, adorned with the beautiful blue and white dinner set we rescued from the auction room. The restorer managed to unstick the middle drawer and inside, he found a family photograph with the names written on the back. It read, from left to right, Mary Ellen, Jane, Rebecca and Sammy. What a find! This confirms that it really is Mary Ellen's Welsh dresser and we now know what Alys' great-grandmother Rebecca looked like as a young woman – not too dissimilar from Alys I think, but then I see her in every generation of family photographs. This photograph has pride of place in our gallery of ancestors, which is hung next to the dresser.

The silver-framed photo of Alys' parents has the place of honour on the mantlepiece. They smile their daily approval at us as we walk busily by. Alys has recently updated the Family Bible, adding our twin daughters, Seren and Eira. We will cherish the Bible and in time will pass it down to our children.

As I look at the photographs, I think to myself matter-of-factly that I have more than fulfilled my original mission to return the Bible to its modern-day descendant of the family tree. I also believe that Mary Ellen would have been pleased to see her house occupied by her family once more. The gardens look magnificent – much as they had in Mary Ellen's heyday, I suppose. Alys has inherited Lowri's gardening skills, with a good eye for colour. At the bottom of the garden, we have put up a sturdy safety fence, so that our twin girls cannot climb over the boundary down to the river.

One lovely balmy evening in late summer, I walk out to join Alys in the garden, carrying our two Dry Martini cocktails. As we sit outside at dusk in the palest, delicate pink light of the setting sun, watching the girls play on the lawn, a car pulls up outside our gate and an elderly woman ducks her head as she gets out of the car. Once standing, she is tall, elegant and regal.

'Is this house called Bodhyfrydle?' she asks us in an American drawl. 'Forgive me. I'm not sure if I'm pronouncing it correctly.'

'Yes, it is, can I help you?' I reply, somewhat taken aback, as I walk towards the gate.

'Yes, I'm trying to trace my Welsh family. My name is Mabli. Mabli Knox. My father, Jared, died a few years ago. He left me a letter, explaining that I had a step-sister in Wales called Rebecca, of whom I had no prior knowledge. He said in the letter that Rebecca was born in this house and that he named me after her mother, Mabli.'

Alys looks at her incredulously, totally stunned.

'Rebecca was my great-grandmother.'

'Come in and join us for a drink. We have a great deal we can tell you.'

About the Author

This is the second novel by Eleri Thomas, whose first book, Treasured Valley was widely acclaimed, particularly in the area of North Wales in which her stories are set.

These are extracts from some of the reviews on Amazon of Treasured Valley:

"What an absolute joy it is to read such an enthralling and beautiful book. It is so wonderfully written and peels back the layers of time as the history of this wonderful place and its people unfold. It is written with great creativity and knowledge. A delight to read!!!"

"A fascinating collection of stories from present day back through history, all set in a beautiful North Wales valley. A very enjoyable read."

"I thoroughly enjoyed this book and highly recommend it to those who enjoy a good read. Endearing characters and vivid descriptions of a beautiful area in Wales."

"Loved this book. I didn't want it to end. Fantastic insight to our Welsh heritage."

"A thoroughly good read from the fertile mind of an accomplished author."

A Quick Favour

If you enjoyed this book, would you please take a moment to write a short review on Amazon so other readers can enjoy it too?

It really does help!

Thank you so much.

email: eli@elerithomas.com

Acknowledgements

My great-Nain, Catherine Jones, of Ty Capel, Capelulo, was born in Pontwgan in 1833. On her eighty-six birthday, she gifted her family Bible to my father. Inside the front cover was her family tree, which inspired me to write this book.

Another inspiration was my great uncle, Thomas Jones, of Llan Farm, Eglwysbach, born in 1856 and who died twelve years before I was born. The items he brought back from Patagonia and the letters written to my family after his death in Canada, which inform the book, are in my possession. From the little I know of him, I spun a story about what I imagined his life would have been like. By all accounts, he was a man of energy and good spirit, who sought adventure. But his ultimate goal was to establish himself as a farmer in his own right, guided always by his deep love of God.

Whilst on a visit to the Museum de Gaiman, in Patagonia, the staff helped me to uncover the whereabouts of the plot my great-uncle actually farmed. I will never forget the kind people I met whilst in Patagonia and their great pride in their historical links with Wales.

Thanks also to the staff at the Conwy Archives for digging out useful information about how my ancestors would have lived during the periods I have written about.

My gratitude once more to my enduringly-patient husband, who is editor, proofreader, publisher and general dogsbody. [Hear, hear: Ed.] He has read this book endless times and is my biggest critic.

My thanks to my dear friends, Mary and Derek, who always encourage me, and also to my friend, Anne. They all took the time to read through the draft manuscript and to provide valuable feedback.

Last but by no means least, my heartfelt thanks to my artistically gifted daughter-in-law, Megie, who has once again designed a beautiful cover for the book, from my exacting specifications.

Printed in Great Britain
by Amazon